COURT ORDERED

AN UNHOLY TRIAD NOVEL

C. JACOBY

Copyright © 2025 by C. Jacoby

All rights reserved.

No part of this publication may be reproduced, distributed, or transmitted in any form or by any means, including photocopying, recording, or other electronic or mechanical methods, without the prior written permission of the publisher, except as permitted by U.S. copyright law. For permission requests, contact authorcjacoby@gmail.com.

The story, all names, characters, and incidents portrayed in this publication are fictitious. No identification with actual persons (living or deceased), places, buildings, and products is intended or should be inferred.

No part of this publication may be used for the training of AI or the creation of AI generated media.

Book Cover by C. Jacoby

Illustrations by C. Jacoby

1 edition 2025

For my mother, who always told me 'Write your damn book already'.
Well, here it is, and it's full of smut.
I love you, Momma.

AUTHOR'S NOTE

The themes depicted in this book are dark, and all scenes herein are purely fictional. They were written solely for your smut reading pleasure. I do not condone the illicit actions performed by the characters in this book. ***Court Ordered*** is a work of fiction, with emphasis on the **DARK** aspect of dark romance. Sensitive and possibly triggering subject matter is described **ON PAGE**. For a comprehensive list of trigger warnings, visit my author website via the address below. If this book triggers you or becomes harmful to your mental state, please stop reading. You are important, valued, and loved.   -C. Jacoby

National Suicide Prevention Lifeline:
1-800-273-8255

PLAYLIST

A full list of songs that inspired **Court Ordered** can be found on my author site by using the QR code on the previous page. The premade playlist features all songs listed here in sequential order for you to enjoy while reading Victoria and Shaelene's story.

I Want It All - highasf, Cameron Grey
BANGARANG - KILLEDDY
Almost Touch Me – Maisy Kay
Deep Dive - Zaryah
Eyes Don't Lie - Isabela Rosa
Vixen – Destroy Boys
She Calls Me Daddy - KiNG MALA
I'm Yours - Isabela Rosa
The Devil Wears Lace - Steven Rodriguez
Breathe - Ne-Yo
Nirvana - Sickick
Lilith – Ellise
Meddle About - Chase Atlantic
Freaks (Radio Edit) - Timmy Trumpet, Savage
Sahara - Hensonn
Have Faith in Me - Lauren Babic Cover
Shallow - Lauren Babic, Jordan Radvansky

In For The Kill – La Roux, Skream
Siren - Kailee Morgue
Narcissistic Cannibal – Midnite String Quartet
Like I'm Gonna Lose You – Vitamin String Quartet
Not Afraid Anymore - Halsey
Lilith – Ellise
Blue Blood - LAUREL
One Eye Open - Lola Blanc
Scream My Name – Thomas LaRosa
Pray – Xana
Holy Water – LAUREL
Welcome to the Fire – Willyecho
Be A Hero – Euphoria, Bolshiee
Skyfall - Adele
Big Bad Wolf - Roses & Revolutions

TRANSLATIONS

- Oggi come stai, cugina mia? - How are you today, my cousin?

- Sto bene, Luca. - I'm alright, Luca.

- Piacere di conoscerLa - Nice to meet you

- Palazzo Angelini - Palace Angelini

- Vieni, Luca. Per oggi abbiamo finito. - Come, Luca. We're done for the day.

- La prenotazione è a nome di? - Name on the reservation?

- Laughlin, nessuna prenotazione. - Laughlin, no reservation.

- Benvenuta ad Anghiari, signorina Laughlin. - Welcome to Anghiari, Miss Laughlin.

- Da questa parte, per favore. - This way, please.

- In inglese per favore. - In English please.

- Non è niente. - It's nothing.

- Non mentire, Luca. Parla. - Don't lie to me, Luca. Talk.

- Nulla di nuovo che non abbia già affrontato. - It's nothing I haven't dealt with before.

- Merda. - Shit.

- Prego, Victoria. – You're welcome, Victoria

- Ma fraise - My strawberry

- Davai pobeseduem - Let's chat

- Zaichonok - Bunny

- Pososi moi yaytsa... Kuzen - Suck my balls... Cousin

- Ciao mamma, cosa c'è? - Hello Mom, what's wrong?

- Calmati - Calm down

- Va bene? - All right?

- Dobro pozhalovat' - Welcome

- Feckin smuigín! - You fucking brat!

PROLOGUE

Victoria

"MOM, IT'S ONLY THREE and a half hours. Even less with the jet."

My eyes track her across our large kitchen, watching as she practically carves a path through the tile with how worried she is. Her honey blonde hair rests on her shoulders, appearing shorter since her hands tangle through it in an attempt to calm herself.

I start at Sloane Institute of Law in two months, and she hasn't spent a day stress free since my acceptance letter came. Graduating from Maryland State University a month ago was only the beginning; she knows Sloane has always been my dream. It's the top, most prestigious law school in the country, with a four percent acceptance rate. And I got in.

I'm not giving up this opportunity.

She's only worried because I've never left the state without her or my father. I've been in Maryland my entire life—unless there was a vacation or business trip Dad brought us along for. The vacations were amazing, but it's time I finally get out and explore the world for myself without anyone always looking after me.

New York is the perfect fresh start. *And a chance to get away from the memories that haunt me every time I drive through our opulent circle of the city...*

PART ONE

Preliminary Examination

1

Shaelene

HER FILE LIES OPEN on my lap, the manila folder resting against the steering wheel, while I sit comfortably in the driver's seat, my knee up and leaning against the door.

I flip through the pages, catching myself staring at her photo. *Again.*

I snap the folder closed and toss it onto the dash with a huff. My knee bounces anxiously as I scan the quad another time, and once again cave to temptation and snatch the folder back, scanning through it.

I've read the details in her file front to back ten times over, memorized it even, but the noise of the papers shuffling is the only thing distracting me from my wandering thoughts and Shephard obnoxiously eating fries in the passenger seat. *There's salt everywhere in my car now.*

I roll my eyes; the arrogant prick is completely oblivious to how annoying he is. *Not that he cares, anyway.* He's an ass, while Shaun, my other brother, is at least self-aware and sarcastic with his irksome-ness.

Noting my ire, he smacks Shephard's shoulder to get his attention, the bag-fry pipeline temporarily paused.

"What?" he asks through a mouthful of half-chewed food.

Shaun chuckles deeply from the backseat. "Dude, you're so loud."

Shephard eyes me while purposefully slurping his empty soda. "I'm *bored*. What'd you expect when we have to wait for some bitch to get out of class?" I ignore him, turning my attention back toward the quad.

That *bitch* is a girl named Victoria Fenwick. Our father didn't tell us why, but we've been tasked with verifying she's attending her first year at Sloane. He doesn't ever share more information than needed for us to complete a job, and I'm not in the habit of asking questions. I do as I'm told so only the right people end up hurt.

Or dead.

Today we were told to look for Victoria.

She isn't on a hit list. *Not ours at least.* We're simply confirming she's the one here and not a stand in.

Loads of haughty rich kids like to pay some smart scholarship student to take their classes for them, while they get to live off of their parents' wealth, completely carefree, for the next four years. *Like they haven't been doing that their entire existence.* My lip curls as I watch a group of them saunter past us toward a caravan of Bentleys.

Working isn't for everyone, I guess; luckily for me, I get a particular satisfaction out of my job. Breaking and entering is fun, but the adrenaline-high from taking a life? That's something I'll probably end up chasing forever.

A heavy breath sighs from my nose, muffled by the sound of Shephard's incessant chewing. My patience today is paper thin, every second spent waiting for Victoria to show herself adds to the jolting edge my nerves are dancing on. *Where the hell is she?*

The folder closes with a defined slap, and I discard it onto the dash. *Don't. Pick it up. Again.* My empty hands, too bothered to remain idle, find the steering wheel to hold instead, my nails drumming against the leather in quiet taps.

Shaun's face, identical to my brother's and so obviously similar to my own, save the extra sharp cut of his jaw, pops into my peripheral. He reaches forward, making to grab the folder, but I snatch it first. Only to be met by his annoyingly familiar 'Gotcha' smirk as he lowers his hand and retrieves a fistful of fries from Shephard's bag. *Assholes, the both of them.*

His eyes move past me to the quad he's distracted me from, and when they return to mine, his teasing brows give a quick raise before he ducks back into his seat.

Immediately I turn, eyes honing in. *Her.*

Those bright copper curls are impossible to miss, especially through the misty haze of early October. I jab Shephard in the arm with my elbow, my spine straightening as adrenaline spikes through me. He starts to bitch until he sees who I'm so focused on.

My eyes are locked, tracking her like prey as she crosses the open quad. Like the campus is an open and grassy field, and she's a foxy patch of red running through the brush.

My little fox.

"Oh shit! Go time," Shephard mumbles, crumpling his wrapper and tossing it into the to-go bag on the floorboard.

Victoria hurries from the library doors, clutching a few books against her chest while a large tote bag swings heavily against her small frame. It, too, appears to be full of books.

The glass ahead of me fogs as my breath hits it. *When did I get so close to the window?*

I roll it down, surprisingly unphased by the light drizzle of rain splattering the inside of the door.

Victoria rushes through the parking lot to her Lexus. *Rich kid. Did she get in on grades or daddy's money?* Based on the number of books she's lugging around, I'd guess she's probably smart, but I've been wrong before.

She steps into the aisle we're currently parked in and clicks her key fob. The taillights of her car flash just as her heel catches on a gap in the pavement, making her stumble and drop one of the books in her arms. My hand is on the door handle in less than a second, but movement down the lane stops me. The driver of the car idling next to us, waiting to take her spot, jumps out.

He jogs over and picks it up for her while she's contemplating how to get it herself without dropping the rest into the same puddle. They stand together for a brief moment, and I read the words 'thank you' on her lips.

They're too far down the lane for us to hear them over the rain that's starting to pick up, and I bristle at the bright smile on her face.

"Shae, close the window. I'm getting hit," Shaun complains from behind me. I hadn't even registered the growing puddle on my arm rest.

Does she know him?

Shaun smacks my headrest, pulling me back to reality. I roll up my window. The fog from earlier is gone, but it's quickly replaced with more from the heat my body is emitting. I turn the vent toward it to clear the window this time, annoyed at myself for getting so distracted.

My teeth scrape against the top of my thumb nail while I watch Victoria tuck her hair behind an ear and smile while the guy walks over and places her books in the back seat of her coup. She climbs in with a small wave and another shy smile, her reverse lights blinking on shortly after. Mr. Nice Guy smirks to himself as he gets back into his car, glancing over his shoulder while waiting for her to leave.

The second she does, I slam into drive and pull out behind her, cutting off the douche before he can pull into her spot.

"Jesus, Shae. Tail*ing*, not tail*gating*," Shephard spits.

"It's my fucking car. I'll drive how I want," I hiss, following far closer than Father would accept. He sucks in a knowing breath and shakes his head.

"Women," he groans, looking over his shoulder at Shaun.

We drive for ten minutes before watching Victoria pull into the underground garage of her apartment building in Pelham Bay.

It's a wealthy neighborhood, and the building itself stands about fifteen stories, not counting the private gated garage with an attendant. There's another standing outside the front entrance opening the door for the residents coming in from the street.

The tollbar lowers behind her, and a sharpness hits my chest. I've been studying her photo all morning, impatiently waiting for her to get out of class, going through the routine I've damn near perfected by now, but the second she stepped out of the library, something ignited.

I'm accustomed to the rush that comes with a reconnaissance job, but this was different. It took all of me not to get out of my Mercedes and walk up to her. I suck a quiet breath through my teeth, trying to regain any semblance of my usually level head.

I spent the entire drive here mentally reminding myself this is nothing more than a job and the first rule of a job is '*Don't get attached*'.

But the memory of Little Helper Boy's hand grazing hers flits through my head *again*. An unsettling emotion flashes through me like lightning. *Am I jealous right now? Of* him? The hairs on the back of my neck haven't lain down yet, and that's answer enough. *I'll deal with him later.*

Right now, I need to hunt her.

I park half a block up the street, too impatient to follow all of my father's rules.

"I'll be back," I grumble, white knuckling the steering wheel before opening the door with a violent shove. Hesitating, I lean back in, my eyes zeroing in on my brothers. Shephard looks across the console at me, his hand already reaching for the display. "And don't fucking touch my radio," I order.

He raises his hands in surrender and slumps against his seat. "Yes, boss," he huffs with a mock salute.

I slam the door closed and fix my jacket, glancing both directions before heading down the street. My steps falter as I hear the intro to whatever Missy Elliot song Shephard put on the second the door closed. *Motherfucker is going to get an earful on the way home.*

The majority of the buildings on Victoria's street have awnings with people huddled under them, waiting for the rain to let up a bit. The overcast sky and dampened business folk drown the block in an ocean of gray clouds and suits. The only bit of color brightening my day was Victoria, and now that she's out of sight, I can feel the gloom and cold starting to consume me. I speed past the horde of pedestrians, through the cloudburst, until her doorman puts up an arm.

"Your business here today, madam?" He's older, not a threat. He's also not armed.

I am.

My face slides into its classic mask, a small polite smile lifting my wind-burned cheeks. "I'm here visiting Ms. Fenwick."

He does a quick once over of me, taking in my appearance.

My dark hair is tied back into my usual tight, low bun, and my tailored, black Givenchy suit is sopping from the rain, giving off the impression I can afford to ruin it and get another. Which is true.

When his eyes meet mine again, he gives a courteous smile and nods, letting me know I've passed his measly inspection of wealth.

"I'm glad she's finally getting some visitors," he says, opening the door. A wave of relief washes through me at being the first person that's come here for her. I return his smile walking in.

Too easy. Anyone could get to her here.

I head toward the elevator bay, taking in the high ceilings and gigantic, modern chandelier with a curl of my lip. A panel on the wall lists the names of the residents and their corresponding floor number. There's no button to call the elevator, only an electronic pad the residents scan their key cards with and the buttons beside the names on the panel for guests to buzz in.

Victoria's name is at the bottom, her view of the city further flaunting her wealth.

V. FENWICK
Floor 15

A sharp smile cuts across my face, my heart pounding in my chest. *I'll see you soon, Little Fox.*

2

Victoria

TODAY WAS A LONG day.

I spent three hours in a morning lecture about cyber-crimes and how they can and can't be prosecuted. We also learned what steps to take in order to protect our client-attorney information from hackers. Spoiler, it involves a pen, paper, and carpal tunnel.

Lots and lots of carpal tunnel.

I rub the knot in my shoulder that formed after leaving the library, barely releasing any of the deep ache from lugging the encyclopedic-sized publications on ethics, influential cases, and a lot of other mind-bendingly dry topics I brought home.

This is what you wanted, Victoria. This is your dream. It's not your fault the path to your dream is currently boring as hell.

Glancing around my apartment, I stick my tongue out at the kitchen, shuffling toward my room with a heavy sigh. I'm way too tired to cook, so I swipe open my phone and place a call to order take out for the third time this week. *I'll never be out of the mood for some lo mein.*

It'll be at least thirty minutes before it gets here, so I strip my clothes off and kick them across my bedroom near the hamper, prepping for a quick shower.

My naked reflection looks back at me from the large window encompassing an entire wall of my bedroom.

I wonder what it'd be like if someone saw me right now. If it'd feel empowering to have a say over how much of my body people get to see again. A lot of people have seen me naked, but no one I've ever given permission to.

Right now, though, staring at myself in the glass, I'm granting any wandering eyes the opportunity to see me. *All* of me. It's exhilarating, and my nipples harden at the thought, my breath catching in my chest at the sensation.

I brush my curls back, looking wholly at my nakedness, watching the anxious but equally excited goosebumps shiver awake over my body. My cheeks are rosy from the thrill of being caught, but my eyes are wide with nerves at that same time.

I can't believe I'm doing this.

Taking a half step toward the window, a familiar heat pools low in my stomach. I tighten my legs, fighting the urge to let myself get any more aroused as I glance down at the pedestrian filled sidewalk and bite my bottom lip, failing to hold in my laugh.

"No one is getting a free show tonight," I giggle, turning and prancing to the shower, knowing I'm the only one that actually saw anything.

3

Shaelene

Victoria needs blinds.

I have the most perfect view of her half naked body from my newly leased apartment in the building adjacent to hers. Private penthouse suites mean nothing in a city full of skyscrapers.

Not that I'm complaining.

The windows in her apartment grant me sightlines into her open living and dining rooms and the master bedroom on the other side of the dividing wall. They're floor to ceiling glass and slightly tinted, but not enough to block me from seeing her move around as she settles onto the couch for dinner.

My little fox is a creature of habit, which is far more dangerous than she realizes. I've followed her to and from Sloane every day since my father put her on my radar, and even if I didn't already have her schedule memorized, I would now.

We need to fix that.

He didn't ask for more information after we returned to Laughlin Manor with our intel a few days ago, the three of us officially dismissed until further notice, but I couldn't let her go. I can't leave her alone.

So here I am.

Our firm isn't currently representing anyone, so there's no work to be done there. Shaun and Shephard quickly made themselves busy with one of their favorite girls to share, reverting back to their nocturnal habits. As for myself, I've gotten comfortable in my new high-rise with views to die for.

The lease came with the show furniture, all of it completely opposite my taste. Everything is ultra-modern. Abstract stock art on the walls, an uncomfortable couch, and fake fruit in a bowl on the kitchen island to top it all off. As tacky as it is, I don't mind because this apartment is nothing more than a place to watch for me. I only care about the bedroom. I've made it sparse, lugging the ugly items to the spare room at the other end of the hall, leaving only a king bed against the wall facing the windows looking into Victoria's bedroom. The only other bit of furniture is a small desk in the corner that my laptop sits on, hooked up to the camera I've got precisely positioned on a tripod.

I zoom my lens to get a closer look despite knowing she's lying on her bed with her thin nose in another book. She's read four in the days I've been staking her out.

The translucent cream curtains she has hanging do little to conceal her from me. Instead, they only serve to give my photos a hazy look. *Exactly how my brain feels any time I'm anywhere other than here looking at her.* Which is another reason I've spent every second not at the manor perched right here at this window, watching Victoria like a hawk.

Her pale, ivory skin is dotted with freckles from her face all the way down to her toes. *I'm going to count every last one of them. With my tongue. While she begs me for more.*

Her dainty fingers trace the pages of **The Routledge Handbook of Criminal Justice Ethics** and goosebumps pebble across my skin.

It's adorable how hard she's studying the pages of a book Father had us burn our first year attending Sloane.

I angle my lens further, focusing on the sheer pink blouse she wore to class that's been taunting me all damn day. Except now it teasingly hides her bare chest, the shadow of her nipples barely peeking through the fabric. And right as my camera focuses enough for me to see them, she rolls to her stomach, propping herself up on her arms as she reads.

The curve of her back as her body sinks into the mattress sends another spike of electricity through me. Her ass is begging to be freed from the cheeky panties she's wearing.

She's wearing more clothes tonight than she did the first day I set myself up here. Her beautiful, round tits were on full display for me while she laid in bed with her robe open eating her Chinese food.

If I were there right now...

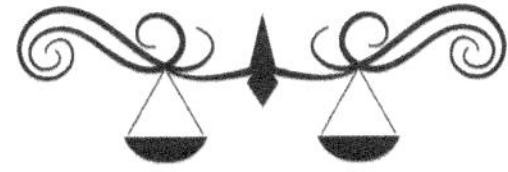

"An intern?" Shaun questions, straightening in his seat.

My father and uncle, the namesakes for Laughlin & Laughlin of today, stand in the grand study, arms crossed and looking down at the three of us in our seats.

"Yes. An intern, Shaun," Uncle repeats.

Laughlin & Laughlin hasn't taken on a student intern in decades. We don't exactly do things the way professors at Sloane teach them to be done.

"Who?" Shephard asks, brows somehow perked and furrowed at the same time. He isn't keen on newcomers unless he sees it as an opportunity to get his dick wet.

A small, exasperated laugh bursts from my chest, my jaw tensing as I put two and two together miles ahead of my siblings. My brothers eye me as I shake my head in disbelief. *This is perfect, but also the worst fucking thing that could happen.*

"Victoria Fenwick," I answer, easily masking the arousal in my voice.

Shephard shifts in his seat, eating up my words and clapping his hands together. "Well, *that* will be distracting." He winks at Shaun, who's also smiling a sadistic grin.

"You're not going to touch her. Either of you," our father orders.

"When?" I cut in, changing the subject before the boys can make any more remarks about my girl.

I look up at him, my chin resting on my thumbs while my elbows are propped up on my legs. A position of power. Ease. Confidence. One he taught me as soon as I understood the influence we had on those around us. His stern brows straighten from their scowl, his face softening into a bland neutral.

"Monday." His shoulders roll back as he walks through the space between the three of us to the back of the room toward his desk. A silent signal our conversation is over. One we're all well versed with.

I rise from my chair and grab my suit jacket from its place slumped over the seatback. Throwing it on, I walk out, the boys riding my ass the second I leave. They both saw her during our stakeout. I saw the way their bodies reacted. I noticed because mine did the same. *If they think—*

"We know what you've been doing, Shae," Shephard threatens from behind me. I turn on my heels so quick his chest hits mine.

"You don't know shit, Shep," I bite back, forcing him to retreat a step.

I'm not a small woman. I inherited our father's height, so I'm an easy six foot without my heels on.

I don't know what possessed me to wear them today, but right now they keep my eyes at the same level as Shephard's. No looking up those few spare inches like usual; we're eye to eye and neither of us is backing down.

His lip twitches in annoyance.

"You're running off to your room to cook up some story to tell that pretty little ginger about us so she won't let us fuck her." His voice is quiet, but accusatory, as he leers, "Too bad it won't work." *And now we're both pissed.*

That's something I did do when we were younger, but I won't need to fabricate anything now. I'll make sure Victoria isn't the least bit interested in my meathead brothers. *She'll be obsessed with me just as much as I am her.*

The boys haven't paid me any attention in the last week, so Shephard has no idea I'm actually grabbing my bags in preparation to head back to my new apartment and resume stalking my little fox.

You're already behind, brother. Better luck next time.

I press my stare deeper into his and feel his hot breath when he scoffs. "It's a good thing Father only needs you for muscle, Shep, because you're a fucking idiot."

Shaun smirks from over his shoulder, arms crossed, enjoying the show.

"Fuck you, Shae!" Shephard yells as I walk away, my middle finger proudly raised over my shoulder.

I have four days before Victoria shows up here and I have to fend them off.

Four days to snare her in my trap.

Game fucking on.

She's naked. Again.

My blood heats, my body wound tight as I stare without shame or remorse.

She likes to look at herself, and I love looking at her. A win-win. *She must know someone could see her like this. Surely.*

Her phone is in her hands, and I zoom as far as I can to see what she's typing. It looks like an ad for a roommate.

I think the fuck *not.*

I pull my cell from my sweatshirt pocket and angrily swipe the screen open. A photo I took of her lounging on the couch the other day shines brightly, illuminating my face in the otherwise dark room. I swallow the all too familiar lump that's taken up residence in my throat every time I look at it, then search the site and quickly find her listing.

**FEMALE ROOMMATE WANTED
TWO BEDROOM HIGH RISE IN PELHAM BAY
PRIVATE ROOM WITH EN SUITE BATH & WALK-IN
CLOSET**

**SHARED COMMON SPACE & FULL KITCHEN
RENT: $0/MONTH & SPLIT UTILITIES
NO PETS PLEASE
INQUIRE AT V_FENWICK01@GMAIL.COM**

The front doorman may be easy to get past, but nobody is getting through me into that apartment.

I make quick work of sending an email from a fake account that looks like an automated message from the site's support team. She opens it immediately, and with that, I'm in. Excitement thrums through my veins as I remotely access her settings while her screen doesn't display a thing out of the ordinary.

Shaun programmed an app a year ago allowing the user to bypass the satellite signal and forward any notifications to a separate device before sending it to the intended person a few minutes later.

We used it to get information about a client's meet up a few cases ago. Now any emails that come through about someone interested in her spare room—*and any texts or DMs*—will come to me first, giving me time to delete them before she even gets a notification.

She tosses her phone to the side and stands with a huff. She looks stressed, her muscles tense and begging for release as her tiny frame—barely shoulder height on me—walks to her window.

It's past midnight. Nearly all the residents in her building and mine seem to be down or out for the night. Hers is the only one with the lights still on.

Mine is blacked out as usual.

The yellowish glow from the lamp on her bedside table lets her see her reflection in the glass pane, her eyes tracing over every inch with careful precision. She isn't stupid. She knows there's a chance someone could see her. My throat closes at the realization... She *wants* someone to be watching.

My little fox is naughty.

I grab my camera and walk to the window, sliding it open the little bit I can this high up. Her eyes are down, looking at her slender legs, completely oblivious to me over here.

Her fingers slink along the curve of her hip, gliding across her stomach to her navel, then up between her perky breasts. Her other hand slides up the back of her neck, getting lost in her wild hair as her eyes glaze over with lust.

CLICK.

A blinding flash shatters the darkness between us.

Her eyes grow wide with terror, her secret fantasy coming to life in front of her. She doesn't move. She's frozen, pondering whether or not she actually saw what she thinks she did.

Her head whips side to side, her body leaning forward on her toes, struggling to figure out which direction her photographer is shooting from.

CLICK.

I shoot another flash straight at her, capturing her mesmerizing profile. A sadistic, satisfied grin twists my face. *She knows where I am now.*

I unlock my phone, keeping my head down so she can't see my face when it's lit up.

> **Pose for me tomorrow.**

She jumps when it goes off behind her, her chest bouncing from the movement. Her nipples are hard. Cheeks flushed. The apex of her thighs slick.

This excites her just as much as it scares her.

Walking backwards, she snatches her phone, quickly unlocking it. Her head snaps back in my direction, her breaths labored. She stares for a long moment, trying her best to see me through the shadows, before she runs over to the lamp and turns it off. The faint glow from her phone is the only thing lighting her face, her sharp cheekbones highlighting her arousal.

Little Fox

Who is this?

One foot in the snare.

I type a quick response, but before sending it, I place my camera back on the tripod facing her. Flipping the light on right as I step into the hall, ready to head back to the manor for the night. All she'll see is an empty bedroom and my camera looking back at her.

See you soon, Little Fox.

4

Victoria

I CAN HARDLY REST, too paralyzed with fear and guilt to get up and dress myself even with the lights off, so I stay hidden beneath the covers, naked and cold, until I feel certain he's gone. But that feeling never seems to come. I have no clue if he's watching me through the camera or from his computer next to it. *And I can't decide whether that scares or excites me.*

At some point I managed to fall asleep, and now the sunlight burns through my eyelids. I sneak around trying to get ready for class—unable to fight the impulse to keep looking over to his apartment.

Why did I stand there long enough for someone to take photos of me? Again...

Someone seeing is one thing, but he could show those photos to anyone. My heart pounds in my chest, my hands shaking as I curl them into fists. I'm so angry. Livid. At myself. At him. At allowing someone to take my feigned sense of control away.

So, why the hell do I hope he texts me tonight?

Classes run long, and I miss lunch because I decide to hide in the library the entire time, distracting myself by doodling in my notebook until my hands are stained blue with ink. I've been checking my phone religiously, worried I'll see a message. *Worried I'll* miss *a message.*

When I finally leave, the sky is an even more gloomy shade of gray than it was this morning, and rain cascades over the windshield on my drive home, forcing me to ignore the underlying adrenaline in my veins so I don't go skidding into oncoming traffic. It's no surprise I found myself stopping for Chinese again on the way. I look at the paper cartons in my passenger seat and laugh at myself. *I'm not an awful cook, just not a good one.* And with everything going on, take-out for the fourth time this week seems like the perfect solution.

Next week will be better.

After parking in the underground, I walk to the stairs leading to the street at the front of the building, curling against the wind and rain, knowing it's faster to go through the main lobby to get to the mail lockers even though my jacket is drenched now. *I am so ready to be safely inside my apartment.*

Well... Safeish.

I smile at Harvey, my doorman, and he greets me with a joyful grin of his own saying, "Glad to see you made a friend, Ms. Fenwick."

My stomach drops along with my jaw. "Friend?" My brain short circuits. *Oh my god! Please tell me Harvey didn't see me naked!*

Harvey stands quietly, holding the door open and looking more confused than I am, so I shake my head awkwardly and excuse myself with a stiff smile. *Of course it wasn't Harvey. Jesus Christ, Victoria. Get it together.*

"Fuck the mail," I mutter as I cross the lobby and swipe my key card, heading straight upstairs and bolting the lock behind me the second the door is shut.

I take in everything with my back against it. The cabinets are closed and the doors down the hall still shut. One of my most recent paintings in the dining room looks off-kilter, but I know that's just from my shitty hang job. The overall sense of rightness in here makes my anxiety dim and I lean my head against the door, closing my eyes and listening to the sound of the rain against the windows.

I keep the lights off in the house, shuffling around in the almost dark. It's still dreary outside, but with the TV in the living room on, there's enough light coming in for me to see. It quietly streams the news while I unpack and sort my food out of its containers.

"NYPD's Chief of Police held a press conference today, urging the citizens of New York to come forward with any information or eyewitness accounts regarding the shooting that occurred last Wednesday in the city's upper west side. The victim, Milano Angelini, age forty-two, was the son of multi-billionaire, Grigorio Angelini, who has since declined giving any statement about his son's murder—"

I step into my bedroom, keeping the light off as I enter. Feeding my newest bad habit, I glance at the building across the way. There's no movement that I can see.

Yet.

Pacing, my stomach churns, my eyes constantly swinging toward the darkened windows. I can't function while on edge like this. In limbo, dreading something might happen. *Waiting for it to happen.*

I set my food down and head back to the kitchen in search for one thing in particular. A bottle opener. *I need this.* Finding it, I make quick work of opening a bottle of wine and pouring myself a drink. A *large* drink. It's not the best pairing for my noodles but fuck it. It's going to help my nerves settle, and I could use the relief.

I'm half an hour into my latest binge show—some trashy reality TV series about fake lawyers in Los Angeles that make law firms seem more daunting than I originally thought. The sky is dark, and the sound of the rain clammers harder against the windows.

My dinner plate sits empty on the bed beside me, and I abandon the glass to drink straight from my bottle since it's almost gone anyway. I jump when my phone vibrates against the nightstand, my breath lodging in my throat as wine soaks into my shirt.

A text!

UNKNOWN

Dragon City for dinner again?

Oh shit. I whirl to face the window, my heart threatening to crack my chest. Even with the lights off, I'm in the spotlight again. *How long has he been watching me to know what I've had for dinner all week?* I reach for the remote to turn off the TV, when another message comes through, freezing me in place.

UNKNOWN

Leave it on.

I hesitate, my thumb hovering over the big red button. I swallow the lump forming in my throat and sit back, glancing at the window out of the corner of my eye.

Who is this?

The same message I sent last night that he ignored.

UNKNOWN

Nobody.

My face reddens, anger building in my chest. He's somebody, and he has lewd photos of me. I should've spent today making a report at the police station, but I didn't. *Why the hell didn't I?* The idea of more intimate photos of myself scares the shit out of me. *He* scares the shit out of me.

The hair on the back of my neck stands on end. I know he's watching me. Waiting for me to feed into his little game, but I'm done. *I refuse to play anymore.* I block the unknown number and toss my phone, resuming my show even though I can't concentrate. *I'll report him tomorrow during my lunch hour.*

My phone vibrates again, my breathing nonexistent as I flip my phone to read it.

S

I'm waiting.

What. The. Fuck?

I blocked him. I know I did. I check the contact to make sure it's the same number I've been staring at for days. It is. And... *S?* He changed his name in my phone somehow too. *Yeah, "S" for fucking STALKER Victoria!*

A chill rushes down my spine and my phone shakes in my hands so hard I can barely type my two-word response.

> **For what?**

> S
>
> **For you to pose for me.**

Suddenly I can't stop my thumbs from moving, heat flaring in my chest.

> **I don't know who the hell you are, but you need to lose my fucking number. You got your pics last night, and that's all you're getting. Do whatever you're gonna do with them, then fuck off and leave me alone.**

I immediately regret sending it. *He knows where I live.* He could easily get to me here or in the garage or anywhere else he's possibly been watching me. He's been here once already, according to Harvey. *What's to stop him from getting in again?*

> S
>
> **Those are only for me.**

Relief settles over me and my shoulders relax enough for me to breathe a little easier. *At least my stalker isn't going to expose me to the entire world.* "What a nice fucking guy," I grumble as my anger takes control again, my thumbs flying across the keys another time.

> Well, thank you, Mr. Stalker, for not sharing your illegal photos of me with the world. That'd really hurt my feelings. How long have you been watching me anyway?

> Creep.

I don't even know why my fingers keep typing. My flight instincts are blaring; a cold sweat covers my body, but something in my chest is salivating at the thought of knowing why he's so interested in me. *Am I just the neighbor that happened to be naked in the window one night and he wants to see more? Or does it go deeper?*

> Pose.

I roll my eyes at his dismissal of my questions and suck at my teeth. *Two can play this game.*

I tear the blanket off and stride to the window. My reflection flashes along with the TV, blocking the view of his darkened apartment, but I know he's in there. I fluff my hair over my shoulder and flip him the bird.

His camera flashes, another white spark of light shattering the night, pissing me off even more.

Well, that *didn't work.*

He's not only getting off from my pictures, but by riling me up too. Turning to climb back into bed, my phone vibrates once more, stopping me in my tracks.

Such a feisty little fox.

5

Shaelene

IT WAS ADORABLY NAIVE when she tried to block my number, but she can't get rid of me that easily. She's scared, trying to wrestle back some semblance of control by flipping me off. I force a deep breath, ignoring the way my hardened nipples scrape against my sweatshirt and make me shiver. Try as she might to deny it, I know I've gotten under her skin. I know I've piqued her interest.

I know she's mine.

And that fact has my pussy throbbing.

Getting her riled up is as enjoyable as watching her perfect ass prance around campus in her pencil skirts and heels, demanding my attention with each clack of her stilettos. But right now, *her* attention is on *me*.

Or the idea of me rather.

She likely thinks I'm some random guy choosing to watch her. Scoffing, I lift my camera and adjust the focus. I don't have a choice. I *need* to watch her. She's held dominion over my mind every second since I spotted her at Sloane.

She's curled up in bed, again, debating whether or not to reply to me. Chat bubbles keep popping up and disappearing over and over as her fingers scurry across the screen then freeze. Scurry then freeze. *Just like a true fox.* I want to frighten her, get her adrenaline surging and watch her pulse skyrocket in her neck, but I need her to trust me too. So, I wait for her to respond.

And wait.

And *wait.*

Finally, she settles on telling me what I already know. What exhilarates and worries me at the same time.

Little Fox

You scare me.

Despite her precious display of defiance earlier, she sinks further under her blanket, my heart lurching as she closes herself off to me. *This hunt isn't over yet, Little Fox.* Drumming my fingers against my thigh, I stand, making a decision I hope will both appease her and help my case. I draw my hood up, shadowing my face.

This better work...

Victoria didn't see me when I first got back into my apartment. I stood by the bedroom door waiting for her to look over, giving her the chance to catch a glimpse of me, but she was too busy finishing her first glass of wine. From what I've noticed thus far, she's not the most observant about her surroundings. *We'll be changing that ASAP. No fox of mine will be oblivious.*

Frustrated—and disappointed—I came in, turning off the light with the pull chain instead of the switch. Now I walk to the middle of the room, standing beneath it, and text her.

Pose for me.

Then I'll pose for you.

She jolts from her spot on the bed, fighting the urge to look my way. Contemplating my offer with an anxious purse of her lips.

She's wondering what she might see. *Am I going to be a crazy perv standing naked at the window jacking off? Is she going to see a face she recognizes?*

Neither.

I'm not showing her my face, but if she sees a person rather than an anonymous texter behind a screen, the hope is she'll get comfortable with me. That she'll *trust* me enough to let me get even closer. Let me fuck— *One thought at a time. Focus.*

Little Fox

What are you doing with the photos?

She's curious. *And no longer threatening me to leave her alone.* Excitement bubbles within me, something I've only experienced on a true hunt before. *She wants to play along with my game.*

What do you think?

Her body is incredible, and the confidence she exudes when she looks at herself naked is the sexiest thing I've ever witnessed. She's a petite, speckled goddess, and she knows it. I know it. The power she wields over my thoughts is excruciating. Desire pools in my stomach every time I see her, and looking at her photos makes me painfully ache to touch her. I want her more than I've ever wanted anything, so much I haven't been able to touch myself to climax because I want my fingers to be inside of her instead.

I want to feel her wetness drip onto my hand. Her warmth as her cunt squeezes around my fingers. *Fuck.* I'm dripping just imagining her giving in to me, but I have to be slow with this or I'll never get her to surrender herself.

Little Fox

How do you want me?

My heart pounds as I look up from my phone and see her standing at the window searching for me.

Naked. I want her naked. *Now.*

She's wearing an oversized t-shirt with the Maryland State University emblem across the front and a pair of shorts painted to her curves. I need her undressed, but I want her to think she's in control. That's when she's herself. That's when she's my enticing little fox.

Her cheeks flush and she glances my way through her lashes, licking her bottom lip and drawing it between her teeth. My breath catches when, finally, she bends forward, slowly skimming her shorts down her legs.

She straightens, the hem of her shirt barely low enough to cover the alluring pink of her cunt. Her chest rises with a shaky breath, but her arms cross as she balls her shirt in her hands, pulling it over her head and dropping it beside her to the floor.

Thank God for the distance and rain sounds between us because the feral growl that comes from my throat scares even me.

Her body is so small compared to mine. My fingers flex around my cell, hard enough it's case groans in protest. *I can't wait to pin her to my bed and hold her there, writhing beneath me while I grind against her.*

I know her phone is on vibrate. I saw it when I mirrored her screen to unblock my number. A wicked smile lifts my lips, power and anticipation making my legs weak. I'll show her a glimpse of who I am, but not until *after* I make her cum.

> **Lay on your bed and put your phone against your clit.**

Her curls bounce slightly from the tremble of her shoulders. Her gaze becoming less searching and more glossy—like she's in a trance. Her brows scrunch, and I can sense I'm starting to lose her.

> **Please.**

Her eyes unknowingly meet mine when she glances from her screen again, forcing a hard swallow before lifting her chin and crawling onto the bed. With her back flat against her top sheet, her hair frames her head in a gorgeous splay of orange curls. She shudders through a heavy breath and holds her phone between her legs. Her eyes closed with anticipation.

I call her, the phone vibrating against her pussy with each ring. Her back arches from the initial jolt, and the showcase of her flexibility makes my core tighten. I end the call when her voicemail sounds. Her breathing slows, her body floating away from my teasing, so I call again, watching her hips buck against the limbo her hands keep her trapped in. *Voicemail.*

I hang up before my shallow panting can get picked up by the recording and redial, calling a third time.

My free hand drifts between my legs, rubbing myself through far too many layers of clothes. Her mouth hangs open, eyes shut tight as she inches closer. *What I would do to hear the sounds she's making right now. To suck that lip between mine...*

She's too close, her chest flushes as she balances on the edge of release. I hang up. *I want her to cum knowing how fucking beautiful she is.*

My thumbs slash across my screen. Sending text after text until her hips jerk before finally sinking heavily back into her mattress.

She turns to face my window, opening her eyes lazily, her lids heavy with pleasure. As promised, I reach above me and flick the light on. I'm wearing the same hoodie from yesterday—my hair tucked down my back to conceal it—and a pair of sweats. Hands in my pockets, none of my curves are on display, and a black neck gaiter covers the bottom half of my face, hiding the delicate line of my jaw. Even if she could see my eyes through the darkness, she wouldn't be able to distinguish me from anyone else. *They're the same as so many others.*

I've revealed nothing, yet I feel more exposed than I ever have before.

I leave the apartment, forcing my gait to remain casual despite the slickness between my thighs. The only picture I took tonight was the one of her flipping me off, but I'm more than satisfied with the way this evening went.

6

Victoria

Somebody *did* get a free show. Somebody terrifying.

He left a few minutes ago, turning on the light before stepping out, his hand barely having to reach over his head to pull the chain.

He's tall.

Really fucking tall, and his shoulders were broad as he stalked through the doorway out of the room. I didn't see his face beneath his hood, but god*damn* if that quick glimpse wasn't enough to make my heart race and my pussy throb again. Then everything blurred as I watched him walk out, tears running down my temples in hot streaks.

I let myself be put in a position for someone to use me for their own pleasure *again*. Memories have been bombarding me since he disappeared, my limbs heavy at my side as phantom ropes trap me once more. I haven't even moved from my spot on the bed.

At first, I was frozen with fear, then bliss. Now I'm lying here, stuck in place with shame and regret, dampened by cum and tears. I started crying after my body convulsed, ecstasy flooding my veins with a nirvana I crave. I couldn't stop the orgasm from wracking through my body no matter how hard I tried. Which, honestly, wasn't at all.

You wanted it, Victoria. Accept that truth.

I can't; my mind is too busy racing with memories.

I blink my eyes open, a throbbing pain in my temple. My legs are numb from the wet cement below me, my cheer uniform is gone, and my skin is riddled with goosebumps.

Beside me is Macy Stewards, my best friend. Her eyes are wide, terror unlike anything I've ever seen taking over them completely. Duct tape covers her mouth, but I can still make out the quiver of her breath as her shoulders shake. Her uniform is stripped from her too. I try to reach for her but my arms don't budge. Something is holding my wrists tied behind my back. When I meet her eyes again, they dart past me, and I turn, my neck stiff.

Jillian Maybeck is on the floor against the wall. Rebecca Townes beside her.

My pulse quickens as I see nearly every girl from the junior class tied up and stripped around me. Most of them awake—their faces a mirror of Macy's—with tape keeping them quiet.

Jillian jolts when she sees I'm conscious. Trying to get my attention, her muffled sobs are incoherent. Manic. Desperate. Then her head is yanked back. Her hair tangled in the tight grip of Sterling Briggs makes her whimper as new tears spill down her cheeks. He laughs when she cries out, shaking her head hard to hear the noise again.

I press against the wall, my foot slipping on the wet tile with a squeak. His head whips my direction, the smile widening across his face.

"Look who's finally awake, boys!" He drops Jillian's hair and stands, cruelty sharpening his features. From the half-wall behind him, Coleson and Parker step around to take their usual places at his side. "Now it's a party."

Sterling's hand snaps out, showing the speed he's praised for on the field, reaching above me and turning on the showers. The water is ice cold, and my already frozen body stiffens further. My nipples ache from how tightly they've peaked, pushing against the thin padding of my sopping bra.

More football players walk into the locker room. All seniors. All smiling. Some still wearing their game pads, with their jerseys slung over their shoulders, others in only a towel from their shower.

My hair sticks to my face and neck. Sterling turns the tap, stopping the barrage of water he forced down. I hear the boys in the back laugh, my skin crawling at the sound. Sterling crouches in front of me, his fingers gently moving a wet curl from my eyes.

Coleson taps his shoulder with something, but I refuse to look away from him. Sterling takes it and flips it open, the blade glinting in the moonlight seeping in from the small windows above the lockers. My breath hitches, and I know he sees my fear.

Another cold smile forms on his face. "I'm not gonna hurt you, Vicky. Just wanna get you a little more comfortable." He traces the blade against my cheek, then down the length of my neck. Over my collarbone and slowly along the top of my chest. The tip pricks the skin of my sternum when he runs it down between my breasts.

I wince at the sharp burn when the edge cuts into my skin, parting the fabric of my bra and making it fall open. Blood trickles down my stomach, forming a small, warm pool in my belly button.

The muscles in my arms strain as they go painfully stiffer, everything blurring around me as tears fill my eyes and fall in hot streaks down my body alongside the blood.

My phone rings between my legs, pulling me from the nightmare and driving me toward another peak.

Is he back?

My eyes dart to the lit apartment across from me. *Still empty.*

Another strong buzz vibrates against me, and I lift my phone to my face, the brightness stinging my eyes as my mother's photo smiles down at me.

"Hi, Mom," I answer, trying not to sound too flustered.

"Honey, it's been a month, and you haven't called."

She and my father helped me move into the apartment at the beginning of the semester and she cried the entire last hour they were here because she couldn't accept me not being in the house anymore. I'd made a point to call her every week to keep her worries at bay, but I was so busy preparing for the internship lottery I neglected calling her.

For five weeks.

I honestly didn't realize it'd been that long. I haven't had time to think about anything else, and now we've been assigned to our firms, so I'll be equally as swamped with work, if not more.

"How are you doing? Everything okay? Are you alright by yourself? You know, sweetie, you can always come home for a bit to—"

"I'm doing good, Mom. I really like New York," I interrupt her. My eyes glancing at my stalker's bedroom again. *He's still gone.* "I start my internship next week."

She pauses. I can hear in the way she's breathing she was hoping I'd come home. If I did, I'd be giving up a huge opportunity for me to actually live the life I want to. To be successful and feel purposeful again. If I quit and go home now, I'll lose myself in the headspace I've tried so hard to escape.

I'd potentially lose the stalker though. That thought nearly makes me want to pack up and head home right now, but who's to say he wouldn't try to find me there too? Plus, then I'd have a stalker *and* a helicopter mom. *So... Two stalkers.*

I pull my comforter over myself and sink impossibly further into my mattress. *I'm staying here.*

"Okay, Vicky, if you're sure," she concedes and my body cringes. She used to be the only one that called me that.

Until Sterling did.

I've never told her about what happened after the homecoming game. None of us told anyone. We were all too scared after the boys threatened to kill us if we did.

They made sure we knew our worth. So many vile insults just for walking down the hall, immediately followed by a wandering hand or eye. Bruises covered my arms. My legs. My chest. All of us lived in fear until graduation. They made sure we stayed quiet, enjoying every moment of our silence.

"I'm sure, Mom," I force out, trying to forget. "I'll call you next week after I start my internship, okay?"

Another pause, but she finally agrees, and I tell her I love her multiple times before hanging up. The line drops and my screen lights up again, displaying all of my notifications.

(3) MISSED CALLS: S
(8) NEW MESSAGES

S

> **I like when you're angry.**

> **Keep flipping me off and I'll show you a better use for those fingers.**

> **You're so close now.**

I can't wait to touch you.

Taste you.

Fuck you.

Come for you.

You're utterly divine, Little Fox.

7

Victoria

THE RAIN HAS FINALLY let up, but the lingering clouds keep the sun at bay this morning, so I dress in leggings rather than shorts for my run. Class keeps me busy during the weekdays and the weekends are the only time I really have for exercise, which is why I opt to take the stairs for a little extra cardio.

I passed out quickly after my shower last night. The anger, fear, adrenaline, and orgasm tolled my body into complete exhaustion, but I still woke up in the middle of the night from a dream about my stalker being in the room this time. I tossed and turned until my alarm went off looking at the texts he sent.

'You're utterly divine, Little Fox'...

I've received plenty of compliments throughout my life—my hair gets brought up in conversation almost daily—but I've never had a positive comment during a sexual encounter before.

Part of me wants to delete the messages. To forget and go back to my lonely life of abstinence. To protect myself the only way I know how. But another part of me likes it. And every time I think about his texts my insides melt, and I have to clench my thighs to keep from dripping into my panties. There's a comfort in being told what to do. To not have to be the one to think. Having someone else know what I need.

He gave me that comfort without hurting me. *Scared me, for sure, but physically I'm fine—*

I drop the thought and greet Harvey when I step outside, putting in my headphones to drown out the noise in my head as I start my jog toward the path that loops around the park behind my building.

The two-lane track runs along the edge of the lush green park. One of the few spots of open grass in this concrete city. On the closest side is a large fountain with tables and chairs surrounding it where a few people sit eating their breakfast, and a couple grandpas play chess while another relaxes a few tables away reading the paper. It's idyllic. Calm. Peaceful after the chaos of last night.

I'm finishing my second lap when a girl runs through me, pushing my shoulder as she jogs past. I catch myself before I stumble to the ground but lose one of my headphones thanks to her shove. Instinctively, I throw out my hands, stopping in my tracks with a jolt that rattles my ankle. An angry, assertive part of me rears her head, one I haven't known in a decade.

"What the hell!" I shout, my heart pounding as my shoulder aches.

She's a lot bigger than me. I definitely wouldn't win in a fight, but that's not going to stop me from cussing her out anyway.

Her head turns, glancing at me over her shoulder. The black hoodie she wears bobs with her shoulders as she runs, covering most of her face, and her eyes are cloaked by the ball cap she has low over her brow. A long black ponytail pulled through the back of it sways as she jogs further away from me.

Her stride is way longer than mine, her steps creating distance between us with ease. She's too fast and too far for me to catch up and do anything about it now.

"Bitch," I mutter through heavy breaths.

I walk the rest of my lap, hands on my hips and eyes peeled for any other park bullies before I finish back at the fountain. My adrenaline is pumping too fast for my body even as I slow and pace by the benches. The push angered me more than I thought it did, and my body is in panic mode while my mind is still exhausted from last night. I look around, trying to focus on anything other than my ragged breaths. *I need to wake up.* There are a few cafes across the street and now seems as good a time as any to get my caffeine fix.

8

Shaelene

"Where have you been?" Shephard asks.

"Out," I snap, as if it's any of his business.

Shaun enters the other side of the kitchen, dressed in only his shorts like Shep. "You reek," he teases, scrunching his nose in mock disgust.

Their taunts mean nothing after joining Victoria on her run, my shoulder still warm where I bumped into her. I pull the orange juice from the fridge, walking to the cabinet to grab glasses before either of them can snatch it and take a gulp straight from the tap. I haven't showered yet, so Shaun isn't wrong. Running in my hoodie had me working up a sweat.

There are far more fun ways to sweat with my little fox... It's only a matter of time.

Too bad patience has never been one of my virtues.

After Victoria finished her laps, she walked to the coffee shop across the street and was there while I snuck into her apartment. I didn't want her doorman to see me and hold me up with questions again, so I went through the garage.

Our buildings share the underground space, divided by a few concrete pylons to stop cars. I walked right through, having no problems accessing the elevators leading up to her building since

I borrowed Shaun's RFID skimmer to steal a digital copy of Victoria's key card.

I swiped it when I ran by her, giving her a nudge for good measure. My hand subconsciously rubs over the spot, a small smirk softening my face. After last night, I don't know if I'll be able to keep my hands off her much longer.

She always spends a good half an hour sitting and drinking her coffee outside the cafe—plenty of time for me to run upstairs and install a few wireless cameras. *And straighten an annoyingly crooked canvas hanging on her wall.*

She got home shortly before I arrived back here, my need to be near her begging me to return to my apartment and the view I know I'd find there the entire drive. Last I saw, she was sitting in her living room reading another one of her library books, her hair wet from her shower and wrapped up in an old t-shirt to protect her curls. I closed the feed before coming into the house, keeping it hidden from any wandering eyes.

I scan my brothers' movements as we maneuver around each other, feeling in my pocket to make sure my phone is still where I left it.

I'm not going to text her tonight. I want to watch her from afar. See how she responds to the silence. See if she aches for more.

"Toast?" Shephard asks from across the island as I pour three glasses. I nod and he turns, setting the toaster for us. My eyes catch his back tattoo, the bold lines stark against his tan skin. A tiger's face snarls across the entirety of his muscular torso, his branding scar artfully hidden beneath a stripe of black fur. The same scar Shaun and I also inked over.

I glance to where Shaun's would be if it weren't camouflaged on his chest, and fight to hide my stupid, spreading grin before either of them notice and take it as invitation to keep asking the details of my whereabouts.

Over the years we've made quite the reputation for ourselves within the elite crime community. Not that Father expects any less of us. Maybe to be a bit more inconspicuous in our early years, but it's all worked out fine. *Though I'm sure he really hates that the nickname stuck.*

Although we've represented a lot of the Dons in court, we don't always stay neutral and occasionally end up sending messages to all major players in the city. They've dubbed us 'The Unholy Triad'. It's fitting given how many sins the three of us have committed. There's no shortage of darkness blanketing our souls—if we ever had them to begin with—and that's how we like it.

Shep snatches the toast when it pops, sliding a plateful onto the island between us. Shaun grabs the peanut butter and several slices for himself, and I take a solitary piece and eat it plain, sipping my juice.

Shephard knocks back half his cup in one swig and eyes me. "Seriously, Shae, where have you been?"

I've slept at the apartment for a few days, and I refuse to let my kid brother make me feel bad about it. When I'd make Victoria think I was gone, I'd really be sleeping on the couch in the living room she can't see.

"I've been out, Shephard. Handling personal business."

Shaun leans on his forearms against the stone top, the eagle tattoo sprawled across his pecs seeming to take flight when he moves. "We know you haven't been getting dicked, so what is it?" He suspects, his eyes missing nothing, but he wants to see if I'll say the truth in front of Shephard.

I won't.

If I mention *anything*, Shep will take it as competition. My need to have Victoria is too strong. I'd maim him before he touched her. He's my brother, and I love him, but she's *mine*. Even if she doesn't know it yet.

I look Shaun up and down, sizing him up in return. I won't fall for his mind games. They're both substantially bigger than myself, but they won't hurt me. I may be the oldest, but to them I'm the fragile sister they have to protect from bad guys even though I'm the one leading the charge most days.

"What you two do in your apartment is your business. What I do in mine isn't your concern," I explain calmly. Praying it satisfies their need for gossip, while also assuring them I'm being safe. Shaun smirks, straightening from the island, effectively ending my morning interrogation.

He rounds the counter and puts a brawny arm around me, kissing the top of my head.

"Seriously, you stink. Go shower."

Victoria made herself busy today, not that it takes much effort in your first year of law school. After her shower, she studied on her couch and ordered takeout for lunch. *I'm going to have to teach this girl how to cook.*

Now she's lying on her bed typing out an assignment on her laptop. Kind of. She keeps getting distracted with her phone. She's been checking it religiously. Waiting for another message from me.

But I'm comfortable under the sheets of my own bed in the manor, content to make her wait while watching her through the camera feed on my phone.

Again, her hands move from her keyboard to her cell, flipping it over and checking the screen. No notifications. Just a photo of her wearing a graduation cap, with her parents on either side of her.

I can't see any resemblance. She's tiny, five foot four as a rough estimate. Her father looks to be about my height, but so are most men so it's nothing special. Her mother's a little closer in stature to her, but that's where the similarities end.

Victoria's bright red hair is the biggest contrast between Mr. Fenwick's dark brown and her mother's straight, blonde locks. Her astonishing green eyes don't match either. Both her parents have blue. *Interesting genetics at play.*

I see her body deflate into her pillows as she lets out a sigh. The cameras don't have audio, but I'll hear that sound in my ear soon enough.

Just a few more days.

9

Victoria

THE PAPER I'M WORKING on is making my brain numb. I can't make myself care about zoning laws when the sun is literally being blocked by the building across the way. I keep checking my phone, hoping there will be a message from my admirer. *Stalker, Victoria. He's a* stalker, *not someone you should be hoping reaches out.*

Groaning, I rub my hands down my face, frustration thrumming through me. I've been working on this paper all week, but now I have my firm for my internship. I'm too distracted to finish. I got the basic info about when and where to show up on Monday, but it's my responsibility to research the firm myself.

Which I haven't started either.

I flip my phone over again. *Still nothing.* His bedroom light has been on since yesterday, but the room remains unoccupied.

I sigh, opening a search browser and bracing myself before typing. The auditorium went deathly silent after Professor Hilton read my name and announced I was going to be interning at Laughlin & Laughlin.

Everyone's eyes lasered my way immediately. Which I used to be able to handle. You don't get to be captain of the cheer team with stage fright, but that isn't the case anymore. Being the center point of everyone's focus had me squirming in my chair, struggling against the phantom chill trickling over my scalp. Students whispered. Leaned away. Only *some* refused to make eye contact.

I'm not ignorant of the reputation the Laughlin family holds. Everyone at Sloane has heard the rumors.

Morally Corrupt.

Juror Intimidation.

The Unholy Triad.

The triplets graduated a few years ago, but their names still decorate the walls of Laughlin Hall, one of many buildings on campus donated by their family over the decades. Scribed into plaques, it's as if the family owns every inch of campus.

I search the firm's name purely for due diligence. Hoping to read something that'll make me less nervous for my initial assessment in two days.

LAUGHLIN & LAUGHLIN ATTORNEYS AT LAW

...

864,327 RESULTS

Okay, wow, that's a lot.

Clicking the first link, an article from earlier this year fills the screen.

KIAN HUGHES FOUND NOT GUILTY, LAUGHLIN & LAUGHLIN DEFENSE UNMATCHED

A photo of their client between the towering twin Laughlins, Silas and Simon, fills the screen beneath the headline. Both of them appear well over six feet tall. The triplets stand, unphased by the media, in the background, the three of them equally as intimidating as their father.

There don't appear to be any editorials regarding the accusations against the firm. None from any legitimate sources, anyway. Only gossip blogs and tabloid news pages. Nothing with facts.

Though, I suppose anyone with the power the Laughlin's are rumored to have would know how to keep their secrets out of the press.

The article itself is vague of any case details other than the ruling and Silas' statement to the journalists outside the courthouse. "Our job was to prove reasonable doubt. We did that. No further questions."

Short spoken and direct.

That's one of the Laughlin's I'll be subjected to down. *Four more to go...*

Simon's name doesn't seem to be attached to anything that doesn't also involve, or more accurately, *revolve* around, his brother. Nothing to prepare me for what he'll be like. I backspace and narrow my search to just the triplets.

LAUGHLIN TRIPLETS

...

116,448 RESULTS

Still a lot, but somewhat manageable. They mostly appear to be mentions of their time at Sloane and the awards they've helped the school achieve. The first link I click is from when the three of them graduated law school.

LAUGHLIN TRIPLETS GRADUATE SLOANE INSTITUTE OF LAW

SHAELENE, SHAUN, AND SHEPHARD LAUGHLIN FINISH FINAL SEMESTER AT SIoL WITH HONORS. EACH PLANNING TO WORK FOR FAMILY FIRM

The next is a newspaper article announcing their birth.

LAUGHLIN TRIPLETS BORN AT ST. GIANNA'S MEDICAL CENTER

SHAELENE MICHAELA, SHAUN KENDRY, AND SHEPHARD NOLEN

BORN 11:49PM THIS PAST SATURDAY OCTOBER 30TH.
MOTHER MIKHAILA VASILIEV-LAUGHLIN PASSED FROM COMPLICATIONS DURING DELIVERY.

I close my laptop with a grunt.

I didn't learn anything more than what I already knew. The firm is esteemed, and they represent a niche clientele. Mostly multimillionaires that get themselves into trouble through shady business practices.

My phone dings and my heart leaps in my chest. Unlocking it, my shoulders sag in disappointment at the sight of another spam email.

I really should unsubscribe from that newsletter.

Swinging my legs off the side of the bed, I walk to my dresser, pausing briefly to peek at his apartment. My body aches to get off again. I haven't had an orgasm as good as the one last night since... Well, my first one.

My mind craves that feeling again, but my watcher doesn't seem to be coming back tonight. It's past eleven now, and the last two nights he texted me around nine-thirty.

The desire burrowing in my gut can't wait any longer. *I'll do it with or without him watching.*

I pull the silicone grinder out from beneath my panties and toss it and the remote onto the bed, shimmying my pajama bottoms off. I kick them toward the wall of glass, airing my frustration at him for not showing up.

If he's not going to be here, he doesn't get to watch through that camera either... I rush over to the lamp and shut it off, clicking the remote to switch the TV off too. The only light in my room comes from my phone screen. *Good luck seeing anything now, Stalker Man.*

Dragging my pillow to the center of my bed, I fasten my grinder into place, my heart pounding as arousal drips between my thighs.

I hover over my toy until I open my messages, then lower myself onto the soft silicone, sliding my knees wider until my full weight presses down onto the ridges. Pleasure zips through me at the slightest tease, my body humming with need. My hands steady me, one on either side of my cell as I click the remote.

The vibrations buzz against my core. The delicate lace of my thong limits how easily I can slide along the rubbery material, dampening the intensity of the rush I'm chasing, so I lift my hips and yank the fabric to the side. My body jerks at the first bare touch, a gasp ripping through my throat into the empty room.

I sit heavily against it, letting the bliss numb my mind and beat rhythmically against my heated center, moaning through the release of the pent-up arousal I've stifled all day.

The tension from the taught lace digs into the crease of my hip, cutting deeper with each stroke. My thrusts turn greedy, craving more pain.

My head dips and my hips buck harder. Frantic. Manic. I reread the messages over and over, imagining him watching me now, thinking of all the things he might say if he saw.

My pace quickens and I straighten, still grinding hard against my cushion. Dropping the remote, happy to let the grinder stay on full blast, I pull my top over my head and free my chest. Squeezing my breasts as my hips continue their relentless dance. My nipples are peaked from the euphoria, and I roll one between my fingers, pinching with my sharp nails.

Father calls my name as I pass the doorway of his private office, his fingers pointing to one of the plush, velvet chairs opposite his desk when I stop and peer inside.

This room is smaller than our shared study, but no less grand. The walls are lined with organized shelves, and an inviting but small seating area fills the space near the door. His large mahogany desk, littered with neat stacks of papers, is centered in front of the back wall.

A bronze Lady Justice statue sits atop it, except her blindfold isn't covering her eyes. It's over her mouth, her eyes peering to the side while she looks the other way. The scales she holds are unbalanced, and her sword rests heavily over her shoulders.

Again. Fitting.

I sit comfortably in my sweats, my duffel laying abandoned by the door. Father's still wearing his suit trousers and white dress shirt, though his open cuffs and collar betray his typically primmed appearance. *He's stressed.*

Behind him are rows upon rows of tomes filled with materials from the thousands of cases our family's firm has taken on.

He closes the documents he's reading in a folder and drops them into the bottom drawer of his desk. I hear it lock when he slides it closed.

I don't speak until he does. Trained not to since we learned to talk, my brothers and I wait until he initiates the conversation, always.

He removes his reading glasses with one hand and rubs his eyes with the other, cracking his neck to the side with a sigh. His tired eyes look me over, squinting when he realizes how late it is. He knows I was up to something, but I'm not prone to trouble like my brothers, so he isn't likely to interrogate me about my whereabouts.

The power of ignorance in our line of work cannot be understated.

He sucks in a sharp breath, his eyes turning to steel. "Tell me taking on this intern won't cause any trouble." My jaw tenses, but he continues before I can voice my unease. "Help me keep your brothers at bay. We need this to keep a..." He pauses, seeming at a loss for the right word. He pops his jaw before continuing. "Reputation."

I nod once, just a single drop of my head, too angry to answer with words. He's quiet for a moment, the air tense with expectation until I begin to stand, and his words cut me off. "You as well, Shaelene."

I lift my eyes to his. He knows I prefer women, and it's never been an issue for the family. We may be morally corrupt individuals, but we aren't bigots.

I stand straight, looking down at him. Victoria won't be trouble because I won't let her be. She won't go anywhere or speak to anyone without my knowledge. She won't betray our trust either. *She'll be too in love with me.*

My face is serious when I say, "Yes, sir."

He hums his approval, putting his glasses back on and looking down at the stacks of paper beside him, dismissing me.

Just before I reach the door, his voice halts my steps. I don't turn around, but my shoulders tense. "I'll have a word with you three in the morning." There's a long pause, his breath heavy as he exhales. "About your birthday gala."

11

Victoria

I woke up for a run again this morning. *Four laps in and no one has shoved me.*

Finishing up my fifth, I'm a gasping, sweaty mess despite the slicing breeze. I skip the quick coffee in favor of eating breakfast at home.

Running a few extra laps today to blow off the steam fuming inside me didn't help anything. He didn't text me last night, and when I woke up this morning, his blinds were closed. A defeated sigh trills my lips. *He's done with me.*

I suppose I should be relieved. Any sane girl would be. But, for some reason, I'm not, and that pisses me off.

I feel like I let myself get used *again*. Except this time, I wanted it to keep going.

And I want *more*. I haven't felt this starved for attention since... Ever. I never dated anyone after the homecoming game. After everything that happened. Back then, I didn't want anyone to notice me. I didn't want anyone else to touch me. It was easier that way.

But now my stalker is all I can think about. After cleaning up my mess, I tossed and turned, only to have another dream about him standing at the foot of my bed, watching me. Encouraging me. Fully enraptured by everything he saw.

I can't shake him. I feel shamefully desperate right now, aching and dripping, pretending I'm not a teasing touch away from exploding. And as good as the orgasm felt last night, I need more than a fantasy and some toys.

But, clearly, he's over me.

When I reach my door, I slide my key into the deadbolt, but my door pushes inward.

It was already open.

My head turns down the hall, looking to both sides of me, but I'm the only one awake this early. I've *always* been the only one awake this early, and I *know* I locked my door behind me. I always triple check. Always. Nudging the door open enough to squeeze myself through, I tiptoe to the kitchen counter and grab a knife from the block.

It shakes in my hand while I go room to room, cursing my mother for insisting I do ballet instead of karate.

The only room left to check is my bedroom.

I creep across the tile in the kitchen as quietly as I can. My door is shut, so I have the element of surprise on my side, but that's it. No training. No calm. Just blind fear and a desperate desire to keep living. I slam the door open holding the knife nervously in front of me with both hands.

No one.

I blink, glancing around and refusing to lower my knife.

No one?

It's exactly as I left it an hour ago. My body relaxes, and I laugh, leaning against my wall as my legs turn to jelly. I look out my window to his apartment, still closed up.

My mother calls again around lunchtime.

"Mom, I said I'd call you after my interview," I try to joke, but her cheery voice dismisses it.

"I know, sweetheart. I just wanted to hear your voice."

She sounds happier than she did a couple nights ago, and my heart feels lighter because of it.

"What are you and Dad up to today?"

She recounts how he had to run to the office this morning to meet with a CEO about a new potential partnership with his company. He's an actuary. Super good at numbers, even better at small talk and shmoozing. *Taught me everything I know about playing cards.*

She goes on about their plans for dinner and the rest of the week.

Finally, she pauses and asks about school, sounding genuinely interested this time.

"I'll be interning at Laughlin & Laughlin starting tomorrow," I tell her, a spark of excitement zipping through me.

She's quiet. Unnaturally so. For a second I think the call drops, but when I go to check, she interrupts me. "That's so great, honey. I think I recognize that name."

Her voice is shaky.

"Yeah. They're big contributors to Sloane. You probably saw the name all over campus during the tour."

When she and my father helped me unpack everything into my apartment, they went on a private tour of the campus with me as well. Not that it helped much. Sloane is huge. I only managed to keep track of where my lecture halls and the library were, everything else on campus is just a blur of granite and limestone.

"Of course. That's probably it." She clears her throat, changing the subject. "So, Vicky, are there any handsome men at school?"

A laugh escapes before I can trap it, my mind immediately thinking of my stalker. But I don't dare mention him to her.

Instead, I counter, "If there are, I haven't noticed. I'm here to *learn*, Mom."

I can feel her eyes rolling through the phone. A door closes on the other end of the line, and my father's voice calls out for her. His voice lifts when she mentions she's talking to me.

"Hello Victoria, dear. How are classes going?"

I smile, knowing I'm making him proud. He was often gone, off making new deals and forming partnerships for most of my childhood, but he always made sure to let me know he was interested in my happenings one way or another.

When I quit cheerleading and dance in high school, he didn't ask questions. He told me it was my decision and if I wanted to do something else, he'd help me find a way. It was then that I really got into painting.

After the night in the locker room, and every horrible school day after, I didn't want to do anything but stay in my room. *Alone.* I was in a dark spiral, unable to claw my way out. Unsure if I even wanted to find the light again. Then a new spark burst within the nothingness eating my soul, something that helped make the oblivion feel less consuming. I'd left one of my notebooks in the car by accident, and Dad found it on his way to the airport for yet another trip.

When he'd gotten back three days later, he had an easel and canvases in tow as he walked through the door. Claiming he loved all the drawings I'd done in the margins between my notes, demanding to see them in color.

I drew because I was sad and felt like I couldn't share what happened with anyone. I drew myself happier, smiling self-portraits covering canvas after canvas for years. An attempt to see my old self again. A fruitless attempt to bring her back into existence. My parents still have the family portrait I painted framed and hanging in the foyer at home.

I haven't painted in years. Law school keeps you incredibly busy, but I do find myself doodling if a boring lecture runs long.

"They're going great, Dad. I start interning tomor—"

"At Laughlin & Laughlin." My words are interrupted, again, by my mother.

The line goes quiet for several seconds.

My father's voice returns, lower and more serious, before I hear his footsteps receding. "Be careful, Victoria. We love you."

My mouth hangs open, unsure how, or if, I should respond since he's already left.

My mother breaks the silence. "We have to get going now, honey. Call us soon!"

The line disconnects, and I stare at the blank screen.

The clock in my kitchen ticks loudly, my body and mind stuck in disbelief and confusion. *Have they heard something worse than I have?* Surely not. My family only deals with lawyers when it comes to my father's business contracts. He's always been above board, not even a receipt or decimal out of place. Nothing criminal.

My father is a good man.

His departing tone sets a pit in my stomach. An all too familiar feeling. *Nothing criminal*, I try to reassure myself. The feeling settles lower in my gut, my eyes finding the curtains across the street. I squeeze my eyes shut, trying to snap out of the excitement building inside me at the thought of danger. I should be worried. I should be careful, like he said, but a piece of me aches for peril.

For my stalker.

For the pain I crave.

12

Shaelene

I BARREL DOWN THE hall that leads to our rooms after Phillip informs me of my father's request. *Meeting. His office. Now.*

Shaun answers on the second knock, keeping the door mostly closed before nodding his understanding and shutting it.

Shephard, per usual, is a different story. I've knocked thrice and I'm not granting him a fourth. I turn the knob and kick the door open with the rounded toe of my loafer, making the girl strung up on his bed shriek before engaging in aggravated eye contact with my brother. Thankfully her entirely bare body blocks his half-naked one before I'm scarred for life like the last time.

I don't move from the doorway; Father's orders are followed immediately, regardless of what any of us may be currently occupied with. Instead, I focus on the intricate details of the crown molding until I hear his zipper.

"Is she the one you said was gonna join?" the blonde slurs, the words running lazily out of her mouth; I don't even want to imagine why her jaw is too tired to work properly.

Shep and I both look at her with disgust, appalled at the fact she can't see the similarities between the two of us.

I'm not identical to him and Shaun, obviously, but we do have indistinguishable features, namely our eyes and dark hair, that show the world our blood relation.

Shephard immediately walks to her after picking up the rest of his suit from the floor and straps a leather strip across her lips, keeping her from talking any further. He crouches beside the bed, pinching her cheeks with barely contained antipathy. "That's my sister, you stupid whore." She whines, and I'm certain she isn't apologetic about her mix up at all.

I roll my eyes when he strides toward me, fastening his buttons and smiling.

"Meeting. His office. Now."

An eternally long and obnoxious walk to the east wing later, my brothers cease their snickering, and we gather in Father's office to hash out the details of our birthday party. While it may be in celebration of us, we aren't the reason everyone is getting together.

We're the decoy.

After Father explains his expectations, Shephard stands from his chair impatiently. "We'll get something prepared." He adjusts his jacket and fastens the top button, his jaw ticking as nerves line his features. My gaze narrows, watching to see if he'll follow through dismissing himself without our father's consent, and I smirk when I see the anxious swiping of his loafer sole over the carpet. I turn my attention back to Father and Uncle, anticipating Shephard's brutal reprimanding.

My father sits, elbow resting on the wooden top of his desk, with his chin in his hand, while Uncle stands behind him with his arms crossed, his serious demeanor matching our father's.

The only discerning factor between them is my father's graying hair. *Probably caused by the stress of raising the three of us.*

Their thick brows are scrunched in our direction, an expression that I've learned to be hesitant against, thanks to my brothers. My father's eyes motion to Shephard's now empty seat, telling him to sit back down. The corner of my lip curls in a snarky grin again when he shifts on his feet, so easily affected by the weight of our father's glare.

"I'm not involved in this secret meeting, and I'm not interested in picking out plate settings. I'll leave that to the ladies," Shephard says, still standing, his head nodding toward Shaun and I. *Such a tragic, blue-balled baby you are Shephard.*

"Fine. Leave us," our father exhales, motioning with his hand toward the door.

With his exit, he dooms Shaun and I to spend the next hour organizing the details. I'm not enthused about the idea of party planning either, but I do intend on making sure my little fox is there. *Maybe I* do *care about planning this year.* I pitch the theme and Shaun agrees, leaving only the guestlist to be settled.

The location is already decided.

The mansion belonging to Grigorio Angelini, the head of the Italian Mafia in New York, is the perfect venue to host all our guests. Our families have been tied for decades, through marriage and the constant gossip rag periodicals alluding to our 'unsavory practices'. Though, three of Grigorio's five sons have avoided charges they were definitely guilty of, thanks to us, so none of it is *totally* unfounded.

Luca, the youngest, has managed to stay out of trouble so far, but danger is never far off when your father is one of the biggest crime bosses in the United States. *And when you're in love with one third of the Unholy Triad...*

His eldest brother didn't follow suit.

It didn't take me long to put the pieces together once it was declared the party would be held at the Angelini's. I learned a long time ago to not ask questions, so obtaining information on my own has become invaluable. When Father said business would be handled during the event, I already knew what it'd be about. *Grigorio wants his son's killer dead.*

Whether or not I'm privy to all their plans now, I will be by the end of it. I'll be there when that piece of shit meets his maker. And if I'm right, I'll get *my* revenge too.

It's half-past one in the morning when I step out of my car and walk through the garage to Victoria's apartment. I haven't texted her for two days. *She's been fiending for me.*

First with her pillow, her eyes locked to the texts I sent, then earlier when she frantically dug through the boxes in her closet for a sketchbook. She drew dozens of variations of me standing in my window.

Then a final one of herself kneeling before a shadowed and vague version of me.

A cold date with my shower wasn't enough to staunch the desire to see her in person again until the morning. *I need her now.*

Exiting the elevator, the corridor is empty, which isn't surprising given the hour, as I make my way to the furthest door on the left.

Victoria's apartment.

Making quick work of picking the lock, I slip my multi-tool away, forcing a deep breath to calm the beast coiled just under the surface. My face is hidden behind a black neck gaiter again; my braided hair tucked beneath my hood.

I gently press open the door, careful to keep it from creaking, and let myself in. The lights are off and the remnants of yet another take out dinner sit empty on the counter. I shake my head at that. *My little fox needs to eat properly for all the fun I have planned for her.*

A small glow flashes from the bottom of her bedroom door. *She should be alone.* I check the cameras on my phone and see her sleeping. Spread across her bed, the sketchbook beside her and a pencil still in her hand, her TV playing a rerun of that cheesy law show she likes. A sharp smile spreads across my face, anticipation thrumming through my veins.

I creep into her room, my footsteps quiet despite my heavy boots.

Her door whines slightly, but she doesn't stir. Her beautiful face rests peacefully on her arm. I could watch her for the rest of eternity. The idea is so inviting I almost don't want to wake her.

Almost.

I shut off her TV, throwing the room into complete darkness. I debate staying in the dark. I debate fulfilling the fantasies flitting through both our heads when there's nothing hidden between us. But I don't want that now. *Not tonight.* I flip the light in her connected bathroom and the bright yellow hue fills the space in front of me. Leaning my shoulder against the door frame, I pull my phone from my back pocket, my heart racing as I watch her take a deep breath.

From her spot on the bed, she won't be able to see the details of my body, only my outline.

I tactically acquired one of Shephard's hoodies to pair with a set of black, cargo pants that smother my curves. Tonight, I want to be just as anonymous as she pictures in her mind, even if she thinks

I'm a man. She'll learn soon enough that I can please her plenty without a cock.

I slide my phone back in my pocket, my eyes glued to her prone form, as a few silent seconds pass before her phone chimes loudly from its spot on the pillow beside her.

She lifts her head groggily, blindly reaching for it, and squints when the screen lights up.

13

Victoria

HOLY SHIT. I SIT up and immediately try peering through the darkness outside toward the neighboring building until something moves in my room, and my eyes widen when I see him. Every muscle tenses and I feel myself begin to shake under their tautness. *I'm not dreaming. He's* actually *inside my apartment.* My stomach twists into a confusing knot of unease and desire, leaving me short of breath.

I knew he was tall, but his head sits just below the top of the door frame despite him leaning against the side of it.

A chill trickles down my spine and my fingers clutch my phone in one hand and grab a fistful of the blanket with the other. *I should definitely call the cops...* My skin cools to the touch, but heat continues to swirl in my fluttering core as I remember what happened the last time he texted me. How shamefully addictive that orgasm felt. A depraved spark of excitement lights inside me, building until I feel it flooding my panties. *Or I could not.*

He pushes off the wall and steps closer, sucking what little breath I have from my lungs and making my chest heave. My nipples press against the cotton of my t-shirt and become a telling sign of my ever-growing desperation.

His face is hidden, sunken deep in the darkness of his hood. A somewhat comforting sight. *My familiar stranger.* Sterling's face has haunted me for so long. *Is that why anonymity feels safer?* Sterling would never hide himself. He enjoyed the torment of knowing I'd have to see him every day too much for him to do something like this. *This is* not *Sterling.*

His gloved hand slips from his pocket and traces along my cheek to my mouth, my lips falling open voluntarily when his thumb rubs down my chin.

He stalks around the bed, but my body is stuck in place, facing the warm light. I let out a shuddering breath when his hand runs along my shoulder and over the back of my neck.

His hand curls in my hair, his touch almost a caress, before yanking my head sharply to look up at him. He lifts a finger, twirling it delicately around one of my curls, using my hair to push my body into motion.

I shift until I can see our reflections in the same window I stood naked in front of the night he took my picture. His shape dwarfs mine in the glass. *Putting up a fight would be useless...*

Through us, I can vaguely see the blinds in his apartment are still drawn, the lights off, and I know the room is empty since he's in mine now.

He isn't done with me.

The small bit of his face not concealed by his mask lights up, my phone ringing again a few seconds later.

Are you scared?

I am. I'm terrified, but my pussy is pulsing greedily. My shivering thighs are slick with sweat and anticipation. *I shouldn't want this, but I do.*

I meet his eyes in the window, my breath still mostly gone. They're striking, staring at me intensely, waiting for a response.

I try to tell him yes, try to appease his desires, but my voice stalls. My lips tremble, every sound trapped in my throat, so I nod instead.

Good.

He kneels on the floor, his broad shoulders still visible on either side of me in the makeshift mirror. *He's so much bigger than I'd thought.*

I swallow the fear building in me, feeling it churn into an even deeper yearning. My fucked-up mind still adjusting to the newly discovered details of my stalker fantasy.

He lifts his arms, drawing the hood from his head and removing the mask covering his face. Squinting at the window, a whine swells within me. *I still can't see anything.* He's hidden, my body blocking the details. Just like before.

Then I can't see anything at all.

He ties the mask over my eyes, cinching it tight around my head. A few strands of my hair pull painfully, my scalp burning when he knots it.

I hear him stand behind me, his boots landing heavily against the wood floor. I don't know how I didn't hear him get in. *How did he get in?* I triple checked it was locked after I found it open this morning.

He shoves me forward, and I barely catch myself before hitting the mattress with my face. I try to push myself up, but a hand presses against my back, holding me down. I arch into the touch, my ass lifting into the air, and his other slaps down on it, setting the bare skin on fire where it landed.

My underwear is ripped off, cutting into my skin before the elastic snaps. He grips my shoulder and pulls me back so I'm sitting on my feet. The dampened lace of my thong wraps around my neck, cutting off my air and sending me teetering over the edge of oblivion.

My face heats, my pussy slick with emotions I don't dare acknowledge, as my already blinded vision speckles with stars.

He reaches around the front of me, pulling my knees apart and I don't protest, letting them fall open for him. Just before I think I'm about to pass out, his hold loosens. A rough gasp escapes me, my lungs heaving for air.

One breath is all he affords me before I'm choking again, pulled tight against his front. The tobacco-y scent of his sweatshirt coating every breath I try to take. His hand rears back and slaps against my swollen clit. The shock makes me gasp and clench, but the spike of pain subsides, and I feel myself drip on his hand.

Leather fingers tug against the wet skin of my lips. The friction only makes me wetter when he pushes one into me. Then two. My hips lift, moving with him. Pleading for more.

The underwear falls from my neck, replaced by his hand. He coaxes a moan from me; the noise no longer clogged in my throat. *I love the feeling of his hands on me.*

His face presses into my hair, his breath heavy and hot against my neck as he takes whiff after whiff of my hair. *I haven't even touched him yet.* His hand twists up into my hair, wrenching it even more. Pulling the skin of my neck tight as he yanks my head to the side.

I scream when his teeth sink into my shoulder, then again just above my collarbone, his fingers working magic inside me the whole time.

My skin burns, the warmth of his spit dragging up my neck as he trails his tongue over me. He hums, soft lips vibrating against my skin. My head lulls against his shoulder as he lets go of my hair and cups one of my breasts under my shirt. *Please take the gloves off...*

The hand inside me pulls out quickly and my legs weaken, all of me slumping against his solid chest as if I'm leaning against a brick wall.

He shoves me again, wrapping an arm around my waist and lifting my ass into the air, flipping me and tossing my legs over his shoulders without uttering a sound. Not even a grunt, like it took him no effort at all.

His arms grip my thighs, gloved fingers digging into my muscle hard enough I flinch. *I'll have bruises tomorrow.*

Heat envelopes me when his mouth meets my pussy. He flattens his tongue, licking me from ass to clit, completely coating me in his spit.

He sucks my clit into his mouth, swallowing until my back arches off the bed and my hands grab for his head. His hands catch my wrists before I even reach him, easily pinning them to my sides.

His tongue disappears from between my legs, his chin scraping against my stomach as he hovers over me. *No facial hair.* It's the only hint I have, other than his height and those beautiful gray eyes, as to what he looks like.

His leg drives mine into the mattress, the other flattening over my bare crotch as he pulls my hands over my head, taking them both in one large hand. Goosebumps prickle my skin, and my mind wanders to what he'll do with me completely surrendered beneath him. Most of his weight is on me, but all I can feel are his hands and the muscles of his thighs. *He was breathing so heavily earlier... Is he not enjoying this as much as I thought? Can he not—*

Something slides across the covers, and I hear the pages of my sketchbook flop open beside my head. The elastic cord that holds it shut wraps around my wrists, tying them together, as the heavy, leather-bound book falls over the side of the bed and keeps my arms in place.

His weight shifts and settles over top my hips and confirms my suspicions. *He isn't hard.* I start to deflate, feeling immensely insecure in my skin. *Why would he be here with me if he isn't enjoying it?* My shirt is tugged up, exposing my bare chest, and a cold breath blows against my already hard nipples.

His hands massage my breasts hungrily before he takes one in his mouth, swirling his tongue around the sore tip, rolling the other between his fingers, pinching and tugging. I moan when he swaps sides, arching against him. Begging for more. Desperate for more. *I shouldn't be enjoying this as much as I am, but fuck it all feels so good—*

Wait. Is this all for me? To make me *feel good and not him?*

His hand trails down my stomach until it reaches my slick entrance again. A finger glides into me, and I can't keep myself from moaning when he draws it back out.

He plunges two fingers into me without warning, the rest of his palm cupping me. My ass lifts from the bed, grinding against the pressure of his hand, and he clears his throat. The noise sounds forced, like he's trying to hide a moan of his own. *I want to hear you too; don't hide it.*

He shifts, and I feel his breath against my face. I know he's hovering over me, watching my face. My eyes uselessly look under my binding, searching for a glimpse of the man pinning me down.

His fingers continue fucking me, rubbing my walls, setting my insides on fire.

More...

The same growing wave of euphoria from the other night continues to build. His body snakes back down mine, moving his fingers harder and faster, pushing my body a few inches back and forth from the force of his hand.

I want more...

My legs shake and tighten, trapping his head between them when his tongue flicks at my clit and I finally lose control. I'm sent over the edge, crying out from the intensity of my orgasm.

I want...

His mouth continues to barrage my sensitive flesh, devouring me until I'm nothing more than a trembling puddle beneath him.

Him.

14

Shaelene

I LICK HER CUNT clean, not wasting a drop of the sweetness she gushed for me. Victoria's legs quiver around me while my tongue glides along her smooth skin, savoring every shiver that jolts through me each time her thighs tighten around my head. Tasting every inch of her until my lips graze over a few ridges.

My eyes widen at the sight of several scars, barely distinguishable against her already pale skin, across the inside and tops of her thighs. I turn my head and survey the other.

A matching set decorates it too, and I choke down the need to interrogate her and figure out why she has them. *I can't ask her questions right now.* I don't want her to hear my voice, but I *will* find out where they came from.

For now, I reward her with a slap to her exhausted cunt. Her body jerks, a satisfied whimper escaping her lips, before she melts into the covers.

I stand, looking over her sweaty, porcelain body, my heaving chest filling with pride. I press a palm across her stomach and pull my phone out to take another photo. Claiming her completely as mine.

A soft sigh floats through the air between us, her response to the sound of my phone's camera. She's still blindfolded, but I don't need to see her seductive eyes to know she's enjoying this.

Her tongue skims her lips before she sucks the bottom one between her teeth.

What is she thinking about?

My hand skims down her body again, running along her thigh and off her knee as I walk around the bed. My boots thud against the floor, letting her know where I'm at, as I round the corner and reach for the book dangling from her wrists.

I flip to her last drawing. The one of me in her room.

I tear it from its binding, ripping it loudly in the quiet of her room. I roll the thick paper and stuff it into my hoodie pocket along with the purple panties I ripped off her before untying her wrists and letting the book fall to the floor.

Her tired shoulders relax, but her arms stay near her head, not bothering to pull her shirt down and cover herself. Her knees fall in place together, no longer twitching.

I lift her shoulders and pull her back to my front so she's sitting up, her legs to the side. We both face her bedroom door, the moonlight shining in behind us fights with the warm glow from the bathroom.

Pulling the blindfold from her eyes, my fingers itch to wrap around her curls and hold her in place, but like the obedient girl she is, she doesn't turn her head to look.

Good little fox.

She can't see me or a reflection from this angle, and since she's not attempting to face me, I risk untying her blindfold and pulling the gaiter back over my face, tucking in my hair and pulling my hood back up.

Moving in front of her, I stare into her lustful eyes and place her forgotten phone in the hand resting in her lap.

The light from my cell illuminates my face, giving her a view she didn't get earlier in the dark, not that it'll do her much good.

My face is free of makeup and my eyes have darkened with the satisfaction of watching her come for me. *On me.*

See you again soon, Little Fox.

15

Victoria

I HEAR THE DOOR close behind him as he exits my apartment.

My body finally collapses, exhaustion warring with euphoria. I laugh in complete disbelief of what just happened. None of my dreams came close in comparison to what it felt like to really have him here. *To have him on me. Over me. In me.*

The air conditioning hums, and a quick breeze hits me from the vent above my bed making my bare stomach and chest prickle with goosebumps again. Sending my entire body into a cold plunge as my mind is invaded by thoughts of Sterling like it did the other night.

Every painful squeeze of his that left bruises on my arms. My ankles. *My thighs...*

I rush into the light of the bathroom and look myself over. Familiar looking handprints are already starting to bruise my legs. I can still feel the touch of his gloves on my skin. My hand lifts to the teeth marks on my shoulder, the movement alone causing an ache to build within my skin. I turn, peeking a cautious glance at myself in the mirror. He indented my skin but didn't break the flesh. *No blood.* Still, I'm completely disheveled, ravished by a mysterious stranger, and somehow feeling utterly satisfied.

For now.

The bites on my neck and shoulder are red and bright, the flesh tight and inflamed. My core clenches around nothing as I remember his intensity. His ease at throwing me around. I huff a wayward curl out of my face, my eyes lighter than they have been in years. *I'll have to cover all of it up before I leave for my interview in a few hours— Shit! My interview!*

I'm exhausted. I only slept a couple of hours before my visitor showed up, and there's only a few more before my alarm is set to go off.

I slink back to bed, my feet dragging beneath me. I don't even bother shutting off the bathroom light.

Tripping over my sketch book, its cord stretched and useless now, I thumb through the pages to see which one he tore out. *Him standing at the edge of my bed with me on my knees.*

My eyes scan the room looking for it. I crouch on the floor to look under the bed, but it's not there.

He took it with him.

A part of me simultaneously leaps and shivers at the idea of him having something so personal. *As if making me orgasm all over his face isn't personal enough.* My art is my safe space.

Now he has a piece of that too.

16

Victoria

I GROAN WHEN MY alarm sounds, my too tired brain unready for today. I need to go into Laughlin Manor with confidence. Poise. Not covered in bite marks from a stranger. I'm sure those sharks can smell fear from a mile away.

Tossing the blankets to the side, I start my usual morning routine, noting how the bruises on my legs have settled into a deep purple.

I rummage through my closet, trying to find something to wear that covers up the fact I was finger fucked senseless a few hours ago.

The sun is shining for the first time in a week. *It'll be warm, so my turtleneck is out of the question.* I spy my collared white blouse hanging and pair it with my striped, green dress pants and a gold pair of heels to match my jewelry.

The front of my hair is pulled out of my face with a simple twist I pin to one side and bring the rest of my curls over my shoulders to help conceal the equally darkened bite marks I tried unsuccessfully to cover with concealer.

I look myself over once more before heading for the door, grabbing my brown leather case from the counter on the way out. It falls open, my notes and a couple books scattering at my feet and bringing all my nerves back to the surface.

Breathe.

I shuffle my papers into a disorganized stack and shove them all into the sleeve inside my case. *I'll sort them later. I* cannot *be late today.*

I'm ahead of schedule when I arrive at the front gate to Laughlin Manor. I was nervous the drive up to Greenwich would be worse than I anticipated, knowing how volatile New York traffic can be. Though punching the address into my GPS did make me realize Laughlin Manor is located in Greenwich, *Connecticut.* Not Greenwich, *New York.*

I wonder if there's a reason for that?

Pulling up to the iron bars surrounding the grounds, I find the intercom system embedded in the large stone wall and reach a shaky hand out the window to hit the buzzer.

"Name?" a man's voice blares through its speaker.

"Victoria Fenwick, here to see—"

The intercom beeps and the gate opens before I can finish my sentence. Settling back in my seat, I take a deep breath, then drive forward through a small wood of trees on both sides of the one lane brick drive up.

The surrounding trees are so thick I contemplate turning my lights on even though it's mid-morning. *Please don't let this foreboding driveway be some sort of omen.*

Finally, the sun cuts through the canopy again and I pull up and around a large circular driveway that surrounds a tiered fountain in front of the house. I gulp, my palms sweaty against the steering wheel. *House is an understatement.*

The estate is massive.

I've never been one to deny how I grew up. Wealthy is a subtle way to put it. My father's affluence got me where I am now, but this is more. Way more. This is *elite*. Untouchable status.

I nearly finish looping the circle before putting the car in park and taking another slow breath to steady my nerves.

My door opens and a white glove waits expectantly in my face. I didn't even see the valet waiting when I pulled up.

I grab my bag from the passenger seat and take his hand as I stand.

"Ms. Fenwick," he greets, bowing his head. He takes the keys and waits for me to step aside before settling into the spot behind the wheel to move my car to a side parking area behind a row of tall hedges.

I suck in a breath nervously, thankful for the moment alone in front of the manor, before forcing myself toward the large, pillared entrance. The stone steps leading up to the door are lined with thick, manicured shrubs. My hand traces the flat top of one as the front door opens.

My fingers retract quickly, like being caught touching it will lead to a prison sentence. *Calm down Victoria, Jesus.*

"Ms. Fenwick?" an older man asks, already knowing the answer based on his expression. His uniform tells me he isn't a Laughlin, but that he works for them. *Of course he does; people this rich don't open their own doors.*

"Y–Yes," I stammer.

He nods and holds the door open for me. "If you'd please." He gestures inside with a gloved hand of his own.

Through the large double front door, the foyer opens to a centered, grand staircase leading to a second story balcony overlooking an empty seating space at the back of the room. A shadowed hallway attached to the side of the entry leads further into the manor.

Another large room, filled floor to ceiling with bookcases, dominates the front of the manor through a wide archway.

"Please, follow me. Mr. Laughlin's study is this way." The butler pauses, waiting for me to pick my jaw up off the polished marble floor.

My heels click against the stone, echoing louder against the walls in the hallway he leads us down.

"I'm sorry, I didn't catch your name," I apologize behind him.

He responds with a curt smile over his shoulder as he raps his knuckles twice on a door. A muffled voice calls from inside, and he ushers me in before turning and retreating back the way we came.

Mr. Laughlin—Silas, to be precise—sits behind a massive mahogany desk. Files, impeccably organized and entirely dust free, fill the shelves lining the walls behind him.

A wall of windows allows bright light from the sun to fill the room, breaking up some of the oppressive organization.

He stands, taller than the press photos let on, towering over his desktop as he rounds it to meet me with a firm hand.

"Miss Fenwick, I presume?"

"Yes. Victoria," I answer, his large hand encompassing mine.

A silver Rolex decorates his wrist, complimenting the silver strands framing the sides of his face below his otherwise short black hair.

"Delightful. Sit." He ushers us to a set of green velvet chairs across from his desk. "Drink?"

"Oh, no. Thank you." I wave my hand to politely decline.

One of his thick brows arches. "I insist," he pushes, pouring a second shot of amber colored whiskey into a matching crystal glass.

The knot in my stomach twists even tighter when he holds the drink out for me to take, his dark eyes narrowing.

"Of course," I concede, slowly cupping it and raising the glass to my lips, taking a small sip. The smokey taste burns my throat, and my eyes burn as I try to stifle the desire to cough while holding the rest of the drink in my lap.

Silas' eyes flash, his face hardening. "No, no, Miss Fenwick. All of it," his heavy voice commands.

My heartbeat pounds in my chest. He must notice because his eyes trace my neck, lingering on my pulse before landing on the front of my blouse, the buttons threatening to pop off from the anxious pressure building inside me. My fingers tug at my curls, brushing them into place, hoping my bruises are still covered.

I swallow the lump growing in my throat before downing the rest of the glass, forcing myself not to gag or cough. A drop lingers on my lip, falling down my chin and making my breath catch. Silas's eyes follow it while he pulls a handkerchief from his chest pocket, his intense stare holding me in place while he dabs the alcohol from my face.

"That's better. Now, tell me, what are they teaching at Sloane these days? You've taken your ethics tests and such?" The hand holding his glass motions as he speaks.

"Uh—mhm. Y—yes, Mr. Laughlin. And I've passed them."

He stands, not acknowledging my reply, instead finishing his glass and turning to pour himself another.

Looking down at the small bar cabinet, he says, "Good." Facing me again, new drink in hand, he follows his approval with, "Now forget all of it."

I blink up at him, confused.

"Forget everything Sloane has taught you about ethics and winning cases. I assume a smart girl like you does her research, so you know Laughlin & Laughlin hasn't taken a student intern in decades. We aren't interested in teaching you how to be a good lawyer. Good lawyers lose cases because of ethics." His brows pinch as he leans closer to me, his voice dropping into a barely-there whisper despite us being the only ones in the room. "We don't lose cases, Miss Fenwick."

"I don't—"

His hand cuts me off. "We represent a very specific *clientele*." He sips the whiskey with an ease I didn't possess, discarding his empty glass on the bar cart. Striding to the front of his desk, Silas leans against it, arms crossed, snaring me once more in his penetrating gaze. "The kind that are more trouble inside jail than out of it."

I knew this firm mostly deals in high-profile criminal cases. Criminal law is my specialty, and that comes with risks depending on who you choose to represent, but Laughlin & Laughlin have represented the worst of the worst.

And *won*.

"You won't make it here if you keep your face in those books." His eyes cut to my leather bag. "If you want to survive in the world of criminal law, you have to be willing to break the very things you vowed to uphold yourself. Can you do that, Miss Fenwick?"

This is it. This is the one chance he's going to give me to leave without fear of consequences. Without the fear of leaving the firm knowing too much.

Is this what my parents seemed so worried about? Me falling in with a dangerous crowd?

Silas has proven himself to be intimidating, fully dominating our conversation, in only the few minutes I've been in his presence, yet something tells me the triplets will be worse... But I've always craved challenge. Something about not conforming to the way the world wants me to be is... *addictive*. And I'm not giving up this opportunity because of a few nerves.

The impatient movement of Silas's finger tapping his suit sleeve pulls me from my thoughts of cowardly ditching.

"Yes, Mr. Laughlin. I can."

His lips turn upwards into a sinister grin. "Good. That's good, Miss Fenwick." He emanates a sort of chilling, old-money glamour as he boasts a prideful chuckle in the air between us. "From this moment on, you're a representative of Laughlin & Laughlin. Do as you're told. I'd hate to have to terminate you."

His teeth seem sharper than they had a few seconds ago as his words sink in.

My body heats again, my heart jolting from not knowing if he means my internship or my life, and I internally scream at myself for falling victim to the rumors for even a second. Silence fills the air between us, but with one final breath, he straightens, turning his back and rounding his desk.

"Phillip will show you out. Be here tomorrow morning at nine."

I instinctually turn in the direction his hand waves, spotting the butler from earlier standing outside the door, waiting for me to follow him.

"Thank you, Mr. Laughlin," I say, standing and offering a polite nod. His eyes stay trained on the papers littering his desk, dismissing me without another word. I smile at Phillip, pleased to have learned his name, as he ushers us back through the hall.

Rounding the corner, the large open sitting area feels cramped with the two large figures now seated in the chairs, both pairs of deep silvery eyes fixed on me.

I glance from one to the other while walking behind Phillip. It's impossible not to recognize the sons. Their staple black suits sit tight against their broad shoulders and powerful arms, highlighting every inch of their presence.

A perfectly shined loafer hangs comfortably over the knee of the one leaning back in the seat nearest me. The men exchange glances, unspoken communication passing between themselves, before putting a hand out to get Phillip's attention.

"Now, Phillip, aren't you going to introduce us?" the triplet closest asks, his eyes sliding up and down the length of my body. He's still sitting but based on the way the chair looks beneath him, he has to be at least as tall as his father.

I've seen the images of them online, but like with Silas, they do nothing to temper the monstrously large men sitting before me.

"Yes, of course, sirs. Misters Shaun and Shephard, this is Ms.—"

"Fenwick," Shephard interrupts from his seat across from his brother, taking a long drawl of the cigar between his fingers. He sizes me up more intensely than his brother, the corners of his lips perking when he reaches my waist, taking in the shape of my hips emphasized by my slacks. He lifts his chin, exhaling his smoke and glancing up to the balcony.

"And Miss Shaelene," Phillip continues.

His face doesn't shift or move, but I can feel her eyes now he's said her name.

Above us, resting her hands on the railing, a third set of metallic eyes pierce into me. This time, they don't stray. They remain engrossed in mine. Severe. Silent. *Striking*.

Shaun stands beside me, pulling my gaze from the loft above. *Oh, he's* much *taller than his daddy.* He adjusts his suit jacket habitually. "Pleasure," he rumbles, offering his hand to me. Mine reaches out while my eyes meet his, lowering his head and touching his lips to my knuckles.

The air feels thick with Shephard's smoke. Hazy from the dark aura I feel billowing off the triplets. The scent is choking me and too reminiscent of last night for me to pretend to be unaffected. I swallow the nerves forming in me, letting them reside deep in my stomach, fluttering and building with every second Shaun's gaze holds mine. Staring in a way that feels too familiar.

"Likewise," I reply anxiously, gripping his massive hand with my own.

A mischievous smile forms on his lips, not as malevolent as the one his father gave me, but still not quite genuine. Movement over his shoulder catches my attention.

Shaelene turns, her tall frame silently sauntering down the hallway beside her, her black hair slicked back into a thick, tight bun.

Shaun releases me, motioning to carry on following Phillip who's already heading back toward the front doors.

My footsteps inauspiciously echo, my face flushing at the sound, as I leave my first of many visits to Laughlin Manor.

"Thank you, Phillip," I whisper when he opens the door for me.

He nods, his face blank. "Ms. Fenwick."

17

Shaelene

My phone vibrates loudly against my nightstand. I walk from my place in front of my bathroom sink, still drying my hair, and tap its screen twice with a free hand.

RENTAROOM (1) NEW MESSAGE

I drop my towel to the floor and hurriedly tap through a few menus on my phone.

ARE YOU SURE?

YOU WON'T BE ABLE TO VIEW THE MESSAGE ONCE DELETED

Positive.

Victoria doesn't need a roommate. *Not unless it's me.* I've deleted every request since I learned about the ad, too possessive of my little fox to let a stranger so near to her.

I toss my phone and pick up my towel, squeezing my soaked hair a few more times.

Returning to the bathroom to brush my teeth, there's a knock on my door I ignore. Shaun enters despite not being invited in, filling the doorway after he pushes it open.

I spit into the sink and rinse my mouth, not bothering to look over at him. "What do you want?"

He steps further into my room, waiting for me to finish and take notice of him. When I eventually peer around the half-open bathroom door, he's no longer in his suit, donning a pair of black joggers with a gray undershirt instead. *I see their peacocking is officially over.* The eagle tattoo on his chest peeks out the sides and neckline, emphasizing his size and showing that his true power lies beyond the courtroom.

"Why'd you run off so fast? It was just getting fun."

I roll my eyes, tossing my towel into the hamper and sliding on my robe. He knows why; he's not stupid. I'm sure he's figured out where I've been running off to almost every night.

He's not the asshole Shephard is, but he still likes to get under my skin. *Brothers.* I mentally roll my eyes again.

"What? You wanted me to stay and witness your sad attempt to fuck the intern?" I scoff walking past him into my closet. "I know you both enjoy an audience, but that isn't a gene we share."

I'd already had enough of Shephard eye fucking her, I didn't need to stay and listen to the bastards discuss all the ways they'd share her if given the chance.

"Shep and I made a bet after she left. Told him I'd have her screaming for me in a week." He follows me and leans against the doorway; his arms comfortably stuffed in his pockets. Waiting for my reaction. Baiting me. When I give him nothing, he continues, "He says he can do it in three days."

The wet ends of my hair whip around my waist as my eyes snap to his, and he meets my glare with a cocky smile, getting the exact reaction he wanted.

"Get. Out," I growl.

He laughs as he goes, too pleased with himself to temper his heavy footsteps down the hall.

They don't know I've already fucked her with my hand and my mouth, my core clenching at the memory. Regardless, that wouldn't stop them from trying to get to her. She's going to have to choose me over them herself.

I'll make sure she does.

I let my robe fall to the floor at my feet, the cool gusts from the air conditioning hitting my bare chest and making my nipples harden. My blood boils at the thought of them, of *anyone* other than me, touching Victoria. Using her. Satisfying her.

Heat flows through me when I think of her again. How tantalizing her body looked fully clothed, hiding the marks I left on her skin last night.

I deny myself the satisfaction of getting off with the vibrator in my nightstand.

Instead, I distract myself by grabbing the pieces of my suit for tomorrow and drape them over the back of the chair opposite my bed.

I glance at my reflection in the mirror strategically placed to see the door from my closet. My tan skin still has droplets sitting atop it from my dampened hair. They drip down the front of me, falling from where black tresses stick to my breasts, and over the top of the tattoo between them. A set of prayer hands holding a rosary, the crucifix upside down on my toned stomach.

My fingers catch a bead, tracing it back up the path it fell from. Rubbing across my chest, along my collarbone, then up my neck. My chin tilts and my head sags as I remember all the places my mouth touched Victoria.

She's mine. I'll have her or no one else will.

The monitors in the grand study show her car pulling up the next morning.

Geoffrey, our valet, opens the door and a shapely leg, tipped with a heel taller than the one she wore yesterday, steps out.

It's cute how the height difference from all of us seems to affect her. Try as she might, my little fox is still over half a foot shorter than me.

I love it.

The grand study is bigger than the one she met my father in yesterday. That's his personal office. We all have one, but this is where we conduct the firm's business together.

We wait on the far side of the manor, the cameras following her and Phillip's movement through the house. My nails tap impatiently on the arm of my chair as my brothers and I stalk her path through the different feeds. All of us equally tense despite our calm exteriors.

My thumb switches to rubbing restless circles into the velvet upholstery with each step they take closer to the door.

Phillip knocks, announcing her arrival.

"Thank you, Phillip," she whispers softly as he disappears back into the hall.

Victoria's fiery hair is pulled messily into a high bun, not her usual tidy style. *Especially for something as important as her first day.* I wonder if it has anything to do with how she spent her evening. She was restless all night, constantly stirring in her bed.

A couple of curls fall in her face as she cautiously sits in the only available scat. Beside Shephard. *Fucking bastards woke up extra early to settle in here before me.* He takes the opportunity to brush them behind her ear, but she shrinks into herself when he does.

My shoulders visibly relax. *Was* he *the reason she didn't sleep?* It intrigues me she liked my rough touch the other night, but not his rare gentle one.

Shephard slides back into the relaxed position he'd been sitting in before, sending a cocky smirk in Shaun's direction, completely oblivious to the fact his gesture didn't win him the points he thinks it did. Shaun huffs, unimpressed.

Victoria looks at him, then at Shephard, before her eyes dart to mine.

They glance over me, hesitating on my legs for only a second before she looks back at her own lap.

I'm sitting back comfortably in my chair, mirroring my brothers. Our waists low and forward, legs spread wide. I may be the only woman in this house, but I'm no lady.

I'm the worst of them; she'll learn that soon enough.

Her mouth opens like she wants to speak but is too nervous to, her teeth clacking closed as her body curls into itself again. I take the growing awkward silence as my opportunity to throw a jab at the boys.

"Did your doll finally leave?"

They know they aren't supposed to bring women here; too much classified information exists in the manor to allow the riff raff inside the walls. We each have apartments for those sorts of affairs. The boys like to test the limits though.

Exactly like they did after Shaun left last night. This girl was annoyingly loud. My teeth grind, fatigue pulling at my limbs. They could've blasted porn through the intercom and it would've been less shameful. They're lucky Father's room is in the opposite wing.

Shephard snickers before tilting his head at me and saying, "She didn't. Must not be a morning person, besides, she had a little trouble getting up and moving today." He winks at Victoria.

Her sprite face turns pink, making my mouth water as my body aches for her to blush like that while I taste her again. *Fuuuuck meeeee.*

Shifting in her seat, she finds her voice and changes the subject. Making small talk with information she already knows, given her search history. "How old are you all?"

"27," we reply in unison, feeding into Shephard's delusion of our triplet superpowers.

She blushes again, not sure who to look at. Her wide eyes finally land on me. *I'll make sure she chooses me every time from here on out.*

"You?" I ask, though I already know the answer too.

She's twenty-four. From Bethesda, Maryland. Attended Old Haven High School, then Maryland State University for undergrad, and now Sloane. Only child to new-money parents, she used to be really involved in extracurriculars, but that all seemed to stop suddenly. *Must've been focusing on applications and school.* I've done my share of research since Father asked us to verify her presence at Sloane.

"I'm 24," she replies, a little less meek now.

She's more confident, thinking she started this conversation, at the idea we're interested in knowing her. *My little fox craves attention.*

In all the time I've been watching her, I haven't seen any obvious signs about whether she's interested in women, aside from me making her come the other night, but even then, she couldn't have known. *Not that it matters.*

She doesn't need to be attracted to one or the other. By the end of it, she'll only be attracted to *me*.

I haven't looked away from her eyes since she answered me a minute ago, and she's held my gaze right back. The boys stir in their seats, and I can feel the rancor sprouting between us with each second Victoria's focus stays on me. But I don't care. Victoria is here, and her attention isn't on them.

I allow myself to glance down at her chest, knowing she'll notice. *Green.*

The color of her bra bleeds through her white blouse, just barely, but enough to make my eyes narrow as I take a deep breath. My chest rises and falls along with hers now that she knows I've seen it. *Her nerves are back.*

She clutches her briefcase in her lap and instinctively I shift forward, not wanting to let our moment sever.

"Green is my favorite color, in case that was your next question."

Her lips fall open with a tiny gasp, quiet but the same randy tone as the other night when I had her on her back. The pink returns to her cheeks tinting them ten-fold.

I sink back into my chair, electricity buzzing beneath my skin, and turn to find Shephard glaring at me. They've never liked it when I played with their toys, especially now, but Victoria isn't theirs.

She's mine.

18

VOICES ECHO FROM THE hall as Silas walks in, Simon in tow. Two more men follow behind them.

Shaelene stands first, finally peeling her eyes off me. Her fierce, calculating stare chiseled through whatever false confidence I thought I had coming into Laughlin Manor today, leaving my knees weak and my breaths short.

The rest of us stand and face them. The patriarchal brothers are identical aside from Silas' graying hair and worry lines. The gold wedding band the final telling difference between himself and Simon.

The older of the two others is sophisticatedly dressed with dark hair slicked back so thickly it makes him look like he jumped straight out of the fifties. His angry, blue eyes sweep across the space in near violent glances, landing on me for no longer than a half-second as he assesses the room before he follows Silas to the desk in the back.

Behind him, a man much closer to my age clasps hands with Shephard, a bright grin on his face as the two of them walk in the footsteps of the others. Shaun right behind them. He fits right into the group of tall, muscular guys I'm surrounded by. *But there's something inviting about that dimple and the shape of his—*

Simon offers me his hand, his gray eyes softer than Silas', giving me the slightest bit of comfort on this already nerve-racking morning.

I take his hand in mine, giving it a quick shake. "Victoria Fenwick," I introduce myself.

His other hand clasps over ours, shaking it once more.

"Simon Laughlin. It's a pleasure, Ms. Fenwick." His smile is genuine, contrasting the one his twin gave me yesterday. "Please." He gestures for me to step past him toward where the others have gathered around Silas' desk.

I stand beside Shaelene just as the younger gentleman releases Shaun from a lingering hug and takes Shaelene's shoulders as he leans in to embrace her, touching his cheeks to hers.

"*Oggi come stai, cugina mia?*" His voice is buttery smooth even if his Italian is completely lost on me.

Shaelene's hands rest under his elbows while he looks at her, and in an unexpectedly gentle voice she responds, "*Sto bene,* Luca."

His smile widens, then his cheerful eyes turn to me. He doesn't size me up like the others, instead he keeps his gaze on my face and lifts his chin, his lively brows raised.

"And who are you?" he asks in English, his New York accent thick and surprising. I've gotten used to the way New Yorkers sound, but his Italian inflection and the way his shining blue eyes lock on mine makes my stomach flutter.

He takes my hand and Shaelene's head turns watchfully. *Am I crossing a boundary? Is this— Are they?* Shaelene isn't someone I want to cross right now. None of them are.

She looks at me with a softened expression that barely makes me feel better and says my name, answering Luca's question.

Luca pulls my hand to his mouth and gives it a gentle peck, looking at me over his lashes. "*Piacere di conoscerLa,* Victoria."

"You as well." I gulp, hoping to God he said something along the lines of 'nice to meet you' and that the residual feeling of his lips on the back of my hand isn't going to be something I'm punished for later. He smiles and moves to stand between Shaun and Shephard.

Shaelene is still looking down at me, her lips upturned in a devious smile while her eyes trail down my face to my lips in a way that makes the butterflies in my stomach swirl faster. *She certainly doesn't look like she wants to kill me. Maybe they're not—*

"Take these and deliver them personally," Silas commands, holding several envelopes in his hand. "Make sure they know their presence is expected." The dour expression on his face makes the hair on the back of my neck stand, the ghost of a shiver rippling down my spine.

Shaun takes them, and the triplets turn to leave without another word. Leaving me standing with three of the most forbidding men I've ever encountered. And Luca.

Simon calls after them, "Take Ms. Fenwick with you."

Oh, thank God...

"You too, Luca," the greaser man says. *Holy shit.* I didn't recognize him until I heard his voice, the same one I've heard playing on the news for the last few days. Grigorio Angelini, one of the many billionaires in New York is *actually* tied to the Laughlins. *His money isn't the only reason he's famous.*

His name litters the tabloids, along with his five sons'. The man runs several companies, doing business all over the world. His most notable being his winery, Vino Santo, which grows its grapes and imports its product directly from Tuscany.

But his recent headlines haven't been about business matters at all.

If you believe the rumors, he's the head of the Italian Mafia presence in New York. Nicknamed the Babau of the Bronx, he's linked to dozens of murders, robberies, and extortion cases, but nothing's been able to stick.

The Boogeyman... And his youngest son is currently seated next to me in the back of a blacked out Suburban.

Luca and Shaelene are on either side of me, filling most of the bench themselves. My legs are pressed tightly together, but even still, I get nudged by theirs anytime we hit a bump in the road.

The third row of seats behind us is gone, replaced with two medium sized kennels secured in place with bolts and metal plates. A panic went through me when I first spotted them, praying they're actually used for dogs. *I haven't thought about God this much in...* Well, a long time. I sort of gave up on that idea after Sterling.

Shephard sits up front drumming against the steering wheel as Shaun turns from the seat beside him and hands me the envelopes to put in my case. My fingers flip through them, noting the names on the front.

I recognize two, Derek Shultz and Bianca Maldonado. The District Attorney and the Governor.

The other is for someone named Barry Kerr, and the fourth is blank.

"Who's this one for?" I ask, lifting it from the others.

"You."

My head whips toward Shaelene, and her eyes pierce into me. The same gut punch feeling I felt when Shaun greeted me yesterday hits my stomach. Those gray eyes and straight brows looking all too familiar. Same with Shephard's peering back at me through the rearview mirror.

The butterflies from earlier dissipate, replaced by a nausea I can't stop. I didn't sleep at all last night; I kept having the same dream over and over.

I'm asleep in my bed when the lamp turns on and wakes me. My stalker is here. He approaches, leaning down and putting his face right in front of mine. I can see his eyes better this time, not just the reflection or through the darkness like before.

They're colorless, emotionless. Nothing like the last time he visited me. The corners of his eyes crease, and I know he's smiling under his black mask.

Smoke flows dramatically through the fabric, drawing my attention to the cigar in his hand. I move in slow motion when I try to run out of the room, but his quick hand catches my arm, yanking me onto the bed.

He climbs over me, too strong for me to buck off. The whites of his eyes are tinted red from the smoke. He's angry this time. He wants to hurt me. Control me. Use me. Part of me wants to let him... But the rational part of me attempts to fight him off even though I know it's useless.

He sits on my hips, crushing me into the bed while his arms pin me down. Taking both of my wrists into one of his giant hands, he pulls down his mask with the other. The face revealed is worse than Shephard's.

It's Sterling.

"Victoria?" Shaelene's voice beside me pulls me out of the nightmare. Her eyes are wide with concern, her perfect brows scrunched in confusion. "Are you okay?"

I shake my head, attempting to brush away the memory, but I can still feel her gaze roving over me.

I peel the wax seal from the back of the envelope and open it, needing to do something to shift my focus.

My eyes skim the gold script on the black cardstock.

***Your presence is requested at the annual celebration of
SHAELENE, SHAUN, & SHEPHARD LAUGHLIN
Saturday, the thirtieth of October at Palazzo Angelini
Cocktail hour begins at Eight O'Clock in the evening
Reception to follow
Black-Tie Masquerade attire only***

19

"Palazzo Angelini?" Victoria asks, turning to Luca.

He nods. "My father's mansion. We host all our events there."

She pauses a second before asking, "Your father? As in Grigorio Angelini?"

She's smart. None of us mentioned Grigorio's name at the house. She put those pieces together on her own. *What else has my little fox figured out?* I want to touch her again so badly. I want to run a nail along the tender length of her neck. To swipe off the concealer hiding my teeth marks from everyone else. But I refrain, opting to open the top button of my dress shirt instead because being this close to her without doing anything about it is starting to suffocate me.

Her mind went somewhere when I said the invitation was hers. She got the same panicked look in her eyes when Shephard moved her hair this morning. *And a similar glossiness washed over them before I called her the other night.*

My brother laughs, his eyebrows lifting in her direction through the rearview. "Why? That scare you, Red?"

She shifts and her leg bumps mine as she crosses it over her other.

I have plenty of room on the door side, but I like making her feel pressured and boxed in. Watching the goosebumps form on the back of her neck when our knees touch.

She swallows a hard gulp. "Didn't his son die recently?" she asks, her eyes aimed toward Shephard until she gasps and turns back to Luca apologizing, "Oh my God, Luca! I'm so sorry! I—"

Luca stifles a laugh. *She's so innocent.* Death isn't something any of us are strangers to. People in our world die all the time. Sometimes they're family. Most of the time they're not. But we're all well aware the risk our lifestyle brings.

He grins and reassures her, "That's part of the business, Victoria." He leans in close and whispers, "You're a curious one. I like that. Careful you don't ask too many questions though."

He straightens, looking at me over her head. I know he isn't interested in Victoria, but I still give him a look telling him not to get attached. His words were meant as advice, not a threat. Asking too many questions around either of our families would get her killed.

I'll die before allowing that to happen.

"Milano," he states, peering out the window, his tone a little more distant. "He was shot last week."

Victoria scans his profile, but she doesn't prod any further. Instead, she turns forward, sitting silently between us.

I can tell the curiosity is eating at her; she's toying with the hem of her skirt, eyes constantly shifting between all three of our laps. She has a thirst for knowledge, even if it's just gossip. I'll have to watch her constantly to keep the firm out of trouble. *Her too, most likely.*

If the information she wants is about Milano, I can't give it to her anyhow.

Our father and uncle haven't shared the exact details with us yet, but from what they *have* said, and what Luca has mentioned, I know one thing: my other uncle, Maxim Vasiliev, ordered the hit.

For that reason alone, Victoria needs to stay in the dark. *I can't let Gedeon anywhere near her.*

The gate guard at the fifth precinct attempts to ask Shephard the nature of our visit, but he doesn't say a word. Instead, he fishes a Laughlin & Laughlin business card from his pocket and flashes it at him. Victoria cranes her neck to see, but like usual, the arm bar raises and the guard heads back to his comically small hut after a couple seconds.

After we're parked, I hold the door open for Victoria as she slides a slender leg out of the backseat. Her checkered skirt is bunched above her knees from the cramped ride here. The black hosiery she wears barely conceals the fading fingerprints I left on her thighs two nights ago.

I offer her my hand as she warily places a heel onto the running board, and she looks up at me with virescent eyes, the two curls from earlier falling in her face and resting against her high cheekbones. I grip the door with my other to resist the urge to brush them away.

She gives me a nervous smile but places her hand in mine. It's cold against my skin, but sparks flare in my palm anyway, only to fizzle out when she plants both feet on the pavement and lets go. I've been on edge the entire ride, purposely brushing her leg with mine and reveling in the miniscule bits of contact that made even more desire take up residence inside me.

I want to tie her down with the seat belts and eat her sweet pussy, but I *can't*. Not until she wants *me* to. I want her to accept me being rough with her as Shaelene, not a masked intruder.

She obeys blindly. I've learned that much already. A few commanding text messages and she was dripping over my fingers, but she's still hesitant around me in person. I won't allow anyone to do anything against her will, not even myself.

The second she gives me the consent I'm working toward, I'll take her to every limit she doesn't even know is possible yet. *And she'll love it.*

Barry is easy. He likes to play as if he doesn't want anything to do with us, but he's been on our payroll since he took his oath as police commissioner.

We meet him in the lobby, a coffee in one hand and the stereotypical sprinkles of a donut stuck in his awful mustache. "Who the hell let you in here?" he grumbles as we step further into the lobby. Before any of us can play along in his stupid game, Barry chimes in again. "Come with me. I'll handle you myself. Tony—" He snaps his fingers at the rookie on the phone behind the front counter. "—Tell anyone that needs me that I'm busy handling some delinquents."

Tony ignores him entirely. Barry's entire performance is overkill given the fact almost the entire precinct knows about his dealings with us. He keeps them from asking questions or patrolling certain areas while we explore business ventures, and we make sure he remains in his gilded commissioner cage.

He leads us past the elevator bay and down the hall to his office. With all of us piled in and the door closed, I feel more cramped than in the car. Barry's incompetence fills what little space is left between the six of us.

"So, kiddos, what can I do for you today?"

Shaun doesn't waste a second. Hating interacting with Barry as much as I do, he turns to Victoria. "Invitation please."

Her hands shake a bit when she opens her case and hands it to him; me grazing by and leaving her beside Shephard and Luca doesn't help her nerves any either. Shaun hands the envelope to Barry and I rip a Post-it from the stack on his desk, pulling the pen from my inside pocket and writing the date and time of the party onto it. I slap it onto the screen of his monitor while he reads the info for himself off the invite.

"Will there be booze?" he asks.

"Enough for all the cops in New York," I deadpan, turning away and striding for the door, making sure to put myself between Victoria and Shephard's wandering eyes as I urge us all back to the SUV.

"Tell your daddy we'll be there," Barry chortles before the door closes between us, and I focus on Victoria's heels clacking on the worn linoleum ahead of me. Shephard breathing down my neck the entire time.

Back in the car, on the way to visit two very important guests, I crowd Victoria as my blood heats and my panties grow damp. An informant told us the governor has a meeting scheduled in Manhattan with another invitee. *Derek Shultz.* I smother the feral grin threatening to break through. It's been a while since we paid him a visit. *This will be fun.*

20

Victoria

Traffic is slow in the post-lunch hour rush. The windows of the car are tinted so dark I have to really focus to see out of them, but the darkness is a welcome solace after so much of what I thought was speculation is being brought to light. The Laughlins are close with the Angelini family. *That could be purely attorney-client based.* They also have a casual rapport with the police commissioner. *Okay, that one's a little harder to rationalize...*

Regardless of the dark though, I recognize the route we're traveling without needing to read the street signs. And with the way my stomach flipped inside the precinct, I can't imagine how I'll feel next.

We make our way through the busy streets of lower Manhattan for several minutes before Shephard makes the final turn I expect him to. Up the road, on our left, is the Manhattan Criminal Courthouse.

Cones and workers in neon vests and hardhats take up most of our lane as they rip up pavement around the giant fountain in the center of the block. Both sides of the street ahead of us are packed with cars and pedestrians alike. *We'll have to park so far down, I should've worn flats—*

Never mind.

Shephard guides the SUV through a narrow spot of cones and parks us right beside the taped off sidewalk directly across from the tall mountain of steps leading into the towering courthouse.

Shaelene holds the door open for me this time too, extending her hand to me again. I take it with a grateful smile, her warm palm closing softly around mine, but she doesn't let go until my ankles are safe from the loose concrete rubble spilling over the curb. Rounding the back of the Suburban, the ionic Roman style columns and white stone walls of the courthouse's grand architecture sticks out so abruptly against the reflective glass skyscrapers surrounding us it almost appears photoshopped.

Shaelene passes me, snapping me out of my daydream, her pace easily matching that of her brothers and Luca as they cross the street and take the steps two at a time. I rush after them before the next wave of cars comes our way, only looking back when one of the construction workers starts to holler obscenities. *We are* so *getting towed.*

The entryway buzzes with people bustling their way through the open lobby.

We head for security, where a small line has formed at the metal detectors, and I take my place in it, emptying my briefcase into one of the plastic bins on the conveyor belt.

A whistle stops me fumbling with my watch. I look up to see Shaelene smiling, the boys chuckling behind her. She jerks her head to the side, hinting for me to hurry over to them.

My eyes fling to the security guard holding my repacked case out in front of him, his expression blank when he mimics the same head tilt as Shaelene.

I swallow the knot in my throat and take my bag, quickly walking through the scanner.

Silence.

I glance back to see the guard's hand reaching around to flip a switch. The green indicator light over the detector comes back on, and he resumes telling the next person to step through. *Unless the city started selling security fast passes to federal buildings, I don't have an explanation for that one. I am in way over my head.*

Shaun and Luca are already making their way down the courthouse halls, but Shephard and Shaelene hang back.

When I reach them, Shephard unbuttons his jacket and gives it a quick fluff, briefly flashing the shoulder holster he's wearing and the gun secured within it. When his fingers finish fastening his suit, he brings one to his mouth, smirking while signaling for me to keep his secret as if it isn't a five-year worthy offense.

It isn't just *his* secret though. Now that I'm aware he's carrying, I can't help but notice a similar shape bulging under Shaelene's jacket too.

The black wool hugs her torso and drapes over her hips, bleeding into the same chic material making up her trousers, elongating her already stretched, intimidating frame. Her shoes, a shined pair of Prada loafers—one with a freshly scuffed toe from kicking aside a piece of broken cement outside—remind me she is, in fact, naturally tall enough she doesn't need a pair of heels to compete with the daunting demeanor of her family.

Which actually makes her scarier. Each of the triplets look like they want to eat me alive, and I can't decide if that scares me. *Or worse.*

My breath catches when something like a smile pulls at the corner of her mouth before she puts a hand on my shoulder. *Worse apparently.* The weight of her hand lingers long enough to light embers inside my already nervous belly.

She lifts her chin and her neck bobs with a swallow before she nudges me down the corridor behind Shephard.

I scan Shaun and Luca when we catch up only to find they're packing too. Shaun's is on his left hip, and the back of Luca's suit sits awkwardly off the rear of him.

It was clear the Laughlin's kept people on their payroll after our visit to the precinct, but I can't help wondering how deep their pockets run if people working in a federal building look the other way when they arrive.

The hairs on my arms stand stiffer the further into the maze of hallways we go.

Our steps echo off the linoleum floors and suffocatingly close walls. The butterflies in my stomach fly at Mach speed, keeping my brain on high alert as we continue deeper into the courthouse. Shaelene's quiet footfalls resonate in my head. I wouldn't know she's still behind me if it weren't for the feeling of her eyes on my back.

Her gaze and the dark, forest green paint on the walls, along with heavily embellished mahogany doors, make the space seem dim compared to the early afternoon sunlight shining outside.

Straight ahead is the office we came for, a bronze nameplate stamped in the center of the door confirming our destination:

Derek Shultz

New York District Attorney

Shaun pushes it open abruptly, not bothering to knock, and the rest of us quickly file in.

It opens into a much smaller foyer where the DA's blonde secretary sits behind her desk, gasping at our entrance.

The boys step around her when she stands, but she places a firm hand against Shaun's chest, telling him the district attorney is in a very important meeting.

"And even if he weren't, he'd decline having all of *you* in his office."

I gulp, preemptively imagining what her wrist will sound like when Shaun snaps it for touching him.

Shephard pushes past the two of them to the door, rapping against it loudly several times.

The woman turns to chastise him some more, saying, "I told you he's in a—"

Shephard pounds his fist against the door three more times before turning the knob and letting us in himself.

Derek's secretary looks back at Shaun appalled. He grips her wrist in his hand, and I wince in preparation, but he only shrugs as he removes it from his chest. "Looks like he has an opening."

His words are playful but cut through her like butter. She yanks her arm from his grasp and takes a frightened step back.

A heavy hand presses into my lower back, and I stiffen, the touch from Shaelene setting my body fully ablaze this time. Her fingertips make the small of my back tingle with electricity, completely opposite the uncomfortable touch from Shephard this morning.

I turn, looking into her brooding expression. Her eyes flick to the secretary then back to me, lightening a bit before she speaks.

"Thank you, Audrey. We'll see ourselves in."

She doesn't look toward her when she says it, her eyes remaining locked with mine. Her voice is husky and intoxicating, but her words feel bitter.

She waits impatiently for me to keep moving, and I spare one last look at Audrey and her desk.

Her things are organized with a seemingly obsessive precision. Her pens sit evenly beside each other on the desktop behind a small name plate with only her last name and title on it.

Secretary Pennington.

Her icy blue eyes turn to me with disgust and disapproval before she sits back in her seat, tucking a strand of loose platinum hair behind her ear while glaring at Shae's hand. I get the feeling they know each other outside of business practices, but I have no idea why Shaelene is so cold toward her. And I'm too scared to ask.

I scurry ahead, not wanting to be caught in the crossfire of an angry legal secretary and Shaelene and walk directly into a tense standoff as two men raise their pistols at the five of us.

21

Victoria

MY FEET GLUE THEMSELVES to the floor; everything around me moves at half speed except the rapid pounding of my heart against my ribs. My mind races to find a logical response to the barrel pointing at me. I don't have one.

My legs turn weak, and I start to stagger back, my body impacting with a concrete wall of a body.

Strong, warm hands brace me from behind, keeping me from falling to the floor. I look up to see Shaelene's calm expression. Her eyes deathly focused on the situation before us.

The heat from her touch thaws the ice circulating my veins enough for me to sink into her hold, but my body still trembles against her stiff frame.

"What in the—" an unfamiliar voice booms from the other side of the room.

Hands slam against a desktop as whoever just spoke stands, their chair scraping the floor with an unsettling screech.

I can't see anything past the three tall bodies ahead of me. My only visual of what's happening is the two suited men, one on each side of the boys, with their weapons trained on us. Unflinching and ready to repaint the DA's office red.

A second person speaks. A woman this time.

"Now, gentleman, it's quite alright. Lower your weapons."

Her voice is even and calm. Not what I'd expect from someone who's just been barged in on during an important meeting. She sounds familiar, though I can't quite place her voice through the chaos in my head.

Her guards wait a beat before they finally holster their guns.

"Madam Governor, this is definitely not *quite alright*," the first voice says, aghast.

The three boys take another step in and make space for Shaelene and I in the crowded office. When they side-step out from in front of me, I get my first glimpse at who we interrupted.

The district attorney stands angrily behind his desk, a light sheen of sweat coating his blotchy, unnaturally orange skin. A pair of wrinkly eyes widen with rage behind a pair of browline glasses, narrowing as he looks to Shephard.

A thin hair piece frames his weathered face, and the shoulders of his navy suit rise as he takes a long breath before returning his attention to the governor.

"Madam Governor, this is *precisely* the type of behavior—"

The governor lifts her hand as she stands. "Derek, we'll continue this another time. Schedule an appointment with my secretary; I have another meeting to attend," she says, checking her watch. Her composure remains confident as she turns to face us and smiles, her teeth shining brightly against full, glossy lips and sandy skin.

This was a very *important meeting.* I should've recognized her voice from all the times I've heard her speak during press conferences on TV. She's a female powerhouse in the political world. New York's youngest governor at only thirty-two, and one of the few female politicians the state has had in the last decade. *She's the reason I chose Sloane for my graduate school.*

She's demanding and uncompromising, needed traits in a profession dominated by men, and attributes she just showcased by silencing Derek Shultz so casually.

Governor Maldonado steps toward us, her pinstripe skirt framing her curves as her heels move silently across the carpet. Shaun turns to me, snapping and pointing a finger to my briefcase. *No 'Please' or 'Thank Yous' in this meeting. Got it.* I pull out the invitation addressed for Bianca, causing the guards to stir.

My eyes nearly bulge from their sockets, but the governor's unthreatened demeanor calms them enough as Shaun holds the envelope out for her. "I'm glad we could catch you both during our trip. We'd love to have you in attendance, Madam Governor," he says, kissing her hand.

She smiles again and her eyes flick to Shephard's. They meet for a moment that feels a couple seconds too long, and a devious smirk tugs at the corner of his mouth before he sends a pointed stare back to Derek.

I guess money isn't the only way to buy someone's trust.

Her manicured fingers delicately open the envelope, her eyes scanning the invitation quickly. She glances at Shaun, a sly smile on her lips. "Thank you, gentlemen... and ladies," she adds, nodding in my and Shaelene's direction.

She pauses beside Shephard with a lethal grace.

"Shephard," she purrs, putting a hand on his shoulder. His palm covers hers and it's the first time I see his knuckles are bruised and scabbed, making his rugged demeanor even more intimidating.

"Save me a dance, Bianca," his hushed voice taunts, tilting his head her way, but his hateful eyes stay aimed at Derek.

The governor doesn't seem to notice, or care, he's making a show of their apparent intimacy to get under Derek's skin. She only smiles wider before leaving, her guards following closely behind and closing us in with the ruddy faced DA.

Somehow, with the armed guards gone, the tension feels thicker. Like they were keeping *Derek's* apprehension at bay rather than ours. Shaelene plants a hand on my shoulder as the other leaves my waist and trails down to the case I'm holding, popping it open with one deft stroke of her thumb and grabbing the invitation addressed to Shultz.

Her face pauses near my shoulder, threatening to rest on top of it, before she stands straight. A shaky breath escapes my lips. The earthy scent of her fills my nose without Luca's overbearing, musky cologne suffocating me. The inebriating notes of something citrus mixed with bergamot consume me. Another whiff hits my senses when she side-steps toward the peacocking DA and adjusts her jacket, leaving me in a cloud of jasmine and amber.

"What is it you want?" Derek spits, his nostrils flaring.

Shaelene's head tips to the side, exposing the arch of her slender neck. "I'm doing well today, Derek. Thank you for asking. How are you?" Her normally cold, sarcastic voice has chilled even further, an icy dagger coating each word of her barbed response.

"Cut the bullshit. Why are you kids here?"

A sharp exhale shoots from Shaelene's nose when she chuckles at the DA's unamused insult. If I had to guess, he's only ten to twelve years their senior, but it's just a way for him to try to assert dominance over the triplets. *Keyword* try.

Shaelene sits calmly in the seat the governor was in not even a minute ago. Shaun takes the matching one beside her, lazily bouncing his ankle on his knee. Like some sort of practiced formation I'm not in on, Luca moves to stand near Shaun, resting his hands behind his back, suspiciously close to his weapon. Shephard locks the door and leans against it, arms crossed and eyes still glued on Derek. Meanwhile, I stuff myself as far into the corner as I can without drawing attention to myself.

"Just thought we'd drop in for a visit with our good friend in his..." She pauses, looking at the overly decorated walls, "...*charming,* little office."

Another heated glare is sent in her direction, doing nothing to melt her icy poise.

Shaelene's impertinence comes as a shock to me. I've known her and her brother's for less than a day, but I hadn't clocked her to be such a bitch. She was certainly nicer than her siblings. *She'd left without a word yesterday on the balcony, but she's been kind to me since I arrived at the manor today.*

Now, the fierceness I'd been seeing in her eyes all day comes sharply off her tongue, each word carefully selected for maximum damage.

"Ms. Laughlin, surely you're not as dense as the rest of your clan here." He jerks his chin at the guys, his jaw clenching. "You know we are no such thing."

Shaelene's eyes narrow. "Forgive me, but I believe you just insulted my brothers."

Shephard's knuckles crack beside me, and Luca lifts his chin.

Derek lets out an unimpressed huff as his head drops, his eyes falling to his desk. His knuckles rap against the surface, anger vibrating through him. Looking up at Shaelene again, he says, "You have twenty seconds to get to the point before I have you escorted from the building."

Shaelene holds his gaze, spinning the invitation in her hands. She flaunts it between two sharply filed fingers before planting it against the desktop and sliding it toward the DA, his annoyance increasing with every second we stay crowded in his office.

Tension ripples around us, an awkward silence growing, before Shaelene speaks again. "We look forward to your attendance, Shultz."

It isn't a request. It's a demand.

They hold each other's glare for a long moment.

"It's really in your best interest to come," Shaun emphasizes, standing alongside his sister. The two of them sink back into the polished and distinguished lawyers they'd arrived as, fluffing their jackets in unison before turning their backs to the DA and heading for the door.

Shaelene's gaze meets mine before she's out, but she doesn't acknowledge me further. Something about the end of this conversation feels different than when we'd first entered. I can still feel her breath on my shoulder, her hands on me, but the warmth is fading.

I turn to follow, all of them striding past Audrey toward the hall.

"Ms. Fenwick." Derek's voice halts me in my tracks. I meet his gaze over my shoulder. His expression has changed to an even, serious one—a shocking difference to the anger he was presenting before. "You'd do well to reconsider your company."

I don't have a response. I know what he's insinuating. He's practically confirming the fears I already had about working for Laughlin & Laughlin. *The rumors... The risk...*

So far, I've met the son of a supposed mafia boss, helped remind the police commissioner of his priorities, entered a federal building with a group of armed cohorts, witnessed the threatening of a high-ranking government employee, and we haven't even stopped for lunch yet.

But what scares me most is that I've been associated with the Laughlins for less than two days and the district attorney already knows me by name...

I am so fucked.

Shephard clears his throat, drawing both Derek and I's attention. He's waiting by Audrey's desk, the look on his face ravenous.

Why would he wait?

22

Victoria

My stomach grumbles angrily the entirety of the painfully quiet drive back to the manor. Luca inconspicuously passes me a stick of gum, the only one taking pity on me, I guess. The attempt to quiet the hungry beast growling inside my gut works for all of ten minutes. If I didn't think Shephard would decline, I might ask if we can hit a drive through, but with our work in the city complete, I'm sure Silas expects us back immediately.

The iron gates outside the property open before we meet the entrance, the interior of the car going black from the shade of the trees and the dark tint on the windows. For a brief moment, I'm blind to everything around me.

Something touches me, drawing a brief circle on my kneecap.

When the elm trees clear and we round the circle drive, Shaelene is still staring out the window on her side, her chin resting on the hand she perches on the door. The other comfortably in her lap.

Did I imagine it? No. Something definitely touched me.

Shaun's elbow is resting on the center console a few inches from my knee, but there's no way he could've touched me and gotten reset quickly enough for no one to notice.

The air conditioning in the garage prickles my skin with even more goosebumps when Shaelene opens her door and we weave through the Laughlin's impressive collection of vehicles.

The Suburban we took today is one of two. The three row SUVs claim most of the space in the parking lot of a garage. I'm not a car girl, but I know the symbols for luxury when I see them.

We pass a few sports bikes too before reaching the door.

I haven't seen this side of Laughlin Manor yet. When we left this morning, Geoffrey had the car waiting out front.

The walls on this side of the mansion are mostly dark wood adorned with art wrapped in gaudy ornamental frames.

We pass through a spacious formal dining room. The table in its center is ready to seat twelve, with fresh floral centerpieces placed every three seats, then another seating room that connects to the main foyer.

Back on a familiar path, we head down the hall to the office I met with Silas in yesterday. The smell of tobacco infiltrating my nose immediately when we get inside.

Grigorio puffs on a cigar, the butts of two others left discarded in the crystal tray on the small table. Simon sits in one of the plush chairs, hunched over a mountain of paper with Silas hovering behind him, visibly stressed.

He rounds the chair and stuffs the documents Simon was writing on into a folder and slaps it closed. "Tomorrow, Grigorio," he states.

Mr. Angelini stands, looking at his son. "*Vieni, Luca. Per oggi abbiamo finito,*" he says, walking toward the door without waiting for Luca to follow. Nodding to me and squeezing Shaelene's arm, Luca bids his goodbyes.

The rest of us remain, quietly waiting to be told what's next.

Silas places the folder, along with a few other files from the table, into the bottom drawer of his desk and locks it with a key.

"It's done?" he asks.

Shaelene nods, and he does the same, muttering a stern approval.

He looks us over before speaking again. "The four of you are dismissed. Miss Fenwick, same time tomorrow."

The boys turn on their heels, trekking off down the hall. I turn too, double checking I have everything I came with before I leave.

"I'll have Phillip tell the kitchen to make lunch before you go." Shaelene faces me, her tone daring me to stay a little while longer.

I'm about to thank her in protest when my stomach grovels again. We both hear it, the sound impossibly loud. A soft smile lifts her plump lips, making my eyes fall to the floor in embarrassment.

"Let me give you a tour while we wait."

I lift my gaze back to hers. *There's still plenty of Laughlin Manor I've yet to see.* Her brows turn up, waiting for my answer.

"I'd like that. Thank you, Shaelene."

Gone are the harsh words I'd seen her sparring with an hour ago, the politeness she'd shown me earlier in the day is back.

She tells me bits of info about every room we pass, the next is an office, almost identical to the one we'd just left, but belonging to Simon.

Turning a sharp corner at the end of the hall, more windows show the resort sized pool and jacuzzi in the center courtyard. From here, we're directly opposite the front door, the backs of the chairs I first saw Shaun and Shephard sitting in are visible through the equally magnificent wall of glass dominating the foyer.

We've made it halfway around the property when Shaelene leads us up a flight of stairs.

A terrace wraps around the outside of the second story, allowing full view of whatever is happening in the water below from every side.

We stop before a door in the middle of another wide hallway, and I watch her put her thumb on a scanner to unlock it.

The room is huge. Twice the size of Silas' office. Three desks line the wall in front of us, and to the right, a large flat screen hangs flush, centered against a wall with shelves full of awards and achievements.

"This is our office," Shaelene says, breaking the silence.

I step in more behind her, admiring the aesthetic. Books and bronze figurines litter the built-ins along the back wall. The beige carpet is soft beneath me, causing my heels to sink slightly. A slice of the room along the back wall is empty, void of any furniture and missing the old money flare the rest of the room possesses.

"We'll have a desk ready when you arrive tomorrow."

My neck snaps her way. "I'll have my own desk?"

I'd half expected to be working in a corner somewhere, mindlessly filing documents and running photocopies I couldn't actually look at. The idea of having my own desk and sharing an office with the triplets hadn't crossed my mind.

Shaelene steps closer, her head dipping low. "Well, now, it'd be a little cramped if we had to share one, wouldn't it? After all, there's only one seat."

The smile I'd seen on her lips earlier creeps across her face in a taunting grin, reveling in my anxiousness. Phillip trots past the door, breaking whatever spell we'd fallen under.

"I'll go order our food. Sit tight."

23

Victoria

I MOSEY OVER TO the floating shelves on either side of the television.

Plaques from the triplets' time at Sloane occupy the first few I scan. Below them, sports achievements ranging from college to middle school fill the shelf to nearly bursting levels.

There are several photos of Shephard and Luca alongside boxing trophies. Shaun's name is scribed onto several framed patents, most of them technology based and far too complicated for me to understand.

Letters of academic and athletic successes from the boys take up most of the shelves. Shaelene's name is tagged on the few they have in common. News articles name her as the valedictorian in her graduating classes from both high school and undergrad, but otherwise it's mostly the boys.

A black belt is displayed with all three of their names embroidered on it and the year they earned it. *Three twelve-year-old black belts...*

What really catches my attention is the shelf below it.

A black and white photo of Shaelene, not much younger than she is now, sitting behind the keys of a Steinway, a gilded trophy proudly beside it.

New York Young Piano Prize

1ST PLACE PIANIST

My chest warms at the thought of the Laughlins enjoying normal hobbies. It makes me wonder what other things they do to fill their time outside of their father's demands.

Shephard boxes. Shaun is a techy. Shaelene plays piano.

Do the boys have a PlayStation in their rooms and stay up all hours of the night yelling at ten-year-olds? Does Shaelene keep a diary?

I laugh at the last one. I can't see Shaelene being the type to write out her feelings any more than I can see Shephard sitting down for longer than five minutes.

The remaining spaces are filled with the feats of the firm. A press photo of them with their uncle and father from the day they were hired sits as the focal point of their time at Laughlin & Laughlin.

Luca and his family appear in a couple pictures, along with other clients I'm not familiar with. *Yet.*

No photos or mention of their mother though. *I wonder if it's something they avoid talking or thinking about completely.*

I'm sure if she were still around, seeing the achievements I'm looking at now, she'd be proud of them. Any mother would be.

I didn't dig any further into the family after that first night. Having met them now, there's no denying they come from Silas. Their looks are obvious, but their confident, *cocky* personality stems from him too. Yet, I can't help but wonder how much they're like their mother.

Does Shaelene share her voice? Do her high cheekbones match her mom? Or maybe they're nothing like her in looks or behavior.

My brain starts to deep dive into their history, desperately wanting to know more about the woman that brought them into the world.

The door opens behind me, and the words fall out before I can stop them.

"Do you have any photos of your mother?"

Immediately, my heart sinks. That was a deeply personal question I randomly sprung on someone it will probably traumatize and who, to my knowledge, is still in possession of a deadly firearm.

Also, Luca literally just warned me about opening my mouth and asking questions.

Then I turn, and my stomach drops alongside my heart when I see Shephard standing inside the office—Shaelene nowhere in sight.

"There you go asking questions again, Red." His low rumble makes my body vibrate as he stalks further into the room.

I back pedal, but that doesn't stop the way he charges at me.

My heels sink into the carpet with every heavy step I take away from him.

"You're a bit nosey, huh?" His eyes narrow as his head tilts. "You must have so many questions. It's been an exciting day for you."

The heel of my shoe catches the leg of the desk behind me, and Shephard takes one more step, caging me between him and the desktop.

"You got to see a glimpse of how we operate. The connections we have. How we can do whatever we want... Wherever we want."

His eyes no longer meet mine. They're on my neck. The vein in it throbbing faster the closer he gets to me. He licks his thumb, then swipes it over one of the bite marks, smearing the concealer I put on it this morning.

His voice lowers, his head looming over mine. "Ask me what you've really been wanting to know, Red." My brain flits through the dozens of things I've witnessed today. *Mr. Angelini. The guns. The governor. The DA knowing my name...*

As if he could hear my thoughts, he confirms my fear. "You even made an enemy today. Shultz has probably had someone tailing you since your car pulled out of the drive yesterday."

"Why would he—"

Shephard shushes me, pressing a finger to my lips. The smell of his cigars lingering on it, making me want to gag. My limbs are stuck to my side. Memories of my nightmare resurface, and I fight to keep them at bay. Tears burn my eyes, my nose itching as I struggle to remain in control.

He leans closer, whispering in my ear, "He doesn't like us very much, Red."

No shit, asshole. But what could *I* have done? *Am I guilty by association?*

"He thinks we're crooked." He gives a knowing smile, loving the idea of scaring me. "That we lie. Do awful things for awful people. He's been trying for years to convince anyone to believe him. He thinks he'll find evidence of our bad behavior and be able to take down the firm and everyone we've represented."

He pauses, just long enough to look over me again. From my trembling lips to the heaving of my chest beneath him. "That's why he was meeting with the governor today. He must think he has something worthwhile on us. Lucky timing on our part. Bianca might have actually heard him out if we hadn't shown up."

His lip curls as he leans into me, his hips pinning mine, his body flush along my own. I feel him stiffen in his slacks, his shaft pressing into my stomach. "She's a little upset with me for not calling her back after a private *meeting* of our own last week."

He winks, his expression hungry and dark. His tongue graces his lips as my billowing chest draws his attention. *Please, no! I don't want—*

"He won't actually have evidence against us though... We don't leave any."

His hands plant on either side of me and I lean as far back as I can without falling, my toes barely touching the floor anymore. Every inch of me shakes beneath him, but he doesn't stop.

"If him having eyes on you is scary, Red, I'll keep watch. You can stay here. With me. Be *protected*. Armed guards outside the doors every night. No one gets in..." His hot breath washes over my neck, inches from my flesh. "Or out."

The first tear falls. The thought of being locked in a room with Shephard, like I am right now, every night shatters the poise I clung to.

My nostrils flare, dread sinking in when my gaze meets the menace in his. *He's right.*

I *have* had eyes on me. Not just since my interview, longer than that. If anything, they stopped once I'd finally gotten *here.*

A terrified croak escapes my throat.

Shephard is my stalker... And he's been fucking with me this whole time.

I can't stop the tears from pouring down my face any longer. They burst from my eyes, soaking my lashes and pooling in the dip of my neck.

Something stirs behind Shephard and his hand freezes before it can brush the streaks from my cheek.

A lustful Shephard is terrifying, but the angry one on top of me is blood-curdling. He looks down at me beneath him, but when he speaks again, it's to someone else. "Hello, Shae."

My breath hitches. Not wasting the opportunity, I round the desk, moving away from Shephard as fast as my shaky legs can.

Over his shoulder, I see Shaelene standing behind him. Poised. Controlled. Enraged. Her darkened eyes laser focused on the back of her brother's head, her pistol aimed unshakingly at the same spot.

"Bet's *off*, Shep." Her tone is fierce, but not irrational.

"Oh, but we were just getting to the good part, weren't we, Red?" Shephard calls her bluff, not taking his eyes off me. "You won't do it, Shae. You can't. Not in front of her."

He's using me as leverage to save his own ass, but something tells me Shaelene wouldn't hesitate to kill someone two feet from me, even if it meant I'd be covered in brain matter.

CLICK. Shaelene cocks the hammer with her thumb.

"No time like the present, baby brother. Touch her again, and I'll put a bullet through that thick ass skull of yours. Call it vengeance for Mom."

Shephard draws in a long breath and lifts his chin as he straightens, scowling at me. Shaelene clearly struck a nerve, inadvertently answering one of the questions I'd had earlier.

Shephard turns, facing Shaelene's gun head on. He lifts his hands sarcastically, stepping into her space. When he looks over his shoulder at me, the barrel is touching his head.

"I told you she couldn't do it, Red," he mocks, tapping a finger against his temple before turning back. "Our triplet telepathy. I know *exactly* what's going on inside her head."

Shaelene doesn't say anything, glaring at her brother, the pistol still in her hand.

"She's all yours, sis. No pussy is worth dying over." His shoulder clashes with hers as he exits, slamming the door on his way out.

Shae drops her shoulder, the gun aimed at the floor as she stares at the door, her thumb trembling as she puts the safety back on.

The tightness in my throat leaves, returning a second later as my breath catches up with my racing heart. "A bet?" My eyes widen, and my cheeks burn from embarrassment. I want to scream. Run. *Hide.* But I want an explanation too.

Shaelene holsters her weapon. "My brothers had a bet about who could fuck you first."

My jaw falls open and I don't have the resolve to pick it up. Shaelene steps closer. "You don't have to worry about them," she reassures me, rubbing her hand up and down my arm. A shaky breath escapes me, my eyes flitting around the room as tears start to well again, and I try to make sense of my life right now. "But you'd be wise to worry about me."

My eyes lock on hers. Gray irises eating away my sense of security. My pulse pounds under the tight grasp of her hand on my bicep.

"Because I plan on being the only one touching you from here on out, Little Fox."

PART TWO

Motion to Strike

24

Shaelene

I DON'T STAY AND watch Victoria sprint through the halls on the monitors. And though I'd love nothing more than to chase behind and drag her to my room, I hunt down Shephard instead. He's right; I wouldn't have killed him, especially not in front of Victoria like that. *But God, did I want to.*

I find him with Shaun in the den, both of them chalking up billiard sticks.

Sauntering over to the table, I grab the cue ball before he can take his first shot. He doesn't say anything or look at me. He holds his chin high, waiting for me to back down and give up.

That will never happen. Him and Shaun may be bigger than me physically, but I'm the oldest. *I'm the revered one.* When the firm gets passed down, I'll be the head of it. He and Shaun both understand that, even if they aren't thrilled by it.

He made a big show to Victoria about knowing I wouldn't pull the trigger, but she didn't see the split-second of doubt in his eyes when he turned to face me. He's my brother and I *do* love him despite him being the world's biggest prick most of the time. He recognizes the fact I wouldn't jeopardize my, or the firm's, future by killing him. *But he should still refrain from touching Victoria again.*

The tick of his jaw and unblinking stare at the wall ahead of him only serve to make each quiet second pass by slower.

Shaun clears his throat, his tone more concerned than annoyed at my interruption. "Anyone gonna fill me in, or am I destined to sit here waiting for one of you to break so we can start this game?"

Still glaring at Shephard's profile, I ask, "Did your stupid bet have any stipulations regarding consent?"

Shaun's head lulls, his shoulders falling in my peripheral. Tapping the tip of his stick against his forehead, his eyes squeezed shut, he groans, "Dammit, Shep. What did you do to Victoria?"

"Nothing she wouldn't have liked after I was done," he replies with a smirk in my direction, but I can see through his false confidence. "She would've said yes eventually. Screamed it even."

I invade his space, pinning his hand to the table with the cue ball and resting my full weight onto it, putting my face inches from his. His upper lip twitches. Other than that, he doesn't let on to the pain at all, but I know he feels it.

I smile. "She wouldn't have, Shep. She's too smart for you."

His jaw tightens, along with my grip on the ball. "Did she say yes to you, Shae? Any of the times you watched her?"

A sense of disloyalty fissures through my chest. *I know he didn't figure that out himself.* I didn't disclose that information to Shaun, but the way he shifts beside us tells me everything I need to know about how much he and Shephard have talked. *He probably rebugged my phone after Shephard's inquisition the other morning, which I'll have to take care of after this.* But still, neither of them know the true extent of my visit to Victoria.

The ball wobbles under my palm, smashing the tendons in the back of his hand, making him wince again.

"She was hard to understand when my tongue was inside her cunt."

His eyes narrow, but I see the hint of respect glinting across them.

I keep him pinned for a couple seconds longer before tossing the ball across the felt, hearing it clack against the others as I turn and walk out without saying another word. I don't have to. They both understand.

Victoria is mine, and they shouldn't try for her anymore.

My jaw is sore from the amount of teeth grinding I've done this morning.

From watching my phone under the dining table and seeing her type then backspace an email to her professor over and over, trying to find the right phrasing for her internship resignation. My plate sits untouched until she finally dials the house and I hear the phone ring.

Phillip answers it in the kitchen and relays the conversation in Father's ear as he sits at the head of the table several seats down from the three of us. I may not have audio on those cameras, but I know from the way she faked a cough and rubbed her neck that she called in 'sick'. *And I'm in no mood to hear Father's reprimands.* Giving no outward expression of his dissatisfaction, he stands and exits.

Shephard massages the bruise on the back of his hand as the three of us walk in sync down the stairs toward our father's office, abandoning the remainder of our breakfast on the dining table.

As expected, Father is behind that damned mahogany desk, his stern face displeased. Stony. Uncle is behind him, his ever-present shadow, leaning against the built-ins with his arms crossed. Two lines notched between his brows. We pause before them, waiting for our father's usual scrutiny.

"Miss Fenwick is ill and won't be joining us today. Any of you feeling under the weather? Being as you were with her all day yesterday, you are the most at risk." His words are guised as sentiment but laced with skepticism. "No?" he presses when none of us answer.

Shephard breaks the silence. "No, sir. We're fine," he pauses, taking the briefest of glances my direction. "I suspect she's frightened from the encounter with Shultz."

What the hell? Why the fuck would that *be what scared her?* My palms cry out as my nails dig into them, an ounce of pressure away from drawing blood. *As opposed to you threatening to assault her, you dickhead?*

Our father doesn't say anything, waiting for Shephard to continue.

"As we were leaving, he called her back. We didn't introduce her, and she didn't appear to have known him beforehand. Probably spooked her."

My breath hitches, and I move my hands behind my back to hide their shaking. *When did Derek address her? How did Shephard catch it and I didn't?* Of course, I hadn't heard it. I stormed from his office as soon as I'd said all I needed to pull a satisfying rise out of him. She'd gone quiet after we left the courthouse—aside from her stomach—which I attributed to her nerves finally catching up to her. *Incorrectly apparently.*

I can't place Shultz saying her name for the life of me. All I could focus on was not making eye contact with Audrey. She incessantly clicked her pen, again and again. *And again.* The heat of her glare burning a hole into my temple.

I couldn't ignore the awkward mix of hatred and longing in Audrey's stare and I didn't want Victoria to see it either, so I took off down the hall, letting Shaun and Luca's conversation drown out everything behind me, which was likely why I didn't hear Shultz call Victoria. *Did he say anything else to her?*

"Did he say anything else? Or do you think simply acknowledging her presence was enough to run her off?" Simon asks like he can hear the thoughts raging inside me.

My eyes fixate on the Waterford paperweight on the desk in front of me while my mind spins, but I still notice when Shephard glances my way with an arrogant blend of pride and—*Is that concern in his eyes?*—before speaking. "He told her to rethink the people she keeps as company," he admits.

FUCKING SHIT!

My nails break skin and the tiny pinpricks warm my palms. *He got in her head.* Victoria is easily swayed, and Shultz did it with just a few vaguely threatening words. And, of course, Shephard spent the day taunting her and showing his ass by flashing his gun in the middle of the courthouse lobby before coming on to her in the office.

Then there's me revealing I've been stalking her... Forcing her to pose naked while I took pictures. Breaking into her house and fucking her.

All of that is more than enough to turn her against us. Against *me*. She has every right to believe we're the bad guys. *Because we are the fucking bad guys!*

She wasn't supposed to know that yet, but Father and Uncle wouldn't have hired her if they'd planned to keep her in the dark. There's too much to hide for us to do that. There's no way she could've found anything to give us up so quickly. There wasn't enough time. *Was there?* She wouldn't do that. *Would she?*

I'm spiraling. I feel my chest filling with air, but I can't catch my breath. My brain can't decide what to be worried about. *Is she in danger from Shultz or our family? Did I lose her already? I only just got her. Does she hate me now? Is our father angry? Will he want her taken out?* I have to calm down. No one is going to hurt her. Not Shultz. Not Shephard. Not my father. Not me.

No one.

My knuckles crack as my fists clench past the point they can stand. Shephard's eyes are notably on me. An unexpected look on his face. *Pity? Concern?* My teeth grit. *That's not like him.*

He can see me spinning out of control. The weight of my threats yesterday must finally be hitting him, seeing me in such distress over Victoria's absence. "I'm sure she'll be back tomorrow," he claims, turning back to Father and drawing any attention away from my face, which I'm positive is a shade brighter than usual. If he can see my panic, everyone else can too.

On my other side, Shaun peeks over without turning his head, moving slow enough to not make it obvious when he gently pries my hand open. Instinctively I grasp his thumb, holding it tight like when we were kids and I'd drag him around by it. *Their hands were always so much bigger than mine.* The familiarness is a gift. The air sticks in my lungs, and my fight instinct settles to a controllable level. Her claws retracting from my chest with each breath.

"Understanding that, your assignment today is of even greater concern."

Father clicks the remote that controls the TV on the wall behind us, swapping the security feed with what's on his computer monitor. Shultz's arrogant face fills half the screen while the other shows a collection of notes and known locations. All of which we're more than familiar with. His home address. His private office. The coffee shop Audrey grabs his daily americanos from. His closer affiliates are highlighted with crisp pictures ensuring there's no confusion, one of which is Governor Maldonado.

"Follow him. Figure out what he wanted to share so desperately with Ms. Maldonado. Do something about it, but don't put us in a worse situation than we may already be. Understood?" His eyes hold mine, waiting for submission.

I dip my chin. He dismisses the boys, ordering me to wait behind.

"Shaelene. It is imperative Miss Fenwick remain part of this firm." *He sounds distressed.* Uncle nervously nips at the side of his thumb, his eyes staring ahead without seeing.

"Why? What makes her so special?" I ask. A piss poor attempt on my part at distancing myself from the reason she's not here. *And a question I can't seem to find the answer to myself.* Uncle remains silent, side-eying Father and waiting for his response.

"It only matters she returns here tomorrow. Do whatever necessary to see she does." He looks at his monitor while pointing back at the TV. The video feed from our shared office yesterday afternoon plays on mute while he continues.

"If fucking her is the mutual interest she needs in order to stick around, *fine*. But if you're going to threaten your brother, take it outside. I don't want blood all over my carpets."

A tight swallow clogs my throat, and I dip my chin at his iron-handed command. "Yes, sir."

I glance at my uncle before leaving, dismissing me with a shallow nod of his own, his brows creased with worry.

25

Victoria

Dear Professor Hilton,
Regretfully, I feel it is in my best interest to withdraw from my internship with Lau—

MY FINGER HOLDS THE backspace key, deleting everything... *Again*.

I should terminate my internship with the Laughlins, but I can't bring myself to do it. It was risky, calling the manor and feigning sick, but I woke up and knew I didn't have the balls to face any of the triplets today. For all I know, Shaelene could've been watching me herself, though I was sure to draw the curtains I'd bought on the way home.

I *ran* out of the manor yesterday, passing by Phillip in the hall, a stunned expression stamped across his face and two of the best smelling gourmet grilled cheeses with a side of soup I'd ever seen in his hands.

I stayed up way too late stressing over everything I'd experienced throughout the day. Thinking about what the DA had said, and how he knows my name. Shephard nearly convincing me Shultz had someone out there watching me. But aside from my stalker—*Shaelene*—I haven't felt any eyes on me.

I don't know if anyone actually believes I'm sick, especially since Phillip didn't sound swayed one way or the other in his short replies, but I haven't received a call ordering me to come in yet. *Which isn't reassuring either, honestly. Shaelene knows where I live; she could break in and drag me there if her father ordered it.* I shudder at the thought, not only because it's horrifying that my new reality has such an air of moral ambiguity, but because I feel my core heating at the thought of her in my space again. *Touching me like last time but whispering her provoking words of reassurance into my ear while she— Nope. Stop right there. Daydreaming about Shaelene will only make an already unhealthy work environment even more terminal.* Which is why I've spent the morning in bed with a cup of coffee weighing the pros and cons of seeing the rest of my internship through.

Pros: Internship means experience and clinical hours, a passing grade for class, recommendations for future firms...

Cons: Damage to my career and reputation, possibilities of dealing with shady and dangerous people, Shaelene has been stalking me, Shephard threatened me, Shaun... has actually been pretty nice, all things considered.

All in all, I know if I resign I'll fail my class. There's no reassigning internships with Professor Hilton. He'll tell me, 'If you can't handle running with the top dogs of New York law, then you won't be good enough to prosecute against them in court later'. He's got a point, but I'm quickly learning it wouldn't matter how good of a lawyer I become myself.

The Laughlins don't lose cases.

If I quit now, I lose any credibility I could gain with other firms. I flunk out of Sloane, and the last six years of my life will have been a total waste. I cup my face in my hands, peeking through my fingers as they drag down my face.

I slam my laptop closed, taking in a long breath then sighing. I'm going to stay on with Laughlin & Laughlin, even if it's the death of me, because living a life without chasing my dreams is worse than risking it every day. *At least then I'd die doing something worthwhile.*

I hope.

I slump onto my pillows and close my eyes, the first bit of silence returning to my head since I left the apartment yesterday. At the very least, making the decision to stay managed to release some of the stress from my shoulders.

As much as I want to soak up the quiet and nap, I'm too on edge to sleep. I roll off the bed and open the built-in storage beneath, digging out my last blank canvas and the rest of my art supplies. *I may as well do something with my free day.*

My brush hovers, and a few drops of over-watered black paint splatter onto the white. *I need to buy a new tube, this one's shot.*

Usually, my feelings inspire something pretty quickly, but I can't quite pinpoint exactly what I'm feeling right now.

It's a potent cocktail of emotions. I picked up the black first so, *fear?* I look at the other half empty paints I pulled out. Green. *Excitement?* Red... The temptation to run lingers in the far back reaches of my mind but... The desire to stay is at the forefront, blocking everything else.

Even when the words left Shaelene's pretty mouth, the truth of her being the "man" next door didn't fully hit me. The truth that my heart raced so lustfully for *her.* That she's who I screamed for as I came. It wasn't until I got home and felt safe not being surrounded by six-foot-something, sexually aggressive triplets anymore that I looked across the street into her apartment. Empty, but the memory of her standing there watching me flashed and everything I felt between then and when she blindfolded and fingered me into oblivion punched me in the gut. I shake my head, unfurrowing my brow and dragging my lip back out from between my teeth.

I'm not gay. I mean, I've never considered myself to be anything other than— *Okay, so you kissed Macy* once *in middle school before Sterling ever happened, but it was just girls being girls, right?*

To be honest, I hadn't done anything remotely sexual with anyone after the attack. *Until Shaelene.*

Granted, I didn't know it was *her*, but it was still her touch. Her tongue. Just *her*, that made me *want* again. I was scared and couldn't figure out what I was wanting, but I wanted all the same. Even seeing her up on that balcony eyeing me, I knew she was different from her brothers. I didn't piece it together then, and I still can't pretend I fully understand, but I think I'm starting to. She terrified me but made me feel safe at the same time. Made it known that if anyone was going to do anything to me, it'd be her, yet she didn't. *She let me leave...* She's only ever brought me pleasure. *I wonder if she'd hurt me if I asked her to...* The wood of my brush crunches between my teeth and I yank it out, splattering even more black onto the canvas. *Stop it, Victoria. Bad.*

Wait, no! That's it! My eyes flare, and I dip into the inky black again. *I know exactly what I'm going to paint.*

My brush swipes the canvas with dark, purposeful curves, around all the drip marks. Black and a muted green, with a spark of red nestled in the middle of it all. I sit for the next few hours on the floor, hunched and concentrated, losing track of everything around me, my feelings and decision becoming more indisputable with every stroke.

26

Shaelene

MY FACE SQUEEZES INTO the tight padding of my helmet as I slide it on and shake it into place, relieved to finally be hidden from the prying eyes of my brothers. Tucking my braided hair beneath the collar of my jacket, I readjust my gloves and double check the laces on my boots. *I wonder if Vic—*

Shaun's voice crackles through my headset. "Lead the way."

We pull out of the drive, upshifting as we speed toward the city, the wind whipping past us and I hear Shepard's *whoop* without the mics. I decided on us riding to the job for a few reasons. Getting through the crowded streets is faster on a bike, so long as you ignore the laws against lane filtering. It's easier to stay covert with a mirrored face shield hiding your identity.

And the weather is nice today.

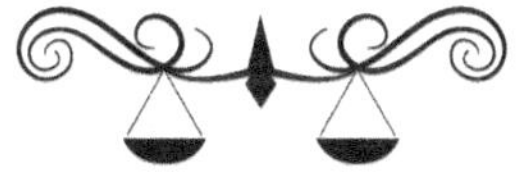

We park on the far side of the fountain flowing in front of the courthouse, more hidden from the constant flux around the building than yesterday. The ceaseless ebb of traffic past us does little to keep me from going stir crazy while we wait, and it only worsens since I can't check on Victoria with Shaun and Shephard always peeking over my shoulders. *She'll be fine for one day. Focus on the task at hand.*

Even as I think it, I catch myself drumming my fingers over the hard outline of my phone in my pocket. *One look won't hurt...*

"There," Shephard's voice cuts through my earpiece. "Coming out the gate."

I curl my fingers over the phone burning a hole against my leg and look toward the parking garage beside the courthouse. Shultz's car is pulling out, driving past the front of the building. *Right on time for lunch.*

I pop into first and speed around the fountain, Shaun and Shephard close behind. "Follow him. I'll check his office," I order, my eyes already locked on the road ahead.

"What about Audrey?" Shaun asks.

"Let's hope she didn't pack a lunch."

Their matching, menacing laughter is cut short when our headsets lose signal.

I quickly dart around the side of the building into the small access alley and park behind the row of dumpsters against the street-level wall. When I pull my helmet off, a few loose strands of sweat-dampened hair stick to my face, my body humming with arousal as I think of the last time I broke a sweat. I stuff my gloves in my jacket pocket and make my way up the tower of steps out front, leaving my helmet perched on the bike seat.

Dennis lets me pass through security just as easily as he did last time.

My riding shoes look like a pair of casual high tops, but the padding in them makes them heavier, and no matter how quiet I try to be, my footsteps pound down the corridor as I head deeper into the building. I stop worrying about the sound of my shoes and pick my head up, striding the rest of the way to Shultz's office as if he's expecting me for a meeting. Sometimes the best way to blend in is to pretend you're not out of place.

I pause, lingering outside the office door to listen, but I don't hear anything except my steady breaths. Hoping that means Audrey isn't in there, I place a soft hand on the doorknob and turn it slowly.

It being unlocked should've been my first clue.

Audrey's surprised eyes meet mine, her lips parting in a silent gasp. Her fork frozen midair in front of her mouth. *She did pack a lunch. Fuck.* I straighten and square my shoulders, hoping she didn't notice my cautioned stance as I entered.

She drops her bite back into her salad and pulls out an earbud, her favorite podcast softly filling the air. "What are you doing here, Shae?"

I can't lie and tell her I'm here for a meeting, she manages Shultz's schedule, and I certainly can't tell her the truth. *Who knows if Shultz even tells her anything anymore?* Instead, I play it off like I'm dropping in for an impromptu meeting. *If you act like you just got caught, she'll rat. Breathe.*

As if I didn't just watch him leave, I ask, "Is Shultz in?"

"He's out to lunch," she replies pointedly, crossing her arms over her chest, her analyzing eyes stormy as she glares at me, then clearing the second after she looks me up and down.

The jacket is tight against my chest, giving me extra definition in all the right places, like my shoulders and back, while narrowing on my waist and creating an hourglass I normally don't possess in my suits. My black pants are a similar pair to the ones I wore the night

I visited Victoria inside her apartment, except these fit me like a glove, outlining the curvature of my hips and giving my ass a nice lift.

She's around Victoria's height, but sitting in her chair, she's eye-level with my chest. Her eyes linger there a second too long before finally trailing back up to mine. She sucks in a breath, fighting for composure I know she doesn't have. "I can take a message."

I need in that office. But I don't have an excuse to give her as to why.

"I'll wait for him," I say, rounding her desk. She's on me quick, grabbing my elbow and stepping in front of me.

I stop, my skin crawling under my leathers. *She never did learn not to touch me.*

"He'll be gone for at least an hour, and I can't let anyone in there while he's out."

I scowl at her hand, but when I meet her eyes, they're pleading. "Alright," I submit, shrugging out of her grasp.

Her shoulders drop and her face relaxes, but her hands still fidget at her sides. "Can I ask you something, Shae?"

My eyes roll to the back of my head as she turns to sit. I don't have time for questions. I need to find out whatever I can on Shultz but seeing as she won't let me into his office unsupervised, I raise a cautious brow and lift my chin when she faces me again.

"Why didn't *I* get an invite to your birthday?"

Jesus H... What are we, five years old?

"Because you don't need to be there." I can tell my words sting harder than intended the second they're heard, her cheeks turning red as if I slapped them.

Something unfamiliar in my chest bristles. *Guilt?* I don't hate Audrey, but I also can't continue having her attached. Our relationship was strictly business at the end of it. She's an innocent. I didn't enjoy hurting her, but I don't regret doing it either.

Sleeping with her afforded us an opening we'd been desperate for, and Shultz has been trying like hell ever since to figure out how we swiped a file from him during our case defending Goldstein a few years ago.

Needless to say, Audrey was a pawn in a game much bigger than herself. She could've lost her job, and any prospective career in the legal community, if Shultz found out about our relationship.

She doesn't know I used her to lift a set of fingerprints from his coffee cup. Reusable cups aren't just good for the environment, they're good at holding the oils from your hand too.

I stayed at her apartment the night before, only planning to sneak a look at her computer and bag for any work files she might've brought home, but no dice. Shultz was smart enough not to trust his secretary with sensitive information, but getting a cup of Joe for him every morning is harmless.

The things people do, putting themselves at risk without realizing it.

I tailed her to the office the next day and sent a text asking if she had time to grab coffee when I knew she was already on the way to grab his. She replied with the name of the cafe and told me to meet her there.

It wasn't hard to steal a few prints off the cup with a bit of tape when she went to the bathroom. We ran them against the governmental employee database when I got back to Laughlin Manor that same day. Shaun used them to crack into his desk safe once he broke in after hours.

But now, I look dispassionately down at Audrey, sitting defeated and on the verge of tears—a million questions scrolling behind her eyes.

She was an innocent, and you broke her. You lied and— WHAT THE FUCK IS GOING ON WITH ME?

"You're too good to be there, Audrey. It's not for people like you."

She sniffs and lets out a dry laugh. "Was any of it real, Shaelene? Honestly?"

I know she doesn't want to hear it and saying it will certainly lose me any chance of politeness from her later, but I need to shut this down once and for all. *Victoria is all I care about now.*

"No," I half-lie. Audrey was a welcome distraction and break in my voluntary abstinence until my father got involved, but nothing in our past even slightly compares to the way I feel about Victoria. One look in her direction is enough to send my heart into cardiac arrest. *And I can never take just* one *look.*

The word is blunt, cutting through her with deadly accuracy. Another sniffle and she turns, her back stiff as her shoulders shake. If the tears are falling, she doesn't let me see them.

"And with her?"

No amount of practice or natural poise is enough to keep my head collected when it comes to Victoria, my jaw clenching at the mere mention of her with such an unhappy tone. I knew Audrey had seen my brazen hovering yesterday; I'd done little to hide it, after all. Every small touch was barely skimming the surface of what I really wanted to do. *The urge to pull her onto my lap in the car. My desperation to press her into the wall and bury my face into her neck and leave my mark again because the soft swish of her skirt over her ass as she walked ahead of me—*

Audrey sniffles again.

The answer to her question feels certain, and the ease at which it crosses my mind is more than a little disconcerting. *It is very much, without a doubt,* real *to me.* Though Victoria hasn't yet made a decision on the matter.

I won't let her choose to say no. I can't. I think it'll kill me.

From the moment her file landed on my father's desk, I'd fallen. And the obsessive pit I've lost myself in grows deeper with every thought I have of her. It's insane. Irrational. All consuming.

But it is real.

"Yes."

She turns back to me, eyes red and puffy. It had been jealousy she'd felt yesterday, but now it's full-blown heartbreak.

I pull a tissue from the box on her desk and hold it out for her, appreciation speckling the disdain marring her face. She straightens, grabbing one of her perfectly aligned pens and a pad of paper from her desk instead. "DA Shultz is out to lunch, Can I take a message?" Every bit of sadness within her turns to spite, her change in tone a clear message. *Fess up or leave.*

"Tell him your lunch hour was uneventful."

I pivot, my shoes squeaking against the polished wooden floor, and head out the door. Using the foregone tissue to clear my prints from the brass knob as I go.

27

Shaelene

"His secretary was in the office, so we didn't get the information we wanted, but we may have another lead." Our father's eyebrows arch in response, his displeasure in my report palpable.

"We shadowed him as he went for lunch. He made a phone call to his wife, and Shaun hacked the signal and traced the number, verifying the call was to her," Shephard informs him while Shaun pulls out his work phone, queuing up the audio recording.

"Darling, hi. No, no; everything's fine. I just now got a minute and wanted to let you know I'll be working late this Friday. One of the meetings I had this morning caused a big hurdle, and we really need to get our case built back up. I know; I'm sorry. I'll make it up to you this weekend. Alright. I love you too, honey."

Our father's eyes move between the three of us, his face unreadable. "Who did he meet with this morning?"

Shaun smirks. "That's the thing; I checked his calendar while I was in his phone. He had nothing scheduled. Now, that's not to say he didn't have them on his work computer or as an off-the-books appointment. I'm handling it."

Father nods. "Right. Follow him tomorrow *and* on Friday. I want to know if he goes anywhere other than his office and home."

"I put a bug on his phone; we'll be able to track him from—"

"Don't be naive enough to believe he'd take his personal cell with him everywhere, Shaun. Track his phone, but I want eyes on him too."

"Yes, sir." Shaun's pride dims, but our father is right. If Shultz is smart enough to keep Audrey in the dark, he's smart enough to leave his phone behind if he's sneaking around to do business.

"Miss Fenwick called while you were out," Father states, grabbing all of my attention, "She's feeling better and will be back tomorrow." His eyes are unflinchingly on mine, silently reiterating our earlier conversation.

The boys run off to the gym after our dismissal, so I take the unaccompanied moment to check on Victoria. She's still on the floor, but moved in front of her bed, the TV on as she paints. I can't see what the picture is of. She's situated overtop the canvas, but she's been furiously slinging paint at it since this morning. *I need to know what it is.*

I've seen her sketches. I have one tucked in my wardrobe upstairs. *I wonder if she's as skilled with a brush as she is a pencil.* Regardless, getting her aggression out seems to have cleared her mind enough to call and update my father.

That in and of itself is a masterpiece.

I spend most of the remaining afternoon swimming laps in the pool. The water is frigid, constricting my lungs but bringing much needed calm. Cardio is my preferred method of exercise. The boys lift and box; I swim and run. They're harder to take down, but I'm harder to catch.

I dry myself under the cabana when I'm finished, the heated concrete warming me slowly from the bottom up.

Inside, I trek up to my room to shower and change until my uncle stops me in the hall, pulling his hand from his mouth. *I've never seen him bite his nails so often.* The sides of his thumbs are raw from his constant nibbling. Something is bothering him, but I have no idea what, and he's not likely to share it.

"Uncle. Everything alright?" I ask him sincerely.

"Yes. Why? Oh— That's nothing." He waves his hand dismissively. "Shaelene, you should keep a close eye on Ms. Fenwick while she's here. She's a welcome guest, but don't let her get too comfortable."

Surely, he doesn't think Victoria is going to do anything deceptive. He'd been more compassionate than Father in terms of treating her like a real person, calling her by her first name and choosing to confide in me about her now.

Is he worried about *her or* for *her?*

He departs without another word, his shadowy form turning down the hall and disappearing toward his wing.

I grunt my frustration at my inability to quickly queue up the live stream with wet fingers. An everlasting minute passes while I drip in the hall, every instinct in my body screaming at me to get eyes on my little fox.

She isn't in her room and her supplies are put away. Her bathroom is empty too, save for the canvas drying against the wall. I still can't see it. Not from this angle. The water on my screen opens the notification panel and I growl, swiping my towel over the screen, accidentally closing the feed in the process. *Oh, my fucking— Take a breath. Dry your hands. Reopen the app.*

MOTION DETECTED: KITCHEN

There she is. IS THAT— Yeah. It is.

She's alive, smothering the fire from a very charred looking grilled cheese. But alive. I laugh to—and at—myself as I continue up the stairs, more than ready to wash the salt water off.

Victoria arrives just as she said she would, the familiar and provocative sound of her heels clacking on the marble is music to my ears. Phillip no longer needs to escort her to my father's office, she knows where it is, but the pace he keeps with her on the monitors tells me he likes to.

"Yes. Thank you; I'd appreciate that, Phillip."

He smiles his welcome as he holds the door while she enters.

My brothers and I sit in the same tufted velvet chairs we'd gathered in on her first day, except this time the empty seat is beside me. And she doesn't miss noting it, her steps hesitating barely long enough for me to register.

She's wearing a white collared shirt beneath a black wool sweater and a blue plaid skirt. It's much shorter than the one she wore the other day; I clench my jaw to keep it in place as she strides into the office. The bruises on her thighs are hidden beneath her dark hosiery. *Unless you know exactly where to look.*

She takes her seat beside me, not making eye contact, though I know she feels all of ours tracking her. Her damp hair is pulled back into a clip, keeping her neck and shoulders dry. My eyes flash as I see a streak of paint left in one of the curls that's fallen loose.

She's as beautiful as ever, more than *I've* seen her yet. She's glowing with the sort of confidence you generate before tackling a big task. For her, that must be simply showing face today. *And I must say, it's one hell of a performance.*

The familiar apple-y scent of her shampoo drifts through the air with every shake of her curls. Another whiff fills my nose when she finally turns to face me head on.

"Good morning."

It's a simple greeting, yet somehow, I come up short of a reply. I can't stop staring at her face. *Those eyes. The freckles dotting her nose. The bow of her lips...*

"Is it?" Shaun asks across from us. Shephard silent in his chair for once. *Good.*

She sucks her teeth, clicking her tongue as she tilts her chin and continues facing me. "It is," she affirms as my father and uncle enter.

28

Victoria

SHAELENE'S STARE PINS ME to my seat, and I manage to hold out long enough to see a glimpse of approval in it before I turn away. My sore neck cracks when I do, an unfortunate side effect of my manic painting episode last night. My couch isn't nearly as comfortable as my bed, especially when my face is smooshed into the arm of it. *Note to self, future artistic crash outs need to happen in bed. With a tarp. And showering immediately after.*

I'm running on three shots of espresso, an everything bagel, and sheer will power this morning. The three good hours of sleep I managed to get after moving to my bed don't help me much either. Waking up edged by a dream feels worse than if I'd just decided to pull an all-nighter.

My drive here was spent convincing myself it's okay to explore all the emotions I've been swallowing over my first week of interning. Even the ones I've been ashamed of. *Like my attraction to the wicked attention of my admi— Shaelene.*

And her silent vigilance beside me is turning those bottled-up emotions into a damn molotov cocktail. I'm ready to explode in my panties by the time Silas orders Shephard and Shaun to resume whatever he tasked them with during my absence, and the two of them leave without another word.

Which I couldn't be more grateful for because even though I try to believe those feelings for her are gone, absolved into the acrylics I had smeared all over me by the time I finished painting, they're not. Goosebumps prickle along my arms beneath my sweater, every tap of Shaelene's fingers on her knee drawing my attention, and I have to force myself to peel my gaze away from her. She grants me no such mercy though. Her eyes stay stuck on me like a tick.

What she did was insane and illegal. *But also desperate and viscerally primal. And so. Damn. Hot.*

Fake it 'til you make it, Victoria.

I cross my legs to stifle my arousal, but the friction does the opposite, and I swear Shaelene is reading every shameful thought from my face alone with the way her eyes darken.

Silas hasn't assigned the two of us with anything to do yet, and our silent contest of wills is growing more and more in her favor as I melt into the velvet beneath me.

Simon stands from his desk, pulling his reading glasses off his face and walking over with a folder in his hand. "I know I usually gather your input and take care of the party details myself, but there's too much we need to prepare right now." He takes a cautious look back at his brother whose focus remains on the notes on his desk.

Shaelene opens the folder beside me and on top is a to do list of sorts. *A very* long *to do list.*

"I need you to handle the orders and reservations."

She doesn't say anything, but I can tell event planning isn't her favorite activity in the world from the way she scrapes a nail down the extensive grocery list of details to decide on.

"Take Victoria with you," Simon urges.

Shaelene's lips curl with a smile before she looks up at him. "Okay, Uncle."

Her rapport with Simon is more casual than with her father. I can only remember her and her siblings calling Silas "sir" when addressing him.

She stands, holding an arm toward the door and peers down at me in a way that makes my legs feel like jelly. "After you."

I vaguely remember my way through the halls toward the garage, keenly aware of the short paces Shaelene keeps behind me. Through the dining room, one side is the entrance to the kitchen with its counters and walls both a spotless white, with marble slabs that match the expensive aesthetic of the floors in the front entry.

The spacious indoor car lot they call a garage is emptier than the last time I was in it. Both SUVs are parked near the far wall, but two of the blacked out motorcycles from before are gone.

Shaelene motions to the sleek, obsidian Mercedes parked beside the remaining bike. A distorted version of my reflection moves along the side of its polished exterior as I reach for the handle. The car chirps and the door opens a few inches on its own as Shaelene passes by me.

She strides around the front, sinking effortlessly into the low captain's seat behind the wheel. I've never seen someone maintain composure the way she does. *Not even her brothers.* Every hair stays in place, her suits freshly pressed and dry cleaned, her body controlled and neutral despite everything around her. Her car is no different.

Inside, the warm scent of leather gives the coup that new car smell even though the mileage suggests it's anything but. The interior is clean, like everything else about Shaelene. The floor mats have fresh lines from being vacuumed, and the passenger seats look as if they've barely been used.

The engine roars to life, and we sit quietly for a few moments letting the engine warm up while Shaelene taps the touchscreen on the dash between us.

A feminine sounding artificial voice states the first directions while she reverses us out of the garage and continues to the road. In a machine nearly capable of a runway take off, she surprisingly keeps us cruising at the speed limit.

The occasional GPS direction does nothing to fill the quiet needling against my nerves. Music would be amazing, but I don't dare reach for the radio for fear of leaving smudgy fingerprints on the screen and incurring Shaelene's wrath. From the bits of it I've seen, I wouldn't wish it on my worst enemy. *Though Sterling definitely deserves it...*

She looks on edge, too, doesn't she? Every time I peek at her, her hand clenches tighter on the gear shift between us. *The hand that's been inside me...* I press my legs together, desire pooling between them again. *Face the window and go to horny time out, Victoria.* I told myself I'd have better control over my emotions since I chose to come back, but I'm failing miserably because of how her fingers are wrapping around that shifter. *How those nails scrape the leather beneath it...*

We're leaving our third stop when Shaelene finally mentions lunch.

So far, we've ordered and reserved enough tables and seats for over two hundred guests, sat down with a DJ and discussed prices and set lists, and left OnSite, a private security agency that makes the triplets look like kittens.

Shaelene hired a small army of seventy-five armed guards to roam in and out of the Angelini's mansion during the gala. *A double entendre of a business name, I'm sure.*

They emphasized their ability to remain discreet in the event of any disturbances or unplanned goings on during the party, and with them being armed, I don't see anyone not invited getting past them alive.

I nod to her in agreement, my mouth watering as my stomach aches with hunger. Thankfully it hasn't decided to embarrass me with its absurdly loud grumbles again. She looks at the list when we return to the car, punching in the details for another stop.

The GPS leads us through the financial district to a parking garage. At least, what I think is a parking garage. The arm bar in front of us is down, preventing us from entering. Unfazed, Shaelene rolls her window down and reaches for the ticket box with a graceful flick of her wrist.

For a moment, nothing happens, an anxious quiet enveloping me. I watch her, waiting for the machine to spit out a parking pass and the arm to raise, but it doesn't. After a couple more seconds, the button turns yellow and a voice comes through the speaker.

"*La prenotazione è a nome di?*" the disembodied voice asks in Italian. New York is chock-full of culture. It really is the melting pot they say it is, but my short time with the Laughlins is the most I've been exposed to languages other than English. I desperately wish I had the ear for it, but on the other hand, listening to Shaelene speak it fluently is mesmerizing.

And arousing.

"Laughlin, *nessuna prenotazione.*"

The silence on the other end stirs the butterflies that hatched in my stomach when I realize Shaelene is likely demanding entrance without a reservation. I don't even know the name of the restaurant she's taking us to in order to pull up my phone and make us one. I check the mirrors to make sure there isn't a line of cars forming behind us when the voice in the box takes what feels like an eternity to answer. *I can't even imagine how Shaelene would handle some road-rager if they honked right now.*

The yellow ring around the call button turns green and the voice returns. "*Benvenuta ad Anghiari, signorina* Laughlin."

Anghiari. That I understood. I whip my gaze to Shaelene, but she stays focused ahead as she pulls us into the shade of the garage. I can only make out the faint rise of her ear as she successfully stifles a grin.

Anghiari is one of the most premier—albeit hard to find—high dining establishments in New York. The news about its grand opening exploded with critiques about the massive entry fee. Twenty-thousand dollars for a yearly membership. Per patron. With a five-hundred dollar, non-refundable deposit for each table reserved.

And the food itself was given a five-star Michelin rating.

Shaelene drives us up the empty levels for at least twenty stories. I lose count on our dizzying ascent. I understand why this place is so difficult to find, but I can't understand why anyone would want to open a restaurant at the top of a giant reinforced steel and concrete block.

We park among a few other cars. Some are empty, but most are running with a chauffeur sitting patiently, or asleep, in the front seat.

Shaelene moves swiftly around to my side of the car, opening the door before I can even clear my lap of our finished chore receipts. I leave my case in the backseat but grab the folder with the rest of our agenda from the dashboard.

"Leave it," she says, and I gulp. When I turn back from the dash, her hand is out, waiting for me to take it. "We'll have plenty of time for work after we eat."

Once I'm standing, she drops my hand and closes the door behind me. The lock chirps, echoing against the solid walls surrounding us.

She rests her palm against my back so lightly I almost think I imagine feeling it over my sweater, but then she falls into step beside me, keeping my slower pace and making for the only wall with an elevator.

29

Victoria

Now I understand the odd location choice.

Floor to ceiling windows on three of the four walls open to the most incredible view of the city I've ever seen. No more dull, cold concrete like below. The sun shines in through the slightly tinted glass and ricochets off the delicate crystal center-pieces on every white-clothed table. Sending the open dining area into a gallery of fractured rainbows.

Servers float down a set of stairs tucked into the wall behind us with trays high on their shoulders, the savory smell of food breezing down from the floor above.

The voice from the box greets us again from behind a small bar, "*Signorina Laughlin.*"

"Elio," she says in return, her eyes roaming the mostly empty dining room.

His throat bobs, and he lets out a quiet breath. I can't tell if he's more nervous seeing Shaelene or relieved to only be serving us two. He's younger than his distinguished tone and accent let on, and taller than me which isn't a difficult feat. The top of his dark hair has him a few inches shorter than Shaelene. *He's like a teenage version of Luca.*

Elio's eyes follow Shaelene's line of sight to a table nearest the far window. *"Da questa parte, per favore."* Shaelene ushers me ahead of her.

The table is small and square, only big enough for two plate settings, and gives the most jaw-dropping view of the harbor.

Shaelene takes her seat as Elio holds mine out patiently. After we're both comfortable, he starts to speak, but Shaelene cuts him off, her eyes glancing my way. *"In inglese, per favore."*

My cheeks burn when Elio looks at me apologetically. "My apologies, madame. What can I get you to drink?"

Shaelene orders a fruity Italian soda I've never heard of while straightening her silverware. "Just water with lemon for me please."

Elio bows before leaving, my gaze following him until he disappears behind the wall and up the steps before I let myself bask in the full effect of Anghiari. The rays pouring in from behind Shaelene give her a sort of shimmering aura, putting everything past her out of focus. *It's... Wow.*

Behind me are rows upon rows of skyscrapers, all different heights, as far as the eye can see, but the window at our side is dominated by the bay. The Hudson River is alive with boaters and the ferry, everything seeming to move together in perfect sync. The Statue of Liberty and Ellis Island are on full display from here, too, the water glistening in the afternoon light.

I suck in a breath, soaking it all in. "This view is amazing."

"Yes. It is," Shaelene agrees across from me, but she isn't looking out the window.

Our surroundings shrink and leave me feeling like I'm under a spotlight. The same way I always seem to feel when she pins her hungry eyes on me. *I don't hate it.* My cheeks start to flush, but luckily Elio returns with our drinks, saving me from making a stammering fool of myself while Shaelene orders us a few appetizers to start.

I wet my lips with my water, steadying the nerves in my hand by squeezing my lemon into it. "The strange location choice makes sense now." I smile, looking out at the city again.

"Have you ever been to Italy, Victoria?"

Shaelene's sun-kissed complexion glows in the afternoon light, making my breath catch in my throat as her right brow arches curiously, waiting for my answer. *She's beautiful no matter which way the sun hits her—* I stutter over my words, my heart erratic as I search for an answer. Aside from the tour and confrontation in the office, this is the most we've spoken. "No, never to Italy. My father took my mom and I to Ireland once for a business thing when I was little, but I don't remember anything except the plane ride..." I cringe. "I threw up."

It's the only reason I remember it. I was so nervous to fly I couldn't help it. It happened at my seat in the little baggy they provide. *And now I'm* word-vomiting *to Shaelene in the fanciest restaurant I've ever been to. Great.*

She sips her fizzy soda with a slight chuckle. It's small, but hearty, and my shoulders bob with my own cautious laugh as I take another soothing sip of water.

"Well," she starts, clearing her throat, "the reason I ask is because, while the view is spectacular from up here, there's another reason Anghiari is at the top of a parking garage." She rests comfortably against her chair before continuing. "Anghiari is a hill town in Tuscany. Dario, the chef, and his family emigrated from there a couple decades ago. The winding drive is meant to symbolize the roads encircling the hillside as you drive up to the city center."

A stunned smile stretches my cheeks. "Wow. That's... Really sweet actually. Here I was thinking it was just another rich person gimmick."

Shaelene's smile mimics mine. "You are one of said *rich people*, are you not?"

I snort on accident and my embarrassment immediately returns. Attempting to stifle the rising heat in my cheeks, I gulp down half of my water. "Uhm, well, my father's job pays good money, and I went to private school growing up, but we didn't have Phillips or Geoffreys helping us around the house."

Shaelene taps the edge of the empty bread plate in front of her and shakes her head, sipping more of her seltzer. *Did I really just poke fun at a Laughlin? And she didn't say something sinister afterward?* Yes, and if anything, her lips are curled up in a smile as she sips her soda. Watching me over the rim of her glass. *I'm blushing again, aren't I? And sweating. Can she— Who am I kidding, of course she can see it. Look at that grin. It's getting wider. Happier. Sexier—*

Elio interrupts my thoughts with a platter of food large enough to have been our main course; it's so big he sets up a tray beside our table to hold it all. *I haven't even looked at the rest of the menu.* Before he can take it from me, I sneak a glance at the entrees. *No prices.* If I had to guess, our appetizers alone probably cost a few hundred dollars. *I'm not Laughlin-level rich and my internship is unpaid... This is by far the most expensive date I've ever been on.*

Not a date!

We're just two coworkers enjoying lunch. *An incredibly luxurious lunch... With each other... While exchanging longing looks...*

Shaelene orders chicken and salmon for both of us and hands Elio our menus, sending him off again at a rushed pace.

Shaelene passes a few of the many plates to me. "Please, help yourself. Decide which you like best and that's what I'll tell Dario to serve at the gala."

The highest rated chef in the city is going to be catering the triplets' birthday dinner, and she wants my opinion on what to have him serve? My mouth watered for half a day just thinking about the grilled cheese Phillip had, but I don't think he'll be able to compete with the dishes scattered before me.

I don't know the first thing about fine dining outside of using the outermost silverware first, but I'm sure everything will taste amazing, and if we're planning for over two hundred guests, I doubt all of them will have the same taste in— *OH MY GOD, THE GRILLED OYSTERS ARE INCREDIBLE!*

I don't care how good anything else tastes, these oysters have to go on the menu for the birthday gala.

We spend the next forty-five minutes tasting and sharing thoughts on the meal before ultimately deciding on the oysters, broccolini, and mozza fritta for the cocktail hour and the baked chicken breast with polenta and a cherry balsamic reduction for the main meal.

The button on the front of my skirt is threatening to pop with how full my stomach is, but I don't feel an ounce of guilt. *Everything was so delicious; I'm still contemplating seconds.*

Shaelene fills my glass from the pitcher Elio left us a while ago, then wipes the corner of her mouth and stands.

"I need to discuss this with Dario. I'll be back."

Elio hurries up to her as he finishes at another table. She says something that makes him laugh nervously, but they're too far for me to make it out. He slows to let her continue on, his eyes watching her warily before he crosses the floor to greet an arriving set of patrons.

I don't know how much time passes because I get lost in the view, watching the tiny ants make their way through the streets and into the base of Lady Liberty before trekking their way to the top. *Empire State can wait; I'm moving that to the top of my New York bucket list.*

Shaelene's reflection appearing in the glass above me makes a shiver trail up my spine, straightening my posture and leaving me feeling stiff after being so relaxed. The sight is familiar and frightening. I know she thinks it too because an eerie grin forms on her face.

"Not the only great view in New York it would seem," she whispers against the cacophony around us now that more diners have piled in during her visit to the kitchen, and even if someone heard, they'd never know her true meaning. Not the way I do.

I spin to face her towering in front of me in my seat, eyes darkening as they look down past my skirt to my pantyhose. I can see so clearly now they were the ones behind the mask. *How did I not realize it was her before?* I can't help but trace the shape of her myself, seeing the strength and power of my stalker within every delicate curve. *And now I'll never be able to picture anyone else when I think—*

The intensity of her stare burns a hole through my middle. I choke down a swallow, electricity settling low in me as sparks rage between my legs at the memory of how the masked man—*woman*—touched me. Teased me. Shattered me.

Her movement brings me back to reality. She holds a doggy bag from Dario in one hand and the other out for me. Waiting. Watching. *Admiring.* Such a normal thing, yet I know she's anything but.

I use her help to stand on shaky legs, easily falling in step beside her. The short elevator ride and walk to the car are quiet, save for the sound of our footsteps pinging back and forth against the concrete walls, but not uncomfortable.

I can't remember the last time I felt this safe around someone.

We slide back into the car, and I flip open the folder to check off another duty from the list. I gasp loudly when I realize; Shaelene gives me a worried look, her keys dangling from the hand reaching for my shoulder.

"We forgot dessert," I say, my hands already starting to sweat. I wipe them on my skirt rather than Shaelene's perfect seats.

The list clearly states cake for the family and close guests, separate desserts for everyone else, but I'm not sure I could stomach another bite to taste test anything. *And if we go back, it'll cost another table reservation and Shaelene already spent so much money—*

Shaelene erupts with laughter. Pure, genuine, tear-inducing laughter. The first time I've heard her unrestrained. Unafraid. Uncaged. It's contagious. I let her joy fill me, releasing a nervous giggle while waiting for her to acknowledge my seriousness about the issue.

She doesn't, instead she starts the car, then reaches for the doggy bag she'd put in the backseat, handing me a small box.

I hesitate for a moment, looking at her before popping open the lid. Inside is a handful of chocolate truffles dusted with cocoa. I look at her again before grabbing one, knowing the dust could go everywhere. She nods, but I do my best not to let any of the powder fall to the detailed interior of her car.

She watches me take the bite and smiles when my eyes light up and I mumble a garbled, "Oh my god!"

She takes one for herself, holding a careful hand beneath it to catch any falling crumbles before popping it into her mouth completely.

She dusts off her hands out the window, covering her mouth with one and pointing to the folder with the other. "Write that down," she attempts to say with her mouth full.

I grab a pen from my case and start to jot down the notes of our decisions.

Oysters.

I list the details of the starters and main meal, my pen hovering before I write down our choice of dessert.

Chocolate truffles.

Oh shit. Did I just load up on aphrodisiacs during a lunch date with my stalker?

30

Victoria

THE DRIVE BACK TO Laughlin Manor goes by quicker than I'd hoped, though I'm relieved to see the bikes are still gone when Shaelene pulls us into the garage.

Inside the kitchen, she tosses the empty doggy bag in the trash, not even bothering to glance over her shoulder to see if I'm following. She knows I am—the small dessert box clutched in my hands as we weave through the west wing to a part of the house I haven't seen yet.

A small square room with an archway opens to a long hallway just like the one leading past Silas' office, and another wide staircase arcs around an alcove in the wall.

We take it up to the first informal area of the manor I've seen. This side feels much homier than the rest. Like someone actually *lives* here. A gray sectional takes up the majority of the open space, and a cushioned ottoman sits in front of it holding a remote and several game controllers. Vacuum lines pattern the floor, but there's an unmistakable foot traffic trail from the couch to the connecting hall. *I'd wager this is where the triplets spend most of their time.* It's comfy, not nearly as polished as the downstairs. *Though it could use some art or* something *hanging on the walls...*

Continuing down the hallway, I take the guess that the doors we pass are bedrooms., suddenly wondering which one leads to

Shaelene's. We round the corner to a familiar stretch that leads to our shared office. Slowly, I've begun to learn the layout of the place. *Maybe one day I'll be able to navigate the obscenity of Laughlin Manor by myself.*

Shaelene starts unpacking my shopping bag of office supplies when we get back to the office. *She wasn't kidding when she said there would be a desk waiting for me.* It's not the same showy mahogany style as theirs, but it's larger than I'd expected. I carefully place my briefcase on top and start unpacking too.

She tosses the empty sack into the bin beside her desk and takes her seat. I hadn't gotten the chance to peek at all the desks in here before Shephard walked in the other day, but now I know hers is the one nearest mine.

Not much occupies the surface of it. Her monitor blocks her from the door, leaving the rest of her desk that faces me wide open. Her cell rattles between us, making me jump as a smirk softens her face. *She definitely caught me staring just now.* I make myself busy organizing my supplies into drawers so she doesn't notice my blushing.

She answers, her fingers gliding across her keyboard. From her answers, I know it's the man she spoke with at OnSite, double confirming details with her.

I power on my laptop, noting the email she sent less than a minute ago.

Floor Plan/Seating Arrangements

I open the attached file to find a virtual rendering of the ballroom at Palazzo Angelini, the guest list with notes of who to seat with whom, and vague details about the band and photographer.

I glance at her over the top of my screen, surprised *this* is my first solo task from the firm. Her head turns slightly, her phone still held to her ear with her shoulder, and she winks, sending a flush of heat across my cheeks again. Too quick and obviously, I duck behind my laptop. *I'm so fucking rosy cheeked right now and butterflies are taking my stomach hostage. Not to mention the warmth simmering between my—* I clamp my legs shut, the lack of friction there driving me absolutely insane. *This is not the time to have a wild office desk fantasy, Victoria!*

She finishes her call and the room falls silent except for the clacking of our keys and the bouncing of Shaelene's leg beneath her desk. Mine rub together to stave the endless need growing between them. *Jesus you horndog, do some work or something to distract yourself!*

Inputting attendee info into the seating plan isn't enough to keep my brain busy, so I click my pen and doodle on the corner of the truffle box. Tracing the stamped filigree around the border, before biting into one of the last two delicious pieces. "Mmmm." *God, these are so good! Not very distracting though, they're pretty orgasmic themselves—*

Shealene moves with so much speed I barely register her before she's behind my desk. She reaches up to the top of the bookcase behind me and grabs a remote, turning to face the security monitor and pressing the power button.

It doesn't turn off.

But one of the feed squares on the TV goes black, and I see a red light fading from the corner of my eye. I hadn't noticed the camera the other day, too entranced at the shelves of trinkets. Foolish of me since I've seen the feed playing in Silas' office every morning. *There are always eyes watching around the manor...*

But not now.

That familiar cold dredge starts to flush down my head and neck. *Was the camera on when Shephard came in? Did Silas see it? Surely not. He would've had to bring it up, right? Have an HR meeting or something? Do the Laughlins even care about that sort of thing?* My mind conjures the answer before I can calm it. *Probably not.*

My body is tense, tied up by the string of thoughts in my head. Only seconds have passed, but the look on Shaelene's face is one of someone that's waited a lifetime to do something.

The remote drops onto the desk, her body bending, caging me into my chair. So close I can feel the soft breaths spilling from her lips.

Her tongue dances across them in anticipation, her focus locked on my mouth. I suck in a breath, my lips trembling as she inches impossibly closer.

Our eyes meet, and she draws back when she notices the tension in my neck. Another wave of shiver-inducing fear washes over me and I start to quiver, but the regretful look on her face stops the sudden chill. *She stopped. She saw, and she... Stopped.*

"Wait!" I call, grabbing her forearm without thinking. *I don't want you to stop.* The cold is replaced with the excited electricity I fight down every time I remember her in my room. Every time I think about the first time she texted me. Every time I think about how her fingers made me feel. Those striking eyes look me over again, trying to figure out what I'm thinking. *I don't even know what I'm thinking. I can't think. Can't breathe.* I can't focus on anything other than her. The acknowledgement in her eyes before she pulled away. *She's not Sterling.*

"Shae..." I whisper, my body drawing toward hers. My lip isn't trembling anymore. It hangs open slightly, waiting, while I squeeze her arm and pray she understands.

She crashes her mouth against mine, the leather of my seat squishing under the pressure of her hand as she squeezes it beside my head. I open for her, not stopping her tongue when it sweeps across mine in an intoxicatingly possessive stroke.

She pulls back and looks at me headily, her eyes narrowed, waiting for my next move. Part of me wants to run, the same nervousness glossing over my skin as when Shephard pressured me, but this time the goosebumps aren't caused by terror.

The other half of me wants to kiss her back as desperately as she kissed me; to relinquish myself to her control the same way I did when she was only my stalker. The battling thoughts are too much to sift through right now, and the only thing I muster is, "I–I'm not gay."

Shaelene's head dips, hiding her face. *Shit.* My heart drops, realizing the side of me that so desperately wanted to give her my mouth will never get the chance to because I can't stop running it.

The leather ripples as Shae's face looks up to mine, the most devious and tingle-inciting smile sprawled across it, pure satisfaction in her eyes. "It doesn't matter what you label yourself, Little Fox. You're mine anyway."

That pet name again...

I sit, speechless under her commanding hover, melting into my seat. *So hot I'll probably burn a permanent ass print into it.* Her lips move in again, brushing mine when she speaks. "Your body seems to be in agreement—" She kisses along my jaw, teasing her teeth along my neck. "—because I can smell the desire dripping off you." Her finger twirls a stray curl when she levels her face with mine again.

No ass print. The chair is gonna catch fire.

Her stare penetrates the sliver of resolve I have left. I draw my bottom lip between my teeth and close the distance between us, my nose rubbing gently against the side of hers.

Her eyes flare before she claims my lips again. Needy and purposeful. The lingering taste of chocolate flavoring both our tongues as she curls hers into my mouth, twirling it in perfect rhythm with mine.

Scratch that earlier thought. We're for sure checking the office desk fantasy off the to do list today. My new stapler crashes to the floor after Shaelene shoves everything aside, not giving me a second to flinch before her hands scrape themselves under my thighs and lift me onto the desktop, dropping me on it with a bounce.

Her mouth doesn't cease its attack against mine the entire time, her hands joining in and coaxing my chest against hers. Her palms rub the length of my back over and over, keeping me pressed firmly against her as my back arches. Her warmth keeping the phantom chill over my head at bay.

She sucks my lip, drawing it into her mouth and pinching it between her teeth. A breathy moan escapes me, filling her mouth, and is met with a delicious groan from her that fills mine. One that I've heard only once, before she tried to cover it with a cough the night she broke in. *I want to keep hearing it.* Her fingers curl in my hair, hot breaths trickling across my skin as she assaults my jaw and neck with kisses, stopping and sucking at the base near my collarbone. Marking me again.

Moans from both of us fill the thick air of the office, her body surging against mine. Her deep, feminine growls vibrate against my throat, her teeth nipping the already abused flesh. She flattens her tongue against my skin, drawing it up and flicking it off my chin in one tantalizing sweep, my core clenching at the reminder of what it can do.

Her hands move to my thighs, scratching softly up the fibers of my pantyhose. The points of her nails tease my nerves until she reaches my center. My quads tense on instinct and my knees flinch to close, but she presses herself harder between us, keeping them open.

She runs a finger down my core, gently scraping the hard acrylic over the fabric covering my clit and between my lips. My wetness has already soaked through the lace of my thong, dampening the thin layer of hosiery over it.

I wince against her mouth at the sharp poke of her nail, and another rush of electricity circuits through me. The fabric rips and I whimper, feeling myself get even wetter. She glides a nail under the seam of my panties, teasing my scorched, swollen flesh. Holding back and letting my body build until it's ready for her. Until *I'm* ready for her. *She's so controlled.* Eager, but patient. Considerate but teasing at the same time. *Exactly how I need her.*

Her fingers tug the lace to the side, exposing my aching pussy to the brisk air of the office. She runs her knuckles over my sensitive folds, playing with the slickness my body made in response to her touch.

She brings her cum coated fingers to her mouth and licks them in front of me. *I want those fingers inside of me. Now.* After sucking them clean, she bites off the daggers from her middle and ring fingers, spitting them to the floor beside her.

Her fingers plunge inside me, my body sucking her in, settling for the first time since her touch in my apartment last week.

31

Shaelene

VICTORIA'S TIGHT CUNT HAS been begging me to finger fuck it all day, and I am happy to finally oblige.

So much warmer without gloves on.

Every ridge is velvety soft against my fingertips. I missed its delicious taste. The hidden strength within her. The delicate responses of her body. *I missed it all.* I'd gotten my nails done less than a week ago, but I chewed them off without hesitation when I felt how wet Victoria was for me. I *needed* to be inside her again.

My fingers work long caresses in her, rubbing the underside of her clit while the heel of my palm presses it firmly from the outside. Cupping her. Keeping her in my grasp. Trapping her exactly where I want her. Her hips rock back and forth, grinding against me in a silent plea for more. Wanting me deeper. Harder. Faster.

Her whimpers bleed into my mouth as she gets closer to climax. Inching me closer to my own with every clench around my fingers.

I loosen my grip on her pelvis and replace my palm with my thumb, rubbing quick, soft circles around her swollen clit, and she lets those quiet moans out.

Her beautiful body jerks beneath me with each flick. Another, louder, moan cuts through the air between us. *If God struck me dead this second, I'd thank her for waiting until I had the chance to hear such angelic music.*

"Look at me."

Victoria's head shifts and she looks at me through half-lidded eyes. I keep my pace, but increase my fervor, pushing into her as far as I can. The knuckles at the base of my hand drip, the webbing between my fingers pained from a stretch it isn't used to.

My other hand drops her hair and grips the side of her neck, holding her body still while I drive my fingers into her. She's struggling to stifle her pleasured mewls now, finally letting them ring out like a symphony.

"Shae!" she squeals. *I lied.* Now *I can die a happy woman.* Still, I clap my mouth over hers to quiet the sound. I want her screaming my name every minute of every day, but I *don't* want anyone to have a reason to walk in and see her like this.

Her tongue is tired and slow against mine as she finishes the waves of her orgasm. When I open my eyes, hers are shut, brows pinched tight while her pussy pulses leisurely around my fingers. Movement on the TV steals my attention.

"Shhhh." I kiss her lips gently from corner to corner, still circling her clit with my thumb. Her foggy eyes grow wide when she opens them again, and she inhales a deep breath through her nose. Her nostrils flare, and she cries out another moan only to be stifled by my lips again.

"We wouldn't want anyone to come in, would we, Little Fox?" I whisper.

Her body shudders and her breath hitches. "Are your brothers back? If they're close we should st—" She cuts herself off, turning to face the monitor.

My teeth dig into her neck, keeping her in place and she writhes beneath me while I lick and suck and mark. Kissing the spot I just pained, her heart quickens, her vein pulsing against my lips.

She thrusts again, seeking more friction as she shudders into me, the walls of her pussy clamping around my fingers so wonderfully tight my knuckles ache.

"Not yet," I tease into her ear. I shift a stray curl out of her face and trail my fingers back down her cheek to her mouth, pulling her lip open with my thumb, before tracing down the lines of tense muscle in her throat. "The ceilings may have eyes, but the walls have ears." My palm presses against her chest, rubbing lightly over the soft tissue of her breast, rolling the taut peak of her nipple through her blouse. Metal thumps from the other side of the wall to my back and her eyes bulge. My hand jolts to hold her hip in place when she starts to hop back down to her seat. "Thankfully Phillip has always been good at keeping his mouth shut."

I pull my hand still inside her out slowly, feeling every inch of her throbbing, ribbed muscles. She whimpers once she's empty, her thighs clamping around my hips. I suck her deliciousness off my fingers again; the carnal taste makes my eyes roll back before I can keep them from doing it. *So. Fucking. Good.*

Her dilated eyes search mine, the pupils so large only a faint, foresty green ring surrounds them. *She's incredible.* Everything about her is decadent.

Her taste, her smell, the way she sounds... But what gets me the most are her eyes. The way she sees everything but tries her best to remain unseen. Doing everything she can to make herself smaller to not attract attention when she is literally the only thing ever on my mind. I take her mouth in mine again, watching her lids close as she melts into my touch.

I let out a breath against her warm cheek. "What are you, Victoria?"

Only a second passes before she replies. Breathless and surer than I've heard her speak yet.

"Yours."

It's so quiet I can't tell if she said it or I imagined it, but the look in her eyes when she opens them again is all I need. They dart back and forth, looking into each of mine. Her expressive brows furrowing a moment, as if she's trying to convince herself more than me, but finally they settle back into the high perch on her forehead.

"My what?"

The conviction in my voice is heavy. She knows the answer I'm looking for, but if she says it, she'll be submitting not only to a relationship, but to *me*. A thick swallow falls down her neck. The nerves I'd worked out of her a minute ago are back. *Please. Say it...*

Her chin dips and she looks at me through long lashes.

"Your Little Fox."

My heart pounds in my chest, ready to explode with relief, but one of us has to remain composed right now. My mouth curls, and my knuckle lifts her chin, tracing the underside of her jaw and trailing to her ear so I can grab the back of her neck again. The tip of my nose skims the side of hers and her breathing evens out.

"I'm going to enjoy hunting you every chance I get."

"You had pantyhose on this morning," Shephard says, perching himself against the front of her desk. I can sense Shaun's smirk growing as he leans over my shoulder.

Victoria's face reddens as she fights to keep her composure in front of the two of them. "No, I didn't," she lies. I eye her hosiery in the trash beside my desk. *I'll dig those out later and add them to my growing collection.* She shifts, crossing her legs beneath her desk.

"Yes, you did. They were nude instead of black this time."

I'll have to remind him to stop eyeing her, again, *but he's got a point.* Her bruises have faded enough they don't need to be hidden behind a dark pair of pantyhose anymore. I drum my broken nails against my desk, distracting myself so I don't smile at the thought of getting to put markings on her later.

"Might as well take the rest off too," Shaun quips beside me, sliding a bottle of sanitizer my way. I reluctantly squeeze a pump into my palm, the alcohol immediately wiping the scent of Victoria from my fingers.

I haven't cum with her yet; I didn't need to this time, though I was close. Watching her curl into my chest while her legs spasmed around me was more than enough. It felt like I died and was shocked back to consciousness getting to experience those too brief moments of heaven with her.

"And it smells like wet pussy in—"

"Here!" Victoria thrusts the dessert box at him. "Go away please, I have work to finish." She looks up at him, holding her breath. Her legs pressed tightly together.

Shephard waltzes back to his own desk, blissfully grinning while he scarfs down the last chocolate truffle. Victoria looks to me for reassurance even though her confidence seems to be at an all-time high today. She kept me on the edge of my seat during lunch, letting me in with every word she shared, and didn't pull herself away from what she wanted when we got back here. *And she just successfully redirected my brother.*

I want to kiss her again. Tell her how much she astonishes me. *Seven feet is too damn far away. I* should *have made us share a desk.* I roll my neck and relieve exactly zero of the tension straining it. I'm trying my best to remain focused, but dammit, she is never *not* clouding my thoughts.

Shaun coughs conspicuously as all hell in my direction.

I roll my eyes even though he can't see it. "Read it out to me again."

I type the coordinates he texted me earlier, too preoccupied losing myself in Victoria to reply. I managed to work her to a second, smaller climax before noticing Phillip on the security feed keeping the boys occupied near the kitchen. By the time they walked in, I was behind my desk, the camera on again, and Victoria's things reorganized on her desk.

"You never let your phone die."

"Yes, well, first time for everything," I lie, sneaking another glance Victoria's way. She chews the inside of her cheek, but it doesn't hide her mouth quirking up into a smile, which only makes the pride swelling in my chest feel even warmer. *She's mine. She said it.*

The search loads and he nods, clapping me on the shoulder before walking back to his desk and grabbing the phone from its receiver, tapping the couple of buttons to connect him to our father's office.

I can hear a warbled version of his voice responding to Shaun's request for a meeting before he hangs up and says to head downstairs. The four of us fall in line, Shephard leading and Victoria bringing up the rear close behind me.

The boys keep such a quick pace ahead they don't care to notice I've fallen back into step with her.

I take her slinky fingers in mine for the short walk we have left. My last comment definitely shook her nerves, but she holds tight to my hand and her breathing stops sounding so shallow. I meant it when I said I'll hunt her. I'll push her to boundaries she doesn't even know exist yet, but I'll always be there to comfort her after. *I'm not a monster.*

32

Victoria

"YOU'RE NOT GETTING COLD feet, are you?" asks a stranger's voice through the speaker on Shaun's phone.

They'd apparently been following Derek any time he left his office. When he'd walked down the street for lunch, the boys trailed behind him, listening in on and recording a phone call he took. *I hope Silas didn't tell Shaun to bug my phone too...*

"You'll be there Friday?" the mystery caller continues.

Derek responds, his voice ragged, "Of course."

"Good. I'll forward you the address."

The call ends with a staticky click and the recording goes silent. Silas is the first to ask the question we're all wondering. "Who was the caller?"

He's matter of fact, like always, his eyes shrewd and penetrating as he stares at his sons. Shephard's attempt to brag about not leaving behind evidence feels dangerously untrue after watching Simon and Silas' faces harden as they listened to the call.

"No caller ID. The number wasn't saved to his contacts, and when we ran a trace, it went to a burner phone in Queens." Shaun answers, his voice a shell of the confident Laughlin I've come to know. *Silas' approval is a big deal in this household.* "But we did learn one thing."

The two senior Laughlins nod in unison. Silas agrees, "We did."

We did? The only thing I'd gathered was that Derek was going *somewhere* with *someone* tomorrow.

"What's the address?" Simon asks, queueing up his brother's computer.

Shaelene interrupts his typing by answering his question. "The Rosary."

That must've been what she and Shaun were going over when they got back. *Of course she's already fully in the loop of this conversation.*

Silas smiles a pearly, amused grin, which makes me even more confused as to why knowing the DA is going to visit a flower shop in Queens is any more helpful.

Shaun starts to plan aloud, "Shep and I will follow him once he leaves his office, Shaelene can—" Silas's hand pauses the rest of his speech. Shaun swallows a lump of pride, the strained obedience stiffening his spine as Silas takes over.

"You're too recognizable in that establishment." He glares at Shephard before continuing. "Your sister and Miss Fenwick will go. It'll be easier for them to get inside." Shaun's face shows his disappointment, but he looks to Shephard, and they nod, their lips thin.

"Victoria doesn't need to be involved." Shae's words slice the air beside me. Her hand is no longer holding mine, but I can feel the protection behind her tone, making my chest swell. Silas' eyes narrow before they flick to me.

He postures up straighter in his seat, his eyebrow cocked and primed in its ever-present austerity. "Shultz is already *well aware* of her affiliation with our firm, Shaelene, and you will not go alone. You'll be admitted faster as a pair, anyhow. She's going with you," he demands, not accepting a millimeter of compromise. "Gather what we need as quickly as you can and escort her back here. We'll discuss further action afterward. She'll be fine so long as you keep focused on the task at hand."

Silas turns his sharp stare back at Shaun and points his finger. "You and Shephard will search his office once you know it's empty for the weekend."

Shaelene's jaw tenses and she releases a long breath out of her nose as she yields to her father's command with a silent dip of her chin, turning and grabbing my hand and pulling me out of the room. I stumble behind in my heels, her long strides too fast for me to keep up.

"Shae!" I call, "Please. Slow down."

She doesn't.

"What's—" My stomach pitches as she scoops me up in her arms and makes quick work of the steps. She drops me back on my feet once we reach the top and stomps down the hall, pausing only to punch in the code to the office door. I half expect her to slam it once I'm in, but she doesn't. Instead, she paces the length of her desk a few times, her hand rubbing her chin and lips. The unusual energy buzzing off her sets an anxious shiver across my skin.

"Shaelene, what's wrong?" I ask. She doesn't speak until I seize one of her arms and make her look at me. "Shae?"

"You shouldn't be going on jobs with us."

I jerk my neck back. I may be inexperienced, but I've lived through my fair share of trials. *If I can handle Sterling, I can handle* this. My damaged ego fades when her gaze softens and I remind myself she doesn't know about my past, so I can't expect her to understand that I can be brave too.

"I'll be okay. It's just a flower shop. I mean, come on, we went to one today." She shakes her head, but I don't stop. "And you'll be there. You'll keep me safe."

A small smile flickers against her cheeks. "You'll always be safe with me, Little Fox." Her words are certain, and I believe her. She's harsh and cold with everyone, but she's been comforting and warm to me, even from behind the glass of our apartment windows.

Her hands caress my shoulders, running down the backs of my arms and reminding me how much I crave her touch. Her grip tightens and she levels herself with me, her sharp eyes pleading. "But I won't be the only one on the hunt there. I need you to stick close to me, Victoria. No one can notice you while we're there."

Her message comes through loud and clear. *I'm severely underestimating this assignment.* Goosebumps erupt over my skin, the hairs standing as a chill rushes through me.

"Shae? It is *just* a flower shop, right?"

33

Victoria

SHAELENE SITS ON THE bed behind me braiding my hair into tight rows so my curls will fit under the brunette wig I'm supposed to wear tonight. The text Shaun read through his bugging mentioned meeting at The Rosary at seven.

We'd spent the day party planning with no mention of the plan for following Derek, and when Five O'Clock hit, Shae brought me into her room to change. I've barely calmed down enough to keep my pussy from pulsing as her fingers graze through my hair. After the way she made me feel in the office, the prospect of being in such close quarters with her makes me excited to say the least.

But sitting on the bed with her, we're anything but cramped.

Her room is about the size of mine, if my living room and kitchen were included as part of it. *So, basically,* half *my apartment.* The space is huge, and the king bed with its four thick banisters does little to fill the space.

Her closet is open, lit across the room, displaying pieces I could never picture Shaelene wearing. Atop a set of drawers are multiple bottles of expensive perfumes and lotions, and a jewelry stand displaying gold necklaces and earrings.

"Do you ever wear anything other than designer suits?" I ask, looking at the two new ensembles wrapped in plastic as her fingers move deftly through my hair for the second strand of braids.

"Of course," she laughs. The sound of her light-hearted chuckle graces my ears, re-stirring the faded butterflies in my stomach. She tosses the finished braid over my shoulder. "I have lingerie too." I can sense her shrug without having to see it. "But they're also designer," she teases against my ear.

I roll my eyes, unable to conceal my smile as she walks to her closet and brings one of the garment bags over, tossing it on the bed beside me.

She lifts the black bodycon dress from it and tells me to stand, holding it out in front of me, surveying. Her lips purse. "I ordered this after you left last night."

I take the dress, and she turns to close the main door, locking it behind her before sauntering back. *Close,* private *quarters...* The butterflies are in a swarming frenzy now.

She's still in her clothes from earlier, except she's lost the jacket. It sits draped over the back of the chair beside her mirror, leaving her the most relaxed I've seen her.

Except for the night she broke into my house and made me come all over her gloves.

I force my eyes to peel from her figure and smooth the dress out over the bed, slipping my heels off, fighting against the arousal warring through me.

She watches me, missing nothing, and I'm suddenly aware of every move my body makes. Wrinkling her pressed slacks, she crouches in front of me, running teasing fingers up under my skirt and crumples the waist of my pantyhose in her hands before pulling them down and off. *Yeah, okay. Her kneeling in front of me is really hot.* My hands reach for her head in an instinct I didn't know I had, my body so desperate to be touched by her again, but I pin them to my sides.

She looks up at me from her knees, her long torso putting her eye level with my stomach. The way her mouth hangs slightly open, like it's poised and ready to strike, ready to devour me, makes me nervous. *But it sets me on fire at the same time.* My hands ball so tight my palms ache. I'm under her spell, but she waits for a cue from me. Something to tell her I *want* this. And after yesterday on my desk, I'm done denying myself the pleasure of Shaelene. *I'm hers.*

I unclench my fists and try to relax enough to give her an answer. It's breathy and riddled with anticipation, but I manage to tell her, "Yes." Her hands move again, her palms finding my ass and squeezing a handful in each before she relieves me of my panties too.

The only thing left hiding my bare pussy from her is my tweed skirt. Her fingers begin to lift it, and I flinch. Shaelene's expression smooths into one of a woman about to take charge. *You want this. Relax and let her show you why.*

"Nothing I haven't seen before," she reminds me, lifting the fabric so it bunches over my hips. I inhale a steeling breath and try to let my mind slip into the dark territory I refuse to fully acknowledge. The one where I don't have to think, where I can just *feel*. The place that terrifies me and always ends in hurt.

Shaelene won't hurt me, not unless I ask for it. Should I? NO. Stop thinking. You're stalling.

Her tongue swipes a quick lick over my clit, pulling all my attention back to her. The heat from her breath melts over my skin and she flattens her tongue, applying sweet, *sweet* pressure to the place I want her most.

Her hands dig deep, her fingers biting into my skin as she squeezes and tugs and rubs my body against her mouth. She lifts my leg, draping my knee over her shoulder to better her angle before pushing her tongue into me and pulling a strangled cry from my chest.

She sucks me into her mouth, the wet smacking of lips filling my ears. She eats me with the vigor of someone drinking the nectar of life, like she can't restrain herself from consuming me.

My moans aren't quiet, and her growls of amusement vibrating through me only make me cry out more. I don't care how loud I am now, and neither does she since she isn't rushing to cover my mouth like before. *Nobody has ever made me feel this good.*

She traces the line between my cheeks with her fingers, feathering over my tensed hole—a place no one, not even *I* have explored—then presses them into my pussy. My standing leg falters when the brisk shock of her icy hand breaks into the warmth inside me.

She stretches me with her fingers, drawing me into a satiated lull. The leg holding me up finally gives out, and I slump against the wooden pillar behind me.

I stare drowsily down at Shaelene, her cheeks hollowing out as she continues barraging me with her mouth. Her eyes looking up, watching every ounce of tension build in my core.

She keeps a steady rhythm, her tongue and fingers coaxing me with a synchronized attack, pushing me closer to the brink of release until I can't hold in the need to explode. My body caves, and my hips thrust, forcing her fingers to keep up with the quickened pace.

I don't stop my hands from reaching out this time, one latching onto the beam above me and the other finding her hair as my head falls back against the wood and my eyes roll back.

My throat burns as a scream of pleasure barrels through when my climax hits, and she opens her mouth, covering me completely and drinking down my cum as it gushes from me and onto the front of her. A garbled, pleased noise comes from her throat when I finish. Every nerve feels burnt out, like all the energy might've actually been sucked out by the woman on her knees before me. She kisses my swollen lips, slow and tender, before she stands, my leg falling heavily to the floor.

The sheen of my cum glosses the skin of her chin, dripping onto my blouse when she speaks. Her voice is scratchy and quiet. "Do you have any idea how fucking good you taste, Little Fox?"

I whimper. It's all I can muster. Her hard body presses into mine, pinning me to the banister, and she dips her head and kisses me, her tongue lapping against mine the same way it did inside of me. The salty tang of cum coats my tastebuds. *Fuck, it's good...* My mouth waters for more every time she steals her tongue back into her mouth, drawing a new fervor from inside me.

The wet silk of her button-down sticks to her chest, vacuum forming to the plump outline of her breasts that're usually hidden underneath all the layers of her suit.

My tongue reaches out desperately for more of her, trying to deepen our kiss.

She rumbles into me, a smirk lifting her lips as she tugs my lower lip between her teeth and backs away. "Now you know why I'm always starving for you."

She runs a gentle hand over my braids before stepping into her closet. Her shirt pulls open and slides down her arms, falling to the carpet and giving me the exquisite view of her wide, toned back through my tired eyes. The front of her bra unlatches, and she shrugs it off too, her chest hidden. I whimper again.

The muscles in her back flex when she reaches for one of the shirts hanging on the rack in front of her. She slips on the silver halter top and changes out of her slacks, pulling on a tight, high-waisted tennis skirt. The pleats flare out over her hips, adding to their curve. They sway when she walks back to me, her hands pulling her long and slightly tangled hair back into several tight twists and jerks her chin to the dress on her bed, still waiting to be put on.

I slip off the remainder of my clothes and drowsily shimmy into it. The hem is cropped short, barely long enough to cover my ass. If I move too suddenly, I'm sure I'll moon someone by accident. The keyhole bust holds my chest high with a perfect view of the cleavage it shapes.

Shaelene kneels again, helping me step into a pair of lacy underwear—*yep, designer*—and boots that come up past my knees, zipping them up the back of my legs.

She leans over the bed and grabs the mesh wig caps and stretches one over my hair, carefully pinning the layered brown bob in place. The new hair falls just above my shoulders in a styled tousle of dark waves with wispy bangs falling into place, hiding my orange brows.

"How do I look?" Her silence feels like answer enough, making me gulp.

"Different."

"Oh."

"I didn't say it was bad." She tugs the hem of my dress down a few inches, and it instantly rides back up when she lets go. "You could never be anything less than stunning."

No disguise could hide the flush she brings to my cheeks. "I'll have to buy you flowers tonight if you keep complimenting me like that," I tease, biting my lip to stifle my giddy smile.

Her pleased expression drops, the reminder of our mission immediately souring her good mood. "Let's go."

Shae's faux blowout stretches down her back in a set of blonde curls resting lightly between her shoulder blades. It's so opposite her normal look I can't stop staring.

Her usually naked face is contoured to chiseled perfection, and even though I watched her apply the smokey eye and rode in the car with her here, I barely recognize her in the crowd of people waiting inside. I do a double take every time I see a glimpse of her.

A sternum tattoo peeks from the bottom of her halter top, teasing me since I can't see more than a few sketched beads and an inverted crucifix highlighting the toned ridges of her stomach. Fitting, given we're doing shady work at a place called The Rosary.

Her breasts are perched high like mine, but fuller, matching her ass and evening out the framework of her lean muscular body. She holds my hand in an inconspicuous girls' night out fashion, but I know the second she senses any trouble, I'll be drug out the door and down the street toward the parking garage we left her car in.

Derek entered the building on his own ten minutes ago. No sign of whomever he'd planned to meet with. We wait in line until the young guy behind the counter motions for us to step up next.

"Order pick up for two dozen long stem Spanish roses," Shae tells him, her voice pitched up an octave.

He looks over the two of us and grins. "Name on the order?"

Shae leans over the counter, accentuating her boobs in his face, and my throat threatens to close. "Shultz," she purrs, and he nods. *I guess that's an answer worthy of entry, if he actually heard what she said...* His eyes don't leave her chest.

I grab Shae's arm with both my hands, tucking in close and try out my best ditsy girl voice, but it doesn't land, coming out sharper than I mean when I say, "We're in a bit of a hurry if you don't mind." Shae turns, her lips drawn tight but the corners ever so slightly perked in a knowing smile. *Real subtle, Victoria. Stop acting like a jealous idiot, she's just working him.* He peels his eyes off her long enough to look me over before clearing his throat.

Shae giggles in her fake voice. "Sorry. We're a little excited 'cause it's our first time," she says.

Is it?

She squeezes my hand still wrapped around her bicep while the cashier grabs a metal box from beneath the counter. "Sure thing. I'll need your phones before I take you back."

Shit. I left mine in the car like Shae told me to— She pulls two cells I've never seen before from a hidden garter on her thigh and drops them into the bin. The guy tucks the box away, leaving the counter under the guard of two buff men in security jackets. With a wink, she takes my hand and leads me through the shop toward the door of the attached greenhouse.

She kind of seems like she knows where she's going— It's fine. It. Doesn't. Matter.

We walk through a few rows of flowers being sprayed with a fine mist before approaching a beefy man with a stern complexion. The bouncer pulls the handle on a cellar door and holds it open for us.

Shaelene still hasn't told me what exactly this place is yet, but I gathered from the oddly large crowd inside this isn't any ordinary flower shop. *What florist stays open past normal business hours and has a secret underground bunker?*

The concrete steps lead down a darkened stairwell, dim LED strips lighting the way.

The bottom of the stairs is surprisingly comfortable; a red rug covers the floor, and the same lighting leads us around the hall to a set of doors. Muffled, bass boosted music pounds on the other side, sending a rhythmic beat through my bones. It feels like I'm walking into a midnight viewing at an expensive theater.

Shae turns to me before she opens them, all traces of the cocky smirk from earlier gone. "Stay close while we're in there, and if anyone touches you, I'll cut their fucking hands off."

I gulp. No matter how different she looks tonight, that familiar fierceness is still under the surface, calming the nerves fluttering within me. She turns, rolling her shoulders, and pushes the door open. The humidity in the room smacks me in the face before the realization of what I'm seeing does.

People. Naked *people. Everywhere.* Some half dressed with their chests on display, while others are completely exposed and being touched by tables full of bystanders.

The Rosary isn't just a random flower shop in Queens; it's a goddamn sex club.

34

Shaelene

COUPLES, TRIPLES, AND GROUPS too big to count mingle closely together, sharing and dipping into each other with wild abandon. Several patrons stand along the wall, faces rosy, and watching everything unfold in front of them, pleasuring themselves to all the sinful sights laid out for them to see.

The first thing I do is head for the bar, pulling Victoria with me. The toned, shirtless tender behind the counter meanders over, completely unfazed by the man receiving head on the bar stool directly beside us. He catches Victoria staring and winks; I gather her into my side, burying her face into my arm. My thumb traces the column of her neck while I order two tonic waters in cocktail glasses, playing it off like we want to stay sober until our first round of fun is over. He says something I can't hear over the music, but I fake a laugh anyway before he turns to make them. I use the mirror behind the bar to scan the room, not caring if my mask slips, because I can feel Victoria shaking against me. She's nervous—*and still a bit jealous*—but she lifts her head when a round of heady laughter bursts from behind us.

Shultz.

It doesn't take long to spot him. He's in a corner booth with two other men, sipping their beers and watching the pairs around them engaging in whatever primal desires suit their fancy.

"Shae," Victoria murmurs, straightening without taking her eyes off the DA.

I kiss the top of her head as I turn back to the room, our drinks in hand. "Stick close to me." She does, attached to me at the hip while we head to the back wall and slide into a booth of our own. Derek still within sight.

"What exactly are we supposed to be doing here other than watching him?" she asks as discreetly as she can over the lustful sounds in the club.

I drop my line of sight on Derek long enough to lock eyes with her, sliding my boot up her calf and hooking the back of her knee under the table.

"Come here," I mouth. She rounds the table meekly. I pat my lap, and grip her knees, pulling her to straddle me. *Shephard was right. Plenty of room in the booths for fun.*

"You're going to ride my hips and make yourself come so no one sees me taking videos of him." I reach into the top of my boot and pull out my real cell, her eyes searching mine. She freezes, stuck in a hover.

"What? But everyone—"

I drop my phone to the vinyl cushion, yanking her ass down, the heat making our bare skin stick together.

I can't fucking wait any longer. I guide her hips until they're moving on their own volition, teasing the bud of my clit through my clothes with each stroke. "Will see two women enjoying themselves and blending in," I whisper, sweeping my tongue along the shell of her ear. My hands cup her perky ass, squeezing with every thrust of her hips. "That's it, Little Fox. Keep grinding. Don't feel embarrassed. Don't feel anything but the pleasure thrumming through you. Get yourself off like a good girl."

Sitting across from each other surveying and taking photos would draw more attention than this. *It has nothing to do with how badly I want to feel her shake against my face again...* My body heats, my desire and thoughts distracting me from what we came here to do. *Dammit!* I pry one hand from Victoria and pick up my phone, keeping only the camera above the top of the table as I record Derek. The way he tugs his dick through his slacks makes me want to hurl. Not at all what I want to see when Victoria is on top of me.

Her moans blend with the cacophony of ecstatic gasps and shouts filling the room, her hands resting on my shoulders to keep steady as her pace quickens.

Her dress is bunched over her waist now, too short to stay tucked under her ass while she dry humps my thighs. The breezy touch of someone's sleeve brushes us as they walk by, and her eyes open in a panic, remembering how many people are around us. Even through the dimness in the room, I can see her face paling. *No. Not in here.* Shivers roll through her with bone bending force, and if anyone is looking it might seem like an orgasm, but I can see the fear.

She stiffens, her body locking in place as her gaze darts through the smoky haze at the other groups. Bodies continue coming together again and again as pleasure rings through the air, the collective release almost loud enough to drown out the music. A gaze or two passes over us, but they don't land or linger.

I grip her cheeks, making her lips pout and force her to face me. "Eyes here," I demand. "It's just us." Her erratic breathing slows, but she stays still. I rock myself against her, pulling us back into rhythm.

"Just us," she repeats, taking a deep breath.

The sweat building between us makes it easier to glide with her, and I'm quickly back under the ecstasy spell from earlier, soaking my panties. Derek forgotten. When I cut back his way, he's up, hands locked with one of his compatriots as they make for the hall leading to the private rooms in the back. *Thank God.* I slip my phone back into its hiding spot and shift my weight so I'm sitting up straight, bending my knee between us and giving her a solid surface to grind against while she leans her elbows on the table behind her.

She strokes herself up and down my shin, her hooded eyes locked on mine. The rest of the room disappears and all I can focus on is Victoria's body moving against mine. The soft bounce of her breasts with each thrust. My clit is screaming for some friction of its own, but I deny myself like every other time. *This isn't about me right now. Victoria and I will get there eventually.* But for now, I want to keep building that same tension inside of her.

Her hips churn until they shiver and her muscles give out, the edge of the table catching her from falling into my lap. I hold her hips in place as she slumps forward, her forehead pressing against mine as she rides the ecstasy of coming hard for a second time tonight. I drop my leg and bury my face into her chest. Breathing in her scent and licking up the soft patch of skin between her breasts as her legs continue trembling on both sides of me.

"You're doing so well. Listening to what I say," I praise into her neck. "But we aren't done, Little Fox. Give me one more."

Her sated eyes widen. "Shae…" she mewls, barely loud enough for me to hear over the club noise. "I–I don't think I can." Her breaths are ragged and deep, but I'm not letting her come down from this high. Not when she's swollen and soaking and plated up on this table for me to feast on.

"Don't think then." I give her zero time to protest before sliding her panties to the side and pushing two fingers inside her, curling them the way she likes. "Just feel," I whisper, blowing a cool breath to her pussy. "Lie back."

My arm wraps around her back to help her lower herself to the table, her back arching from the cool touch of the wood on her exposed skin. I lift one knee over my shoulder and the other follows suit without me having to pull my fingers out and put it there.

The evidence of both her previous orgasms drips out of her pretty cunt into my palm and I've never seen such a beautiful sight. I blow another cool breath at her clit and she shudders, her fingers curling around the lip of the table when I lick the breeze away. Sucking her clit into the warmth of my mouth and drawing slow circles on it with my tongue. My hand digs into the meat of her thigh to keep her in place as she squirms. She's more than wet, but I want her to leave this place a damn puddle.

Her hips jerk, forcing my head to bob along with the motion to keep my mouth on her. When her orgasm hits, her ass tenses and her knees lock against my head, squeezing me so hard I can feel the blood rushing in it, then straight back to my clit as she gushes into my mouth with a scream that's the loudest she's been, yet still barely audible enough to be distinguishable from the other climaxing patrons.

I place one parting kiss to her exhausted clit and put her underwear back into place. When I lift my head, her barely open eyes meet mine as I wipe the wetness from my chin off with the hem of her dress. She's practically dead weight when I sit her up and back into my lap.

She sags into my neck, and I kiss her there while petting her head. "I knew you had it in you, Little Fox. You came so hard for me. You drenched both of us."

She whimpers and I grin, scooting us from the booth and pulling her dress down to keep her covered as she wraps her legs around my hips. I carry my tired fox out the side exit—*Thank you again, Shep*—and the rest of the way to the parking garage.

35

Shaelene

VICTORIA'S PHONE RINGS THE second we reach the car. It's half-past ten, and our trip to The Rosary was a success. *In more ways than one.*

I managed to capture Shultz cheating on his wife with not just two other women, but whoever the man was he'd met with too.

I wait to pull out of the lot and text the videos to Shaun, keeping my hands and ears busy as I strain to hear who's on the other end of the line since I couldn't intercept the call with my phone stuffed in my boot and Victoria half-conscious as I buckled her into the passenger seat.

DS_ROS(1-4).MPEG

Shaunie

Good work.

Damn, what'd you give her to make her so loud?

Do your job and get the stills.

On mute.

Victoria's moans infiltrated the audio in the recording while she got herself off. Her body wasn't in frame, but her presence was well apparent.

It's her mother. The tinny voice on the other end of the line asking questions about her first week at work. I throw the shifter into reverse with more force than necessary, causing Victoria to flinch and peek my way anxiously, looking much more awake than a minute ago. *Fuck. I hate that I've made her uncomfortable when I know she's already there talking to her mother. I've seen the texts between them. Blocked a few overly harsh ones from going through to her phone. No one is that short with a parent unless they're hiding something.*

She keeps her answers vague. *Probably a little embarrassed to be talking about what's happened at work since it's been mostly sex and dangerous meetings.*

Her mother's voice cracks while reminding her to be careful.

Dropping her phone into her lap, Victoria turns to me, apprehension marring her face. "Sorry about that."

"Don't be."

"She just worries about me. All the time." She sighs, biting into her lip.

"She has good reason to." We lock eyes before I turn back to the road. "You're her only child."

"Yeah, that's true— Hang on. How do you know that?"

The foot I just put in my mouth tastes like the sole of my Tom Ford boots.

"Did you social media stalk me?" she grills.

I can't help but laugh at the exasperated expression on her face. *The shock in her eyes is ridiculously adorable.*

"I rented the apartment across from yours and took pictures of you naked. I don't think internet snooping should be your main concern, Little Fox." Her jaw falls open and another laugh brews as her face turns a bright shade of pink. "But to answer your question, no. I did not."

What I did *do was lose myself in a black hole of unanswered questions regarding her parents and why she doesn't resemble them at all.*

"Why did you start watching me?" she asks, more curious than fearful. *Why did I?* Another question I'm not fully sure the answer to.

In the beginning, it had been a job. Until she stepped out of that library and I caught a glimpse of the only person that's ever made my composure falter.

The only person I've never been able to draw myself away from fully. The only one I've ever felt paralyzed by grief at the thought of someone else having them. All within the few seconds of seeing her walk through the courtyard on campus.

I knew then I was in trouble. This fox would be the end of me. Either by destroying my soul with a denial or my own inability to keep a clear head with her around. Letting my heart take the reins from my brain will cause my first—*and potentially last*—slip up of my career.

But now that I have her, I can't fathom giving her up. Regardless of how dangerous being together could be for the both of us, I want her with me because even when she isn't, she *is*. Victoria is always there, every second, clouding my judgment. She's the only job I've ever feared.

Because I don't know what it is yet.

"Shae?" She gasps, pulling me back to reality. The engine is screaming, somehow revving faster than my heart. I ease my foot's heavy weight off the gas and pop the clutch, switching gears to stop the noise, then easing us back down to the speed limit.

When I look at Victoria again, her neck is tense, like her stomach is in her throat. *Point proven. Dangerous.*

Which is why I look away, straining to keep my eyes on the road and answer her the most honest way I can.

"My father ordered us to."

"Ms. Fenwick, you're free to go. Get some rest; we'll see you bright and early Monday morning," Uncle says, clearing the tea settings from the table between us.

Victoria's half-lidded eyes meet mine like she wants my permission too. I do *not* want her to leave. What I want is to carry her upstairs and settle her into my bed so the both of us can recover from the all-nighter my father forced us to pull. With our intimidation script fully written and roughly fifty hours before we use it on Derek, there's plenty of time for her to sleep. *And some more after for me to give my undivided attention to her pu—*

She yawns, her entire frame shivering in an attempt to stay awake. Uncle clears his throat after he moves my saucer and cup to the tray in Phillip's hands.

I can't make myself say the words for her to leave aloud, so I nod in her direction, hoping the small smile I force is enough to mask my disappointment as she collects her things and follows Phillip out.

Shaun's laptop slams closed from his seat across from me. "I cannot look at these any longer," he mutters quietly so Father doesn't hear from his desk where he's berating Shephard. "I don't know how you stomached seeing it in person."

I didn't. Half the time I was filming, I kept my hand steady to keep everything in frame, while my gaze kept diverting to the exquisite, writhing red head on top of me. Which turned out to be a blessing because I managed to avoid seeing Shultz grope the women in his booth while he tangled his tongue with the man beside him.

Shaun grabbed the best stills from the videos, but Father demands he clarify the images even more.

Technically none of what we captured Shultz doing is illegal; all of them were consenting adults, but since none of them were his wife, blackmail is still an effective option to keep him in line. Destroying his marriage isn't the only problem he'll have on the line either. The nature of his actions directly opposes the 'family-man' morals he's preached his entire career. An infidelity scandal is a sure-fire way to lose him voter support in his current position as district attorney.

Shephard huffs as he slumps himself into the seat next to mine. He too mutters under his breath to avoid our father hearing. "Did the doctors tell him the two of you absorbed my brain cells at birth or something? Or does he truly believe I'm incapable of doing anything without my fists?"

Shaun chuckles, and Shephard trills his lips on an annoyed exhale. I glance down at his bruised knuckles—a couple cracked and scabbed too—but ignore the urge to quip at him. *Father did more than enough.* I pull out my phone and track Victoria on her drive home. *I should've driven her. She's too tired.*

I watch until her little blue dot drives into the garage beneath her building, the knot in my stomach finally loosening.

36

Victoria

I BARELY MAKE IT inside the manor before Shaelene is on me.

Her polished loafers practically float across the smooth marble floors, advancing on me so fast I can only smile before her hand tangles into my hair and her lips slam onto mine, still flavored with the lingering taste of her sweetened morning coffee.

"Hi," I say breathlessly against her mouth.

A wicked grin curves her lips as she draws her face from mine. "Hi," she replies, her voice low and sounding relieved.

Our visit to The Rosary only piqued my desire to keep coming back to work every day. I want to understand why my body responds to Shae. I want *more*. And as exhausted as I was after Simon finally told me I could go home, I spent yesterday bored out of my mind. The only thing occupying it was the thought of Shaelene and all the things I'd let her do to me.

Heat floods over me, casting away the morning chill from outside with her body pressed against mine. With the way she kisses me, I think she might've been as miserable as I was this weekend.

She takes my hand and pulls me back to her father's office. He and Simon are seated in the green, velvet backed chairs instead of their usual place behind Silas' desk. Shephard and Shaun stand across from them, their backs to the door. The security monitors are on like always, and my cheeks flush knowing everyone in here definitely saw Shaelene kiss me. No one mentions it though, and the four of us are immediately sent off to the courthouse.

I arrived at the manor an hour earlier than usual, since we'd had this meeting planned for two days, but Shephard still speeds through downtown traffic.

We bypass security and barge through the heavy door where a shocked Audrey is waiting for us. She jumps to her feet and starts to round her desk, her eyes locked on Shaun, but he holds his hand up, cutting off her reprimand before it can start.

"We have an appointment this time."

Audrey swallows a hard gulp. "There's no meeting on his calendar today," she starts just as Derek opens his door.

He gives a quick nod to Audrey, confirming Shaun is telling the truth, before he turns and gives an exasperated sigh. "Let's get this over with."

Shaelene squeezes my hand before shoving her way between her brothers, and I fall in step quietly behind them.

"Mr. Angelini couldn't join us today?" Derek huffs.

Shaelene doesn't take the bait, instead she retorts with a sarcastic jab of her own. "No, fortunately for him, he had better plans."

Derek remains quiet behind his desk for a beat, sucking his teeth. Finally, he clasps his hands and leans his elbows against the desk, eyeing all of us with derision.

"What, pray tell, brings you lot here for the second time in a week? Surely it must be important since you took the time to schedule an appointment *for once.*" The edge in his voice leads me to believe we won't be getting the full thirty minutes we're scheduled for. My hands wring the handle of my briefcase to hide their trembling.

Shaelene takes a seat in the same chair as last time, leaning back comfortably and intertwining her fingers. Her thumbs patiently tap together. Shaun mirrors her in the other chair, rocking a lazy ankle over his knee while Shephard stands next to me, arms crossed with his glare locked on the DA.

"Actually Derek, it was our last visit that got us interested in seeing you again. Our deepest apologies for cutting your time with Ms. Maldonado short." Shaelene's words hold as much sincerity as an unsigned 'get well soon' card. "It was your meeting with her that put you at the top of our list of people to see. Why don't you tell us what the two of you were discussing?" The last bit may have been framed as a question, but her tone and expressionless face don't imply much choice in the matter.

He dips his head and when it lifts again, a bleached, white smile spreads across his face. "We were simply two colleagues, *friends* really, having a chat before lunch. Not much to share, I'm afraid." His composure stays steady under the pressure of the triplets leering down on him, but his lie is unconvincing to us all.

"I find that *very* interesting to be quite honest, Derek."

Based on the snarl of his upper lip, Shae's continuous disuse of his title when they're on anything but a first name basis is eating away at his resolve. Especially since it's going up against the blank slate of a mask Shaelene wears most of the time. I might not think she was capable of emotion if she didn't impose that hungry smile of hers on me so much. There's no such expression there for the DA though. She detests him. And he hates all three of them.

And me by association.

His jaw tenses, but he doesn't get the chance to respond before Shaelene starts in again. "See, Ms. Maldonado is a close friend of ours as well. We know firsthand how busy of a woman she is. It's not an easy task to arrange time to see her. You must be something special for her to make the trip downtown just to chat." Shaelene pauses, reaching out and straightening the ornate nameplate at the front of his desk, ignoring his growing hostility. "Are you special, Derek?"

I'm sure if he was glaring any harder, his eyes would pop right into her lap.

He grits his teeth and asks, "What do you want from me, Miss Laughlin?"

Shaelene matches his hateful energy and leans into his stare, testing the beast inside the DA. "Cut the bullshit, Shultz. Tell us whatever half-ass *irrefutable evidence* you think you have that might finally convince someone to take you seriously."

Derek's eyebrows rise, his face full of shock before he lets out a laugh. An *unnerving* laugh that sends goosebumps pebbling across my skin. Followed by a long, overly drawn-out sigh as he bares his teeth. "You poor little bastards. For a family so good at being corrupt, you kids really are paranoid."

All three of the triplets' eyes narrow. My head spins trying to keep up, but I'm lost as well. *If he doesn't have anything against the Laughlins, why was his meeting with the governor so important?*

Derek slides his eyes from Shaelene to the boys and then me, gauging if the rest of us have any idea what he's saying.

"I don't need to convince anyone of anything anymore. I know enough about your dealings that when I win the election, I'll have the power to cut your family down myself."

"Election?" Shaun growls, fighting for the composure slipping through his fingers.

Derek turns to him, smiling more menacingly than before. "Yes, Mr. Laughlin. I'm announcing my campaign for the open senate seat later today."

No one speaks. No one breathes. We're all too busy contemplating what could happen if he were able to win and gain that level of governmental power. What that could mean for the firm and the Laughlins themselves. *How much prison time would they serve? What crimes have they committed that the DA is able to prove? Blackmail, for starters, but what else has Shaelene done?*

37

Victoria

"YOU WERE RECRUITING THE governor for your campaign. Hoping she'd endorse your candidacy."

The words spill out before I can swallow them down, everyone's attention turning to me. Shaelene's eyes rest on mine, holding me in place. There's no hiding the shaking in my hands now that I unintentionally brought awareness to my otherwise small and quiet presence. Derek already knows who I am, but that doesn't mean I wanted to give him any reason to keep further record of me.

He straightens and points a finger my way. "A smart one you've picked up here. Perhaps you should send *her* next time you go phishing for information."

Shaelene stands, putting herself between Derek and I, fury simmering in her eyes as she shields me from him. She snaps a finger, and I open my case, letting her reach in and grab the folder. For the briefest of seconds, she looks at Shephard near the door before nudging her chin his direction. The eye contact with her is the only thing keeping me grounded right now, so I don't dare break it as I step back, Shephard shifting to block half of me with his body. Shae runs her fingers down the side of the folder for a moment before slipping her mask back over her vengeful expression.

"Well, that settles this then. Should be an easy decision for you now."

I can't see much from behind Shephard's massive back, but I know Derek's confidence is faltering by the timorous chuckle he makes.

Shaelene goes on, "You can go about this one of two ways. Ruin your spotless reputation by publicly attending our birthday gala and showing the world you drink and party with *supposed* criminals in your spare time. Hell, that can even help your campaign if the right people see it. After all, Bianca will be in attendance too." Shephard plants his feet deeper into the carpet in front of me.

Derek remains silent, but the mood in the room has already shifted, the tense back and forth transforming into a suffocating cloud of hostility that has my lips quivering and my breath hitching.

Shae leans further into her threats. "We'd be able to get you those ballot votes easily, Derek. If you're willing to put aside the morals you claim to uphold so dearly, and from what I've seen... You are." I hear her nail scraping along the folder, then the sound of photo-paper ruffling. It slides across the top of his desk, shoving everything he had on top of it out of the way. "So, it shouldn't be a problem to find common ground."

"NO! That's not poss—"

"Option two," Shaelene interrupts, and I dare to peek around Shephard and see another photo in her hand. "We can ruin it for you. Along with any chance you have at holding a senate seat—now, or in the future—by sharing *these*." Shaelene flaunts the folder in her hand for emphasis. "The public will crucify you. Naming you a lying, adulterous, fornicating bastard that secretly dismisses all those family values you so openly preach. Tell me, Derek, does your wife know about Friday night?"

A murderous anger scorches behind the DA's eyes, threatening to melt the glass in his readers. Beads of sweat glisten on his forehead and upper lip, and a sharp breath hisses between his teeth when Shaelene thrusts the second photo at him.

"Which is it going to be?" she asks.

As if there is any real choice in the matter, Derek sighs. "Fine. Get. *Out.*"

Shaelene leaves the file of incriminating images on his desk with a sarcastically gentle pat. The secret is his to keep, for now, but they can always print more copies.

By the time Shaelene reaches me, Derek's anger turns to fear, then triples into guilt. Before we're out of the office, he slams a photo of his family face down onto his desktop, a tear slipping down his cheek. The last I see of him is his face buried in his hands. I'm sure he'd have pulled his hair out if it wasn't glued on. *I'll be surprised if he shows up to the Angelini's with eyebrows.*

"I'm telling you. He. Won't. Talk," Shaelene says for the second time on our drive back to the manor.

"I'm just saying! It's even harder to talk with a broken jaw," Shephard retorts from the front. Shaun laughs, his shoulders bobbing as he turns his attention back out his window.

Shaelene rolls her eyes next to me in the back, muttering, "Brain cells."

"I heard that," Shephard says through clenched teeth.

"What?" I ask.

She shakes her head, facing and draping an arm over me. My hesitance at sitting in the middle earlier feels childish now that I have the comfort of her touch on me again. "Nothing. Just a dumb triplet thing." She settles her hand on my shoulder, her fresh set of nails absentmindedly running over my sleeve

She's already made the point that she's confident Derek will behave until the gala, and how he'll likely spend his time before then trying to cover any evidence confirming his visit to The Rosary instead of seeking retribution. 'That will come later' is what she'd said, but for now we have time to prepare.

Shaelene and I go through the list of what's left to do for the party. The gala is in thirteen days, and most of everything is covered. The only bits left for her are overseeing deliveries and replying to emails confirming details with the bakery and florist.

Luca enters the office, looking exhausted and making Shaun and Shephard perk up in their chairs. "Up for a box?" he asks with a thicker accent than usual, his words slow to form.

His eyes are sunken and dark as if he's already been through a few rounds. *And lost.* His broad shoulders hang low under the weight of whatever's bothering him.

Shephard stands and loosens his tie. "Always."

Shaun follows, holding Luca back by his elbow as Shephard heads for the gym. Shaun's eyes frantically search Luca's sullen expression, fear sharpening his features. "Luca. What happened this time?"

Luca's attention flicks to Shaelene and I. "*Non è niente*," he whispers back.

Shaun's gaze doesn't waver, his voice dropping when he responds. "*Non mentire, Luca. Parla.*"

Luca's eyes narrow, his shoulders tensing as he pulls out of Shaun's grip. "*Nulla di nuovo che non abbia già affrontato!*" He follows Shephard's long since faded footsteps, leaving Shaun frozen in place. He rubs a heavy hand over his face, throwing a worried look in our direction.

"Go. We'll finish up here," Shaelene tells him, without looking over her monitor.

Shaun sighs and pulls his jacket from the back of his chair. His lengthy strides take him out of the room, quickly catching up to Luca. Their voices fading the further down the hall they go.

For the first time since our kiss this morning, Shae and I are alone, but she doesn't rush over to me. Her fingers move like lightning over her keyboard, and I try to focus on the seating chart sprawled across my own screen.

An hour or so passes until I feel my eyes starting to cross from staring at the endless table assignments. *Who knew people dealing in illicit business practices had such a hard time getting along with one another?*

I stand and stretch my arms behind me. "Do you want a coffee?" I ask, waiting for her eyes to finish slowly climbing their way up from my ass.

"I'd love some."

I haven't ventured through the halls of the manor on my own yet, but I'm confident enough in my ability to find the kitchen by myself, and after rounding the bottom of the stairs, I finally do.

The sleek marble countertops gleam under the blinding white recessed lighting, giving the kitchen a showroom feel. It's so sterile and clean, it's hard to believe anyone ever eats or cooks in here. *My stovetop could only dream of being this spotless whenever I do cook.*

After opening nearly every cabinet, I find what I need to start brewing our coffee.

I freeze, searching through the fridge, when voices in the hall begin arguing. They're hushed and biting, my skin crawling at the pain within them. I know it's Shaun and Luca without having to see them.

"Let it go, Luca," Shaun's voice rings from the hallway. There's a second of silence before something clatters to the floor and a loud crack comes from their direction.

I close the fridge door and place Shaelene's labeled bottle of hazelnut creamer on the counter. Quietly as I can, I tiptoe to the archway on the other side of the kitchen.

When I peek around, I see Luca pinning Shaun to the wall with a forearm against his chest. The bouquet of lilies that'd been beautifully arranged on top of the hall table lies in pieces on the floor beside them. Petals and stems scattered under their feet.

"Just admit it. You've got one foot out the door."

Shaun's hands are quick when they shove Luca off him, showing his hidden strength. He's not as built as Shepard, but that doesn't make him any less deadly. Shaun closes the space between the two of them and grabs the fresh, white t-shirt Luca has on now, holding him in place while he yells.

"I'm not half out of anything! I've been all in since the beginning, but *you* won't let me show it. And now you're doubting me."

Luca snarls, but he doesn't try to get out of Shaun's grip. He levels his chin and sneers back at him. "You've been tag-teaming girls with your brother! I'd say that's the *definition* of half out."

"We agreed on not being exclusive until *you* worked up the courage to say the truth out loud, so don't use that excuse on me." Shaun's fists loosen, his voice lowering. "I get that you're scared, but don't ever say that shit to me again or I won't just be 'half out'. I'll be done." His shoulder slams into Luca's as he walks past him toward the stairs.

"Shaun," Luca calls brokenly, grabbing his elbow. "I'm sorry. I... You know how my—" his words are cut off, a choking sound filling the space.

Shaun's fingers curl around Luca's neck a split second before he presses his mouth against his. The vein in Shaun's neck is so prominent, it could pop any second. I cover my mouth to conceal my gasp and silently watch as Luca's stiff, adrenaline filled body relaxes under the pressure of Shaun's hold, their lips and tongues swallowing each other's until Shaun pushes Luca back.

He hasn't released his neck yet, and his face is beet red from the lack of oxygen, but neither seem intent on breaking their standoff.

"I know, Luca, and I don't care what he thinks. Now get your head out of your ass about my feelings for you because I've made them *abundantly* clear."

With that, Shaun lets go and turns back to the stairs, his footsteps fading as he walks away. Luca catches his breath, slapping himself on the cheek a couple times before heading up the stairs behind him.

I let my body fall against the kitchen wall, leaning on it for support while I attempt to make sense of everything that unfolded in front of me.

Seeing Luca struggle under Shaun's control reminds me of Shaelene choking me the night she came to my apartment. How exhilarating it felt for her to take the reins. How open I was to submit to her will, but she's been gentle with me since her confession.

My stomach still flips every time I catch her staring, and her touch sends my resident butterflies into a frenzy, but she hasn't made me feel any sense of danger since that first night. She's given me my control back, which is exactly what I've wanted since Sterling stole it. *So why does part of me want her to hurt me again?*

Need ignites in my stomach, but my heart breaks at the same time. *Am I so damaged that I can't be satisfied unless my sex life is traumatic?*

I hate the idea that Sterling still somehow has a say in how I live my life.

My head falls back as I slide to the floor. The cool stone biting through my stockings, aiding the cold that's starting to wash over me.

None of this is right. I shouldn't keep letting myself fall into these situations. I shouldn't have drunk after the game. I should've fought him harder. It shouldn't have felt so good. I shouldn't have let Shaelene touch me that night. I shouldn't let it happen again.

My trembling hands find my hair, tugging strands loose from my clip.

Sterling was dangerous as a kid. The Laughlins do worse as adults.

Macy would be so disappointed in me...

I swallow my self-pity like a big pill painfully scraping my esophagus on its way down and stand decidedly, finally listening to the logical part of myself I keep shutting out. *No longer will I allow myself to fall for the temptation of Shaelene or the sinister allure shrouding her family. I'll keep my head down, create some distance between us, and push through the next few months of my internship. No matter how difficult it gets to be around her.*

I pull myself from the wall and put away the creamer, adjusting my hair back into place before heading back to the office to finish my work.

All three of the boys are back in the office when I return, their loud conversation already filling the previous silence Shaelene and I had been working in.

She doesn't question me about her missing coffee, but I know she can sense something is off.

"Everything okay?"

I don't look over, knowing my newly found resolve will break if I do this soon. I keep my focus trained on my computer, forcing stiff words past numb lips. "I'm fine."

I do my best to finalize the seating arrangement, the hours ticking by in an awkward flurry of ignored glances and keyboard clicks.

I finish my first draft of the chart and send it to her inbox around a quarter to five, and she shifts in her seat from the comfortable position she'd been watching me in to open it.

The second the clock on my computer reads **5:00**, I close and pack it into my briefcase. Simon told me during our all-nighter that he appreciates me staying overtime, but I'm allowed to leave any time after five for the remainder of my internship, so long as we aren't dying for manpower.

I'm taking advantage of it while I can, but I barely make it down the hall before Shaelene catches up and spins me to face her.

Her brows are scrunched low on her face, trying to figure out what to say to me. She has no idea where my mind has gone since witnessing Shaun with Luca.

After opening her mouth and changing her mind a couple times, she finally says, "Don't worry about getting here tomorrow."

One of the muscles in my neck pulls with how quickly I rear back at that. The look on my face must be one of horror, because she holds both of my shoulders in her hands to reassure me.

"I'll pick you up in the morning for our appointment with Maciej."

Shit. I'd completely forgotten about that. We're meeting with Shaelene's favorite designer for a fitting tomorrow so he can get our measurements for the gala.

Sighing, I nod and gently shrug out of her grasp. *I just need to get home and lose the feeling of her eyes on me.* I turn and meet Geoffrey outside at my car. *I'll deal with Shaelene's presence tomorrow.*

38

Shaelene

MACIEJ WORKS OUT OF his apartment on the upper east side with his two assistants. The Polish born fashion royal rarely works commissions, liking to keep his pieces rare by only offering up a few to the runways for New York and Paris fashion week every year.

I met him a decade ago when my father asked him to prepare a wedding gown for me. Coincidentally, there'd been an *accident* in Maciej's previous shop, and I never had to wear it. He's been helpful to me in more ways than just fashion ever since.

One of his assistants is giving Victoria a tour of the high rise, showing off one of their recent projects and explaining their plans for the next one.

Her awed expression is the most emotion she's shown since she left the manor yesterday. She's barely spoken to me and is alarmingly more relaxed now that I'm sidelined across the loft with Maciej brainstorming dress details.

I haven't told Victoria I'm the one designing her gown, but I've had the image in my head since the day she showed up to the manor and I saw that teasing green poking through her blouse.

Maciej and I sit for half an hour discussing the details. I want it corseted tightly on her torso with silver and emerald crystals beading down the boning and mesh on her stomach, scattering down onto the shiny silk of the train we've decided to cut high on one side to expose her leg all the way up to her hip. He pulls out some fabric swatches, and I find the perfect color hidden among them.

It's the ideal shade of deep green to compliment her fair skin and eye-catching curls. She'll look exactly like I imagined when I'd seen her for the first time on Sloane's campus. A heart stopping flash of red in a field of green. *My Little Fox.*

I run an idea for her mask by him once he finishes his notes for the dress, doing my best to scribble the shape onto the bottom of his sketchbook page. I'm no Victoria Fenwick, but the drawing is decent enough for him to work his magic off of.

"Your ideas are great, Shaelene. Shall I teach you to sew while you're here?" he teases.

He laughs as I shake my head. He's one of the few people that know me well, but anyone could see I'm not the housewife, sewing, and baking type.

"I'll leave that to you, Mach."

He laughs again and flips his notebook to a fresh page. "And what of you? Don't make me do another suit, Shaelene, please. My heart can't take it."

My eyes roll and find Victoria as she paces around the open flat, distracting herself with anything she can to avoid coming back over here. "Surprise me," I say, standing. He already has all my measurements, so there's no need to discuss my fitting any further, though I add in one stipulation. "But keep it black, please. Or *my* heart won't be able to take it."

His cheeky grin stretches further across his face until his eyes are smiling wide too. "Yes, Ms. Laughlin," he jests.

I turn, smiling myself. Maciej has always been able to bring out genuine joy in me, even though we met under less than happy circumstances.

The smile sticks until I see Victoria staring at me with sad eyes. She all but rips my heart out when she turns away, blinking and shaking whatever thought she'd had in that gorgeous mind of hers. I've scoured my brain for clues as to what could be bothering her since she left for coffee yesterday, but I've come up empty every time. The not knowing pains me almost as much as her cold shoulder.

Maciej passes by me and joins her, explaining the measurements he needs and that it'd be better if she undresses. Her eyes slip back to me when he says it, but she agrees and turns to place her jacket on a chair behind her.

39

Victoria

SHAELENE SITS IN THE seat where I left my clothes, settling the folded pile onto her lap. Her protective eyes watch me stand half naked on the platform in the middle of Maciej's open apartment.

It's an interesting place, meant to look industrial with exposed walls and beams while the concrete floor amplifies the cold from outside. Kat, one of his assistants, mentioned something about the open air and cool temps being better for the fabrics. *As if I'd know anything to the contrary.* My mother had gowns made for me growing up, but never anything of Maciej's caliber.

Racks of designer pieces line the wall beside the giant mirror in front of me. The one I catch Shaelene staring at me in from her seat.

It feels like time slows and hours pass when our eyes meet, but after a couple moments Maciej is between us blocking our view.

He works quickly, measuring the length of my legs in and out of heels. Then my waist and bust from the front. When he ducks to measure another part, I get a glimpse of Shaelene.

Her eyes haven't moved, the intensity in them still fierce.

"I apologize. Katerina insists I keep it exceptionally cold in here." Maciej draws my attention from the mirror, making me aware of my shivering.

"Oh, that's... I'm okay."

His eyes leave his tape measure for the briefest of seconds to peek past my shoulder. Shaelene's unblinking eyes don't meet his. He centers himself, using me as a wall between him and her, and whispers, "I'll be quick, darling."

I look away from the both of them and up to the ceiling. *God, I've made my confliction so obvious, haven't I?* I know I'll have to talk to her at some point, though I've tried my best to avoid it so far. The silent ride here was agonizingly painful, but her glaring at me is worse. I've seen her agitated, confident, and slightly surprised, but never vulnerable. Now, a glimmer of confusion passes behind her eyes before they narrow further in the glass.

Maciej taps my elbows, and I instinctively lift my arms so he can wrap the tape around me, measuring my bust again.

"Katerina, the bodice please," he says. She runs by and retrieves the piece from one of the worktables. "If it's alright, Victoria, I'll need you to take off your brassiere and try this for me now."

I pause, glancing at Shaelene's reflection again. Maciej turns, pursing his lips at her, before forcing a smile back at me. "I'll leave you a moment to get changed. Katerina." He nods and the two of them walk toward the back room his other assistant is working in. Their muted voices whisper over the makeshift wall of shelved fabrics after they disappear behind it. The droning of a sewing machine back there suppresses the rest of their conversation, further dividing them from Shaelene and I.

My fingers twist the back strap of my bra, and it falls loose around me. I try to keep myself covered while I slide it off and toss it to the side, but since Shaelene is still holding the rest of my clothes, it lies alone on the floor.

"Don't do that."

For a second I think she's reprimanding me for putting my bra on the floor, until she shoves the clothes in her lap to the ground and comes up behind me. "Do what?"

"Act shy," she says, looking with contempt at the arm covering my chest.

She's got a point; she's seen more of my body than just my breasts. *Seen it. Touched it. Kissed it. Photographed it.* She's mistaken though. I'm not hiding myself from *her*. I'm avoiding the look she makes when she sees me. Those damn eyes become so full of light and desire, they melt every inch of my defenses as they rake over me. *Like right this second.*

She reaches around and takes the white bodice from my hand, trapping me between her arms and unfolding the corset in front of me. The strings down the back loosen when she spreads it apart. She looks at me impatiently in the mirror, waiting for me to lift my arms.

I do, and the light I'd been dodging flickers in her eyes. I swear she can see my heart pounding under my ribs as she waits an extra second before hoisting the corset over me.

It's tight and makes my breasts overflow out of the rigid boning when she pulls the cords taught around me.

I can barely breathe in this thing, but wearing it or not, the look on Shaelene's face would steal the air from my lungs regardless. The muscles in her neck are tense, but not in the way they get when she's peeved. It's the look she gets when she's trying to contain herself, and her desire is winning. Her jaw clenches, her fingers flexing restlessly at her side.

Her hands caress my cinched waist, but I can hardly feel it. Her touch is so gentle I wouldn't know they were there if I wasn't watching them move up my sides in the mirror.

Goosebumps form on my arms, adding to the anxious anticipation of Shaelene's hands sliding up my body. The warmth of her palms is a stark contrast to the ice cold feel of my skin when they rub over my shoulders and pin my arms to my sides.

She ducks her head, leveling her face with mine in the mirror, her pupils eclipsing those devious gray irises as she takes in every nervous move I make until they disappear behind her lids when she buries her face in my neck.

One kiss is more than I should allow, but I don't pull away until the third. Her bottom lip drags against my neck when I do. I can't bring myself to meet her stare in the mirror, but her slow heavy breaths are enough to signal her displeasure.

She straightens and drops her hands. I finally lift my eyes when I hear her footsteps walking away, but she's already out the door before I can say anything.

The room is quiet and lonely, the fabric seeming to absorb all sound. Ten seconds ago my heart was thudding so loudly in my ears I thought my eardrums would burst, but now the silence feels heavy enough to break me. My eyes burn, but the quick chime of my phone echoing around the room saves me from myself. I hop across the cold concrete to retrieve it, reading the text.

Shae

Someone will pick you up and drive you home once you're done.

She left. *She actually fucking left.* The corset aches as it stretches with each of my frantic breaths, my stomach feeling hollow. I scratch at my back to loosen the strings as my vision darkens at the edges.

Nimble fingers catch mine and Maciej whispers, "Darling, allow me." He makes quick work of the laces, and I take a deep breath, my vision clearing except for the tears pooled in my eyes. "Take your time," he says, patting a gentle hand on my back. "We're on your schedule, darling. Katerina! Would you please fetch Victoria some water? Do you need anything else?"

Her...

I sniffle, shaking my head, the clog in my throat still too thick to talk through. I swipe the tears from my cheeks as they fall. *No. This is what I wanted,* I remind myself. This is what my brain has been trying to convince me is best since her camera flashed. This is how it needs to be.

So why the fuck does it hurt so bad?

40

Shaelene

I DON'T KNOW WHAT the fuck is going on with Victoria, but I'm going to find out.

The mudroom door slams so loudly behind me one of the maids yelps from the kitchen—*Marcella by the sound of it*—while I make my way up the stairs.

Shaun and Shephard are both sitting on the sofa, Luca between them, watching a movie until I stand in front of the TV and block their view.

"Shae, what the hell? Move," Shephard garbles through a mouthful of popcorn. When I don't, he pulls his feet off the table and reaches for the remote to pause whichever Rocky movie they have on for the millionth time with a sigh. "What do you want?"

I turn my attention from his shitty attitude to Shaun, who's sitting in front of me, equally annoyed and confused. "What did you say to Victoria?"

His brows raise, still unsure as to why I'm fuming before him. He glances at Luca, then back to me. "What are you talking about? I didn't say anything to her."

"Then what did Luca say?" I press, turning my rage at him now.

Shaun's face instantly switches from perplexed to angry, his protective boyfriend mode overshadowing the usual brotherly savior one. Shephard, on the other hand, revels in any and all sibling rivalry. His previous annoyance is replaced with the giddy look of anticipation, his eyes bouncing between the two of us.

He claps his hands together and turns to face us better. "Oh, here we go. Thousand bucks says Shaun wins." He nudges Luca with his elbow, shoving another handful of popcorn into his gullet.

I put up a hand to stop the rest of his stupid commentary before it can begin. "I already had this conversation with you once, Shep, and I pulled a gun. If you make me say it again, I'll fire it."

He laughs, hearty and deep, and it's the absolute last thing I want to hear right now. "Ah, but you didn't! Which is why my money's on Shaun."

I ignore him, keeping my focus on my other brother, who's growing more furious by the second.

Stop looking so fucking clueless, Shaun.

"I find it interesting that yesterday Victoria went to make coffee, and ten minutes later Shephard's sweaty ass returns from beating the shit out of him," I say, pointing an accusatory finger at Luca. "While the two of you were off doing God knows what. And when Victoria finally comes back from the kitchen, she's not acting like herself. Like she's scared to *look* at me." I pause to collect myself before gritting out, "And without. Any. Coffee."

Realization settles over Shaun and the fury leaves his eyes. Dead air hangs between us while I wait for his explanation, but I grow impatient. "What did you idiots say to her?"

"We didn't say anything," Shaun starts, his body sinking deeper into the couch.

I don't believe him.

Then Luca's expression falters, plagued with worry and guilt as he pinches the bridge of his nose. "*Merda...*" He sighs.

Neither of them has given me an answer yet, but I don't have to ask again because Shephard does it for me.

"What am I missing here?" he asks, swapping glances between the three of us.

"She probably saw us fighting," Shaun finally admits, no longer looking at me but down at his hands instead. That answer doesn't clear up any of my confusion or anger.

"That doesn't make any sense! Why would seeing them box change anything?" The ball of impatience and annoyance swells in my stomach. *I just need fucking answers, not more questions. There are already too many damn questions.*

"Not boxing," Shaun says, rubbing his hands over his face. "She probably saw Luca and I arguing in the hall."

"Arguing *how*?"

I know how he gets. Shephard may be the one with the shortest fuse, but Shaun is still a hothead. If pushed, he'll snap fiercer than anyone. He bottles things up, more than either of us, but one final straw will send him over the edge, and if he doesn't get his emotions out soon enough, not many can survive his wrath.

"We'd just finished hosing off in my room and we went down to grab some food. We were in the hall, and Luca..." His voice trails off but picks up with less than an explanation. "Then I—"

"Goddammit, Shaun! *What?*" I shout.

"We were fighting about us!" Luca yells, jumping to his feet. His tall frame sags next to me, clearly still upset about whatever caused them to fight in the first place. "I said some stupid things, and I pushed him against the wall. Shaun fought back, and the next second he was choking me."

Them dealing with their bullshit however works for them is one thing, but letting it get physical around Victoria is unforgivable. *If she'd been caught in the middle and been hurt—*

I turn my back to keep from wringing my hands around both their throats myself. *Something. I need to break something.* Shephard holds his popcorn bag over the back of the couch out of my reach when he sees the wild look in my eyes.

"Don't you touch those controllers, Shae," he orders when my gaze moves to the ottoman. I let my head fall back and face the ceiling, sucking in a calming breath. Unsuccessfully.

"Then we kissed. That's it," Luca finishes, and I turn to see his usually expressive hands settled across his chest.

Shaun stands too, putting himself between Luca and I. "We didn't know she was there. We didn't even make it to the kitchen."

"We came straight up afterwards," Luca seconds Shaun's claim. "You don't think she'll say—"

I cut off his asinine question, some of my anger returning. "Jesus Luca, I've been fucking her for the last two weeks. She's not homophobic," I huff. He looks to Shaun who isn't finished fuming at me apparently. I roll my eyes and give Luca a more sympathetic assurance. "She won't tell anyone. She wouldn't be so distant if she was planning to rat on you two."

I shoot Shaun an annoyed glance and he nods, pulling Luca in tighter. I'm not going to ask any more about their little lover's quarrel—*that's none of my business*—but what I really need to know is why it bothered Victoria so much she doesn't want *me* to look at her anymore.

I leave the boys to their movie, my thoughts spinning a web of clues, trying to thread together what her issue is.

She isn't scared off by violence; my holding Shephard at gunpoint without her fleeing is an indication of that. Sure, she took a day off after, but the next she was melting into my hand. *That only leaves two options.*

She could be heartbroken over one of the boys, which is unlikely. I'm certain she doesn't have any feelings toward them. *She did nearly buckle over the first time Luca introduced himself to her though.* But that's par for the course for any woman that makes his acquaintance. I'm almost positive she lost any hope of a deeper connection when he warned her about asking questions.

Leaving only one other option, which is her liking what she saw. *That could be promising.* Getting her to surrender control will be easier than I thought. She just has to let go, and I'll take care of every want and need she has. I'll make her understand I can fulfill all of her deepest, darkest desires.

But she'll have to stop running away from herself first.

41

Victoria

SHAELENE ISN'T SPEAKING TO me.

It's been four days since our appointment with Maciej, and four days without any contact from her.

A driver picked me up after my fitting and drove me straight home, and I haven't seen Shaelene at the manor since. I thought the pressure of being under her microscope was too much, but not having her around is worse.

Shaun and Shephard don't talk to me unless they need something done or signed. The firm still doesn't have any current clients, but Silas keeps me busy in his office while sending the boys off to keep eyes on Derek.

Now it's the weekend, and I'm not due back for two days.

Two days without Shephard sizing me up when I arrive in the morning.

Two days without the dizzying smell of Silas' cigar smoke penetrating every piece of paper I file for him.

Two more days without Shaelene...

Orange juice dribbles onto my sketchbook as I cough, choking from the thought of not hearing from her for so long. From thinking that unlike before when she was watching from across the street, she might *actually* be done with me this time.

My phone chimes next to me, my heart rocketing to my throat, and I snatch it up quickly. Too quickly. I grapple with the air before my cell can fall through my fingers.

SIoL Library Services: You have (5) books past due

Crap, I forgot about those. I haven't been back to Sloane since I started my internship. I rush getting myself dressed and load the books into my tote since the library closes early on Saturdays.

"Your late fee is sixty-two dollars and fifty cents."

When I raise my eyebrows rather than hand over my card, the grouchy woman behind the counter chastises me some more. "Sloane's policy for overdue books is two-fifty per book. Per day. And these were due back Monday. "

"I know, but—"

"And since you've accrued over fifty dollars in late fees, you'll be suspended from checking out books until next semester." My jaw falls open in surprise. "You can still read them, but you must do so in the library," she reassures me in the most nonreassuring tone possible.

I probably won't need to borrow any more books until then anyway, especially since Silas explicitly told me to forget everything I've been taught. Defeated, I dig around my bag for my wallet and hand her my card.

"Ah, *Blue's Guide to Jury Selection*. I should've grabbed that from you when you dropped it. I've been trying to check out a copy for a week now," a voice behind me teases.

I turn around and see Nathan, the guy who helped me a few weeks ago in the parking lot. The tight, dark curls of his hair are pressed into waves on the top of his head, fading into his brown skin on the sides as his hazel eyes look playfully down at my embarrassed face.

"Shhh! I don't need her charging me for damages too," I poke back.

He smiles, one of his teeth on the side noticeably sharper than the others. It's cute and gives him a sense of youthful adorableness I've been deprived of lately. He's in the same lecture as me, but I don't remember what firm he got assigned to, and aside from his help a few weeks ago, I haven't spoken to him much. *Or anyone else for that matter. I really should make some friends...*

The clerk clears her throat impatiently, my pride deflating as I take my card from her. I toss the receipt in the trash on my way toward the exit.

"Hey, Victoria! Wait up!" Nathan calls after me. I hold the door open as he catches up, the copy of *Blue's* I just returned in his hand. "You wanna get some coffee? I'll pay."

It's probably a dumb idea, but I agree to it anyway. *Shaelene isn't speaking to me anymore, so maybe she's given up stalking me too.* I didn't fail to notice her apartment has been dark.

It's a meaningless cup of coffee with a classmate filled with uninteresting small talk, nothing more than a distraction from the pathetic side of me that can't stop thinking about her.

"So how is it being at Laughlin & Laughlin?" Nathan asks.

Never mind. I sigh silently. *I should've known she'd still somehow be the topic of discussion.*

"Uhm, yeah, it's good," I half-lie, taking a sip of my latte.

"Oh, come on!" He leans across the table, dropping his voice, "You've gotta be working on some exciting stuff. Any high-profile clients?"

I shake my head. Even if there were active cases right now, I wouldn't be able to share because of confidentiality. "No, nothing too exciting. I've been more of a party planner than anything."

"Party planner?" His eyebrows perk.

I laugh at how ridiculous it sounds. I don't mention blackmailing some attendees, but I tell him about everything I've been overseeing the last few weeks.

It's surprisingly nice talking with someone that isn't intimidating and cold, and I catch myself smiling for what feels like the first time in a week. Nathan is only slightly taller than me—*maybe five-ten?*—and he's got the build of an average college-aged, athletic guy. He'd be dwarfed by the triplets if they were here, but there's something comforting in their size difference. *Nathan feels more human than the Laughlins, less... Ethereal.*

"Well, that's some *interesting* legal work you've done." He squints at me, unable to keep a straight face before laughing with his whole chest. I spend a moment watching his Adam's apple bob in his neck and taking in the adorable stubble on his chin. It takes me far too long to realize he's stopped laughing and is staring back. At my lips. I stupidly fill the awkwardness with words.

"You should come see it."

I regret the offer the second it leaves my mouth. *He absolutely should* not *come see it.* I don't even know why I mentioned it.

Maybe because he's the first person in weeks to talk to me without commanding me?

Just because the fine print on the back of the invite mentioned plus ones, doesn't mean I should involve anyone else with the Laughlin family, but it's too late for me to retract the offer.

His innocent eyes glint with excitement. "I'd love to."

Shit, this was only supposed to be coffee.

"Great!" I force out, finishing my drink to keep from talking anymore. We exchange numbers, and I agree to text him the rest of the info later tonight before making the short drive home.

I notice something in front of my door when I step out of the elevator into my hall. It's a large black box with the letter "M" beautifully scribed on the center of it with a smaller, velvety case on top.

Not waiting to bring it inside, I pop it open, and a note falls to the floor.

Per Shaelene's request. –M

Tucked snugly inside the soft casing is a metal mask, silver wires intricately wrapping around several emeralds.

I rush inside with my surprise packages, hardly pausing to close the door before heading for my room and slipping the mask from the box. Stepping in front of the mirror, I hold the surprisingly light masterpiece up. The cool metal chills my flushed cheeks, somehow fitting the curves of my face perfectly.

The wires bend up into points at the ends, and with it held up in place I see clearly what it's meant to be.

A fox face.

42

Victoria

I'VE BEEN MINDLESSLY STARING at the same email for twenty minutes, none of the words making sense, and I can't take it anymore. I cease clicking my pen and finally ask the boys the question that's been killing me all morning.

"Where's Shaelene?"

It's been just the three of us all week. I assume Derek has decided his best course of action is *not* to talk since they haven't been tailing him the last few days.

Shephard doesn't look over at me, continuing to watch the highlights of whatever fight was on last night. I don't think he hears, so I clear my throat to ask again, but he says, "She's at the Angelini's making sure the security detail knows their routes," without looking up from his phone.

All this time she's been finishing the planning, and she still sent me the fox mask. Maybe she isn't ignoring me. Maybe she's just giving me the space I acted like I wanted. Nathan's life flashes before my eyes. *And I've gone and invited a date to her birthday...*

"It's okay for me to bring a plus one tomorrow, right?"

Shaun's humming of whatever is playing in his headphones stops and he glances at Shephard, whose growing smirk kick-starts my goosebumps. None of it makes me feel good.

"If you think that's a good idea, Red."

Fuck. I already texted Nathan the details, and he told me yesterday he found a suit and mask to wear. Shaelene's going to kill him—*me too probably*—but it's too late to cancel.

I should've just had coffee at home.

The clock on my computer clicks to twelve and I stand, grabbing my bag and rushing to the door. "I'm getting lunch," I say to no one in particular, needing to get away from their weighted glances and silent, telepathic judgement.

I fly down the stairs, rounding the banister, and run face first into Shaelene. She doesn't budge an inch, only looking up from her phone with an eyebrow raised in eerily calm surprise. "Going somewhere?"

The impact knocked the air from my lungs, but so does the sight of her after an eleven-day absence.

"Lunch," I spill. "I was, uh—"

My cell chimes in my bag. I peek at it and cringe when I see a text from Nathan. When I peer up again, Shaelene is slowly looking up from my screen.

"Phillip, have Geoffrey bring Ms. Fenwick's car around." The way she says my name is cold and dry, the hollowness in her words making the pit in my stomach deepen until it feels like it'll swallow me from the inside out. *Is this heartbreak?*

I hadn't even heard Phillip walking up behind her, my ears too muffled from my pounding heartbeat, but I see him turn and duck down the hall toward the garage without hesitation.

She doesn't mention the text I'm positive she saw. She simply looks down her nose at me, her brows no longer arched on her face. She looks even more calm, but in a scary sort of way because I can still see the hurt behind her eyes even though she refuses to show the emotion fully.

This time, *her* phone vibrates and breaks the tension. She taps the screen a couple times then puts it away, all while maintaining her composure and brushing past me up the stairs.

My phone dings after I finish the uneasy walk through the front of the manor. It's another text from Nathan—a picture of him in an untailored tux to go along with his earlier message.

Nathan D.

Dry cleaned and rdy 2 go! 6:30 work for u tmrw?

I send a thumbs up emoji and turn my phone to do not disturb for the rest of the day. I head home, not intending to come back after lunch. Silas and Simon are out today, so there's hope they won't care since there's no work for me to do anyway.

Except there is. I've got to figure out how the hell Nathan and I are going to survive the party tomorrow.

By the time I buzz Nathan up twenty minutes earlier than planned, my only solution is a bottle of liquid courage.

"You look incredible!"

"Thanks." My stomach churns, and I practically run into the kitchen, leaving him at the door.

Maciej worked wonders with this dress. It's tight enough that it feels like a second skin without suffocating me. My boobs are hoisted to high heaven, and the slit on the side makes me look taller than I really am.

The beaded jewels are the same cut and color as the ones in my mask, everything flawless as it catches the light. I did myself a favor and moused and diffused my curls this morning, so they've got extra bounce around my shoulders while my bangs are twisted back into two intentionally messy top knots. Altogether, I look like Shaelene's perfect little fox. *Just like she wanted me to be.*

Then there's Nathan, the perky, naive rabbit I'm leading straight into the viper's nest.

He's sitting in one of the bar stools across the island blissfully unaware of the looming danger, struggling to peel his eyes from my chest while I pour us both a shot. I slide his over, downing mine with a grimace.

"Oh. Thanks, Victoria, but I gotta drive," he reminds me.

"Right, sorry." I down his too.

His face furrows partially impressed but mostly concerned. I pretend not to notice and look around for anything I might've forgotten to squeeze into my clutch, biting the inside of my cheek so I don't ruin my lip gloss.

When I'm sure I have everything, we leave for the Angelini's.

The security Shaelene hired is no joke. There are at least two dozen guards working the entrance checkpoint. I surrender my clutch at the door, so the spare shooter of vodka I'd packed for when the first two shots wore off stays at the coat check, the steely man running it remaining silent as he gestures for us to keep making our way inside.

Palazzo Angelini looks like a stone mansion plucked straight out of Tuscany and dropped into the lush countryside of the American Northeast.

There are no corners in the building. Every wall is rounded with rustic plaster and columned archways one after another down every curve.

We follow the rest of the crowd to the main ballroom. It could easily fit four to five hundred people, and tonight it's packed with tables and masked guests dressed to filth in high-end couture.

Nathan sticks out like a sore thumb in his slightly too big tux and cheap Zorro mask. Nobody pays him any mind though, they're all too enthralled with the decor.

"Woah? You did all this?" Nathan asks, taking everything in.

Long black and red drapes fall from the ceiling around the edge of the room, elegantly complimenting the arches and pillars while also providing added direction to keep guests from wandering down the maze-like corridors.

Each table is topped with a towering feathery, floral centerpiece over its black satin tablecloth.

At the back of the ballroom, between a set of wide double stairs, is the stage where the live band has their instruments set up and ready for later. Shaelene told me she handled the arrangements for them already, so I have no idea who's performing. For now, the DJ blasts house music so loud my mask vibrates against my nose and cheeks.

The place looks fantastic, better than I'd imagined after only deciding on colors from an array of swatches and Shaelene agreeing with every opinion I offered. *I can't take all the credit for this.* "I had some help," I admit, my throat tightening as I search the room even though I know I won't find her. Not if they're sticking to the routine.

The crowd around us bumps along with the bass of the song, but Nathan catches sight of someone and raises his hand to flag them down.

"Mr. Shultz! I didn't know you'd be here," Nathan shouts over my shoulder.

I turn to see Derek, his blood-shot eyes scowling through the holes in his generic white half mask and a false smile showing his veneers. His burgundy tux making him stand out among the crowd of black and white ones. "Nathaniel, I could say the same." His tone conveys the same feigned confidence he had in his office the last time I saw him. "What brings you to such a *select* kind of party?"

"Victoria invited me. We share the same lecture hall with Professor Hilton."

"Did she now?" His eyes cut to mine, rage roiling within them. "That's very thoughtful of you, Ms. Fenwick." Nathan doesn't notice Derek using my last name without either of us having said it yet, nor the deep crease between my brows. *How is it they know one another by name too?*

"I'm sorry, but how do you two know each other?" I ask, scooting closer to Nathan's side. His mouth opens to answer, but the DA does it for him.

"Mr. Davis was assigned to my office for his student internship." His practiced confidence slowly grows cockier as the obvious discomfort on my face spreads. "He's been a great help."

"Mostly just small administrative stuff." Nathan modestly brushes off Derek's compliment, fidgeting with the cuffs of his coat.

The DA's eyes skirt around the room before settling back on me. "For now."

It's not so much a hint about upcoming work for Nathan as it is a threat. Just because he was forced into coming tonight, doesn't mean he's going to give up his senate campaign *or* his hatred for the Laughlins. I don't know what he's planning, or how he could've done it with Shaun and Shephard watching, but if he managed to stir something up it can't be good. *And I might've made it easier for him by unknowingly bringing his intern here as my plus one.*

Something behind us catches Derek's attention, releasing me from his pinning glare.

He claps a heavy hand on Nathan's shoulder and departs, telling him to enjoy his evening and melting into the crowd of guests filling the ballroom.

We wait a while, standing awkwardly under one of the columned archways at the back of the room, until the loud conversations around us grow hushed and everyone starts to notice the same thing.

Six large, statuesque men stand guard over the party like a group of masked gargoyles. Two on each end of the line of muscular tuxedoed bodies wear Venetian jester masks, smiling unnervingly stagnant grins down at us. *Yellow, red, blue, and green.* All in place on their respective sides of the wide second story landing.

A matching purple mask completes the set from atop a table at the front of the ballroom, reserving a place for Milano.

A different color for each Angelini son.

Between them are the two masked brothers I'm more acquainted with, their identical faces hidden behind twin black, devil masks sporting curved horns like a ram's skull. Shephard is beside the red jester, managing to dwarf the giant that I know is Giovanni because of the tattoos covering his neck and hands. Shaun is next to Luca wearing blue, their hands on the railing closer than the rest, pining to touch but forced to keep up appearances.

"Holy crap," Nathan gasps beside me and I realize it's the first time I've heard him curse, *sort of.* I can't blame him. The team upstairs has such a powerful presence, looking down at all of us, that I'd forgotten he was standing next to me.

His hand slides around my waist and my body stiffens. I'm not sure if he's trying to claim me or comfort himself. Regardless, the last thing either of us needs is Shaelene seeing him holding me, and right on cue, the music changes—the mood in the room shifting again.

The party lights dim, leaving the ballroom under the soft, warm glow of the six crystal chandeliers hanging high above our heads and the shining light from behind the menacing figures above us.

The six of them straighten and split into two groups, walking down both staircases in a synchronized pace, stopping on their marked steps just like I'd planned.

Orchestrating their entrance doesn't stop me from being enamored while seeing it in action. There was no rehearsal, just a brief explanation to Shaun and Shephard about what they need to do. Shaelene was still gone when I'd told them everything, but her silhouette slowly struts into view onto the landing, timed perfectly, and my heart hits the floor.

Oh. My. Fucking. God.

I didn't think it was possible for Shaelene to be anymore terrifyingly beautiful, especially with a pair of horns.

They don't curve like her brothers'. No, hers stab their sharp points out into the air above her, widening her outline and forcing people to move out of her path unless they want to risk losing an eye.

The lights transition, cascading down the steps so they each have a spotlight beaming over them.

Shaelene's spotlight is last, her figure focusing into view as she somehow finds me in the back of the crowd. The moment feels too similar to the first time I saw her at Laughlin Manor—except this time, she doesn't turn her back and walk away from me.

For a long while, it's just her and I in the ballroom, eyes glued on each other. I'm her prey, caught in the snare she's built with texts and touches and camera clicks. She's the snake that hunts me. *Tempts* me. Feeding me the right words, followed by the sinful strokes of her forked tongue.

Her velvety, gloved hands perch themselves wide on the banister. Another homage to one of our firsts, but instead of cum stained leather, the black fabric stretches from her fingertips to her biceps, clasping delicately to her shoulder pieces before continuing down to the sweetheart neckline that exposes more of her chest than I've seen since meeting her.

Somehow, her dress shirts manage to hide the plump roundness of her breasts, but tonight they're roosted high on her torso from a bustier like the one in my dress.

Her waistline is cinched narrowly beneath a few perfectly placed pleats just above the curve of her hip, and a high slit shows off one of her mile long legs. The weight of Nathan's hand slips away and the crowd parts in front of me, my eyes never leaving her as I step forward.

Silas' voice in the microphone startles me back to the present.

"Ladies, gentlemen… New York's finest." He pauses when a roar of cheers erupts from the side of the room; Barry Kerr and several of his payroll deputies bask in the praise of his greeting.

The double meaning is lost on them, but not me. More than a few of the other faces in the crowd glance in their direction, their sneers barely hidden under their masks. The bought off cops barely register when it comes to the worthiness scale of the Laughlins. *They're only here as a show of power, nothing more.* I look around the massive hall at the other guests.

Goldstein and his wife, both of whom Shaelene begrudgingly gave me the rundown on during my first draft of the seating plans, are near the bar with rubies dripping from their clothes. Wu Bó Chéng, leader of the Silent Dragons, and a group of his men—rumored to be guns for hire—collect themselves in a tight formation near the hall, all of them with a scaled mask diagonally cut over half their face.

Huh. Apparently warring crime factions can *put their differences aside when an open bar and the Laughlins are involved.*

"We want to thank you for coming out tonight to join us in celebrating the twenty-eighth birthday of Shaelene, Shaun, and Shephard Laughlin."

The triplets and Angelini brothers move to stand behind Silas, waiting for the applause to die down before he continues.

"Dinner will be served shortly; in the meantime, grab a drink, enjoy a dance, or take a moment to say hello to our guests of honor." The siblings bow their heads to the crowd, their movements precisely controlled. Silas gestures to the stage behind him, recapturing the attention of the room. "Our good friend, Bobby, from the Times is also here. Introduce yourself and get a photo. I'm sure he'd be happy to take a statement as well." Silas winks and it sends a chill down my spine that makes me I hope I never have to see it again.

Bobby looks terrified. The young journalist has the appearance of someone thrown into the back of a van and forced to come here—which I wouldn't put past Shephard to have done.

The camera he's holding shakes so forcefully any pictures he takes will be too blurry to publish, but that doesn't mean the threat of being photographed alongside the worst gangsters in New York won't still scare the guests it's meant to.

Derek Shultz, to be precise.

43

Victoria

NATHAN AND I SIT near the head table, the centerpiece mostly blocking him and Shaelene's view of each other, but it doesn't get in the way of my hidden peeks to where she's sitting, eating the third course of Dario's incredible meal and sipping bubbles from her champagne flute. Her eyes off me for the briefest of moments while she talks to a member of the waitstaff.

Servers circle the table, bringing trays of desserts around, and the one Shaelene spoke with brings a plate of chocolate truffles directly to me. I last all of two bites before risking another glance her way, only to be met by her intense gaze. It makes my mouth water and body heat. I rub my thighs together, hidden beneath the table, craving her familiar friction. *Don't lose your control over a damn dessert, Victoria. If Shae kills Nathan because she notices you're horny in his proximity, you'll have to explain that in a eulogy.*

Our table remains quiet through dessert, only bothering one another with occasional small talk. *How do you know the Laughlins? That Shephard gets bigger every time I see him. Such a shame about the Angelini boy...*

Eventually, the conversations throughout the room fall as we all recuperate from multiple servings of five-star cuisine.

Silas stands from his seat at the head table, capturing every ounce of attention and raising his scotch glass high.

"A toast," he starts, "to my three children. You've embodied the strength and resilience the Laughlin family has carried for generations. You three may have given me the hardest challenges of my life over the last twenty-eight years, but you're also my greatest achievement to date. Happy birthday."

"Happy birthday!" everyone else cheers in unison, raising their drinks and celebrating.

Silas turns a smiling face back at us. "Traditionally this is where we'd sing to them, but I believe the triplets have something of their own planned."

Dread shoots through my veins, cooling the heady warmth the alcohol poured into me. *Did I forget to schedule something?* I planned this entire party, but I have no clue what Silas is talking about. *Does this* thing *involve killing my date? Surely not in front of everyone... Right?*

The three of them stand and head for the stage, taking their places. Shaelene is behind a microphone with Shaun—a guitar strapped across his chest—at the mic beside her. Shephard tosses his jacket and sits behind a set of drums.

They're the fucking band?!

I nervously wipe my sweaty palms off with the hem of the tablecloth. *Everything is fine. Singing is better than public assault and the execution of Nathan.*

I hope.

All the other guests stand and gather near the front of the stage. Nathan starts to as well, but when I don't follow him, he stands timidly ahead of me. "Do you want to—"

"No! Uhm, sorry Nathan. I just... I'd rather watch from here."

His hands dig into his pocket as he forces a smile, rocking on his heels in place beside me.

"It means a lot that you all came out tonight. To say thanks, we're gonna play a few songs," Shaun says, keeping his sight focused past the gathered crowd. When I glance back, it's Luca, still standing near the head table, though it's who's gone that worries me.

Silas, Simon, Grigorio, and the rest of the Angelini's are no longer at their seats. I scan the room while the drums start in the background. *They're not here, and I'm the only one that's noticed, which is exactly what they wanted.* No one saw them slip away because they're all focused on the triplets.

Shaelene sings the opening line to the song I've purposely been skipping in my playlist all week, and my neck snaps back to the stage. To her pained, lovely voice. And just like everyone else, I'm a victim in the Laughlins' trap because I can't look away from her up there.

I ignore Nathan's offer to dance, so he shuffles off to get a drink. He could drive home right now for all I care. *Shae is incredible.* I've never heard so much raw emotion out of her. She sings with her whole voice, fully belting the lyrics—screaming some too. Her focus is entirely on singing, her eyes closed and brows knitting as she and Shaun hit the chorus.

"Such lovely words," someone says ahead of me.

He turns and I'm met with the bronzed face of a wolf. Light brown hair waifs over the top of it, and a pair of jarringly dim, blue eyes peer down at me from behind the mask. They're frighteningly pale, like gray clouds just before a massive storm. Nothing like the calming slate of Shaelene's. The goosebumps already pebbling my skin prickle harder, the hair standing up on the back of my neck.

"It's a shame a voice like that is stuck inside the devil herself, though I suppose that's what makes her so tempting." He sneers against the rim of his mule glass.

He doesn't look familiar. Not from the guest photos and descriptions Shaelene provided me with at least, so he must be a plus one. A pale scar cuts across his mouth and down his chin, so faded I almost didn't notice. His smirk drops when he catches me staring at it.

A new song starts, slower this time, and despite the warning bells ringing in my head, I look past him to the stage at Shaelene again. Every word feels like it's meant for me, and the way she sings them makes my heart leap even if it shouldn't. Shaun's accompanying vocals preach to Luca too, and I can't help but smile.

"She's not so bad," I say, glancing over, but he's gone—vanished like the others. Spinning around, I search for a flash of bronze in the crowd without success. He's disappeared completely, leaving me with only the faintest remnant of a scar and the memory of his accented account of Shaelene's dangerous character. *Maybe he was one last ditch effort on behalf of my subconscious telling me not to give up my self-imposed abstinence of Shae.*

My heel slips on the marble flooring, and I barely catch myself after whirling again to look for him. Nathan must be able to read my thoughts because he returns to my side, grabbing my hip to steady me. "You okay?"

I don't have time to answer. The song ends and movement from the crowd catches both of our attention. Shaelene disappears from the stage and gracefully bulldozes our way while Shaun and Shephard start the next part of their setlist without her. Everyone parts, clearing a path directly to me.

My heart races, the thumps so loud blood might start pouring from my ears. Everything comes crashing down around me, and I'm suddenly very conscious of Nathan's hand squeezing my waist. I pray a silent apology to his parents for getting their son murdered.

The soft fabric of Shaelene's glove wraps tightly around my upper arm as she spins me around and pushes me toward the back of the room, forcing herself between Nathan and I. Her shoulder smacks him as she passes, and I hear him grunt before we disappear behind the wall of drapes.

I have no idea where she's leading me. If Laughlin manor is a maze, the Angelini mansion is a labyrinth. We pass dozens of hallways and doors before she finally pushes one open and shoves me through. I don't have time to catch my breath before I'm slammed against it, her lips capturing my gasp.

Her tongue sweeps over mine, kissing me with two weeks' worth of pent-up aggression. "Don't ever make me stay away from you again," she gasps. "I can't."

Her voice is hoarse, and her groans are quiet whispers against my neck. My knees buckle and I lean my head before thinking, giving her better access. I want so badly to give in, to let her show me what I've been missing, but if I do there's no going back. She'll break me. She'll leave me when I end up admitting the fucked-up things that happened to me and how I want them to happen again.

"Shae, I have to." My voice cracks as I push her arms off. She grabs my wrists and pins them above my head, pinning me in place with her face stern above mine as chills seep into my skin.

"I know you saw Shaun and Luca," she croaks. "They fight and are rough because they're angry. At each other. At the world. At themselves. Who knows?" Her eyes soften as she tries to convince me to let her back in. "But I'm physically incapable of being mad at you, Victoria. No matter how hard you try to drive me away. So, why are you?"

I don't say anything. I can't say anything. I have an answer, but I'm too scared—*too ashamed*—to say it out loud. At least in my thoughts the only person that can judge me is *me*.

"Haven't I shown you enough for you to know how much I want you? That I don't care who knows it?" She drops her shoulders, her forehead resting against mine as her body folds in on itself. This is the first time I've heard her question herself. I *hate* it. "Do you want more?"

I freeze, and Shaelene lifts her head. She watches the knot force its way down my throat as I swallow, then takes a deep breath through her nose, straightening to her full height. With her heels on, she's almost a full foot taller than me. *She's daunting. Menacing. Comforting...*

I muster enough courage to nod, but I don't dare look away from her, keeping eye contact through my lashes. I do want more, but not from anyone else. I don't want another Sterling. I want—no, *need*—more with Shaelene.

She unknits her brows and slides her hand down my arm, wrapping her fingers around my neck. Her nose grazes the side of mine as she leans in, squeezing my throat.

"Is this what you want, Little Fox?"

"Yes," I choke out. I feel her smile as she tightens her grasp.

"I may not have a cock swinging between my legs, *ma fraise*, but I can still be a dick." Her tongue teases past my lips, stealing what little resolve I have left. "All you had to do was ask."

44

Victoria

SHAE CARRIES ME TO the pool table in the center of the room, my legs wrapped tightly around her hips, fisting a handful of my ass through the cut of my dress.

She spreads my ankles, putting a foot in each of the corner pockets like they're a pair of stirrups as both her hands run the length of my legs, meeting at my center. I clench on nothing, desperately ready for her to be inside me. *Thank you for such a high slit, Maciej.*

She teases me over my underwear with her thumbs, rubbing long, firm strokes. I run my hands over the back of her dress, holding her close while she claims my mouth with her tongue again.

"How much pain do you want?"

As much as you can give me. But I don't know my limits yet. I've never explored this side of myself before. All I know is that I want to be hurt, I want to be pushed, but I don't want to feel *used*.

The thin strap of my dress falls down my shoulder, and Shae takes full advantage, freeing one of my breasts from its designer prison. Her warm tongue swirls around my nipple before she nips it between her teeth.

I arch further into her, wanting every pinch and bite she'll give me. But my answering gasp isn't enough.

She hollows her cheeks and sucks my breast into her mouth, loudly breaking the suction with a sharp tug. A growl rumbles deep in her throat before she licks her way up my chest and neck, flicking her tongue harshly off my chin.

"How much?" she asks again, dipping past the hem of my panties and massaging a fleecy thumb against my clit.

"I don't know." I press against her, seeking more friction. More pleasure. More pain.

Her hot breath wafts over my face when she looks at me, searching my eyes for an answer. When I say nothing, she stands up straight, leaving me open and slack in front of her. "I'm going to do things, but *you* are in charge. Understood?"

I swallow a nervous gulp and nod.

"Use your words, Victoria. Do you understand?"

My words get stuck before I can say them. My thighs shake and my knees knock together. I can feel the vein in my neck pulsing. I want to feel this way; the adrenaline is already making my panties slick, but my shame is putting up a fight. My eyes squeeze shut, blocking out the room while I wait for the memories to come. *You can get past it. Shaelene isn't going to use you.*

I keep waiting for the rush of ice to freeze me over, for the dreadful cold wash to start. But it doesn't. *Where is it?* When I focus on what's in front of me, I realize. Shaelene is there, *waiting*. She hasn't touched me, and she won't. Not until I give the okay. *She isn't Sterling.*

"Yes."

She lets loose the breath she was holding, her wicked smile returning sharper than before. "I'm going to hurt you now, Little Fox." She waits, only a second, for me to take my last chance to stop her.

I don't.

Shaelene's palms are harsh as she pushes me back, and my head smacks the hard top of the table, sending a throb bursting through my skull. When I open my eyes again, I'm looking at myself in the mirrored ceiling.

She yanks one of my hands up and ties it in the gaudy, braided fringe of the side pocket, then stalks around the table to do the same to the other. In the reflection, I'm crucified across the red felt.

Her fingers untie the back of her mask, and she places it next to me on the table. *And now the devil is looking down at me too...*

My eyes follow her to the side wall, watching as she runs her palm across the sticks hanging in the rack. Plucking one from its casing, she twists it until it separates in two.

She sees the look on my face and reaches for me; I greedily lean into her palm, some of my anxiety melting away. "Blink hard twice if it's too much." Her thumb traces my chin and pulls my mouth open. "Bite."

The stick groans between my teeth, gagging me like a horse bit.

She tugs my thong to the side and spits, her warm saliva hitting my clit and making me flinch. My body is tense, but I know she can see how excited it is too. Her eyes don't leave mine for a second.

The rubber bumper presses against me, pinning my clit against the bone beneath. I arch and writhe against the twisting cue, every ounce of my attention focused on Shae's malicious glee.

When she deems me ready, she spreads me with her fingers and pushes the shaft inside. Slow at first. Teasing. When it starts to glide easier, she pushes further, stretching me beyond anything I've ever experienced.

The grip pinches something inside me, and I groan from the burning pain it causes, but I don't dare blink for fear she'll stop. Every stroke is met by a delicious bite of torment.

She drives the cue further in, over and over, slowing when it's almost out, then plunging it back in relentlessly.

My shoulders drive into the table, rubbing themselves raw against the felt when my back arches. My mask slips up my forehead and my eyes water, but my body caves to the pleasure, a heavy moan erupting out of me, drowned by the muffled music coming from the ballroom.

No one out there would hear me even if I screamed.

A flood starts cresting in me, so close to bursting free. Several more drives of the stick have my legs shaking, falling closed from exhaustion, but Shae shoves them apart with her free hand, keeping her view of my face clear.

I'm so close to coming, my teeth threaten to crack from the wood between them, the varnish sour against my tongue.

I suck in another breath through my nose when Shaelene rips the rod out of me, letting it clatter on the floor. Her soothing mouth takes its place, sucking and kissing every place she was rough.

Her moans and the sounds of her lips smacking against mine send me over the edge. I come against her face, my hips searching for more pleasure as my trembling legs hold her head tight against my pussy, and she laps me up while I convulse below her.

She looks up at me from between my tired legs and I see hints of her smile spreading on her face, lifting her cheeks and reaching her eyes. They're glossy. Ravenous. More pleased than she normally is after making me come.

She finishes with a peck to my swollen, overstimulated clit—my body following her touch—and stands. I gasp at the sight of her.

Her chin and mouth are smeared with red. For a second, I think it's her lipstick, but I remember she isn't wearing any.

It's my blood.

She kicks the half of the cue she used to fuck me across the floor, and I follow it in the mirror as it rolls. A good bit of it is coated in the same scarlet glaze that covers her mouth and chin. The pinch I felt must've been a tear, ripping me on the inside.

Shaelene lifts my feet from the pockets and brings my legs together, then moves to untie my wrists. Snagging a polishing rag from the cabinet on her way back around.

After cleaning her face, she takes the stick from my mouth and twists the pieces back together, wiping the handle and returning it to its previous polished state, then back on the rack it goes. *Okay, we* have *to make sure that gets cleaned before we leave tonight.*

Beside me, she fixes her mask back onto her face. It's a sight to see, the sinful smile shining beneath the dark vision of her horns. The only trace of our mess on her is the slightly red tinge of her teeth. When she's in front of me again, she lifts one of my heavy legs by the ankle and cleans me. Her hands feather light with the rag.

I'm still riding the high of my orgasm, the adrenaline fueling my words. "Why are you okay with this? It's insane. I'm insane for wanting this... Aren't I?" I plead, half-hoping her answer is yes, but desperate to hear no at the same time.

She sets my leg down, letting it dangle over the end of the table and settles herself between them as she leans over and pulls me up to sit. She brings a soft, gloved finger to my face, gently swiping a tear away and adjusting my mask back into place.

I'm ashamed for wanting such a messed-up sex life. *But fuck, if Shaelene didn't make it feel so normal...*

"No, Little Fox. You're not crazy," she reassures, placing the softest of kisses to my other cheek.

I lift a hand, holding onto her wrist while she twists a fallen curl around her finger. "What am I then?"

Her smile widens, baring her sharp teeth in a hungry, slow smile. "Mine."

I sigh, letting my eyes close and my head fall back. The rhythm beating fast in my chest begins to slow, but I don't want to lose this ecstasy yet. Eagerness grows in me again. My sore walls clench on nothing, wishing she'd fuck me again. Fill me with her fingers and banish all the self-deprecating thoughts with another swipe of her tongue.

One question stays stuck in my head though; she didn't answer it, and I *have* to know the reason.

I open my eyes, meeting hers as they watch me, dipping my chin to look up at her through my lashes. "Why are you okay with this? With hurting me?"

She's silent, tracking the rise and fall of my chest, the pace of hers starting to pick up too before she says, "The same reason you want me to."

I go stiff, my mind racing a million miles an hour while she looks back at me as cool and collected as ever. *Something horrible happened to mess with my brain chemistry this badly, so... What happened to her?*

My heart shatters at the thought of anyone hurting Shaelene. It's not something I thought was even possible. She's so strong, and more than capable of protecting herself. *Who could've damaged her like that?*

Her hand slides up my neck and into my hair, grabbing it tightly at the base. I whimper at her strength, the ease at which she could make me do anything if she wanted to.

"One more thing, Little Fox." She pins me in place as her eyes scan down the length of me, taking in every inch of my exhausted body, held up only by her fist in my curls and the metal boning in my dress. "Green is your color. Not mine. I won't be made jealous." My skin strains and a few hairs pull out of my scalp as she tightens her grip. "Fix your makeup and get rid of your... *Friend...* Before I do it myself."

She lifts me off the table, and I wobble on my heels, barely managing not to fall on my ass.

She turns away and saunters out of the room while I regain my balance and composure, heaving a few deep breaths in and out. The ceiling tiles confirm Shaelene's truth about my tattered appearance. My hair is a tangled mess and my mascara is smeared.

I also have no fucking clue where the closest out of sight bathroom is in this goddamn castle of a house. But I brace myself and step out of the door anyway.

Thank God! After too many locked doors, one finally opens and it's a large communal washroom with a row of stalls and a counter full of sinks.

My heels clack loudly against the tiled floor as I rush to one of the raised, glass bowls, flipping on the faucet and splashing a handful of cool water on my cheeks. I tear several paper towels from the dispenser and rub my under eyes raw washing off my smeared makeup.

Glancing in the mirror, my eyes look puffy and red, like I've been crying. Which would be a good enough excuse if Nathan asks where I've been for the last— I have no idea how long we've been absent... *I'll just tell him I don't want to talk about it and need to go home; that should get him out of here.*

My hair looks like a rat's nest, so I ditch the buns since they've fallen limp anyway, thanking myself for doing my curl routine before pulling it up tonight. I pull a few knotted strands apart and bounce the ringlets around my shoulders.

I look passable, and I feel better. Clear-headed.

Until I see it.

My body jumps and I whip around to make sure I'm not imagining anything. *I'm not. There is definitely a foot there, sticking out from the bottom of the furthest stall.*

A shiny, brown leather loafer attached to a leg draped in an all too recognizable pair of burgundy slacks. A puddle of blood surrounding it.

45

Victoria

"Hello?" I call. *Please don't answer. Please don't answer! But also, please be alive. God, if you're there,* please *let him just be drunk and injured.*

Through the quiet, I creep to the stall, hoping to every divine power in the universe it's just someone passed out. I tap the foot with the toe of my shoe, and it falls to the side, limp and heavy. Goosebumps bloom across every inch of my flesh as I afford myself one breath before pressing a clammy palm against the steel door in front of me, forcing it open so I can peer in.

I scream before my brain can tell me not to.

Cloudy-eyed and bloody, Derek Shultz lies splayed across the stall floor, more blood outside than inside of him. My body buzzes, my hands shaking as I cover my mouth, muffling the rest of my shrieks. I back away slowly, my eyes locked on a new nightmare set to haunt my dreams.

The door to the hall slams against the stone wall, making me jump, and I panic thinking someone is about to catch me alone with the district attorney's dead body. But it's Shae. She rushes around the corner and locks eyes with me.

"What's wrong? Are you hurt?" she asks, holding her hands out as she comes closer.

"Shae, I swear. I–I didn't..."

I can't even say the words, another sob bursting out of me as I turn to look at Derek again.

"*Fuck*. Okay, look—"

I faintly hear her words, but I can't look away. I can't look away from the dripping body. I can't look away from his twisted face. *I can't—*

"Victoria, look at me!"

She's yelling, but I barely hear her. It's like I'm underwater. Frozen. Drenched. Sinking deeper and deeper and deeper. My vision narrows, growing dark around the edges until her hands are on my shoulders and she's shaking me. My brain spins. My chest feels too tight. My skin tingles with adrenaline again, but this time it's urging me toward flight. I want to scream and run, but Shaelene is holding me in place.

"Victoria, I need you to listen to me!" She cups my face and pulls me close. I do the best I can to not spiral, keeping my watery eyes locked on her powerful features. I try to focus on anything but Derek and the smell of iron clogging my nostrils.

Shae's eyes dash back and forth between mine, a look of worry softening them. She isn't the least bit distressed about the dead government employee lying in a pool of his own blood in the stall next to us. No, her angled jaw is clenched tight waiting for *me* to settle.

I suck in a shaky, broken breath through my teeth, avoiding the stench as much as possible.

"Good girl. You're alright, see?" she coos. "I'm going to go get the others, okay? I need you to stay here and lock the door behind me."

I shake my head, my vision blurring with fresh tears. "Shae, I can't!" I sob, begging her not to leave me alone.

"Yes, you can. Lock the door and wait by it until I get back."

She doesn't let me protest again, dragging me by the arm toward the exit. "Shae, wait!"

She turns one last time, keeping the door cracked between us. "Lock it."

The bolt slides into place and the heavy click echoes through the empty bathroom, leaving me with only the sound of my ragged breaths.

I'm a shaking, crying, snotty mess on the floor when someone bangs on the door a couple minutes later. I freeze. *How do I know it's Shae and not someone else looking for a place to pee?* Silence follows, no one begging to be let in. *Maybe they walked away...* The door crashes against the frame with three more loud, heavy knocks. *Oh my god, Victoria! People don't knock before entering bathrooms like this!*

"Victoria, open the door," Shae's muffled voice whispers, and I jump to my feet, stiltedly sliding the deadbolt out of place.

She storms in, Shaun and Shephard stepping in behind her just before Silas, Simon, and Grigorio barge in too. The door shuts with a much quieter click behind Luca as he enters last. He eyes me silently, sliding the bolt back and locking us in. For the first time, his reassuring smile doesn't meet his eyes as he gently grabs my elbow and leads me back to Shaelene's side.

"Shae, what's the big emerge— Oh shit! Now it's a party." Shephard smirks through a mouthful of cake. How he's keeping it down is beyond me. Another look at Derek's bludgeoned face has me gagging.

He snickers and ends up catching a lethal dose of Shae's side eye, before looking at me. I see the moment he realizes I'm paler than usual and on wobbly knees. He stuffs another forkful of cake into his mouth without another comment.

Simon takes the handkerchief from his pocket and pushes the door open wider, giving us all an unwanted look at the DA.

His forehead is split, caved in with pink bits spilling out onto the toilet seat beside him. The wall he's leaned against has a bloody splatter at about head height, and his nose is crooked and bloody, staining the hideous tint of his spray tan even darker.

His eyes are open, staring blankly at us. *Well, one of them anyway.*

"Where," I start, stifling another gag. "Where's his other eye?"

Shaelene pulls me into her, trying to shield me from the sight of him, but I'm too morbidly curious now, even if the sight of him makes me sick. I'm not alone with him anymore; there's no more fear of being mistaken for killing him. My hands shake as I grip her biceps, my body still pushing me toward flight, but I know the safest option right now is to stay in Shae's arms and fight it out.

"Keep this bathroom locked until everyone leaves; we'll deal with this then," Silas orders. He looks back at Grigorio and Simon. "We need to continue our meeting. Thanks to this *enlightening* information—" He waves a pissed off hand in Derek's direction. "—we have more to discuss."

The three of them storm out without a second glance.

"That's it? We're just going to leave him here and–and..."

"And what? Drag him through the ballroom for everyone to see?" Shephard laughs through another bite, leaning against the sink and shaking his head. "You think that's a better idea, Red?"

I stay quiet, nuzzling into Shaelene's neck and letting my brain play catch up. *Us going back out there and pretending nothing happened is the smartest thing to do. It'll give us all an alibi; witnesses can attest to us being present. No one will raise suspicions unless the party gets shut down early.* It's smart.

Shaun steps toward Derek's body, tiptoeing around the puddle and into the stall. He peeks around the walls and the backside of the door, a small scoff filling the air. "Found it."

"Found what?" Shae asks.

He turns, yanking a long strip of toilet paper from the holder beside Derek's head and folds it in his hand several times. The door closes slightly while he maneuvers around, blocking everything he's doing.

When I see his hand again, I nearly wretch. Pinched in the cotton between his fingers is Derek's other eye. The dark brown iris is a sunken hole, like a fleshy, pitted olive.

"Whoever did it wasn't leaving anything up for debate. Probably smashed his nose against the wall there first," he says, pointing a thumb to the splatter. "Then threw him against the hook back here before finishing him off on the seat."

He tosses the wad to the floor and it hits the tile with a disgusting splat. My stomach churns, and I start to lose my battle against it.

Shaelene sees it on my face and snatches the cloth from Shephard's breast pocket, trapping the vomit in my mouth. "Swallow it," she demands. "We don't need to worry about cleaning you out of here too."

They all watch, waiting for me to do as she says. Watching me lose it in front of them.

Acidic chunks burn the inside of my cheeks, but I manage to swallow them back down, my eyes watering and melting my mascara all over again.

"Good. That's my good girl," she whispers, kissing my clammy forehead.

"We *do* need to clean him off her though," Luca says, taking note of the small line of blood trailing along the floor from my dress.

"Oh my god..." I tremble, my knees fully giving out. Shaelene's arms cradle me as she carries me to the counter, gently placing me down beside the sink and running the back of her fingers down my cheek. Luca wastes no time gathering up the train and soaking it under running water. He takes the pocket square from his jacket and soaks it too, handing it to Shaelene who presses the cool cloth to my forehead. She whispers words of assurance into my hair while she rubs a hand over my back. I don't hear much of it, everything is too fuzzy. Too warped. Too tunneled. My breaths come out ragged, my entire body alight as the fear-fueled cold wash starts trickling over me again.

Shephard and Shaun are having their own conversation by Derek's body, but my world is too busy spinning for me to notice anything other than their lips moving and their hands gesturing around the mess of blood and dead DA.

The loud whirring of the hand dryer beside me helps clear some of my senses, and I realize Luca is now standing beside me while Shaelene rushes to dry the end of my dress. The stains are mostly on the underside of the train—*Thank you, God*—but the mop-like streaks I'd leave behind if I left with it wet would be just as noticeable as the blood. Especially on the already slick, polished floor of the ballroom.

Luca looks over me while Shae continues drying, forcing a wincing smile that's even less reassuring than before. He ruffles inside his jacket and pulls out a stick of gum, handing it to me without a word.

"Thanks, Luca," I whisper.

He wraps his arms gently around my shoulders and hugs me, resting his cheek against my hair. "*Prego*, Victoria.'

The dryer quits its endless humming, and Shaelene turns our way. "Let's get you out of here."

46

Shaelene

Nathan Davis is at the bar unknowingly chatting up the man his dead boss most recently tried in court.

Watching him put his hands on Victoria like she's anything other than a classmate has kept me on edge all night, and now my nerves are fucking shot. Annoying as it is, finding Shultz dead has been a pleasant distraction from Nathan's presence.

If Victoria weren't a trembling piece of glass on the verge of shattering, I'd have removed him from the party myself. Unfortunately, Nathan has now become useful. *I need her as far away from the Palazzo as possible, and the best course of action is to remove them together.* I have to stay and be seen. Keep playing the gracious guest of honor to ensure everyone remains unaware of the body growing cold in the bathroom down the hall.

I grip his shoulder when we reach him, trying my damndest to rein in my desire to remove his arm from its socket, while my other hand continues holding Victoria's.

"Ms. Fenwick isn't feeling well. Thank you for coming, but she needs you to take her home. *Now.*" His stupid face looks up at me, clueless and confused, before he turns to her and softens at her puffy eyes and sweaty skin. *I hate him.*

I hate her looking like this. I hate him looking at her like that. *She doesn't need your pity, douchebag. Or your comfort. She needs me. I helped her through the panic. I keep her calm.*

She's still shaking but is holding herself together well enough. *Maybe she* can *brave the shit storm of my family's lifestyle*—even if I'd rather keep her out of trouble all together.

I reluctantly surrender my little fox, my hand empty and cold without her, and walk away, finding my brothers in the crowd.

"I don't trust him," Shephard sneers as we watch Nathan lead Victoria out of the ballroom.

"That makes two of us."

"Three," Shaun adds.

Luca appears at his side, brushing his arm against my brother's. "Four."

When their heads disappear around a wall, I pull my phone from the garter on my thigh and type out a quick text before fixing a fake smile to my face. "Let's get the rest of this shit over with."

I have to clear my head so we can figure out how to handle this.

Shephard winks. "Who wants cake?"

The entire spectacle of us cutting our too big cake in front of a crowd that couldn't care less makes me want to roll my eyes, but I keep them on my brothers at all times instead. I am in no mood to receive a face full of buttercream courtesy of either one of them. *I do* not *want a repeat of last year.*

"Ladies first," Shaun croons, as if there isn't already a gorilla-fist sized chunk hacked out of the back of this monstrosity from Shephard earlier.

I'm so on edge I need both hands to steady the giant knife as I force it through the layers of cake. As much as I want to plunge it through Shaun and his smug ass, we already have one dead body on the grounds, and I'd rather not clean up another. I place my slice onto the dish a waiting server holds out beside me, and the boys do the same before passing the knife to a member of the staff who'll continue cutting pieces for the line of guests.

The first bite turns to ash on my tongue, my fork clattering against my plate in disappointment. I swap plates with Shephard after he inhales his slice, ditching the empty one on a nearby table.

Every second of this performance of a birthday drags by with Victoria absent. Every planned charade feels pointless since she isn't here to witness her handiwork. The silent auction goes by quickly at least, though Father isn't pleased to see *my* name as the highest bid on the full day tour of New York City.

"Shaelene Laughlin!" he announces into the mic, crumpling the auction card in his hand and shoving it into his pocket. All heads turn to find my barely concealed grimace behind my mask as I dip my chin in acceptance.

Once all this is settled, I'll enjoy an entire day out of the manor with her. *No annoying brothers. No scolding father. No dead fucking politicians.* I'd been planning to take Victoria out ever since seeing the awestruck look in her eyes when we were at Anghiari, then again after seeing the searches on her computer after we'd gotten back to the office. *Before I sunk my fingers—*

"He is *so* pissed," Shaun snickers in my ear from over my shoulder.

"He can get over it." I shrug, swigging the last of my champagne then darting my gaze to my father. He's seething with no mask to hide it even if he wanted to. *Stubborn for no damn reason.*

He's not angry I won; he's annoyed I took away his chance to pull money out of someone else. *And a chance to earn favors in return.* The tour is an extravagant all day excursion, privately chauffeured on our helicopter during the day and utilizing our yacht in the bay in the evening.

Victoria's eyes are going to light up even more when we're actually on the water. I can't wait to see it.

And just like that, I'm back to being pissed she isn't here. That Nathan Fucking Davis is the last person she'll see tonight. *I have to get out of here already.*

Shephard trudges back to my side from the bar with my tonic water disguised in a flute glass. "Could tonight take any longer?" he asks, picking up on my thoughts with his so-called telepathy. He drinks back half his scotch with a singular gulp, sending a furrowed brow across the slowly filling dance floor as our father concedes the mic and the dance portion of the evening begins.

"For fucks sake, Shep. Go ask her for a dance," I utter, rolling my eyes when I see it's Bianca he's making himself miserable over. "Be grateful *your* girl is still here."

He scowls in my direction this time. "You know I can't do that."

"I know you think you can't." I groan. "And you were supposed to be done drinking two scotches ago."

Shaun snorts beside me, injecting himself into the middle of our conversation. His fun is cut short as our father slices through the crowd toward us. I already know what's coming because it's the very next bullet point from Victoria's meticulous itinerary. *Damn, I wish she were here to dance with instead...*

"Shaelene," my father says expectantly, extending a hand when he reaches me. I pass my glass to Shephard, and take Father's hand, following him onto the dance floor.

"You need to smile. People are watching," he insists as we make our second lap around the carousel of other dancers. My lips lift involuntarily as I glance around the floor. Shaun stepped in and asked Bianca to dance after Father and I started, leaving Shephard a fuming pillar of rage standing hatefully along the edge of the crowd. They spin around near us, Biance's eyes rolling playfully at something Shaun whispers into her ear before he leads her straight into Shephard's arms for him to finish the dance. His smile is too strong not to poke through the self-imposed agony he subjects himself to when it comes to her.

I have no such affection for my dance partner. I know if I were to look at the guests clapping as my father twirls me around, I'll see smiles and everyone taking in a special moment on a daughter's birthday. *A bunch of fools.*

What they don't see is the scrutiny in his eyes as he analyzes my every step. Insisting they're all perfect. Robotic. His eyes narrow in annoyance, and I know I haven't done enough to appease his ire.

I blow out a soft breath and tilt my chin higher, slapping a polished grin on my already tired cheeks.

"Better, but you need to stop worrying about the girl and think of your family."

I stare at him through every one of our steps. "She's a part of this now."

"I'm aware."

It takes every fiber of my being not to pull myself from his grip and trudge away to my car so I can go to her. *He involved her in this.*

He brought her into the firm. He's the reason she nearly shattered tonight.

"Why did you hire her?"

His eyes harden, but the apples of his cheeks lift like I said something sweet. Hiding his irritation to everyone but me. "It was time."

"Her specifically," I clarify. If this were just about bringing on an intern for appearance purposes—which it never would be because my father values trust and obedience above all else—then he wouldn't have had us stake her out in the first place. He chose her. I know he did. *I just don't know why.*

"She is only a girl, Shaelene," he hisses through another forced smile.

"You trust her?" I ask, waiting with bated breath. Either of his possible answers will set me on edge, but only one requires me to choose her over him. *Which is getting easier to come to terms with every passing day.*

He quirks a brow. "Should I not?"

Oh, no. He isn't turning this investigation onto me. *He* is the leader of the firm. He knows the ins and outs of every decision, and I'm sick of being left in the dark. "You said her retention is imperative." My grip on his hand tightens.

He says nothing, simply sends me into a turn, forcing me to submit again. Before I come back into his hold, he sets his face into the stony, cold look I'm intimately familiar with. He's clearly finished with this topic of conversation and too irritated to care if anyone else sees it.

He should have worn a mask like the rest of us. Then he wouldn't have to fake a happy face all night.

"You need to smile. People are watching," I sneer, parroting his earlier sentiment.

His lip curls. "Shaelene Mikha—"

"Don't middle name me. It's my birthday."

The vein in his forehead pops, his control straining. "Stop speaking like an insolent child and—"

Uncle taps Father's shoulder, cutting him and our dance off. "May I?" he asks, his eyes shining brightly behind his silver-plated phantom mask.

Father looks between the two of us, giving a curt nod to his twin and striding across the room toward the bar.

"Don't push him, Shaelene," Uncle urges, pulling us back into pace with the other dancers. The music has changed since I last cared to listen, the tempo much softer than earlier. When I glance around, Luca is bounding his nieces around the circle, one balancing on each of his feet as he sweeps them into turn after turn, their infectious giggles spreading into the crowd.

"He knows something, and he isn't—"

"He *always* knows something. Secrets are his favorite toys, but don't confuse his complacency with you right now for something else. He's irascible, Shae. More than usual. And *you* are not the only one with questions. Asking them and feeding his contemptuousness isn't going to help."

"I—"

"Have done all you can do tonight. Exceptionally well, I might add, given the circumstances," he assures, meeting my gaze with a genuinely kind quirk of his lips. "Let us handle the rest."

An odd sense of relief pulls the weight of this evening off my shoulders. Uncle's confidence in me removes my discontent of falling in line again. It's as if tonight might not be the horrendous shitshow it was shaping up to be. *Everything will be alright. He'll make sure of it.*

"You told me I needed to keep an eye on Victoria…"

"Now more than ever," he admits, setting just enough of a pit in my stomach to put my ass back into high gear. "I'm going to twirl you."

The dance doesn't call for it, but before I can protest, he sends me spiraling in front of him, our hands clasped high in the air above our heads. Steadying me with a featherlight hand on my back, he looks truly overjoyed to be dancing with me. And I feel a pang of *something* when the song ends and he wraps me in a hug.

"They've seen enough of you. Go to her."

47

Victoria

Getting into Nathan's car, I dig in my clutch for two things. My phone and the vodka shooter. I down it with a shaky hand and a humiliating cough.

"I don't know if that's the best idea if your stomach is hurting."

I ignore him and unlock my phone.

Shae

> **Pack a bag and hang tight. I'll be by to get you after the all clear.**

I press myself into the passenger seat, trying to get every muscle to relax. Leaving the Palazzo without Shaelene feels like a mistake. Like she's the only thing that can hold me together and on my own, my shivers are only the start of my mind breaking down. I know Nathan is here, but he won't be able to help me if I have another panic attack before we get to my apartment. For all he knows, I've got an upset stomach and need to go home and sit on the toilet for an hour. He has no idea his direct supervisor was just *murdered*.

He pulls the car over in front of my building, and I'm unbuckled and out the door before he can put it in park.

"Hey, are you sure you're okay? You need help up?" he asks, desperately leaning over my seat to see me standing on the sidewalk.

"I'm fine. Thank you, Nathan."

"Alright, uhh... I'll text you in the morning to check on you—"

The door slamming cuts him off as I rush inside. Harvey isn't out front tonight and the guy that is must be new because he asks for my resident pass before letting me in.

I breathe through the shakiness in my hands as I clear the lobby and step into the elevator alone. *I'm home. I'm alive. I'm safe.* But questions about tonight start spinning in my head as I stare at my reflection in the door.

Security was tight. How did Derek's killer get in? I watch my eyes widen. *It had to have been someone with an invitation.* My stomach churns. *Everyone there probably wanted him dead... But why risk doing it at such a high-profile event?*

The elevator dings, barely saving me from what is absolutely starting to feel like a panic spiral I won't survive, and I rush down the hall, locking my apartment door behind me the second I'm inside. Resting my forehead against it, I look at the floor without really seeing and force myself to take deep breaths. But near the floor is my dress.

Before I can stop it, I fixate on its hem and the dark edges that aren't fully dry.

Did Luca get all the blood off? Oh my god, there could be a blood trail leading from Derek's body to my apartment! Would that make Nathan an accomplice?

My dress suddenly feels infinitely tighter, caging me within my panic as my breaths turn shallow and unsteady, sweat slicking my brow against the door.

How long does it take to clean and cover up a murder? How long before the heat dies down? Is there even heat yet? Is this just paranoia kicking in? I squeeze my eyes closed, but I still see the phantom stains on green silk. *Shaelene knows what she's doing. I'll be fine. Wait... How* does *she know what to do?*

I can't breathe. I'm suffocating. Drowning. My throat is disgustingly hoarse with every gasp as my stomach churns again.

Will the killer come here next? Try to keep me quiet by killing me too?

Shaelene isn't here to stop me getting sick this time, and I spill most of Dario's courses onto the door as I vomit. Cold, clammy panic grips me. Terrified, the edges of my vision start to darken, my body covered in goosebumps from a shower I can never forget.

On the verge of passing out, I brace both hands on the door frame, rocking in place a few times before finding my balance.

Vomit trickles down to the floor, some chunks landing around my feet, the smell enveloping me and making my throat burn. Rushing to avoid a third round of five-star Michelin flavored puke, I sprint through my bedroom to the bath, cranking the shower knobs until they're full blast. The spray cascades down onto the back of my head, drenching me with icy water. I flinch away, my hair dripping and stuck to my face as I stumble back against the wall. I go limp, sliding down it and instantly transporting from my bathroom to a nightmare.

"Vicky, come on," Sterling singsongs. *"I know you like this. Open your eyes. Stop hiding."*

Even with my eyes squeezed shut, I know he's smiling. I can feel it.

Just like I can feel him inside me. Rubbing harshly with two fingers, adding an excruciating third as my body betrays me just like it did when he started. I feel like I'm at war, not only against Sterling, but myself too.

My teeth ache from how tightly they've been clenched for the last... Too long. The fireworks behind my eyelids faded into a deep blackness a while ago, serving as my only shield from him.

I don't want to see the way my body is giving in. Hearing it is bad enough. The abhorrent squelches with every thrust and twist of his fingers in and out, over and over and over, is somehow worse than his voice purring in my ears.

"Look at me, Vicky. It's okay. I'm liking it too."

I'm not *liking it. I hate every bit of it, and every instinct in me says to run, but I can't with my wrists tied to the shower head, my shoulders numb from the constant stretch. Still, my body responds against my will, my thighs clamping around his wrist as my back bows, and he chuckles as I lose the battle against myself. A singular groan passes my lips before my body goes slack and the tears I tried to keep at bay finally slip.*

I didn't want him to see me cry. I didn't want to come either. Not like this. Not for the first time...

Sterling's hand slips out and trails up my stomach, spurring goosebumps that make me wince. I keep my eyes shut, my body curling away from his touch. I don't want to open them and see what I've let happen.

"See, Vicky? See what I can do for you? Open your eyes and look what you did to my hand."

No. I won't. I refuse.

He grips my jaw hard enough to bruise, and I can smell myself on him. "Look at me." I shake my head, and he digs his nails into my cheek. "Open your fucking eyes, Fenwick."

If my mouth wasn't so damn dry, I'd spit on him.
"VICTORIA, OPEN YOUR EYES!"

The hands on my face soften, but I hear my name again. "Victoria, please. Open your eyes."

Shae?

When I finally blink them open, squinting past the blinding light and the tears, I see her.

"*Ma fraise...*" she murmurs.

"I'm sorry—"

"You're safe. I'm here." She scoops me from the puddle I've melted into on the floor, the shower head still going, and the tub filling faster than it can drain. *How long was I stuck like this?* Shaelene sets me on the counter and grabs a washcloth from the cupboard beneath, soaking it before turning the water off.

"What time is it?"

"Almost midnight," she says, dabbing the cloth over my forehead and across my chin. *Right. The vomit...*

"Did you see the..."

Her eyes stay focused on wiping chunks and sweat from my mouth and neck. "I'll clean it. Are you alright?" she asks, finally meeting my gaze with open worry in hers.

"I am now."

The corners of her mouth perk up with a forced smile. "You're safe, do you hear me? Nothing is going to happen to you." She steps closer, wrapping her arms tightly around me, taking a deep breath in time with me. "I didn't get the chance to tell you tonight," she whispers, her voice muffled against my neck, "But you look incredible, Little Fox."

More tears well in my eyes, burning down my cheeks when they fall. I cling to her as she lifts me again and walks me into my bedroom, pulling the strings at the back of my dress so by the time she sits me on the bed I can breathe easily. *Minus the same anxiously excited inhales I always take when Shae undresses me.*

"Can you change yourself?"

I nod, slipping my feet out of the pile of dress around my ankles, my fingers still trembling as I undo the straps on my heels. "How much should I pack?" I ask, finally responding to her earlier text. I don't know how long I'm going to stay with her. *One night? Two?* I don't even know if it's safe for me to be at my apartment anymore. *I found the body after all. Never mind, I don't actually know anything other than the fact that Derek is dead and it definitely was not a suicide.*

Panic rises within me once more, and I can't help but look across the room at the woman I seek in every space I go. *That's not true; I know more than that.* I know Shae is going to protect me, but her calmness throughout all this forms a smaller, second knot in my belly.

"Don't worry about packing; we don't have a lot of time. Change into something comfortable while I clean up. We can always come back for whatever you need, or I'll buy you something new."

She presses a kiss to my sweaty, tangled hair and walks out of the room, keeping the door open so I can see her until I finally get up and pull my comfiest pajamas out of my dresser.

When I meet her in the kitchen, all remnants of me getting sick are gone and the few dishes I'd had soaking in the sink are being run in the dishwasher.

"We could've done those when we come back," I tease.

She doesn't attempt to hide her gawking as she slinks her eyes over me. "You could've done it after you used them," she taunts. I don't hide my gaping either now that I feel level-headed enough to fully take her in. Her hair is tied messily in a bun on top of her head; the black hoodie and sweats she's wearing are somehow competing with her suits on the sexiness scale.

She said you don't have time, Victoria. Put the dirty thoughts away; she can probably smell the pheromones wafting off you. When I make eye contact with her again, she winks. *Oh yeah, she can definitely smell them.*

"Come on," she says, extending a hand for me to take while picking up a bag of trash with the other. "Everyone's waiting."

48

Shaelene

THE LONGER WE WAIT to take care of Shultz's body, the more problems could arise.

Everyone is gathered in Grigorio's study, already discussing options, as we arrive.

"The boys can handle the body. As for residual forensics, Simon, do you have any suggestions?" Father asks.

"Grigorio, how do you feel about home renovations?"

Signore Angelini has already been at the brink of his sanity since Milano's passing; I'll be surprised if he doesn't wage an all-out war now. *Whatever business he and the others had been discussing tonight is going to have to wait until this situation is handled.*

"We'll play it off as if the bathroom was under construction and blocked off from the party. Shaun, you'll handle the security footage. Loop the feed so the hallway stays empty, but make sure the time stamps line up," Uncle orders. "And mute it for good measure."

I lean near his shoulder and whisper, "Wipe the footage from the billiards room too." He looks back at me with a curious brow, then over to Victoria, before rolling his eyes.

"We'll arrange for a demolition crew to be in early tomorrow morning. They'll back-date the paperwork and schedules," Uncle continues.

Victoria's arm tightens around mine, and I pull my hand from my hoodie pocket, linking my fingers in hers. She squeezes me, keeping her voice hushed when she asks, "What are they going to do with... I mean how—"

I stop her before she gets herself worked up again, my thumb consistent and calm across her knuckles. "It's better you don't ask. No one is going to find him, and they can't get answers out of you if you don't know."

Of the dozens of corpses my brothers, the Angelinis, and I have disposed of, none have been found. Every case goes cold eventually.

Laughlin Manor is embedded at the front of two-hundred acres of forest thicker than the patch of trees that leads up the sides of the driveway. Venture far enough past the tree line and you'll run into one of the coyote packs living out there. *They'll eat anything.* After a few days, the only parts left are the bones, and those get broken up and thrown out with the deer carcasses our chef butchers in house. *No one bats an eye when rich people eat venison for dinner a couple times a week.*

Without a warrant, time, and a large enough search party, no one is going to find what's left of Shultz.

"We can't scrub his face and pretend he didn't show. There are too many people able to attest to him being here," Father argues.

"But we can downplay his overall attendance. He was invited, yes, but so were a lot of other influential guests. Not noticing him leave wouldn't be out of the ordinary," Uncle counters. "Anything to add?" he asks, looking around the room at the rest of us.

"Nathan," Victoria whispers, but the room is too quiet, and all eyes turn to her. She looks past them, directly at my father, his scowl deepening.

"Has your date become aware of our current predicament, Miss Fenwick? If so, he is not the only loose end we need to handle." My father's eyes narrow on her and I feel her hand begin to tremble in mine.

"He hasn't, but he was Shultz's student intern," I interject, drawing his ire to me instead. She stiffens, likely wondering how I knew that. My father unleashes a nuclear-level glare at the both of us, and I shift a step to block her from it. I feel her lean into my back, scared but also probably pissed at me again too.

I didn't just watch them get coffee. I used his contact information from her phone to find him anywhere I could. Online. In person. The fucking DA's office.

A classmate? Whatever. Her plus one? Royally pissed me off, but fine. She wanted space; I can respect that. Shultz's intern? That's troublesome.

So, I took it upon myself to have a look through his emails, sifting through thousands of spams and subscriptions—*and porn ads*—looking for anything sent between him and the DA's office. He's essentially an assistant to Audrey, and I'd already checked her files. She doesn't know anything other than us showing up a couple of times.

"Will he talk?" Father's temper is no less flared than earlier, but at least now I can protect Victoria from it by talking him down.

"No."

He isn't so easily convinced. Like when we'd told him Shultz wouldn't be a problem after The Rosary; he doesn't compromise. "Make sure of it. Keep an eye on him." He flicks his hand, dismissing us without another word.

I pull Victoria by the arm, leading us both out to the hall out of sight of everyone else. She needs to leave and get as far away from the scene as she can safely be for now. She's still shaking as I rush us down the stairs, but I can feel her pleading stare digging into me.

"The last person you guys kept an eye on is *rotting* downstairs," she whisper shouts, her nails digging into my arm. "Please don't hurt him, Shae."

I don't give an ever-living fuck about Nathan or his wellbeing. He's lucky he still has both of his hands after he kept putting them on her tonight, but he's an oblivious idiot with no harm coming to him unless he starts asking questions.

"Shae!" she begs again, forcing me to stop at the bottom of the stairs, making her collide with my back.

I spin to face her, jaw tight. "I won't. I didn't hurt him before; I won't do it now."

She looks up at me with aggravatingly adorable doe eyes, wondering what I mean. The pieces take a second to sink in, but then she rips her hand from mine, shoving a finger into my chest.

"You've been watching us."

Fuck, she's so beautiful when she's riled. She's in her own world most of the time, forgetting how different the one I reside in is. She doesn't look over her shoulder when she's out or notice when things are fixed in her apartment after I visit, but if given the slightest bit of insight, she'll piece everything together on her own. *Like she did with Shultz's senate campaign.*

I smile, my pride overshadowing the festering jealousy. Her jaw drops, but she doesn't step back when I advance on her.

"Did you think I'd let you go that easy, Little Fox?" So many thoughts swirl behind her clever eyes, the gears turning so fast the tips of her ears turn pink before she takes a breath. I laugh, amused by the revelation spreading over her face. "Let's get you home."

49

Victoria

APPARENTLY BY HOME, SHAE meant Laughlin Manor.

I'm in her room, sweeping my hand through the clothes hanging in her closet. *Suits on suits on suits.* Some with Maciej's tag still attached. Steam pours over the bathroom door when she opens it, crossing the room in a few strides and pressing her body into my back. The soft silk of her robe brushes the side of my neck when she leans down.

"Water's ready," she whispers, grazing my earlobe with her lips. Her hands run up my back beneath my shirt, her warmth spreading through me with each tender skim of her fingers.

Kissing my neck, she sinks her teeth into my pulse point before pulling my shirt over my head. Then the elastic from her hair, letting it drape over both of us. She cups my breasts in both palms, pulling me into her hold and rolling my nipples between her fingers. Right as I feel my body begin building with anticipation, she slips her hands away and walks to the bathroom.

The glass shower door is foggy when I step into the bathroom, but I can see her silhouette shifting through the steam clouds on the other side.

The black tile covering the walls and floor compliment the dark paint from her bedroom. *There's so much space. Her bathroom is the size of my kitchen.* A huge vanity and claw foot tub take up two of the walls, while the toilet and double shower fill the other.

I step under the second shower head, blocking the water from raining down on Shae's back. Her skin is smooth over toned muscles, defining her figure. Her shoulders are bulky but still feminine, leading down to her dimpled, narrow waist. Beneath that, her ass sits *perfectly* over her thick legs.

Suds from her shampoo run in foamy lines over a dark blotch of ink on her hip. The tattoo I barely got to glimpse when we went to The Rosary, now fully exposed. *A hissing snake, coiled around a bouquet of roses, bleeding where thorns dig into its scales.* It reminds me of the one I painted; not an exact replica, but I couldn't have been more right in my likening her to a serpent. *My temptress.* Always convincing me to stay in her catastrophic wake.

She spins, facing me with her eyes closed as she tips her head back to rinse her hair. I stroke a cautious finger through the suds and over the tattoo, tracing the design and curve of her hip, and— *Is that a scar?* I cup a handful of water and rinse away the bubbles, tracing the shape with my thumb, trying to decipher what it looks like since it's covered by ink. *Curved, but with points? Something inside a circle.*

"Sly little fox, aren't you?"

I don't know how long she's been watching me take in her body. Her chin is tucked and the water washes over her face, dripping off the end of her nose while she stares down at me. Big as the shower is, she takes up most of the space while I'm nuzzled in close, her sternum tattoo inches from my face.

Prayer hands with an upside-down crucifix, another mockery to the faith stamped on her skin. Maybe Wolf Man wasn't wrong, and she is *the devil incarnate. Either way, I don't care anymore.* As much as it scares me, I'm all in.

I lift my hands, ready to take her breasts in them, but I hesitate when her nostrils flare. Before I can back away, she pulls my wrists up, forcing my hands to her chest. For a moment I only hold them, heavy and full in my hands, until her breathing settles back to a steady rhythm. Kneading them, her nipples pull taut from my touch. Both of us rippling with goosebumps despite the heat from the water spraying down on us. The platinum barbels stuck through her stiff peaks glint against the dark rouge of her nipples.

I tease one with my thumb, mesmerized by the look of it. Her stomach tightens against mine and her chest heaves. I stop again, but she holds me in place, keeping herself planted in my palms as a breath shudders through her. "Anywhere else you'd like to explore?" she asks, her mouth slow to close and her jaw tense.

Everywhere.

Shae is the only woman I've been with. I've taken care of myself plenty, but I have no idea if she likes the same things I do. *But I want to find out.* I suck in my lip, desire pooling low in my belly. "Yes."

"Let me show you." Her hand covers mine and together we slide down her stomach and between her legs, the skin there softer and paler than the rest.

She guides my fingers over her slit, gliding us through her wetness and spreading the folds of her heated center. She pushes two of my fingers in, along with two of her own, the ribbed walls sucking us in and making my knees weak as her fingers curl mine over and over inside her in steady waves while her walls start to clench. The silkiness I expected, but her pussy is so tight even with her arousal coating the both of us. Like it isn't used to penetration.

"Mmmmm," she moans, her eyes still locked with mine, the gravely change in her voice making her so much sexier. She pulls her fingers out, leaving only mine inside, fluttering against the same spot that feels so good inside myself.

Her fist slams against the wall, hitting a button that changes the shower setting. It switches from pounding into my back to waterfalling on us as she rushes me, pressing my back into the cold wall and seizing my mouth. I flinch away from the biting tile and press into Shae's front. One of her hands bridges the space between me and the wall, keeping me warm and our bodies together.

She sucks on my tongue when I swipe it over hers, our moans fighting for dominance. I lift my foot, finding the bench for balance, and she dives her fingers into me, winding inside me faster than mine in her.

"Do *exactly* as I do," she commands, not breaking our kiss.

My knees buckle, but Shae slips a leg beneath mine as she plants a foot on the bench beside mine, making me hook around her to keep upright. I try to focus enough to follow her rhythm and pace, circling her clit with my thumb the same way she does mine, but it feels too good. *Multitasking is fucking hard when half of it involves feeling every stroke of Shae's magical fingers.*

My other leg battles to keep me standing as my muscles shake, trembling through the first waves of my orgasm. Shaelene breathes into my mouth, her smirk nearly lethal.

"That's it. Come for me, Victoria."

Every stroke is bliss, sending pure, *hot* adrenaline through my veins.

"I'm right there with you, Little Fox. Don't—*mmm*—don't stop. You feel so fucking good inside me."

God! How has it taken so long for this? This is what I was running from? "Please keep talking. I'm–I'm so close, Shae." Her grip on my back tightens and I pray she leaves bruises.

"You're doing so well. Do you feel how wet I am for you?" she asks, her fingers moving impossibly faster. "And you're built for me. So soft. So tight. So *greedy*. Is three better?" A third finger stretches me, stirring the pain from the rip earlier as she pushes it in, knuckle deep, with the others.

"Shae!" I scream, falling apart in her hand. I'm a mess, quivering and gulping for air as she keeps going, my leg tightening around her waist and riding her hand through the rest of my orgasm. I scream again when her teeth clamp on my shoulder and she growls, pulsing around my fingers as she comes in sync with me.

She slides out of me and cups my face in her hands, putting all her weight into me. "You're perfect, Victoria." Her breaths are as ragged as mine, the vein in her neck throbbing faster than I've ever seen it. "Fucking perfect."

She spins us, pulling me onto her lap, and kisses me until the water runs cold and leaves us shivering in each other's arms.

50

Victoria

NAKED BESIDE ME, COVERED only from the waist down by the blankets, Shae's arm stretches over me. Her fingers graze my back through her old Sloane t-shirt.

I run my nails over her chest, tracing circles around a nipple. "Did these hurt?" I ask.

Her breasts bounce when she laughs. "No."

"Wait, really?" I shift up onto an elbow and search her face for any sign of teasing, convinced she's lying.

"Really. I did them myself."

What! I chickened out when Macy wanted to pierce more holes in our ears at cheer camp freshman year. "Like, with ice and a sewing needle?"

"Safety pin."

My voice catches with a choke, then I let out a laugh as she grins at me.

"I was seventeen and immature. Happens to the best of us."

I doubt that. Even at seventeen, I can't imagine Shaelene being any less calculating and sure in her actions. *She found something sharp and raided the freezer to pierce herself because she wanted to, not as some teenage rite of passage.*

The quick flash of her, ten years ago, with a rag in her mouth to bite through the pain makes me giggle, then I think about doing

310

something so similar earlier at the Palazzo. My body heats at how good that pain felt.

"What about this one?" I ask, inching my hand down her stomach to her hip.

"It hurt *more,* but only because it took longer."

I shake my head, second guessing my question. "Not the tattoo." I skim my fingertips over the roughened patch of skin, too nervous to meet her eyes. *Is this too personal? She's seen my scars. Kissed them. But never asked how they got there.*

"Ah. *That,*" she sighs. "Hurt very much."

"What happened?"

"We were rebellious and drunk, wanting to do something for ourselves." When I look back, her eyes are watching my hand move beneath the blanket, a small devious smirk splitting her lips. "And *sixteen.*"

"We?" I ask. She smooths a thumb over one of my pinched brows, drawing it down my cheek and jaw before cupping my cheek in her calloused palm.

She tips her head back against the pillow, closing her eyes as she tells me the story, that damning smile never leaving her face. "The firm won a big case, and all the adults were celebrating. Shephard swiped a bottle of our father's vintage scotch, and we hid out in Shaun's room drinking as our own celebration of sorts. After it was half gone, one of us hatched the genius idea to solidify the 'Unholy Triad' rumor. So, while they kept watch, I snuck into Father's office and stole his wax seal."

"You *branded* yourselves?" *I'll need Botox by twenty-five with the way this family makes my brows raise.* "What even is it?"

"Our initials. And our father's. And Uncle's. Really bad for business in hindsight."

I drop my head back to her chest, enamored but horrified. "How did your father react?"

"You've met him." She shrugs, losing a bit of the light in her eyes.

I have, and I can only imagine the ass chewing that came from him after.

"I'm—"

The door opens a half second after someone knocks. We both perk up as Shaun enters, still in his tux, throwing his arm up over his eyes while Shaelene pulls the blanket up.

"Oh, goddammit, Shae! Jesus!" He flusters, keeping his eyes pressed behind his elbow.

"Knock next time!" she barks, annoyed. She pulls the comforter further over top of me, making sure my bare bottom half stays covered.

"I did. Just— Get dressed. I need to show you something." He walks out, the door falling closed behind him.

When she gets up, I see it's almost three in the morning. "Get some sleep. I'll be right back," she says, kissing me and slipping into a pair of sweats and a t-shirt.

I wake up to the bed still empty beside me. I don't know how long I've slept, and my eyes are too hazy to read the clock, so I turn over and reach for my phone. Pulling it off the charger, the bright LED display burns my drowsy eyes.

4:27 AM

It's been over an hour since Shaun came to grab Shaelene. I pull the covers away and swing my legs off the side of the bed, ready to go look for her, but a shadow at the other side of the room stops me. "Shae?" I call out.

The glow of my phone's screen makes it impossible to see anything in the dark room clearly, so I shine it toward the closet. The black mass forms into shape as it steps into view. Tall shoulders wrapped in an expensive wool suit tower in front of me before he leans down to meet me face to face.

The snarling face of a golden wolf lunges for me, metal teeth sinking deep into my cheek.

I open my eyes again, the room bright from the table lamp and Shaelene hovering over me, eyes panicked. And my face on fire.

My chest surges beneath Shae's hold, trying to come down from my terror. *In through the nose, out through the mouth.*

"What's going on?" I croak through the cotton-thick dryness in my throat.

"You were screaming, and I couldn't get you to wake up," she murmurs, her shaky hand finding mine.

It was just a dream. Another fucking nightmare... But the pain felt so real. My cheek is warm when I run my hand over it, a twinge of guilt sweeping across Shaelene's face when I do. "Did you hit me?"

"*Ma fraise...* I had to. I tried calling your name and shaking you, but you wouldn't snap out of it," she confesses, her shoulders rounding in an unusual sign of defeat. I'm not angry, not even a little bit. I know she'd never hurt me from a place of anger. *She must've been desperate if she resorted to violence when I didn't ask for it.* "You scared the hell out of me," she whispers, pressing her forehead against mine. "What happened?"

I shake her question off, wanting to forget the horror that just played out in my head. "Nothing. Just a bad dream," I lie.

She doesn't buy it, refusing to budge when I try to sit up. *I really need her to move because my mouth is so damn dry. I need water.*

I sigh when she raises her perfect brows at me impatiently, scooting myself up to sit beside her. "It was about someone I spoke to at the party. He was attacking me, and I don't know why."

"Who?"

"I don't know. He kept his mask on. His eyes were pale like yours, but looked..." I trail off, pulling my knees to my chest and burying my face between them. I really, *really* don't want to talk about this anymore. My tongue feels like it's stuck to the roof of my mouth, but she keeps pushing for answers.

"Looked *what*, Victoria?"

I stammer a bit before finding the right words. "Dead? I guess. Kind of soulless, like he had no emotion at all except for this weird smirk. And an old looking scar on his lips I saw when he was talking. He had an accent too. Not like Luca's though. Some other European country, maybe? I don't know, I only paid attention to what he said, not so much how it sounded."

Her face stills, but the heat of a thousand suns blazes behind those merciless eyes. She takes a useless calming breath. "What. Did. He. Say?"

I don't want to tell her. His opinion isn't mine, but saying the words out loud makes me feel guilty—like I'll hurt her feelings. I shy away from her face, picking at the sides of my nail, as I think.

I'm sure she's heard worse, but I don't want her to think I believe him. She's not the bad person he says she is; she's a survivor. She all but said the words in the pool room. She needs to take control just like I need someone to control me. It's how we've learned to cope, and

Mr. Wolf doesn't know the slightest bit of what she's gone through to become the fierce woman she is.

She notices my hesitation and rubs her thumb over my knuckles, a silent reminder that she can't be angry with me. That she won't be upset at me for repeating it.

"He said you were the devil," I admit, my voice barely a whisper.

When I peek up at her, she squints with a chuckle, looking down at our laps. She shakes her head, glancing back up at me, the light-heartedness gone from her expression. "What did his mask look like?"

"A wolf."

Her neck pops as she slowly turns, jaw locked tight. *If she's this hostile, I need to be more worried.* Alarm bells blare in my head, sending my heart racing. *She knows who I'm talking about. She knows, and she isn't happy.*

"Come on," she says, pulling me out of bed and cinching a pair of shorts tight around my waist. She bangs a heavy fist on both Shaun and Shephard's doors while we stomp quickly down the hall.

"The fuck, Shae?" Shephard groans when he opens his door, rubbing a bruised knuckle against his eye.

She doesn't stop to explain, pulling us through the manor. The boys fall in line behind us before we reach another closed door. Shaelene pushes it open without knocking, smacking the knob into the wall with a *crack* that sounds like plaster breaking.

Silas is at his desk, working out the minute details of his plan, Simon behind him sipping from a steaming mug of coffee. *Clearly neither of them has slept since leaving the Angelini's.*

"You need to tell us everything you and Grigorio have been discussing in secret. *Now*," Shaelene demands.

PART THREE

Sentencing

51

THE BOYS GO STIFF hearing me address Father with such an aggravated tone. Usually, I'm the one keeping the peace, never asking questions and always following orders, but I'm pissed. Formalities no longer matter.

His eyes narrow, anger filled but maintaining their resolve. "No."

The tension in the room is so thick it threatens to suffocate us all, but I'm not about to cower now. *Not when* he *was here. Not when he was close enough to speak to Victoria. Close enough to hurt her—*

Shephard finally cuts the silence. "Shae, it's fucking early. Get on with it."

"He's here," I snarl.

"Who?"

"Shae," Shaun urges, reaching for me.

I swat his hand away. I don't want to hold his thumb and calm down. I want some fucking answers.

I lean across the desk and keep my gaze locked with Father's, waiting for him to stop shutting us out before someone else ends up dead.

"Gedeon," he says, confirming everything I've suspected.

Of course he knows who I'm talking about. The asshole has been holding out on us for weeks, but thanks to Victoria, it's all falling into place.

"He was at the party. I'm willing to bet he's the one that killed Shultz," I say, already sure what his response will be.

"*That's* who you think was in the wolf mask?" Shaun asks. Beside me, Victoria turns sharply, swapping her gaze back and forth trying to figure out how he knew about it.

That's the reason he barged in and stole me away from my little fox. While altering the Angelini's security footage, he was deleting the feed of the billiards room like I'd asked but saw something else in there. Something neither of us expected.

After Victoria and I left, someone came in wearing a mask identical to the one she described.

I foolishly hoped he wasn't who I thought he was, but Victoria's recount of their conversation was the unfortunate final nail in the coffin.

"Sorry. Who—who is Gedeon?" she asks, her voice meek.

My brothers answer at the same time, their voices monotonous and dry. "Our cousin."

Our goddamn cousin. Gedeon Vasiliev is the only son of our uncle, Maxim, the head of the Russian mob in Moscow. *And the bane of my fucking existence.*

He hasn't been stateside, to my knowledge at least, since my brothers and I were fifteen and him a year younger. It was the first and only time any of us can remember being graced with his insufferable presence.

Our mother was Maxim's younger sister and aside from their not so courteous visit in our youth, the Vasilievs have been distant all our lives.

Until the sick fuck managed to sneak his way into our birthday party, talk to my girl, and steal the bloody rag I tossed aside in the pool room.

The footage showed Gedeon entering the billiards room from a door on the south side, which means he somehow managed to escape the crowded ballroom unnoticed. He must've just finished killing Shultz, ducking into one of the other hallways to avoid being seen, and been waiting for us to leave.

Who knows how long he stood in the dark watching us. My blood boils at the idea of him seeing even an inch of Victoria. Then he went and took the rag I cleaned her up with. *He's a sadistic bastard, and now he has a piece of her.* Thinking about it sets a pit in my stomach, which is why I won't tell Victoria the truth of it.

"It would seem you don't need me to tell you, Shaelene. Anything else you'd like to share?" my father asks, baiting me. Prodding me to learn what else I've figured out. He's well aware I don't know the details of his discussions with Grigorio since it's all been behind closed doors. Even Luca doesn't know more than it having to do with Milano's murder.

That's it. Another piece falls into place.

"I know Gedeon killed Milano, but he doesn't do anything without Maxim's order. Tell us why he'd order the hit along with whatever retribution you and the Angelinis are plotting."

He smirks with a huff, proud of me for being so smart, but more than upset with my insubordination. He stands, smoothing his hands over his chest, making no progress flattening the wrinkles in his shirt, and rounds the desk. "Sit," he commands, pointing to the same four chairs we all sat in on Victoria's first day.

Robotically, we collapse into the seats, my fingers hastily tapping on my thigh.

He's grappling for control. Making us sit while he and our uncle stand and look down at us is a tactic I see right through. "Maxim has been trying for decades to run guns through Grigorio's wine shipping routes. Wanting to put them in casks to bypass customs. Grigorio refused, and it put them on bad terms," he says, angry, restless knuckles rapping against the desktop behind him. "Those terms have grown decidedly *worse* in recent weeks. Maxim is tired of waiting."

"Guns for who?" Shaun asks.

Uncle sighs and places his mug on the desk, running a tired hand through his hair. He opens his mouth, but Father gets the words out first, "We don't know. He wouldn't apprise Grigorio of that information, which is partly why he refused." His knuckles crack loudly before he crosses his arms, hiding them beneath his biceps.

I don't miss Uncle's split-second, narrowed gaze at my father before he speaks. "Vasiliev has been attempting to tank Grigorio's trade as a way to get him to change his mind, but none of it has worked. The Angelinis' ties to their motherland are strong enough to thwart off Maxim's threats thus far."

I nod in understanding. "He sent Gedeon to make it personal."

"Yes," he confirms. "Shooting Milano in the middle of the city while he was out with his kids made this *very* personal. Grigorio wants to turn to war."

Victoria has lost all color in her face, the usual pink flush under her freckles washed white with shock. She's taking it all in—the scandal, the particulars of our family's tie to the mob, the casual way we talk about hit men and international war between gangs—probably wondering how she ended up in the middle of it all.

I'm still wondering the same thing. *Why the hell, of all the times to take on a student intern, did my father choose* her? *Why* now? A lump of unease forms in my throat.

She raises her hand like we're in one of her lectures, waiting to be called on to ask her question. My father raises a brow. "Yes?"

She lowers her hand, chewing the inside of her cheek before she asks, "How does the DA fit into all of this?"

He smiles at her initiative. "Excellent question, Miss Fenwick." His praise eases some of the anxiousness stirring inside her and her shoulders relax, sinking the weight in my gut deeper.

He knowingly put her in danger by allowing her to work here.

"A frame job. District Attorney Shultz was building a case against the Angelinis, claiming business tax fraud as a means to dig for more information on all of us."

With Shultz missing, investigators will no doubt go through his case files to look for suspects. *What better motive than stopping someone from sending you to prison and destroying your family's livelihood?* Doing it at the Palazzo threw means right into Grigorio's lap. *He'll be the FBI's first suspect.* And we don't have a lot of feds on our payroll right now.

My phone buzzes against my leg, but I ignore it—too invested in how we're going to stop Gedeon without landing ourselves in a shit ton more trouble.

"Our original plan was to arrange a meeting with Vasiliev *here* where we could mediate a possible solution that would benefit all parties," Uncle explains. "But our ties with the Russians aren't what they used to be after—"

My phone buzzes two more times, and I draw it from my pocket with an irritated growl to silence it, but the notifications from the cameras in Victoria's apartment steal all my focus.

(1) MOTION DETECTED: FRONT DOOR
(2) MOTION DETECTED: KITCHEN
(3) MOTION DETECTED: BEDROOM

52

Victoria

SHAELENE GROANS, CUTTING OFF the rest of Simon's explanation of frayed ties with the Russians.

First, I get acquainted with the Italian Mafia, then I plan a party with most of New York's biggest gangsters in attendance, and now I find out my girlfriend's—Are we labeling ourselves?—uncle heads the Russian mob, and his son is in town murdering people for revenge. Great first month of my internship...

Everyone is looking at her, but she ignores us, a frenzied look on her face as she stares at her phone instead.

"After Shaelene's refusal," Silas states, keeping his eyes pinned angrily on Shaelene.

Refusal? Until ten minutes ago, I didn't know Gedeon Vasiliev existed. "Refusal to do what?" I ask, trying to fill in the bits everyone is conveniently leaving out. No one answers, making the anxiety rolling around in my gut grow.

Shae is still lasered in on her phone, and Silas is the same but on her. Shaun's face is red, and his knuckles are white as he grips the arm of his chair. Shephard turns away from everyone and up to the ceiling, his eyes pinched tightly shut. The only one that acknowledges me is Simon, but his eyes are full of defeat.

"To be with him," Simon deadpans, his shoulders falling as he looks at his niece.

I can't contain the laugh bubbling out of me. This is all completely ridiculous. *Of course she refused! That's her cousin... And she's gay!*

Silas' unsettling glare shifts to me, unamused by my *apparent* amusement. "Oh... Y–you're serious?"

"Very," he answers. "Maxim lost his sister when the triplets were born. His solution for keeping the families on the same side involved arranging for Shaelene to marry Gedeon and relocate to Moscow," he says, shooting a sidelong look at Shae. Her eyes still glued to her phone, not hearing a word he's saying.

"But he's her cousin..."

None of them bat an eye.

Simon sighs. "Kings used to marry their sisters, Ms. Fenwick. The Vasilievs are Russian royalty, and if pairing Gedeon with his cousin meant Maxim had a way of keeping us in check, he was going to do it," he says, explaining things in the gentlest of terms.

My heart breaks at the thought of Shaelene being subjected to an arranged marriage and shipped off against her will. To be a pawn in her uncle's game. She wasn't though. *She refused*. But I get the feeling it was more than her just saying no.

'*The same reason you want me to...*'

The words she said to me last night. *It all comes down to control.* She needs it, and I think Gedeon tried to take it from her the same way Sterling did me.

She jumps out of her seat, charging from the room without a word. The rest of us watch, listening as she heads further into the manor. The boys stand, ready to follow her, and I follow suit right as Silas speaks behind me.

"Leave. We'll continue this later."

53

Shaelene

Someone was in Victoria's apartment.

Someone was in Victoria's apartment, and it *wasn't* Gedeon.

No mask. No disguise at all, but I didn't recognize his face either. He left while Uncle was busy talking, and I refuse to waste any more time sitting and discussing my unfortunate engagement. Victoria and my brothers enter my room as my head slips through my hoodie.

"Where are you going?" Shephard barks.

I don't look at any of them, grabbing my gun from the table beside my reading chair and checking the magazine before racking a round into the chamber. "Someone was in Victoria's apartment."

Victoria's eyes go wide. "What? How do you—"

"I put up cameras. My phone alerted me while we were in Father's office. I watched him ransack the place."

"Gedeon?" Shaun asks, and I shake my head. His hand claps Shephard on the shoulder, the two of them heading back to their rooms to gear up. They'll come with me to check things out; the hard part is going to be convincing Victoria to stay here. It isn't safe for her to go back there. I chance a look at her while stuffing my pistol into the waistband of my pants.

If she'd been at home, she'd be dead. The cameras wouldn't have helped. The drive from the manor back into the city is too long, even if I raced there on my bike. *I could've lost her tonight.* My teeth ache from the tight set of my jaw.

By herself and locked in my room is the safest she can be right now. If this person is working for Gedeon, it's bad enough I led him to her in the first place. *They could have all her information already.* It was easy enough for me to get a hold of myself, and whoever this was had access inside of her home. Who knows what they found or why they want it.

"You what?" Victoria screams, her arms flailing. "When? *How?* You don't even have a key!"

Slipping my boots on, I fish in my pocket for my wallet, pulling out the key card I made with her stolen data. I flash it at her, and she gasps, her jaw hanging open as she thinks of what to yell at me for next.

"Shae! That is such an invasion of pri—"

"Did you forget I got you off from the window across the street? I've been watching you for *weeks*. Even after you didn't want me to. I can't stop." I run a hand over her shoulder, grounding myself more than her. "I *have* to see you. To make sure you're safe."

It's the truth. The doormen in her building don't offer any security, and she's too blindly naive to be left in charge of her own care. *Look where one night and a few phone calls got us.*

"Be angry if you want, but those cameras just saved your life," I start, an image of Victoria bruised and bloody and broken flashing through my mind. "I can't let you out of my sight. I just... *Can't.*"

Shaun and Shephard return, knocking on the wall beside the open door.

"Stay here. We'll be back soon," I tell her.

She scoffs, crossing her arms over her chest. "You just said I can't leave your sight, and now you want me to wait *here* while you go on your own?" I don't say anything, knowing it'll only take her a couple of seconds to realize. "Oh my god! You have cameras in here too?" she yells, rolling her eyes and searching the ceiling.

I let a smile lift the corner of my mouth. *The tip of her nose turns the same shade of pink as her nipples when she's angry and it's fucking adorable.* Sometimes I hate that I can't bring myself to be angry with her. Even when she's refusing to listen, she makes me feel at peace and stressed as hell at the same damn time. *I am so in love with this girl. Too in love.* My smile evaporates, my spine straightening. *My feelings for her are what led someone straight to her apartment.*

She grabs the sweatpants I changed out of and drags them over her shorts, pulling the drawstring as tight as it can go before cuffing the legs a few times. She's swallowed by my clothes, and I can't help but soften at the sight.

"I'm coming with you," she insists, striding toward the hallway and refusing to look back.

"Vic—"

She's already out the door, pushing herself between my brothers as she marches off. I want to argue, to call her back in here and tie her to the bed because *something* in my gut knows that whatever is happening isn't coincidental. But we don't have time. The longer we wait, the more time Gedeon has to set up whatever plan he's hatching. I take a deep breath through my nose and roll my shoulders, yanking a second hoodie from a hanger in my closet.

Shaun and Shephard stand in the hall, all three of us able to hear Victoria stomping down the stairs. They wait for me, brows perked and arms crossed, waiting for an order.

"You heard her."

54

Victoria

SHEPHARD BARRELS PAST ME in the garage, taking the front seat before I can jump in, leaving me stuck sitting in the seat behind Shae as she races us into the city. My stomach pitches when she hits eighty on the freeway, but it's the recording Shaun watches beside me that really puts me at unease. *Seeing that creep wander around my apartment, throwing all my things around...* I can't watch after he enters my bedroom. *Shae's right.* If she hadn't put in the cameras, we wouldn't have even known he was there, and I might've been home the next time he or Gedeon came snooping. I untuck myself from my spot against the door and lean forward, resting my chin on the seat back beside Shaelene.

She tilts her head, her cheek brushing my nose. "What is it, Little Fox? You finished sulking?" she teases.

I am, though I don't want to admit it so easily.

"No," I taunt. "I have a question."

Her ear wiggles slightly when she smiles, eyes still on the road ahead of her. It's cute and soft, such a stark contrast to the side of her that matches the rumors. *I want more of this.*

"How long have the cameras been there?"

Her sneaky smile widens before she answers, "A while."

I roll my eyes. She knows that isn't the answer I want. I want a date. *I want to know what she's seen.* Her eyes meet mine for a second before she looks back at the road.

"Don't worry, Little Fox," she whispers. "Your secret toy stash is safe with me."

I flush at her wink in the rearview mirror, embarrassment written across my cheeks. *That means they've been up since before she visited me. She still watched me the days she wasn't stalking me from across the street.*

A memory flashes of a runner in a bulky hoodie like the one she's wearing now. Her hair swaying after she bumps into me. *God, she's been everywhere, and I've never noticed.* I spent—*wasted*—so much time thinking she wouldn't want me when she hasn't even tried to stray.

Shephard clears his throat, splitting the growing sensuality between Shae and I, and I curl back into my seat, pulling the hood of the sweatshirt she gave me over my head for the rest of the drive.

She opens my door and gives me her hand like usual, keeping me tucked close against her side while we make our way up the elevator.

My front door is cracked open, the wooden frame splintered where the deadbolt used to be.

Shaelene steers me across the hall, my back rattling the art framed on the wall. "Don't move." Every muscle in my body stiffens, and I don't stray an inch from where she put me as she turns to face her brothers. "Shephard first. Clear the open space then the left rooms. Hallway, spare bedroom, then bath. Shaun, take the half bath and laundry closet." They nod, pulling their guns and quietly making their way inside. Shae keeps herself in front of me, eyes trained on the doorway with her pistol ready in her hands. A knot forms in my throat as I look around the corridor. *What if my neighbor comes out and sees her with a gun? Or someone comes out of the elevator and—*

My eye catches the security camera in the corner. "Shae, there's a camera." My hands shake as I hold the backs of her arms, her muscles tense beneath her hoodie.

"Not an issue," she says, not taking her eyes off the threshold. On the other side of her, Shephard and Shaun emerge from the hall, giving her a subtle thumbs up before disappearing past the doorway toward my bedroom. She whirls on me, her face hard and focused. Embodying every bit of the nefarious triplet she's rumored to me. All sense of flirtation from earlier struck from her expression. "Keep your hand here," she orders, forcing my hand to ball up the fabric on the back of her jacket. "When I move you move. Say yes so I know you understand."

"Y–yes," I say with a swallow.

Her steps are slow and quiet when we get inside, gracefully dodging the mess of utensils and other things strewn across the floor. Mine aren't nearly as graceful, but I keep up with her until we meet up with the boys near my bedroom door.

Shae's head juts and Shaun falls in line behind me, close enough that I can feel his stomach against my back. Shephard surveys the front door one final time before looking to Shae, and mouthing a count to three. She rears back, and I hear the sound of her boot connecting with the door and then the knob slamming into the wall inside.

Before I can take a step to follow her, Shaun wraps his arm around me and spins us away from the open room, his body crouching over mine until we hear both Shae and Shephard shout. "CLEAR!"

Shaun stands, and I feel hands on my shoulders, but they aren't his. Shae pulls me into her chest, the slightest of hitches in her breath as she kisses the top of my head.

"I'm okay," I say, though I'm not sure why because I feel anything but. My heart feels like someone is holding tight and squeezing, like an emotional version of the way my apartment looks. I feel violated in a way Sterling never made me feel.

"Yes. You are," she murmurs, squeezing me again. The crunch of glass has me moving to see the catastrophe in my room.

My mattress is flipped upside down, hanging halfway off the far side of my bed frame. The built-in storage beneath is open and my art supplies thrown everywhere. My dresser is scooted out from the wall, all of the drawers pulled out and my clothes litter the floor. Nothing was left untouched.

"At least they didn't take the good stuff," Shephard laughs, pinching a lacy, pink thong between his fingers near my dresser. I squeal, jumping over the mess to reach for it, and he tosses it to Shaun before I can snatch it out of his hand. I slam the drawer closed, but he moves his hand just before his knuckles get smashed. *I swear to God, if he saw everything beneath my underwear, I will pass away before Gedeon gets the chance to kill me.*

Shaun holds the panties out for me, an annoyingly handsome smirk on his face. I yank them from his grasp, tossing them onto the pile of clothes on the floor.

Stepping over it, I hear the crunch of glass again, realizing one of the picture frames I kept on my desk is in pieces on the rug. I bite my lip, instantly recognizing the frame and that my graduation photo is missing. *The one of me and my parents.* So far, it's the only thing I notice is gone.

Until I survey the disaster of my bed closer. The pillows are scattered and blankets tossed. My journal nowhere in sight. I pat one of the pillows in hopes it stayed in the case when it got thrown across the room. *No, no, no.* The only other place it'd be is my bedside table, but both drawers are empty, the contents dumped onto the floor in front of it.

The thief took the only two things that could ruin me. I choke on the knot growing in my throat. *He could use that photo to find my parents, but what would he do with them? Ransom? Blackmail? Worse?* And the notebook. Every. Single. Detail. Of Sterling and his friends' abuse jotted down in ink, blotted by tear drop stains on half its pages. *What if that gets out? I'll never recover. I'll lose myself again...*

I glance at Shaelene, icy chills dripping down my back. *She* cannot *find out about Sterling.* I don't want her looking at me differently. She already thinks I'm something I'm not. She thinks I'm strong for letting myself crave what I really want, but that isn't true. I'm weak for needing pain to give me pleasure. *I should be able to fall into bliss without it; like someone fucking normal.*

I don't think she's noticed my small freak out yet. She's by the windows, staring through the bright glare of the morning sun at her old building. She turns, pulling her phone from her pocket and tapping at her screen without looking up. "Anything missing in here?"

"Just a picture."

Her head shoots upright at the same time she locks her phone and slides it inside her pocket. "What picture?"

I pick up the broken frame and turn it over in my hands. "Me at graduation with my parents. Shae, you don't think..." I start, my bottom lip beginning to tremble—my breath getting shakier with each word. *I need to make sure they didn't take anything else!*

I run through the mess and back into the kitchen. Pulling open the freezer and flinging a pack of frozen waffles into the sink, I slide a stack of pizzas out of the way.

"Victoria, what're you—" Shae starts behind me, but when she sees me holding a frosty freezer bag she stops. I break off the chunks of freezer burn and peel the bag open, letting out a relieved sigh when I know everything is still there.

I grab a new bag for all my papers—one that won't melt in my lap on the drive home. Shae leans over my shoulder, looking at the documents laid out on the counter, while Shaun and Shephard take turns eyeing me like I'm crazy for keeping medical records and my birth certificate beside a bunch of TV dinners.

When I finish repacking it all, I let my nerves settle and explain. "In case there's a fire. I don't have a safe, and apparently burglars don't check the freezer when looking for stuff to steal." I shrug, more than a little embarrassed with the way the boys keep looking at me.

Shae grips my arms from behind me and kisses my cheek. "It's smart, *ma fraise.*" I lean into her hold, feeling better knowing she isn't secretly laughing at me too. "Is anything missing?"

I shake my head. "Not from here." I look toward my bedroom, my thoughts still on my journal.

"Good. We need to check something," she says, an ache in her voice.

55

I LEAD VICTORIA INTO my old apartment.

I hadn't thought to check the camera in here until I saw the state of Victoria's place. They were looking for something, anything, they could use against the family. I know it. *Gedeon and his minions have been following us longer than just last night.* If he's been in the states since the attack on Milano, he could've been tracking us this whole time. Of course he'd know about my apartment too.

My suspicions were all but confirmed when I checked the camera. Unlike the ones I used in Victoria's, this one ran a live feed instead of a recording, so I didn't catch anyone on it, but I can see something on the corner of the desk that wasn't there when I moved my belongings out.

Technically, my lease isn't up until the end of the month, which makes today the lucky last day I have to get in here. *Gedeon did always like to play games... Happy fucking Halloween.*

Sometimes I hate being correct all the time. On the corner of the desk is a folded-up slip of paper. An origami rabbit. When I unfurl it, there are two words scribbled across it in his unmistakable handwriting.

Davai pobeseduem.

Let's chat.

No way in hell am I speaking with Gedeon, and he sure as shit isn't getting anywhere near Victoria again.

She walks into the room quietly, but her eyes say more than her mouth could as she takes in her stalker's bedroom. I crumple the paper in my hand and shove it into my pocket before she can see.

"Wow," she says on a sigh. "You really can see everything from here."

Her back is to me while she looks across the small alley toward her own apartment. With her curtains torn down, we can make out the features of her trashed bedroom and the disarray of her couch in the living room. She follows my brothers as they bounce around her space, fixing everything back the way it was.

She faces me, her somber eyes round with anticipation of what I'll do or say next. *She's scared. So scared, and it's all my fault.*

I step on the bed, wrinkling the old comforter as I reach up and pluck the camera from the vent. Victoria watches me, her eyes lingering on my stomach where the hem of my hoodie lifts and exposes my waist before crawling up the length of my arm, watching my fingers twist and pull the camera out of place. Goosebumps trickle across my skin. *There are bigger issues at play. Fucking her on this bed while in your brothers' line of sight isn't going to solve them.*

I wait an extra beat before slipping the camera into my pocket, then drop from the bed directly in front of her.

Her shoulders are tense, my mouth thinning at the sight. They've barely relaxed since she found Shultz. I brush my fingers along her neck feeling all the tension she's carrying. "I won't let him hurt you, Little Fox."

Tears flood her eyes, threatening to spill over at any moment, but she wipes them away and turns back to the window. Slipping my arms around her from behind, I rest my chin on the pillow of curls her messy bun forms.

We both look silently at her apartment, watching my brothers put her living room back in order. Well, Shaun anyway. Shephard is on the couch helping himself to the leftovers from Victoria's fridge. She laughs when Shaun snaps a dish towel at him, but it's sharp and quickly turns into a stifled sob which makes me clutch her harder.

I told the boys to keep the cameras intact in case Gedeon or his associate decides to return, making sure Victoria knows it's safer to remain at the manor.

I doubt Gedeon will return though. Trashing Victoria's place was a scare tactic to get us here and for me to find his note. My hold tightens until Victoria gasps. *Chat about what? After all these years, there's nothing to discuss.*

Whatever his father and the Angelinis are planning has nothing to do with Victoria, but he's smart enough to know he can use her as a weapon against me. *And I know he's not above doing so.*

We have to figure out a way to stop him from getting any closer. If that means taking him out and potentially making the rift between us and the Russians worse, then so be it. *I'll kill all of them if it means keeping Victoria safe.*

My eyes meet hers in the glass. They're still watery, but she's lowered her guard, letting herself sink into my chest and relax.

"Let's get you home. We have a lot to talk about."

56

Victoria

HOME. THAT DAMN WORD again. Laughlin Manor is starting to feel like the only one I have now.

Shaelene assured me she'd restock my wardrobe since I didn't pack anything. I just wanted to get out of that apartment as soon as I could. It doesn't feel like it's mine anymore. But the only clothes I have at Laughlin Manor right now are Shae's. *I can't show up to Silas' office in another of Shae's tees and sweats.*

The four of us sit comfortably on the floor in Shaun's room, my legs sprawled across Shaelene's lap while we chow down on our drive-thru breakfast. Shae pulled over without me having to ask the first time she heard my stomach growl from the passenger seat, the boys perking up from their squished spots in the back. She made them cram into the rear row on the way back, keeping her hand entwined with mine the whole drive.

Between bites, the three of them toss around ideas of how to handle our Gedeon situation. Shaelene pulls a wrinkly paper from her pocket, translating the message for me and making it blatantly clear she has no intentions of speaking with him ever again.

"He left that note for you, Shae. Not Father. Not Grigorio. *You.* You're not the least bit curious about what he has to say?" Shaun asks.

Shaelene shakes her head, chewing through the last bite of her pancakes. "I have no desire to listen to a word he has to say." She swipes her napkin across her lips. "In fact, it'd please me more if he were unable to speak ever again."

I wash down a choking bite of bacon with my drink and turn to her, concern etched across my face. "Wouldn't talking to him and finding a resolution be better than letting him continue to torment us until he gets what he wants?" The words come out a bit more brazen than intended, and Shaun and Shephard are on the same page as her, leaving me once again in the dark because of my lack of knowledge. Aside from their quick explanation of Shaelene's marriage refusal, I don't know anything about Gedeon except that he's their cousin and they *loathe* him.

All three of them cast their eyes on me in surprise, and I sit up straighter as I steel my spine. "I only ask because you've all made him out to be dangerous enough he's got both Grigorio *and* your father rattled. He already came after me once." Shaelene flinches, looking away from me to the floor. "I need to know what I'll be facing if he decides to do it again."

"You won't be facing anything because I won't let him near you," she growls still not meeting my eye.

"An entire army of paid guards didn't stop him from killing Derek, so excuse me if I feel a little exposed with only you three there to stop him!" Silence envelopes the four of us, and my legs shake in her lap. "Shaelene, I'm sorry. It's just— I..."

Shaelene's eyes gloss with hurt, the sting of my words hitting her by surprise. But just as quickly as the pain appears, it's replaced by fear. "If you want to know something, ask it."

She doesn't actually want me to. I'm sure she wants me to move on and forget Gedeon exists just as much as she wishes she could.

But if I'm going to be any help in this situation, I need to know whose target I am.

"What happened between you and Gedeon?"

Seething. That's the word I'd used to describe Shae's demeanor to anyone that could see it right now. Her jaw is flexed tight, fighting to find restraint to keep from lashing out. She said she couldn't be mad at me, no matter what, but Gedeon brings out the worst in her. *Even just mentioning him breaks her control.*

The floor creaks beneath Shephard and when I look over, he's looking at me with his arms flexed, ready to reach for Shaun, whose face is glazed with pain as he looks at his sister.

Her hands wrap around my legs, and she shifts them like she's about to stand, but then decides against it, putting them in her lap again and tapping her nails against my shin. Every silent second passing without her talking only works to cement my suspicions about Gedeon.

He's her Sterling.

"We were teenagers the last time he was here," Shaelene starts, eyes unflinchingly locked with mine. Shaun and Shephard both straighten as she begins the backstory I've been ignorant of this whole time. "Maxim showed up, unannounced, telling Father his expectations for the engagement. He'd been planning something. I don't remember what, but he made it clear he needed the firm on his side. Always. Whatever it took for Father and Uncle to represent the Vasiliev name, regardless of whom they may go against in court. It didn't make much sense at the time. The three of us thought all of his business took place in Russia, but I believe it was all a very *long* game. And he's only now making his next move."

Her eyes flick to her brothers, something unsaid rippling between the three of them and giving me only a second of respite before she's boring through me again as she continues. "I was to marry Gedeon and be relocated to Moscow as insurance for our father's cooperation."

My heart squeezes painfully, her resigned acceptance tearing me apart. The heat of her stare no longer burning its way through me.

The shame in her voice does.

"Shae, no one blames you for refusing. For him to threaten your family with such an outrageous proposal—"

"I accepted."

I blink, confused and blindsided. "What? But I thought... But Simon said..." I stammer.

"I accepted," she says again, her voice quiet. "It was the right thing to do, or so I thought." Her nail traces the length of her thumb, her eyes unfocused. "If it meant keeping the peace and pleasing Father, I was going to go along with it. The marriage contract was drafted that same night. Gedeon and I signed it."

I shake in place, the floor feeling like slick tile beneath me as I reach my hands to her for mutual comfort. "Shae, you were a minor. Surely you knew—"

"The fine print stated the nuptials wouldn't go into effect until I turned eighteen," she interrupts. "Until then, I was permitted to remain in the states."

None of this makes sense. "But Simon said you refused. I don't understand..."

She tilts her head toward the ceiling, sucking in a slow breath. My hand, still placed on her knee, not held. Her distance and guard are up, hating having to explain her past to me.

"They were staying at the manor a few more days before flying back." She takes another deep breath while the boys hold theirs across from us. "Gedeon found me in the library." She sets her jaw tight again, holding the rest of her words in.

"Shae," I whisper, gently pulling her chin down to face me. "Tell me."

I plead with her silently, desperate for her to trust me with this truth. Through the tears starting to pool in my eyes. Tears not of pity but of assurance that she can tell me anything. That I'll understand. That I will love her through anything, the same way I have faith she'll do so for me.

She swallows, and I watch the lump of insecurity escape down her throat while she takes her hand in mine.

"He tried his best to flatter me, but I remained indifferent. It was just another job I had to complete." Her voice cracks, and the boys shift uncomfortably. "He told me he couldn't wait three years to have me. That he'd make right on his *husbandly duties* before he left. He grabbed both my wrists and tried to pull me into him, and when I shoved him away, he laughed. It was the worst noise I'd ever heard. It wasn't angry or nervous... It was like he wanted me to put up a fight. He wanted me scared."

My heart strings are officially torn. Ripped apart with every triggering detail of Gedeon's assault on her.

"He closed in on me and clawed at my shirt, ripping the buttons apart. Before I could scream, he put his hand over my mouth and pinched my nose. He threatened to suffocate me until I passed out. Said he'd take his fill whether I was awake or not."

I close my eyes, taking it all in, trying to brave my own fears to be strong for her.

Beside me, Shaun's knuckles crack, his balled-up hands shaking. Shephard—sitting angrily beside him—keeps his eyes narrowed on the wooden slats of the floor.

"After that, he threw me onto a chair and pinned himself against me. Grabbing and licking where he could. Moaning and talking to me so casually, like he wasn't threatening to rape me. When he started to tug on my pants, I knew I couldn't cooperate with him anymore. I couldn't sit back and let it happen, so I grabbed the letter opener from the side table..." Her breaths are controlled but still rise and fall heavy in her chest.

My eyes widen, knowing what she's about to say next. "His scar."

Her lips curl before they flatten into a thin line. "Before he could put his mouth on me any lower, I kicked him off and slashed it across his face. He screamed, blood gushing down his chin onto me. That's when Shaun walked in."

I turn and see him white knuckling his fists in his lap. Head down, eyes blank with rage. Beside him, Shephard's discomfort turns to disgust.

"Shephard had to pull him off before he killed Gedeon. Father and Uncle came in after that, whisking him back to Maxim. They left the next morning and haven't been back until now."

"Shae, I'm so sorry."

"Don't," she pleads. "Don't be sorry for a damn thing. You had no part in that. I should be apologizing for getting you involved in this mess."

"You didn't. Your father—" I try to say.

"Did what he had to. Maxim gave him no choice, and I went along with it." Her solemn eyes are dull with grief. "I should've refused before making things worse."

She can't change the past, no matter how much she wishes she could, I know that from experience, but what we *can* do is plan for the future. *We are going to come up with a plan to get Gedeon out of the U.S.*

"Can I ask you one more thing?" I look cautiously into her emotionless face. She stiffly nods, her body seemingly empty. "Why do you think Gedeon sent someone to my apartment?"

She hesitates, and I know the answer won't be good.

"He wants to hurt her." Shaun grimaces. "They never came back to collect her. Don't you find it odd, now knowing the whole story, that Shaelene is still *here*? Gedeon is pulling the same strings his father did, and he'll use *you* as leverage to take her."

"Take her?" I ask, attempting to convince myself he doesn't mean what I think he does.

"The contract went into effect ten years ago," Shaelene's confirms. "Legally, I've been married to him ever since."

57

Victoria

I CHOKE ON A piece of egg that threatens to escape my gut-punched stomach after hearing Shaelene admit the truth.

She's. Married.

To her cousin. A man. *Her abuser.*

My heart aches for her, knowing she's still attached to her monster. At least I was able to escape mine and never look back, but I'd be lying if I said I wasn't also hurting for myself. Selfish as it may be, I can't help but feel the twinges of jealousy forming in my gut at the idea of Shaelene belonging to someone else, the same sensation I felt when she spoke with Audrey in Derek's office. *Multiplied by a million.*

I know Gedeon holds no part of her heart, that the only thing she feels for him is hate, but he has her in a way that I don't, and an unsettling itch spreads under my skin in response.

"Maybe that's why you should talk with him," I suggest, my voice hoarse.

Shaelene's appalled expression stares back at me. "What?"

I contemplate how to explain myself, looking to the guys for help, but they stare at me with equally shocked faces. I sigh, facing Shaelene once more. "Maybe if you speak with him, you can tell him you want a divorce?"

The unease breaks with Shae's tense laugh, but my confusion remains. She's so damn difficult to read sometimes, but I want to know every chapter of her story and help her write the rest.

"What am I missing?"

"The contract doesn't grant me the option of divorce. The only way out of the marriage is if *he* breaks it off or if either of us die," she explains, grinding the rest of my heart to dust.

"Then he dies," I blurt before I can think better of it. Shephard claps, breaking my focus from the mixture of surprise and pride on Shae's face.

"That's the spirit, Red," he gloats, standing and dusting crumbs from his lap. "I knew you'd finally come 'round."

"No." Shaelene stands, glaring at Shephard. I rise too, grabbing her arm and looking up at her. Her stern brows soften for only a second. "No," she says again, trailing her fingers down my cheek.

"Shae, why? If you won't speak with him, and that's what it takes to pull you out of this hell—"

"I've involved you in too much already. I'm not risking him getting any closer to you." Her voice is even, but I can see in her eyes she's pleading with me to stop. *She's hiding something.*

"Fine. No killing. So, let's set up a meeting," Shaun tries, but Shaelene shakes her head, tripling down.

"No, Shaun. Leave it. *Please.*" The last word comes out harsh, but I can see the slight tremble of her chin before her jaw locks and she rushes out the door, leaving the three of us in her wake.

I look to them for something, *anything*, that will help, but Shephard's usual hard demeanor is traded for one of anguish, for what I can only assume is disappointment mingled with the need to be a protective brother.

Shaun shares the same sentiment across his face, but he lifts his hands to my shoulders, forcing me to face him. "Shae is stubborn, you know that much. She locks her emotions away into a fortress. She won't let us past her walls." My vision tunnels on him. "She needs *you*, Victoria. We can end him, but you have to help her first."

I don't know what else I'm supposed to do. She's kept herself closed off until now. "What should I do?"

"Talk to her. She'll let you in. Then you open the door for us," he assures, like it's an easy task to get Shaelene to let her guard down. *If it were, they wouldn't need me to scale the massive barriers surrounding her heart to convince her killing Gedeon is our best option.*

"What if she doesn't?" I ask, tears streaming down my cheeks.

"She will," Shephard insists beside us, his bulky arms crossed over his chest as he stares out the door at Shaelene's invisible trail.

Shaun straightens, his hands still holding me in place, and he nods at Shep before turning back to me.

"How do you know?" I ask.

Shaun wipes a tear away with his thumb. "She already has."

I find Shae pacing in her room, her hands wringing through the hair she's pulled out of her bun.

"Shae," I whisper, closing the door behind me.

She whirls and sees me. "We'll figure something out, but I can't—"

"Shae," I fight, yanking her arms down and holding them at her sides. "Look at me." She resists, pulling out of my grasp. "Shaelene, *please*. You can do this. You can be free of him."

"No! I'm not putting you in any more danger!"

I rear back from her outburst, flinching away from the arms she throws out wide. The flames in her eyes extinguish the second I do, and she reaches out to try and hold me, but I avoid her touch and hold my ground. "Why won't you even consider it?" I ask, stepping away.

Her hands find her hair again as she spins on her heel.

"Do you doubt your ability to protect me? Because I don't. I never have. And we'll have Shep and Shaun to help us. We—"

"Victoria, please... Stop. Just... Stop," she croaks, still facing away from me.

My nails dig into my palms, my thoughts spiraling as I stare at her trembling back. *I'm making my way over this damn wall one way or another, but she's already built another one by refusing to look at me. If my confidence in her won't make them disappear, I'll demolish her entire fucking castle a different way.*

I hate arguing, it only pisses me off more. I'd much rather concede and move on, but that's not an option anymore. I can't ignore this, or Gedeon, because then I'd be ignoring my feelings for Shaelene too. *And I'll walk through the flames of hell for her.*

My own fury bubbles, barely staying at the surface, but the longer she keeps herself locked away from me, the hotter it boils until it finally blows the lid of the pot. I rip her hoodie off over my head, already feeling myself beginning to sweat, and throw it at her. It bounces off her with a light thud on the floor.

"You can't protect me from anything if you keep hiding!" I yell, my heart shattering some more. When she finally turns around, her watery eyes meet mine, my rage disappearing instantly. "Shae..."

58

"Don't you know by now you can trust me? We're both fucked up, Shae. Stop trying to hide yourself from me," Victoria scolds, her voice the strongest I've heard it. I'm a pulverized version of myself looking down at her berating me.

When did my little fox become the strong one?

"Just fucking talk to me for once!" She pushes at my chest, her hands doing nothing to force me back.

Her ire matches her hair, bright and unmanageable and entirely her own. *Beautiful.* Despite what she's thinking, I'm not angry at *her*, and the tears welling in my eyes aren't from the harsh truth she's spitting at me.

I haven't spoken to her about myself much at all.

My infatuation has been entirely one-sided, stemming from a need to learn about her. As a person. What her body responds to. How to keep her mine. *But I haven't afforded her the chance to be mine. To know me.*

Last night was the first time she touched me, and it was everything I could've envisioned and more. We talked a bit before Shaun barged in, but even then, it was merely reminiscent small talk. I haven't let her know *me*.

Not until I told her about Gedeon.

She's watching me with tearful, pleading eyes. Imploring me for more. *I should expect nothing less.* She's been a sponge for information since her first day. She may not know what to do with half of what she learns, but she doesn't miss a thing we say. *Such a clever girl.* Yet, I've continued to deny her even the tiniest of scraps about who I am. Whether it be from selfish neglect or for her protection like I pretend it is, it's time to stop. *No matter how much it scares me.*

Her eyes bounce between mine, waiting for me to give her something. Anything. *Everything.*

I brush past her and into my closet, toward the deepest, most haunting part of my past.

Tucked away on the furthest shelf is a box I swore I'd never open again. Stowed away and plaguing the back of my mind for years. I slow my breathing as I pull it down, holding it in front of me.

The water in my eyes evaporates, leaving only the swarming nerves buzzing in my stomach to fully engulf me. I can feel Victoria's hard, yearning stare boring into my back, only softening when I turn and she raises a quizzical brow.

"What's that?" she asks, breaking the silence blanketing us. I let out another breath, settling myself to keep my hands from shaking as I bare all.

"Letters," I murmur. "From Gedeon."

Her eyes drop to the box again, the cardboard musty and faded and covered in half a decade's worth of dust.

Setting the box on the table, I run my fingers along the edges, willing myself the strength to open it. Victoria waits at my side, lightly stroking my arm and tucking in close. Her warmth, either from the short-lived rage she just unleashed or her naturally inviting and caring personality, is the confidence boost I need to lift the lid and toss it aside.

"He sent me the first one a few days after he and Maxim returned to Moscow."

Her thumbs brush gentle, reassuring lines along my bicep, but her eyes don't stray from the dozens of envelopes stacked in the box.

"Like clockwork, every month Phillip would call me to the kitchen to receive one from the mail. And every month I was tormented with Gedeon's enthusiastic musings of all the ways he'd imagined being with me that day and in the future. Morbid curiosity got the better of me the first few times, but I never opened another one after the fourth."

When he told me how much he longed to feel my pulse quicken under his grip. How he vividly remembered the softness of my skin against his lips, and that even though he left bloody and bruised, he'd happily be the end of both of us if it meant he could own me.

"After that, I started shoving them straight into the box." My voice catches, the edges of the letters blurring. "I don't know why I kept them. I should've burned them... But I didn't."

Maybe *this* is the reason. Maybe this is why I've been hoarding them away. Victoria can read them. She can learn every horrifying detail about the type of monster Gedeon is, and hopefully that will be enough to convince her keeping him at a distance is our safest bet.

I only hope she can see past the gruesomeness of my dark life and still want to stay. *But if she wants to run away as far as she can, I'll let her. Because the further she is from me, the further she'll be from Gedeon too.*

Twenty minutes. She's been hunched over the pile of letters scattered across the bed, ripping them open one after another, for twenty minutes. Meanwhile, I've been in my chair, the leather cushion crying with every uncomfortable and impatient shift I make, watching her face meld through a constant rotation of emotions. She's gasped twice and cried once before glancing over to see me nervously waiting for her to say something.

Whatever Gedeon wrote is clearly affecting her, but I can't strip her of any more knowledge. Not when it's my only hope of making her understand.

She folds the last letter back into its envelope and looks at me. Pain ricochets through my chest from the despaired, hollow look in her eyes. *I need her to tell me she'll stay.* She stares at my fidgety hands in my lap, hesitating before looking me in the eyes again. *This is too much for her. She's going to leave me.* It won't be like the other times she let her nerves get the best of her and tried to stay away. This time it'll be forever. *And I'll have to find a way to be okay with it. For her sake.*

I shift again, the quiet abruptly interrupted by the groaning seat beneath me. Victoria's face gives nothing away as she uncurls her legs and swings them off the edge of the bed.

Now *I* can't meet her eyes. I hate that I've allowed so much to fester between us that I can't even permit myself to look at her when a couple hours ago we were lost in a fathomless depth of passion in the shower. I can picture her wet strands of hair curled and stuck to her gorgeous face while she worked me with her hand, the two of us exploding in sync.

It's going to fucking kill me when she leaves...

59

Shaelene

"I WAS RIGHT. YOU can't protect me."

My chest becomes nothing more than a crater, ruptured into a million, inhabitable shards.

But it's not the crushing blow I thought she was going to hit me with. Victoria must see the confusion and pitiful relief on my face. *At least she didn't just tell me to go to Hell and stay there. To stay far away—*

"But I also don't expect you to believe me when I say I want you to try."

"What?"

She closes the last bit of distance between us until she's standing in front of me, our knees brushing.

"I've been witness to a lot of terrifying things in the, what? Three weeks since I first came here?" She chokes out a laugh.

Three weeks since her first day, and already she's been through enough chaos to make it seem like years. Not even a month has passed since the whirlwind of emotions sparked inside of me at the sight of her, and less than that for the dangers of my life to sweep her up into its cyclone of consequences.

"These aren't the first nightmares I've faced, Shae," she confesses, her voice a whisper. "I know you've seen my scars."

I take her hand—her nimble, shaky fingers interlacing with mine by instinct. The warm touch thaws the anxious chill encapsulating me.

Yes, I've seen them. Their pattern is forever ingrained in my memory. The faint remnants of old cuts across her inner thighs, made hastily and shallow. The raised white skin, more noticeable because of their lack of freckles, a stark contrast to the rest of her beautifully speckled body.

"You've never asked about them. I'm thankful for that, but I haven't shown you a similar kindness. I've pushed you, asking for more over and over again, just to feed my own selfish curiosity. Even when you might not have been ready to share it with me. But today... Today you showed me everything."

I did. I showed her the chewed up and spit out shreds of my soul I didn't think I cared enough to try healing.

Not until her.

But I'll still gladly destroy myself to the bitter end if it's what she needs to be happy.

She hesitates, her tongue wetting her lip before her teeth crush the soft flesh, and I squeeze her fingers, bringing her eyes to mine. She doesn't need to cut herself open for me now. We don't have to be fair in our trauma exchange for her to feel worthy of my approval, for her to be worthy of me. *God, of course she's worthy. She deserves more than I can give her. Freedom from hurt and any more that my life will throw at her.* My grip loosens, reality washing through me. *She deserves peace.*

"I'm damaged, Victoria. I can't protect you if I can't even save myself from—"

"I'm damaged too, dammit!" she yells, throwing her arms to the side as she leans in close. *Why am I pushing her when the idea of her leaving hurts so fucking bad?* "Damage doesn't make some-one unworthy of happiness! *You* showed me that. Let me do the same." Her eyes plead with mine. "Please."

"You don't have to tell me," I insist, shaking my head.

I've long since surmised where her scars came from anyway. It wasn't hard to deduce she carved them herself; that particular spot is easy to hide from her parents, her friends. Baring her chest and reliving that pain to tell me something I already know would do more harm than good when she inevitably decides she wants to leave my fucked-up life.

Her past moments of weakness aren't the big concern. Gedeon is. *And he'd hurt her worse than she ever could if given the chance.*

"I will if you ask me to. I'm not a weak little girl anymore. I've learned to be brave. You've been brave," she says, looking over her shoulder to the discarded pile of letters on the bed. "Let's be brave together."

My heart stops. My lungs seize and I can't breathe. *She isn't ashamed of the skeletons lurking in my closet? She isn't scared?* I suck in a shaky breath, my eyes burning as I refuse to look away from her. She's right, about all of it. My lips twitch. I can't believe she's actually saying this. *Believing that would mean she's either completely lost all her senses or she's as deep in this, in* us, *as I am.*

I don't say anything. Words to express the relief—the grati-tude bounding inside my chest—don't exist.

She looks to the bed and lets out a long, calming breath before moving. The empty feeling immediately rushes in, inhabiting my chest in the absence of her closeness.

The miserable papers crumple as she snatches them up and throws them to the floor. Another shaky breath bursts from both of us as I watch her, standing on tiptoes, reach across the bed and under my pillow.

In a trance, I watch her slide the sheathed Ka-Bar from my hiding place, click the fastening open, then pull the knife from its casing as she faces me again. The black metal glinting in the small rays of morning sun peeking through my curtains.

'Let's be brave together...'

"Victoria..." I say breathlessly, locked in place like never before.

Lost her senses it is then.

Our eyes lock as she kneels on the floor in front of me, hands shaking as they tightly grip the handle and raise it above her head before she drives it into the chair between my legs.

My knees ring out from the force of them hitting the arms of my chair as I flinch away from the blade. Inches from my flesh, it fully embeds into the leather, notching into the wooden bones below with a creak.

Victoria stands and peels the layers of her bottoms down her legs. My shocked, widened eyes take in every millimeter of the woman standing in front of me with mesmerized intensity. She's as beautiful as ever, slender and fragile and otherworldly. The epitome of the visceral way I feel about her. *This isn't about making us even. This is for her.* To prove her strength to me. Her courage.

I cup her thighs as she climbs onto my lap, hovering over the knife's handle, her hands firmly placed on my shoulders to steady herself. Her hesitance lasts only a second before she closes her eyes and drops.

She winces, curling her lip as she lowers. *Too dry.* Her mind is there, but her body isn't prepped for this. I lift her away and help how I can. With my hand splayed across her lower stomach, my thumb traces slow circles on her clit.

A quick gasp and I can feel her tense muscles relax as her grip on my shoulders loosens. Her eyes find mine, admiring and unwinding as she lets me coax her body into compliance.

I twist my wrist, the heel of my palm pressing firmly against her, my fingers curling along her slit, feeling her slickness pooling and readying her to take the handle.

Victoria's head falls back, her jaw opening lazily, setting her moans free as she absorbs every bit of pleasure she can from my fingers. Her hips sync with my hand, each flick met with a thrust against my palm.

My free hand slinks along her supple skin, over the plump curve of her ass and under the hem of her shirt, grazing along the dimples of her back and working its way up until it reaches the smooth, hard plane of her shoulder, holding her in place while I work inside her.

When her walls tense around me, clenching through her first orgasm, I slide my fingers out and grip her hips again, helping find her balance so she can lower herself down effortlessly. The pommel of the hilt puts up little resistance against her tender and slick flesh, sliding easily into her heat. Adjusting her weight, she falls heavily on my thighs, already tired from her first climax.

Soft moans slip between her nervous-laden breaths, but Victoria's hips churn steadily on my lap, pumping my arms along with them as I hold her.

My head slumps against her chest, needing to breathe her in to force my mind into accepting this is real. That *she's* real, and still here. *She hasn't left. She won't.*

Her nipples harden from my breath against them, forming stiff peaks beneath the fabric of my t-shirt. She arches into me, sinking my face between the plush mounds of her breasts. Soft kisses through the cotton are all I can manage, my arms unwilling to let go of her weight, but she leans back, crossing her arms and pulling the shirt over her head, tousling her curls in the process.

The second her chest is bare, my mouth is on it, sucking deep swallows against her curves, drinking in the scent of her skin. Warm, woodsy notes left over from her using my soaps invade my senses. *She smells like me mixed with the scent of her own arousal.* The two of us blended together perfectly. A groan hums through my throat, her body arching into me further as she chases the sensation.

Her eyes are heavy with pleasure when I meet them, a satisfied smile lifting her lips. *I need her closer to me.* Peeling my hands from her sides, I cup her face, stuck in a moment of pure bliss.

My lips clash against hers in a hungry kiss, her tongue slipping between them, eager and claiming, while her hips keep their steady rhythm.

Closer. I need her closer.

I pull away long enough to gasp a breath before taking her mouth again. The inconvenient need for air is the only thing capable of drawing me from her right now, and even so, I'm pushing my limits to say. The hard, passionate kisses shared between us are all I can focus on. *Her tongue tangling with mine. The feel of her skin. The heat of her own heavy breaths against my face.*

The symmetry in our movements, our fervor indistinguishable in who it stems from, builds. Nothing else matters. *It's just her. Just us. Just this.*

"I love you," I confess, not even sure it was loud enough for her to hear. Not until I feel her pull away.

She stops moving, sitting idly atop the handle, eyes fixed on me. Her body frozen save for the quivering hands she holds my face with.

Too long of a moment passes before her throat bobs, the soft click echoing in my ears. *I'm giving her all my truths.*

"I love you, Vic—"

Another vicious attack of her lips against mine pushes me against the chair, except this time her movements are speared and separated by sobs. "I love you too, Shae!" She cries each word against my mouth, her eyes clamped tightly shut and her body shuddering.

I pull my head from hers, scanning her face so exquisitely cast in the light from the window behind us. The tears spilling over her high cheeks—laced with relief and felicity—drip off her chin, painting her chest with sparkling droplets.

Gently, so tenderly the movements don't feel like my own, I wipe them away before cupping her face and pressing my forehead to hers. Soaking in the essence of our shared truth. Believing it.

My little fox doesn't want to run. She wants to fight. Together.

I lift both of us from the chair, careful of the knife, and walk to the bed. The forgotten letters ruffling as I step through the scattered pile and lay Victoria on her back.

Climbing over her, I repeat her words from earlier, "Let's be brave together."

60

Victoria

THE BOYS ARE CLEARING their plates from lunch when Shaelene and I finally emerge from her room, telling them to meet us in the office.

Shae spent the last couple of hours between my legs, making me admit all the things I loved about her. Her tongue being one of them.

On weak knees, I hobble over to one of the velvety chairs near their trophy shelves and plop down, Shaelene's devilish smirk earning her an eye roll.

When Shaun and Shephard find their seats beside me, Shae sighs, her nails drumming against her leg. "Let's finish this."

Shephard cracks his knuckles as he sits up with excitement. Shaun looks at me with a questioning brow raised, but I'm too exhausted to respond with more than a slight nod. His lips curve into an all-knowing smile before he shakes his head and turns back to Shaelene. "Lead the way, Boss."

She uncrosses her arms and clicks the remote, turning off the camera in the corner.

This is the Shaelene I've missed seeing. Decisive. Genius. In control.

The next several hours are spent ironing out every detail, no matter how insignificant they seem. *Gedeon is too dangerous to leave anything up to chance.* Shaelene knows his past, but she declined having me tell her anything written in the letters she hadn't opened.

I know how demented he is *now*, and what he'll do if he somehow gets out of this unscathed. *We can't let him live.*

"Absolutely not," Shaelene refuses, continuing to pace beside us.

Shephard counters, "We'd have every advantage! If he's desperate enough to talk, he'll come."

He makes a solid point. Laughlin Manor is as good a place as any to lure Gedeon to. *The seclusion could work to our advantage.* At the thought of it, my eyes turn to the windows facing the back of the property. Through the tinted glass, the looming silhouette of the thick pine trees stretches on for miles. The ghost of a shiver trickles down my spine, wondering if that's where Shephard and Luca's brothers hauled Derek's body out to. If his ultimate punishment is having to be stuck with them forever.

"I don't want him near the house." I feel her eyes scanning over me even while I look outside. Sure enough, they're pained with guilt as I turn back and meet them. "We need somewhere familiar but hidden. Not just from the LEOs. Father too."

Last night's outburst and her insistence of working behind Silas' back are the first bits of defiance I've seen from her. She senses the recognition on my face and shrugs. *Better to ask forgiveness than permission.* We'll deal with the ramifications after Gedeon is taken care of.

"The Rosary," I suggest. All three of them turn, annoyingly wide-eyed, but don't shoot the idea down immediately so I explain myself further, ticking each point on my fingers. "It's familiar and far from the house. It's already under the radar of the police, and from what I remember, there were only two exits. We get him inside and have men outside both doors once he's down there."

Shaelene's look of approval—a salacious mix of pride and intrigue—sets my enervated insides on fire again. *I want her to look at me like this all the time.* "And what of the patrons inside?" she asks, ever the Devil's advocate.

"We use them as cover. Part of the ruse this will be a peaceful, bloodless meeting. While he's down there talking, our guys can keep anyone new from coming in, and whoever is watching the back can grab him as we leave."

"You're forgetting Gedeon shot Milano in the middle of Fifth Ave. He isn't going to be reluctant to try something for fear of civilian casualties," Shaun cuts in.

"We go outside of business hours," Shaelene says, the commanding energy she presents keeping both of her brothers from barking any counters. "Gedeon won't know the difference, and once he's down there we can deal with him the way we need to. Without wandering eyes watching."

"How are we supposed to get ourselves in there without being recognized? You two stayed below radar because you were undercover," Shephard reminds us.

Shaelene looks at me like she's remembering our trip too, making my already reheated body blush further. "We won't worry about doing this covert. We'll make a deal with the owner." Both of the boys nod in agreement. "If money doesn't do the trick, we'll let the Angelinis convince him to let us in the hard way."

Shaun called Luca to fill him in earlier, and all four of the Angelini brothers are on their way over now. They have reason enough for wanting Gedeon dead. *Besides, the more backup we have the better.*

"How do we get Gedeon there?" I ask.

"I have no doubt he has eyes on us. They're likely watching the manor as well. We'll get in contact with him the same way he did us."

A note. My brow furrows, confusion tilting my head.

"When his cronies spot us going back to my old apartment, he'll make his way there soon enough. Then he'll find a card with the time and location specifics waiting for him," she explains. An aloof assuredness pours off her, the Shaelene from this morning once more buried deep. "In the meantime, we have to secure The Rosary for ourselves."

Someone pounds on the office door, and I jump in my seat. Shaun looks down at his watch and nods to Shephard who gets up to open it. *The Angelinis.*

The four of them squeeze through the doorway, each barely smaller than the last. Finally, Luca enters, his eyes meeting mine with a grim grin. A baby by comparison, though his tall frame and broad shoulders still fill the hollow space leading out to the hall. His body instantly relaxes once he sees Shaun.

Am I ever not *surrounded by suits anymore?* The usual blackened three pieces the triplets wear are nicely complimented by the varying shades of blue the brothers sport, each piece impeccably tailored to fit the larger-than-life men. But the shared rage simmering beneath their white button downs threatens to burst the seams just as much as their muscles.

If the owner of The Rosary isn't one for taking bribes, the Angelinis sure fit the intimidating description Shae hinted at earlier. I can't say I'd expect him to withhold the club from us if it came down to him versus them.

61

Shaelene

VICTORIA PUSHES HER WAY past Shephard to claim the front seat as the Angelinis get into their own SUV to follow us. I was going to tell him to sit in the back anyway, but watching her boss him around is too enjoyable to get in the middle of. The prick's knee is stiffly pressed into the back of my seat while he sulks behind me, but I couldn't care less. Even the weather clouding over couldn't dampen my excitement. Though Victoria shivers beside me, nervously mentioning her bad omen conspiracy.

Her proposal of using The Rosary is genius. *So long as we can convince Gustavo to let us in.*

I catch him noticing us as I round the car and open Victoria's door, finding her hand to help her out and tucking her closely against me while we lead the way inside. Gustavo is the one behind the counter today, and although he's doing his best to remain nonchalant, his avoidant eyes skimming over his bookkeeping and the set in his jaw are a dead giveaway.

"I've made my stance clear, Ms. Shaelene," he grumbles without looking up. The bell on the door rings again when Luca and his brothers enter, finally getting him to lift his eyes and acknowledge us with a barely concealed scowl. "You are not welcome."

His quick and heavy accent makes his insult sound almost sultry. *Almost.*

"There was no issue with our presence here the other day." I smirk, which earns me an irritated glare.

"A simple oversight from a new hire, I assure you. He won't be making that mistake again." Gustavo turns his angry eyes to Shephard. "And you choose to further disrespect me by bringing your brother here as well?" Victoria stiffens next to me, but I've already prepared myself for the battle Gustavo Contreras is going to put up. "Your time here with Señorita Maldonado and the rumors—"

Shephard grunts, crossing his arms across his chest. "Exactly. *Rumors*. They were never proven to be true."

Gustavo sneers an insincere smile. "Yes, but the existence of those rumors is the reason I found myself in hot water with many of my regulars. The threat of exposure is not good for business."

"You know what *is* good for business, Gustavo?" I ask, recapturing his attention as his sidelong stare grows testier and more suspicious the longer we stand in this fluorescent hell. "Money."

I pull the first of two stacks from my inside breast pocket and place it on the glass counter between us.

"Even money has a price, Ms. Shaelene. Don't think I'm too naive to assume otherwise."

Gustavo can keep up the tough guy act all he wants, but I don't miss the way he takes in the sight of those bills before dragging his eyes back up to mine. The quick purse of his lips tells me everything I need to know.

I pull out the second and double the bribe, holding both beneath my palm, and wait.

He breathes a heavy sigh through his nose and looks past me to the four burly Italians growing restless in the aisle—surrounded by potted orchids and bushels of gardenia.

"What do you want?" he finally asks, and I can't contain the snarky grin festering to be let loose.

"Your club."

Gustavo's eyes go wide with refusal before I go on.

"For two hours, before you open for the night. We just need to discuss some things with an... *Associate*," I say, giving all the information I'm willing to share.

I shift the bills toward him, and he shuffles the top one in his hands, sniffing the crispness as they ruffle beneath his nose.

"When?"

"Tomorrow. Noon."

62

Victoria

SHAELENE IS BY THE window while I finish packing some clothes and art supplies.

Across from us, the vase of oleander she left for Gedeon sits lonely on the desk where he left his note to her. Gustavo didn't bat an eye when she grabbed one of his bouquet cards without paying, writing **12 PM** on the back of it and tucking it neatly between the stems.

Gedeon's lackeys were probably tailing us like Shaelene said, so if the business logo on the front of the card isn't enough for him to know where to meet, whatever intel they feed back to him should be.

"I think that's everything," I huff, hands on my hips as I look down at the bags. She turns and does the same, scoffing at the overstuffed suitcases before us.

"Are you sure?" she jests.

I cross my eyes and stick out my tongue at her teasing, my initial shyness long since faded. I'm in this now. After this morning, I realized I love her more than I'd originally let myself believe. *There's no going back on that even if I wanted to. Even if she told me to.*

My mask isn't nearly as well practiced as hers and the happiness slips from my face. I can tell she sees the discontent painted where it used to be. *If something were to happen to her...* She steps past me and reaches into the top drawer of my dresser.

I choke out a strangled gasp when I see her holding the rose toy hidden in there. She laughs, and I feel my face cycling through every shade of pink as she stuffs it into the main pocket and zips it closed. The heavy case thumps against the floor when she slides it off the bed, giving me a wink. "Lots of flowers today."

I hide my smile, looking to the floor while I turn and pull the other one off the bed. I take one last look out the window, catching a glimpse of Shaelene and her outstretched hand in the reflection behind me.

She leads us out of the room, back to where Shaun is emptying my fridge into the trash—Shephard intercepting what he can before it gets there. He ties the garbage with a tight knot and shoves it into his brother's chest, grabbing the suitcase from me as we head for the elevator and faking a grunt as he drags it into the overly crowded steel box.

Shephard slings the trash bag over his shoulder with a nasty *slosh*. "Grabbed all the good stuff right, Red? The pinks, the blues... The *purples*?" The pestering smirk he gives Shaelene is distorted in the metal doors, but her teeth clicking beside me is clear as day.

I react without thinking, and Shephard snorts a laugh after I lift my foot from his now scuffed loafer, releasing his smashed toes from my heel. Shaelene intertwines our fingers, and the rest of our descent is filled with the quiet jazz leaking from the speakers.

I don't know when the next time we come back here will be, if ever, but I'm happy that this time at least, we're walking out together. Returning home, hand in hand.

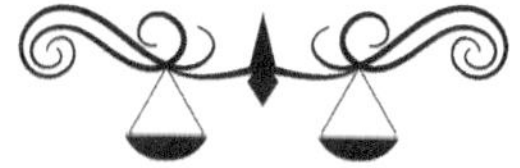

"It's a less detectable version of wearing a wire," Shaun explains, the seven of them gearing up in the office.

Luca, Massimo—the second oldest brother—and I will be in the car waiting near the back of The Rosary while Shae, Shaun, and Shep meet with Gedeon inside. Giovanni and Alessio are set to watch the front from the building across the street. Both street level teams ready to intercept Gedeon if he attempts to leave. My job is to *'Stay. In. The. Car.'* as Shae repeatedly reminds me.

However, she did spare me the details of what they plan to do once they have him secured. *Which is fine by me; I rather enjoyed breakfast, and I would prefer to keep it down.*

Shaun lets me hold the cable he's talking about while he pins several tiny clips to the underside of his shirt collar. It's flexible, like most wires, but clear as glass and so thin it feels like I could snap it in half no matter how durable he claims it to be.

"Fiber optic wiring. It's stronger, lighter, harder to see, and *faster*. These little nodes at the end—" He points to the chrome cap that's smaller than my pinky nail. "—are the microphones." He holds the recorder up so I can see the tiny piece that splits the wire into two halves "And this block is the Bluetooth that sends the signal to the laptop you'll have in the Suburban." He tosses a small flash drive to Massimo. "There's almost no lag time between when someone speaks and when you'll hear it through the speakers. Only downside is it's one-way. You'll hear us but won't be able to respond."

I twist the device over between my fingers. "Wow," I finally say. I knew Shaun was tech savvy, but I never understood what that meant until now. Silas putting him in charge of scrubbing the footage from the birthday party was a bigger task than I realized, and I can only assume he made it possible for Shaelene to swipe my key card information forever ago. *He probably made the cameras she put up too.*

I shoot her a look, catching her already smiling like she can read my thoughts and knows I'm still annoyed by them even if they did prove helpful. I scrunch my nose at her, handing the device back to Shaun. "What made you settle for being a lawyer? I'm sure you'd make a fortune off this stuff."

He shrugs off my compliment, but the faintest trace of a smile shadows his lips. "Probably, but it'd make our job harder if everyone had access to the things we do," he jokes.

"It's a good thing no one with any *illegal schemes* is going to use them then," I tease, poking his side. This time a broad smile forms and he chuckles. My own grin flashes across my face in response.

He clasps the wire in place, the tiny magnets clicking before he flips his collar back down. My eyes widen as I lift onto my toes, trying to get a closer look. The device is completely hidden from sight or a pat down. Even from my angle below him I can't see it because of the clear cables.

"What?" he asks, lifting a thick brow, the silly smiles still plastered on our faces.

I shake my head. "It's just nice seeing you guys not so serious all the time. I was starting to think you were robots." Another hearty chuckle bursts from him as I pat his chest and walk over to stand by Shae.

63

Shaelene

VICTORIA BUCKLES INTO THE seat beside me, picking at her thumb and looking over her shoulder into the trunk.

"What is it?"

She meets my worried eyes, chewing the inside of her cheek before she says, "There are no dog cages in this one."

I glance back as if I need to double check. "Still plenty of space for Gedeon to be tied up and contained back there though."

She shudders slightly. *She's held her nerves well so far.* Shaun kept her occupied talking about his gadgets while I quadruple checked our exit routes with Mass and Gio. *Once we have Gedeon, we'll take him to Grigorio's shipping docks and take care of him there. We can't risk bringing him back to the manor still breathing.*

"Those are *dog* cages, right?" she asks.

I scan her face, remembering her horror seeing them those few weeks ago. "Yes, they're for dogs, Little Fox."

Her shoulders sag in relief then tense up worse than before. "I haven't heard any dogs at the manor."

"You won't. They're guard dogs that patrol with the sentries. If you hear them barking, it's a *very* bad sign." She doesn't say anything, likely still learning the limits of her bravery. *Today might very well be one of her biggest tests.* "I can show you the kennels when we're done. If you'd like."

She nods, and I let her collect herself in silence the rest of the drive.

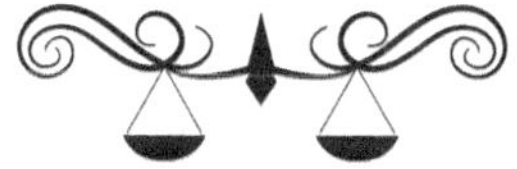

The heart of The Rosary looks the same during the day as it did the night I brought Victoria, minus the hoard of heavy petting patrons fornicating in every corner of the room. The dim table lights barely illuminate the space making the polished wood floors meld with the matching scarlet pleather covering the booths wrapping along the walls.

The small round tables scattered across the space are bare save for the one in the center where four whiskey glasses and a pitcher of water sit waiting for us.

The mirrored wall behind the bar makes the club appear bigger than it actually is, but even when it isn't packed with dozens of horny members, the room is claustrophobic.

The usual heavy bass filtering out of the speakers is replaced by the low hum of jazz. *As if any regulars of this club would come for a matinee.*

Shaun returns from securing the side door, leaving it cracked open to ensure the audio receiver's signal can reach the others, and takes the seat beside me while Shephard puffs his cigar.

Three minutes past noon.

Shaun checks his watch, feeling the same restlessness I am. Not that I expected Gedeon to be on time.

After a few more lengthy minutes, the hatch at the top of the stairs opens and light from the greenhouse spills down into the hall, followed by Gedeon's menacingly slow footsteps.

The three of us turn, but don't stand, as he saunters into the room. His tailored, slate-gray suit fitted to his shoulders. He's not as broad as Shaun or Shephard, but he makes up for it with his cunning ability to be an absolute fucking insufferable asshole.

His vacant eyes trail over my unbothered form sitting in my chair. I don't look away. I don't shift a millimeter, no matter how much my body aches to shield itself from his gaze.

He won't see weakness from me again.

"It's polite to stand and greet your guests, you know," he purrs, his sickening tone berating my head with memories of the things he said in my ear all those years ago.

Shaun stands, breaking our stare, and meets him a few feet from the table. Gedeon rolls his eyes, lifting his arms and letting Shaun roughly pat him down. He turns back and shakes his head, lips thin as he returns to his seat.

Gedeon waits. Still watching me. Still waiting. *That's new.* My foot finds the leg of his chair under the table and gives it a hard shove, kicking it out for him to sit.

"Ever the lady, Shae," he quips, taking his spot opposite us.

More silence. None of us stir, only shooting glares across the divide before Shaun says, "I believe you were the one that had something to discuss. Why don't you begin?"

Gedeon feigns a smile, giving us a casual shrug as he settles further into his seat. "I wasn't expecting an audience." Cold, emotionless eyes lock on me. I keep up the quiet game, still not saying a word since he entered. "I had business in town and thought I'd make time to catch up with my wife."

A flash of disgust crosses my face before I can hold it in. Claiming me after so many years of absence I can handle, but the gall of referring to killing Milano and Shultz as *business* is asinine.

The Angelinis are likely foaming at the mouth to get a piece of him after that dismissal.

Gedeon returns my snarl with a sneer, the scar slashed across his lips mocking me. I used to picture it as a permanent reminder of my victory over him that day, but now the faint line of pink skin traitorously taunts me by adding to the dark essence of his smile.

"She is *not* your wife," Shephard growls.

That unfeeling stare slinks from me to him, my body feeling lighter. "Thank you for your input, Shephard. Though, per usual, your ignorance is showing." A long, heavy pause thickens the air between them. Gedeon ignores the tension and checks his watch, seeming entirely unbothered. "She is whatever I choose to call her." His eyes lock on mine once more. "Aren't you, *Zaichonok?*"

Bunny. As if I'm a small, easy meal for the Big, Bad Wolf of Moscow's son to feast on as he pleases.

Shep doesn't flinch from Gedeon's tough guy act. Instead, he plucks the cigar from his mouth, snuffing it out on the black tablecloth, and spits. The insult runs down my *husband's* cheek. Gedeon reaches into his jacket and both boys instinctually reach for their guns, every muscle in my body constricting until Gedeon lifts a hand in surrender as he draws a handkerchief from his pocket and wipes his face clean.

"Make your point or we're leaving," I finally say, my voice measured and controlled.

Gedeon's brows raise, his signature light brown pouf of hair swaying with the jilted tick of his head. "She speaks!" He claps, dropping the spoiled cloth into his lap as the sound echoes around us. "I was beginning to think you'd lost that ability too."

My eyes widen imperceptibly. *He means those damn letters, since I never wrote back. I must've bruised his ego. Good.* The boys tense, frustrated at the obvious secret knowledge between Gedeon and I.

Gedeon reclines in his chair and checks his watch again, disappointed I didn't take his bait. "I have no point other than wanting to see you, Shae."

"You've seen me." I stand, ready to head for the door. His eyes scan me top to bottom, soaking me up, no shame in the pauses he takes at my chest and hips.

"Yes, I have," he purrs again.

I start to turn from the table, and his jaw ticks as he falls for my bluff. Raising his hands in surrender. "Alright, alright," he urges, looking the direction I was heading, then at the double doors he came in from. He sucks his teeth. "Fine. Please. Sit, Shae."

A bitter tang fills my mouth when he says my name a third time. I roll my eyes and huff, making myself sit again.

"I leave in two days."

"Good."

Shaun and Shephard share a cautious look.

Gedeon leans in close, his snarling face to face with my indifferent gaze over the table. "I want you to come with me."

A horrifying and unexpected laugh bursts from me. "Why the hell would I ever do that?"

"You've had your time here, *Zaichonok*. And I'm only going to ask once." He makes a point to glance at each of my brothers before continuing. "Next time, I'll skip the niceties and take you myself."

Shephard jumps to his feet, the table shaking from his strength. Gedeon meets his eyes immediately, his stare as angry and unflinching as my brother's. "Your brutishness will only seal your sister's fate further, *cousin*."

Shephard huffs, his knuckles white. "*Pososi moi yaytsa... Kuzen.*"

I don't bother hiding my smirk.

We all stand, Shephard bouncing on his toes and Shaun shaking out his arms. Gedeon rises from his seat slowly, tossing his handkerchief to the table and fluffing his jacket, noting the time again. *What the hell is he waiting on—*

Shouting and the sound of glass shattering down the hall draws our attention.

Gedeon straightens, fastening the button of his suit, unphased by the commotion upstairs.

"Anonymous tip. I told them they may want to bring reinforcements." With a final wink, he lifts a hidden pistol and shoots, the mirror behind the bar exploding as the three of us duck to the floor.

More glass and what I assume are ceramic pots shatter above, followed by the sound of heavy boots and another round of shouts, covering up the slamming of the side door behind Gedeon.

"SWAT," I growl, reaching for both my brothers as my mind whirls.

The hatch opens and a hiss fills the hallway. *A smoke screen. Dammit! We need to leave. Now.*

I tug Shaun's shoulder, and the three of us dash for the other exit to find the door shut, the brick Shaun used to wedge it gone. Shephard doesn't hesitate, pulling the security box off the top of the door frame and ripping the wires out of the wall to silence the alarm before shouldering it open.

Glancing around, I search for Gedeon in the shadows, but he's vanished, disappearing somewhere and leaving us alone in the crumpling alley, the Suburban waiting around the far corner away from the main street.

Shaun pushes me onward and directs everyone keeping guard, "Mass, start the car. Ale, Gio, find somewhere across town to set up. We'll meet you there."

More shouting comes from the road behind us as we sprint past the dumpsters and towering brick walls toward the car.

I catch a glimpse of an armored truck screeching to a hard stop right before we round the corner and pile into the open doors of the SUV.

Massimo doesn't wait for them to close before taking off and pulling into the heavy lunch hour traffic.

"The jetty!" I shout, panting and keeping watch through the back window.

No patrol cars behind us.

Yet.

64

Victoria

SHAELENE DOESN'T TAKE HER eyes off the road, my heart unable to fully settle until I check her over. "Shae, oh my god! Are you alright? We heard... Are you hurt?" There isn't any blood on her that I can see, and the pulse in her neck is quick not weak.

"I'm not injured," she says with too much pain in her eyes to be true. She isn't hurt physically, but I can tell being around Gedeon has done its damage.

I grab her hand, the sides of her nails raw from her biting and picking, holding tight to it as I bury myself in her side. "I thought I lost you..."

"Shhhh, shh. I'm here. I'm right here, Little Fox."

Traffic is heavy until we get through downtown, and Massimo makes a point not to draw attention by speeding, instead utilizing a few stomach whirling maneuvers around other cars that has me gripping the seat ahead of me—setting my shot nerves even more on edge.

The occasional patrol car goes screaming past us toward The Rosary, its sirens and lights blaring, but none of the units on site seem to have noticed the SUV tucked away in the alley.

After another fifteen minutes of zigzagging down back streets, the sun glares through the windows as it bounces off the surface of the harbor. Rundown buildings with dilapidated brick exteriors block our view of the city on one side and tall steel fencing along a large expanse of concrete dock separates us from the bay on the other.

Massimo stops in front of one of the gates dotted along the fence and a buzzer sounds. The metal grate slides silently on its tracks as he pulls forward.

On the water, several ships carry giant cargo containers, some unlabeled, others bearing the logo for Vino Santo. *This must be what Shaelene meant by the jetty.*

Pulling between two unloaded shipping crates, Massimo stops the SUV and steps out with Shephard, and Shaelene lets out the first breath I've seen her take since getting in the car. The ache in my chest settles with each calming rise and fall of hers.

Outside, Shephard tosses something to Massimo at the front of the SUV, then rounds the back of it, dropping below the view of the window behind us.

"What're they doing?" I whisper.

"Swapping the plates," she says. I look over my shoulder and see Shephard's head pop back up. When they both get back in, Massimo hands him the front plate along with something else.

At first it doesn't register, but I look to Shaelene after Shephard slips the two bright yellow New York license plates and a gold and red Cadillac grill emblem into the seat back pocket in front of him.

She smirks, the only sign the tension she's worn all morning is starting to fade. "Insurance. In case anyone saw us."

"And the Cadillac ornament?" I ask.

She settles into her seat, throwing her arm along the back and idly tracing shapes on my shoulder. "Witnesses tend to remember makes better than plate numbers. In the chance they managed to get both, the plates will show up registered to a black Cadillac Escalade. Since those descriptions match each other, they'll have no reason to suspect a Chevy Suburban," she explains.

I can't even attempt to hide the amazed look on my face. *They really do cover all their bases... But how did Gedeon get out?* Shae must know what I'm thinking because she says, "He's who called SWAT."

I blink, my brows drawing together. "Why would he do that? He has more at stake for getting caught than you do."

She sighs, raking a tired hand over her face. "I don't have any idea why he'd set the raid up. To scare us into cooperating?"

"Into going with him, you mean."

The air sits heavy between us. Between *all* of us. Massimo and Luca were primed and ready to explode when Gedeon referred to Milano as 'business'. Their collective rage festered so hot, I thought they'd set the car ablaze. Then Gedeon's offer came through, and I felt the same, my skin burning at the idea of Shaelene being subjected to him more than she already was.

And when he said he'd *take* her everything went cold. I'd never felt more intense dread than then, until that gunshot rang through the speakers and I thought I'd lost her. Shaun's voice was the only thing keeping me in the car because I knew he'd never leave his sister behind.

"How did you guys get out?" Luca asks.

Shaun shakes his head, and Shephard keeps his eyes pointed out the window.

Shae sucks in a long breath. "The same way Gedeon did," she says.

His name from her mouth makes me wince.

He must have scouted the club after getting our message and seen there were only two ways in or out. If he pulled this stunt as some sort of power trip, to prove he had the upper hand, he wouldn't have left himself pinned in the trap as well.

"He must not have mentioned the other exit in his tip," Giovanni murmurs, coming to the same assumption we did. "The sadistic prick really wanted to scare you that bad?" He shakes his head, leaning back and swirling his coffee.

The small iron table between us wobbles unevenly as Shephard shifts his weight, leaning on the back legs of his chair. "It would appear so."

Giovanni and Alessio chose a small, well-known cafe for us to meet at. Shaelene insists we need to appear unbothered and give ourselves the best attempt at an alibi we can. So here we are, all eight of us, outside a bakery in upstate watching the early afternoon pedestrian traffic filter by and letting various cappuccinos grow cold, too rattled to even pretend we're drinking them.

"We won't let him take you, Shae," Alessio swears, putting a hand on her wrist. "He's not taking anyone else from our family."

Tears well and it takes every bit of my concentration to hold them back. *I need to be strong.* Everyone looks at Shaelene with reassuring eyes, but she turns to me and gives my knee a squeeze beneath the table with her free hand. Her voice is low, soft enough for the thrum of the street and the idle chatter of other patrons to nearly drown it out. "Still brave?"

On a long breath, I stare at her hand. Willing the sting in my eyes to fade until I can blink the wetness away. I lace my fingers with hers, her skin warm and calloused and gentle. When I look back at her, my underlying fear for both our safety collides with my desire to save her from Gedeon, which is exactly why I tell her, "Still brave."

We don't get the chance to see the kennels after returning to the manor.

The Angelinis trail behind us through the garage when Massimo's phone rings.

"*Ciao mamma, cos'è? Mamma. Mamma, calmati.* Took him where? Okay just— We'll be there soon, *va bene*?" he says, trying to stay calm, but there's panic in his voice. When the line clicks, he looks at each of the triplets before turning to his brothers. "*Papà* is in custody."

All of us collectively suck in a sharp breath, scouring our thoughts for how the police could have so suddenly gotten to Grigorio, when a pair of voices from the hall pull our attention.

Shaelene and her siblings lead the charge, barreling through the dining room and attached tea room, our rushed footsteps echoing off the polished floor of the empty foyer.

"Sorry to cut this short, but I'm glad we could come to an agreement," Silas apologizes, rounding the corner with Gedeon behind him.

"Yes, well, that's for my father to decide. I'll relay your message and we'll be in touch," he says, not a trace of surprise on his face when the rest of us see him.

What the fuck is happening right now?

Sweat pools in my palms; my throat begins to close. My first real look at Gedeon guts me completely. No more mask. No party lights or loud music to muffle the evil making its way toward us.

His previously hidden scar is on full display, tauntingly splayed across a wicked smile that matches his equally sinister eyes. The embodiment of posh arrogance duels with the primal wrath radiating beside me, his hubris matching that of the seven angry cousins.

He says nothing further, at least nothing I hear over the pounding of my heart in my ears. *Can he see me shaking?*

If he does, he makes no outward note of it. His eyes stay locked on one person, *my* person, until his slithery form walks out the door, hands casually perched in his pockets.

"What the hell was he doing here?" Shaelene seethes.

Silas ignores her, looking to Massimo over her shoulder instead. "You've heard?"

Massimo nods.

"I'm heading there now," Silas informs. "Go check on the house. And your mother."

The four of them don't hesitate before obeying Silas' order and heading out the door. From the lack of shouting or fighting, Gedeon must already be gone. *Again.*

"Why was he here?" Shaelene asks again, practically splitting the words. Her father finally meets her gaze, narrowing angrily at her tone before he shoots me a sidelong glance, slowly looking back and scanning his three children.

"The four of us will speak later," he clips out, walking out the door.

The four of them. I am not a welcome part of that discussion, which means it has to be really bad.

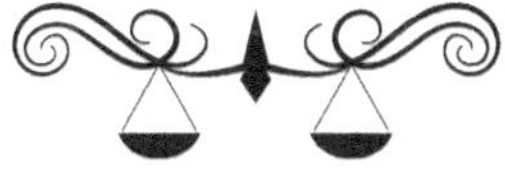

"Wave it over everything like a metal detector. If the static becomes a high-pitched whine or if you see a red light inside whatever you scan, then it's probably bugged," Shaun explains, turning on the device for me and handing me a set of headphones. He and Shephard split off to sweep the front of the office, leaving me and Shae near the built-ins and Silas' desk.

I wave the small box over a few of the volumes on the shelf beside me, hearing nothing but quiet, white noise. Shaelene moves Silas' chair, swiping her receiver in the space beneath the desk.

"Do you truly think Gedeon could've planted something without your father noticing?" I ask, moving past her to scan the next shelf. *Nothing.*

"Him being here instead of tied up and thrown off the docks makes anything possible."

She crouches, scanning the drawers and groaning when they don't budge open. I hold my scanner over the desk as I move around it, the static crackling but not spiking when it's over the monitor.

"But Silas never lets anyone out of his sight, so it'd have to be something he wouldn't realize is off, right?"

Her head pops up from behind the desk, lines forming between her brows as she stands to her full height. "You are *absolutely* right. I purposely placed the cameras in your apartment on the vents because they blended in with the screws," she starts, glossing past my widened eyes. "But I had time to move around without being noticed. Gedeon would need to hide it somewhere he could reach without being obvious." Her gaze shifts to the seat behind me, then to her brothers across the room. She rushes over to them while I feel around the underside of the desk's ledge with my hand, finding nothing.

Shephard flips the chair behind me, searching the bottom of it, while Shae and Shaun follow a set path into the room, starting with a thorough sweep of the doorway.

"It would need to be camouflaged too, right? If it's not hidden well?" I ask over my shoulder. "What normal things can be bugged?"

Shaun answers, a little too enthusiastically for our circumstances. "Anything. Lightbulbs, coins—"

"Pens?" I ask over the screeching in my ears. I rip the audio cable from the device but keep it hovering over the fancy pen display beside Silas' name plate. The loud whine pulling everyone over to me.

"Yep. Pens." Shaun sighs, turning the dial of my receiver to **Off**. Shaelene's face pales while her brothers' redden.

"Is there something special about that pen other than it being bugged?" I ask. Shaun pulls the elegant cap off to reveal a quill tip still stained with ink.

"It belonged to our great grandfather. He used it to sign the contracts that established Laughlin & Laughlin. Father never uses it except for—" Shaun stops, turning his attention to Shaelene. Her face a mixture of confusion and horror.

"Gedeon signed something before he left," she mutters. I search the desktop for any papers, before remembering the locked drawers Shaelene pulled on. My mind wanders through thoughts of whether or not we could break into Silas' desk without him noticing, but with Shaun at his disposal, I'm sure he's got some way of knowing when his things are tampered with. *The rest of them not suggesting trying probably means I'm right.*

"Is that the only one?" I ask, my eyes still scanning the top of the desk, recalling what looks familiar from my interview. *Lady Injustice, the name plate, the—*

My stomach drops at the small, folded fox tucked beside a large glass paperweight. "Shae..." I gulp when I pick it up, turning it over in my hands and finding where to open it. The photo slips through my trembling fingers after it's unfolded.

"What does it say?" I barely hear Shephard ask behind us, my senses already beginning to tunnel.

Shaelene wraps an arm around me before bending down to pick it up, grabbing hold of me when she realizes what it is. She pulls me tightly against herself as I violently shiver in her arms, too numb to calm myself. Too in shock to even cry as Shaelene holds up my graduation photo for her brothers to see.

65

WHEN I COME TO, I'm in Shaelene's arms, my face tucked into her neck while the two of us are lying in her bed, her hand petting my hair. "*Ma fraise,*" she whispers, when she feels me stirring.

A headache threatens to split my skull, and I squint against the light coming in through the window. "I'm okay, I think. I just—"

"Fainted," she finishes for me, reaching for a glass of water sitting on the nightstand. "Drink." I do as she says, chugging the glass to get rid of the same cotton-like dryness I felt the other night.

"Shae, why would he—Was that photo for me or you? You don't think he'll go after my parents, do you?"

"I think he left it to taunt us."

A reminder of how easily he could get to me. Use me as a weapon against her like Shaun said. I hold my head in my hands, blocking out the light and pleading for the pounding in my head to stop. "How long was I asleep?"

"Thirty-two minutes."

Of course she'd know the exact time. She pries a hand from my face, and I whimper as another flash of pain rebounds inside my skull. "I need something for this migraine," I say at the same time I feel something drop into my palm. *Midol. This woman is a godsend.* Shae takes the glass from me and refills it with the pitcher it was next to.

"Where are the others?" I ask, resting my forehead against her shoulder.

"Back in our office. Shaun hacked the transmitter but said it didn't record anything other than Father receiving the phone call about Grigorio's arrest and our voices while we searched for it."

Gedeon was smart enough to wait until his shady dealings were done before turning it on.

"What about whatever he signed?" I ask, feeling her go tense beside me.

"Father likely had it in his briefcase when he left, or it's locked in his desk."

I think about my earlier assumption and ask, "We can't open those drawers without him knowing, can we?" She shakes her head glumly.

Then our only option is to wait for Silas to return and demand the information from him. Great.

Phillip brings dinner up to the office, but none of us touch our food. Shaun is asleep, the disassembled replica of their great-grandfather's pen spread across his desk, while Shephard continues his relentless pacing back and forth. Beside me, Shae's knee bounces under her desk, ticking along with the clock on the wall.

At twenty-three after six, Simon knocks on the door. "I have news."

According to Shaun, Luca called him with an update after he and his brothers had gotten back to the Palazzo a few hours ago. The police were still there, ransacking their way through the Angelini mansion. For what, they weren't sure. Shephard and Massimo swear they left no evidence, and with the bathroom half destroyed from the contractors, there was nothing for the police to find or dust for prints. Luca said that didn't stop them from searching the rest of the property and taking the security footage.

Shaun confirmed, *again*, nothing would be found and, as expected, Signora Angelini was distraught over her husband's arrest, switching between sobbing uncontrollably and asking the police what they were looking for. They'd abruptly stopped and cleared out without a word after searching the master suite, leaving all of us in the dark about what they could've found that was proof enough for Grigorio to be taken into custody.

"A pocket square with the Angelini crest embroidered on it," Simon tells us, his face grim. "That's what they're using to keep him in holding."

"A pocket square? How is that suspicious if they found it in his home? Wouldn't that be where you'd expect to find one?" I ask.

Simon dips his head, pushing his glasses back up his nose with a sigh. "They didn't find it at his home. It was found during a raid on The Rosary club this afternoon."

The color leaches from all four of our faces.

"Do you know anything about that?" Simon asks.

A trick question based on the accusatory tone in his voice.

Shaelene doesn't miss a beat. "The club was raided?"

Simon's head cocks, his eyes narrowing. He's better at letting his emotions simmer just beneath the surface compared to his twin who's always primed to explode. "You're better off not lying to me about this, Shaelene." They square off with one another now, testing each other's resolve. Shae's straight back and rolled shoulders against Simon's pinning stare and crossed arms. "Tell me what you know."

"Tell me why Gedeon was meeting with Father first."

Simon is the first to break, his jaw clenching. "Gedeon?"

Shaelene doesn't deign him with a response—her intentions entirely set on learning what business Gedeon had here.

"Gedeon was here?" he asks, and I'm starting to believe he actually had no idea.

Shae nods. "They walked out of his office as we got back from lunch."

Simon's eyes widen so subtly I might be imagining it because his usual soft gaze reappears behind his glasses. "I'll look into it." He sighs, definitely upset about not being informed of Gedeon's visit. He turns to leave, and I can't help but wonder what other things Silas hides from his brother. *And the rest of us.* He's made it obvious I'm not welcome in whatever further discussion he plans to have when he returns.

When he reaches the door, he looks over his shoulder, his lips thin and eyes tired. "The handkerchief was soaked in blood. Labs have been ordered, but I'm certain it'll come back positive for Shultz," he says, his voice low.

Fuck.

66

Shaelene

Fuck. Fucking FUCK!

This was it. This was the reason Gedeon called in the tip. Of course, it wasn't just to intimidate us. He had the upper hand and wanted to rub it in our faces. He showed it, flaunting it straight at us. *That fucking handkerchief was right there for all of us to see and left on the table for the agents to find. Dropped so nonchalantly after he'd used it to—*

"Shep," I breathe, the realization hitting me like a mortar round to the chest. That same feeling washes over his glazed eyes as he stares at the floor between us.

They're testing the handkerchief for DNA. They'll no doubt discover the blood belonged to Shultz, but they'll get a match for Shephard too.

"FUCK!" he roars, pitching the ashtray from his desk at the wall. The glass shatters, gray flakes and crystal shards cascading over the carpet. Victoria flinches beside me, my body blocking hers instinctively.

"Settle down. We'll—"

Shephard whirls to face me, pointing with a deadly calm. "Don't *fucking* tell me to settle down, Shae! That piece of shit played us. We walked right into his trap, and now *my* head is on the fucking chopping block."

"We'll call Barry. Have him—"

He laughs. A boisterous, delirious laugh devoid of any warmth, and my lungs fight for air. Even though I know how unreliable Barry Kerr is, he may be our only option.

Shep runs a hand through his sweat slicked hair, shaking his head. The truth is, Gedeon tricked us all. We did exactly what he wanted us to, and it put my brother at the top of the suspect list alongside Grigorio.

Shephard. My youngest brother and my biggest protector. Both boys were there the night Gedeon assaulted me, and both of them pleaded with my father to reconsider the contract, but it was Shephard who pulled Shaun away and broke Gedeon's nose. *And ribs. And nearly his own hand. Shephard, who beat our cousin half to death for touching me...* And now the cocksucker let my brother destroy himself by banking on his affinity for anger. Violence. Revenge.

Gedeon made it harder for Shephard to stop him from coming and fulfilling his threat. '*Your brutishness will only seal your sister's fate further*'.

He sniffs, barely holding onto his bearings as he rushes out the door.

"Shephard!" I call after him, but he dismisses us with an angry wave of his hand. *Don't run again... Please.*

Something squeezes my hand. Victoria looks up at me, so much worry in her eyes my knees almost buckle.

"Father's back," Shaun mutters from beside his desk. I glance at the wall, holding tighter to my little fox. Sure enough, the camera feed shows his car pulling in.

Time for some damn answers.

67

Victoria

Silas walks into his office to find the three of us and Simon waiting for him, ready to demand an explanation.

His already bristled expression pinches further. "Miss Fenwick, if you'd please," he orders, his hand motioning to the open door behind him. "You're not needed for this discussion."

Not needed or not wanted?

"Needed or not, she's staying," Shaelene insists, her disobedience on display once more. I swear I can hear Silas snarl as his upper lip curls. "She's proven herself to the firm. She can and *should* be trusted."

Shaelene trusts me. Not just with her secrets, but with all inner workings of the firm. *A big step up from the student intern I started as.* Silas must not find it worth his time to try disputing my presence because he storms across his office and drops his briefcase on the desk.

"What was Gedeon doing here?"

"Shae," Shaun's hushed voice pleads, but Silas silences both of them with a wave of his hand. The locks on his case click loudly in the quiet, making me flinch as he opens it and throws a stack of papers on the desk beside him.

I can only assume what's on them. *And what's hiding in the fine print.* Copies of everything the authorities have on Grigorio which, based on the height of that stack, is *a lot*.

"This is just the start of what we have to work around," he says. All our eyes track his hand as it hovers over the stack, each of his fingertips dropping heavily on the pile. "Witness statements."

Witnesses?

The rest of them must be wondering the same thing because Shaun says, "That's a lot of paper for a case that just broke this morning."

"The police have been looking for Shultz since Friday."

Shae, Shaun, and I hold our breath.

"According to his secretary, he hasn't come into the office and didn't bother to reschedule any of his meetings. His wife corroborated and added he didn't come home Friday evening. She hasn't been able to get a hold of him since," Silas continues.

"Where did he go on Friday?" Shaun asks.

Silas clicks his tongue. "Figure that out. Where is Shephard?" His tone is laced with annoyance rather than genuine curiosity.

"Out," Shaelene answers, catching Silas' side-eye.

"Where?"

"We don't know," Shaun offers, failing to ease the tension between them.

"Why?" Silas' eyes don't stray from Shaelene's intense glare.

He still hasn't answered her question.

"Likely to speak with Kerr," she lies.

"Why would your brother need to speak with Barry Kerr before hearing everything we have to say?" Simon jumps in, his typically neutral tone harsh and disappointed, as if he knows what she's about to say will make this situation even worse.

"Because his DNA is on the handkerchief along with Derek's blood."

Unsurprisingly, the elder twins look as if they could murder the lot of us without remorse, their quiet anger scarier than any of the illegality I've heard from them.

Silas fists his hands so tight his knuckles crack under the pressure, stretching the skin near to splitting. Simon closes his eyes, trying to still himself with a long, slow breath. "How?"

Before Shaelene can give an explanation, Silas cuts in with an unnerving calm. "Kerr can't help us. Call him back before he puts us in more trouble."

Shaun does just that, pulling his phone out of his pocket and using the opportunity to walk out to the hall.

I restlessly shift on my feet beside Shae, not wanting to risk Silas' wrath, but I *need* to know. "Why can't he help?"

He reaches into his briefcase again, this time pulling out photos. Copies of the ones Shaelene took of Derek in The Rosary, along with a few others. *Derek leaving his office. One of him in a parking garage with the same man from The Rosary. One of him speaking to the valet at the Angelinis'.* From the angle it's hard to tell if he was arriving or leaving, but we all know he didn't walk out of that mansion.

"Delivered to the precinct this morning. Kerr was working to get rid of them until they received an anonymous tip which led to the raid on The Rosary. It would have raised too much suspicion for those photos to be *misplaced*."

Fucking Gedeon. He had to have all this planned before ever agreeing to meet with us. He was one—*two*—steps ahead this entire time. Then he had the audacity to show up here like nothing happened. Rubbing it in our faces. Flaunting his victory.

"Why. Was. Gedeon. Here." Shaelene sounds like she's using every muscle in her body to keep her feet in place instead of hurdling her father's desk and asking with her fists.

He meets her ferocity with his own. "Like we said, our original plan was to meet with the Vasilievs *here* and arrange a deal. That meeting was cut short when Grigorio didn't show, and I received the call he'd been taken in."

"What deal?" she asks, her tone desperate and short.

"The particulars of Maxim's trade do not pertain to the mess we currently find ourselves in."

"That's bullshit and you know it," she spits as Shaun enters, his face wan and eyes even more tired than before his nap.

"He didn't say where he went, only that it wasn't to Barry."

Apparently, that's enough for Silas—or at least all he can stand from us—because he doesn't press it, instead taking his jacket off and making himself comfortable.

But Shaelene isn't satisfied with his answers. "What was the deal?" she urges, taking a step toward his desk.

Shaun looks to me concerned, but I can't do more than offer a nervous shrug and head shake to him.

Silas sighs, running his hands down his face. The darkened circles forming under his eyes age him more than the gray hairs framing his head do.

"We meet with Maxim at the Vino Santo warehouse in two days. Grigorio has agreed to the offer. The meeting will happen with or without him present." He extends no details to what he discussed with Gedeon or what information he'd be relaying back to Maxim. "Which is why *you* are going to go and keep him tempered. Fight for bail. Do whatever necessary to get him out before they find something to keep him past the forty-eight-hour hold," he says to Simon.

Simon's jaw ticks, but he doesn't argue.

"You three," Silas starts, glowering at the rest of us. "Keep your asses in this goddamned manor until Wednesday. Get your brother here and tell him the same." He lights a cigar and begins the plethora of troubling paperwork around him, dismissing us.

"Shaelene." His voice stops her in her tracks beside me. "This deal is good for you too."

I know she's thinking the same thing I am. I can sense it by the tense strain of her neck. *Her contract. Silas actually found a way to work in her freedom with whatever deal Grigorio agreed to.* She says nothing, only lifts her chin and rolls her shoulders, leading us out.

68

SHAELENE'S EMPTY SIDE OF the bed pulls me from sleep. The black satin sheets cold and the blankets thrown aside from where she'd been lying. I shoot up, finding the rest of the room in place. The lights are still off, but there's no trace of Shae. Frantically rushing out of bed, I drape the fleece duvet over my shoulders and make for the door.

The rest of the manor is quiet, sleeping like it should be, but that doesn't stop the ominous feeling growing in my gut as I pace through the empty hall in search of her.

I pass Shephard's room first. The door is cracked, lights off, and I can tell he hasn't come back yet because his bed is still neatly made. After we left Silas' office, Shaun called again, but in the few moments Shephard answered, he didn't say much. *Yelled much, rather.* Loud enough for us all to hear that he was handling what he could on his own and to leave him alone for the rest of the night.

Pissed off and annoyed, Shaun phoned Luca and left Shae and I to each other. We cuddled up on the couch, but without the details of Gedeon and Silas' meeting, we came up empty about what to do next besides mentally prepare to face the lot of them in two days.

I tried to keep a positive outlook, reminding her of what her father mentioned. That in a few days she'll be free of him. We both will be. *Apparently, that wasn't enough to settle her mind and let her sleep.*

Something scuffs inside Shaun's room, and I jump, wrapping the blanket tighter around myself. Rough sounds—like fighting and furniture being thrown—echo from inside and I pause. *That can't be him and Shaelene arguing, right?* They were both heated today, but I can't imagine them being physical toward each other when Gedeon is the one behind our collective anger.

I reach for the doorknob, but the door opens before I can turn it. Luca stands inside the doorway, shirtless and in a pair of briefs so tight and short he might as well have been naked.

His chiseled features twist into a sly grin, the toned muscles of his abdomen flexing as he chuckles. "Looking to join the fun, Victoria? Here I thought you were spoken for."

He peeks at my hand, still firmly wrapped around the knob between us. I yank it back, my palms sweating as I try to think of how to explain myself. "I–I thought someone was fighting in here," I say, digging myself into a deeper hole. I close my eyes as the look on his face widens into an even more smug and catastrophically handsome smile.

"Something like that." He winks.

Shaun's stoic face appears behind him. "Luca, leave the poor girl alone."

His bulky, muscular frame fills the rest of the doorway, blocking what I now realize is probably a tangled mess of sheets and the rest of their clothes because he, too, is shirtless. A large black and grey eagle tattooed across his chest and wearing only a pair of sweats slung low on his hips. They do about as much for covering him as Luca's underwear, the semi-hard remnant of what they'd been up to staring right at me.

The fact that neither of them seem to be bothered by my gawking only heightens my embarrassment, and I have to physically shield my eyes with my hand in order to get any words out.

"What is it, Victoria?" Shaun asks over Luca's snickering.

God, now they've both said my name in husky, post-sex voices! Each of them is attractive in their own right, but damn! Do they have to rub it in like this? Fuck, I'm so flustered. Them staring down at me like that isn't helping. Don't look down again. Oh my— I need to get the hell away from here and find Shae.

When I finally risk a peek through my fingers again, they've crossed their arms over their chests, not helping my confidence in the slightest. "I'm looking for Shae," I manage, my voice pathetically breathy.

"Try the pool," Shaun suggests. When I squint up at him, all hints of humor are gone from his face. "She swims when she's stressed."

I nod and race down the hall before the burning in my cheeks starts to blister, not daring to look back or slow my pace until I'm down the stairs and through the sliding doors to the center patio.

The heated slabs are a welcome gift to my bare feet as the cold November air gusts through the blanket, instantly chilling the flush in my cheeks. Despite the chill and the shiver racking through my shoulders, I step through the breeze to the pool.

Sure enough, there's Shae.

Finishing a turn and pushing off the wall, she swims away from me—her strong legs kicking and helping her arms pull her with each stroke. She makes quick work of the distance between us, steam rising off her body as the water shimmers on her skin under the dim outdoor lights. She must have been out here for some time if her body is that warm. *Or maybe the pool is heated too.*

I dip a toe in and immediately jump back from the water. "Jesus, Shae! It's freezing!"

She plants her hands on the edge, hoisting herself out and sitting on the side of the pool. "The cold clears my head." Slicking her hands down her hair and wringing out the water, she stands. "Go back to bed, Victoria. You need sleep."

I don't move. Not even when she walks past dripping chilly droplets on my feet. She grabs her towel from the patio table and dries her face, then looks back at me sternly.

Her hair hangs heavy down her back, leaving her shoulders and chest in view. The straps of her sport bikini dig into the pumped muscles in her shoulders. All her exposed skin prickles with goose-bumps in the night air, her nipples and their rings pushing against the thin rectangle of fabric covering her breasts.

Watching the beads of water cascade down her body, seeing the way her bottoms rest low on her hips, washes away all memory of the way Shaun and Luca stood in front of me upstairs. Her broth-ers, both blood and not, are undeniably handsome and would be the type I would've found myself drawn to before, but Shaelene... *She is irrefutably perfect.* I'll never understand how I didn't notice it sooner. Even after all the moments I've spent wrapped in her arms or nestled under her, the sight of her never lessens.

So many days wasted avoiding her, and now all the ones ahead of us are becoming more troubling and unsure than the last. So uncertain that I don't want to focus on anything other than us. Here. Now.

She sets her towel down and steps into the hot tub. The lights beneath the surface making the water glow a turquoise-y shade of green, her tanned body suspended in the middle.

"You're shivering. Go back inside," she orders.

I'd been too busy watching her, not at all paying attention to myself or the chill seeping into my bones. My whole body shakes under the blanket, my teeth chattering through every breath. "I'll bc alright."

I drop the blanket and walk to the jacuzzi. Sitting on the edge, the water is substantially warmer than the pool as it wades around my legs, and the comforting heat of the pavement on my ass sends a relaxing shiver up my spine. My body stills as the warmth snakes through me.

Shaelene watches me the entire time—her eyes skimming from my knees to my chest—heightening the heat within me as the winter cold perks my nipples into hard buds beneath my silk night-shirt, the light breeze keeping them taut and desperate.

Her eyes are tired, like her swim has done nothing to dull the stress waging war in her mind, but when they reach mine, they grow alert. On edge. Keeping me protected in her sights since I'm making it clear I'm not going back to bed without her.

She rolls her neck, relieving what I can only imagine is the ache from her laps already setting in, and slowly floats toward me. She hesitates, only for a second, before draping her wet arms over my thighs and resting her head on them, soaking my shorts.

It's such a vulnerable position, one I so rarely get to see her in, that my heart lurches, my body instinctively hovering over hers. Her eyes close, content to sit with me and listen to the lapping water against the ornately tiled walls.

I place a hand on her head, my fingers tingling from her over-heated body. "Talk to me."

There's a pause, and she lets out a long sigh, her body fighting the helplessness of her confession. "I hate not having all the an-swers."

I don't have any of the ones she's looking for, so I sit quietly, running my fingers over the sleek sheet of her hair and wait for her to go on.

"None of this has gone like we planned..." Another deep sigh and she opens her eyes but doesn't look up at me. Tracing the doors of Silas and Simon's offices hidden behind the mirrored glass.

"Shultz. Gedeon. And now Maxim. Everything is going to shit, and it feels like there's nothing I can do to stop it."

"We don't know that, Shae. This meeting could be the fresh start we've been hoping for. We can crisis manage everything else when that's finished." I try to sound reassuring, but it comes out like the broken record it is.

She shakes her head, her hands starting to tremble as she wipes phantom water from her face. "It will never be finished. Not with them. They're wolves. They don't stop hunting just because the rabbit offers them something tastier to eat." She stares blankly down at the water calming in the pool. "I don't know what my father is offering them, and that worries me more than any of the possible scenarios I can come up with."

She releases a long, shaky breath through her nose and glances up at me through her lashes. "I can't stop thinking that they're doing this to weaken us. Forcing our hand into a lopsided deal only to finish us off anyway..."

Her words run on a loop in my head. The way she feels small and helpless when it comes to Gedeon yet lets herself be open and vulnerable with me. Both show her strength. She may not know the twisted things Gedeon wrote to her, but the damage he inflicted that night in the library was enough to fester the fear and insecurity he wanted. She came out here to take control of what she could, even if the chill and ache she'll feel tomorrow might not be worth it.

I hate the way she shrinks herself in comparison to him. They may call themselves wolves, but Shaelene is no rabbit. She isn't anyone's prey. Not anymore.

Cupping her face, I keep her eyes focused on me. "Listen to me. You can't control what anyone is going to do and stressing over what *could* happen isn't going to help keep your head clear. You are iron, Shae. He didn't weaken you. He made you stronger. You won't let your guard down again. You think everything through in ways you may not have before." I take a moment, looking deep into her eyes, trying to think like her. Think of what she'd say to take my worries away. "Instead of trying to strike first, shift your thinking. We don't know what's heading our way, so keep yourself aware. That way we can pivot and adjust as the blows come."

Her eyes flare in surprise, but it doesn't take long for her lids to lower into that sinfully seductive look she's prone to sliding my way. "Have you been talking to Shephard?" A hint of pride coats her question, making my cheeks heat.

"Not particularly. He just talks. Really loud," I joke. "Especially about boxing."

It earns me a laugh, some of the chains around my chest loosening, but my point is more than serious. "I mean it, Shae. Whatever we're walking into is going to be a million times more intense than The Rosary." Her face sobers, the reality pressing in around us once more. "We have to be brave." I say it for the both of us. "And if control is what you need to keep your head from spinning, take control of what you can now." Her arms are still resting on my legs as I spread my knees for her. "Control *me*, Shae."

There's only one quick, foggy breath between us before she rises to her full height and wraps her arms around me. Burying her face and catching my neck in her teeth, she lifts and pulls me until my ass is at the edge of the tile.

Her fingers trace the waistband of my shorts, tugging the elastic down until I lift myself enough for her to slide them and my panties off.

Her palms glide along the inside of my leg before she tosses both over her shoulder.

I'm wet before her mouth even touches me, my back arching with need. She rubs her thumb over the line of my lips before kneading my clit with rhythmic strokes, my mewls of pleasure echoing across the water. She swipes her tongue over the same path, parting me slightly with its warm, gentle caress.

Her hand slides up my shirt the same moment my hand tangles in her hair. *I want her here.* I want her distracted, not plagued with thoughts of the last few weeks.

I want her satisfied and in control, and I only let go when she presses her palm flat against my chest and pushes me back. Savoring the quick bite of pain from the cobbled texture of the concrete below me, I hold her tighter with my legs.

I want more. I need *more.*

Her kisses and licks are hungrier than usual. Needier. Less forgiving. My thighs are already shaking, but she doesn't slow the torrent of lashings from her tongue, easily sending me over the edge with a cry. The sound only makes her more ravenous, her hands finding their way back to my legs with bruising force as she plunges two fingers deep inside me before the final surges of my climax end.

She's relentless, teasing and curling in the same perfect rhythm as her tongue against my clit, guiding me right back up until I'll inevitably nosedive off the other side into another quaking orgasm.

I hope the rest of the house has actually gone to bed because I'll die of embarrassment if they caught me earlier *and* are hearing the primal sounds Shaelene is forcing out of me right now.

"Shae! Oh god, Shae, that feels so fucking good!"

Her answering groan sends a shockwave through me, catapulting me near the top of my sense threshold.

A few more licks and I'll be in free fall until she makes me start climbing again.

My hips buck against her face. *I don't think I can last. I don't want to last. I'm right there. I want to feel her while I—*

She pulls away, staring down at me with cum glistening on her chin and a feral, predatory look in her eye.

"What? Why'd you sto—"

The words die on my tongue, the water enveloping me as she pulls me in and spins me away from her.

Shaelene shoves me into the side of the tub, pinning my ribs against the hard ledge. Her hand snakes around my throat, forcing my head back so I'm looking straight up at her face. Terrifyingly and beautifully looming over mine.

Her eyes darken with desire. "This time I want to watch you come."

She doesn't break her gaze when she reaches over and taps the display panel built into the ground. The jets turn on, taking me by surprise, and filling the hot tub with current. My hips jolt when one makes perfect impact with my bare pussy, pulsing a hot, constant stream against my clit. *Like my apartment's shower head on steroids.*

It only takes a couple seconds for my eyes to roll back and I impulsively rock into her, the pressure building as I start to climb again, but a sharp squeeze on my throat makes them pop open.

"Ah, ah, ah, Little Fox. I watch you, and you watch me."

Another wave of heat flows through me, my body arching into hers as I seek release. I don't close my eyes again except for quick, anticipatory blinks when she moves her free hand between us. Her forearm and wrist settle between the crack of my ass while her fingers pound my pussy from behind.

My bucking doesn't stop. There's so much sensation all at once that I can't focus on anything. My body is on autopilot, driving itself toward its basest need while my brain scrambles to form a coherent thought. Only one solidifies. *I hope Shaelene is feeling this same sense of lustful void too.*

The dominating look in her eyes only works to push me closer to the edge. The confident, in charge woman I love is back and she's leading me toward another devastatingly euphoric climax.

"Such a good girl. You're close again, aren't you?" she purrs, but I can only muster a garbled moan in response. She leans into me, her lips so close her breath brushes against mine. "You can't come yet, *ma fraise*. I'm not done playing."

She plants a mercifully slow kiss to my mouth, then another, and one over my cheek before pulling back to watch me again. Her fingers slide out, and I whimper at being left hollow and wanting. But with one less distraction my body relaxes from the tension it'd been building, the barrage of water and her hand on my neck are the only things I feel.

Until her fingers rim my sensitive, untouched hole.

Pacing slow circles on my ass, I feel myself clench. My body goes stiff. Rigid. But she keeps her hand in place. "Relax for me. I want to feel every part of you, Little Fox."

I fight through a swallow, everything feeling rough under her grasp, but I obey—spreading my legs a couple inches wider and damning myself in the process. Shaelene smirks, knowing damn well the jet smashing against my aching clit is also flowing along my slit, surrounding every inch of my pussy in a warm, bubbly frenzy.

Shae's finger presses in again, and this time I force my body to agree. To give her leeway to push into me. Then a bit further, and a little more until her finger is fully in my ass and making me lose all sense of control.

My whimpers and squeaks turn into rumbling, rambling moans that don't cease until my eyes roll back and Shaelene's face blurs out of focus. Sound fades and fireworks erupt as her finger works magic inside me. My soul leaving my body as I explode.

When I finally recover, the jets are off and she's drifted us over to steps, sitting with me on her lap, kissing reassuring words of lust and pride into the side of my neck and top of my shoulder.

"Thank you," she whispers beside my ear. Turning to face her, the worry and sadness from earlier has faded into satiated content, but something prickles at me. *She didn't come.* She was in control, and no doubt felt the same rush I did watching it unfold. Watching me surrender to her. But she didn't come.

I want to give that same high to her.

"I want to do that for you." *Clearly not the 'you're welcome' she was likely expecting if her brows perking up tell me anything.*

"Someone's feeling *very* brave tonight," she purrs.

"Brave. In love. Yours," I add. "I want you to feel that too."

Her full, gorgeous lips tick up in a smile. That same damn smile that melts me every time I see it. "I've always felt like that with you, Victoria." Her arms squeeze me tighter. "Always."

I spin until I'm facing her completely, my knees on either side of her hips, bracing my hands on her shoulders. "I want you to have every part of me. Body. Mind. Soul. Let me give you the final piece."

Her eyes flick to my mouth in understanding. If I didn't know better, I'd think she was about to turn me down. That the quick pause before she wraps my legs around her waist and walks us out of the hot tub was her deliberating a rejection.

But I *do* know her better; I know how much she insists on control. She was convincing herself to relinquish part of herself to someone. To me. *I'd gamble to say she's never let anyone please her orally before.*

Her towel wraps around the two of us as she walks us inside, crushing her lips against mine all the way to the stairs. When we reach them, movement down the hall catches my eye over her shoulder.

Shaun and Luca watch us from the kitchen, both of them wearing shit-eating grins while they pile food onto a pair of plates.

Shae's long strides pull us out of view before I can return their smirks with an eyeroll or middle finger, but the memory of them completely vanishes when Shaelene uses her back to push open the door to her room and sets me on the bench at the foot of the bed, stripping me of my wet tank top.

She hesitates again before crossing her arms, her biceps flexing as she rips her top off over her head, splashing my face with water that drips down the side of my nose and over my mouth. Her beautiful, full breasts bounce free, the rings glinting on both sides of her pert nipples.

I reach forward, tugging on each side of her bottoms, the fabric tight against her skin until she pops a hip and I peel it down her legs, letting it fall to the floor between her feet. Her chest heaves when she's bared in front of me.

"You're still in charge," I remind her. "Teach me."

She holds my chin with her thumb and forefinger, gently tilting my face up. Her eyes search mine, flicking back and forth before she nods. Urging me onto the bed with a jut of her chin. "On your knees."

I do just that, crawling off the bench and pulling my legs beneath me to sit back on my calves. She climbs forward, closing the gap between us, the toned expanse of her stomach at face level with me. Her piercing eyes pinning me in place from above.

"Start here." She taps a finger to her collarbone, and I rise up on my knees to fulfill her command. Kissing softly along the delicate bone and into the crease of her neck, then over the spot along her jaw that makes my body shudder when she kisses me there.

Her head tips back in surrender, both our nervous breaths in sync.

"Lower," she says, her voice slightly shaken.

I listen. My head roaming down—my tongue trailing across her chest and flicking over her nipple like she's done to me so many times before. She inhales sharply through her teeth, holding the air deep in her lungs. When she lets it out, I suck in as much of her breast as I can. Exploring every bit of pebbled skin and perked nipple my tongue touches. Palming and squeezing the other as my heart races.

Slowly, I kiss and nip my way to the other, giving it the same attention while twisting the glinting ring I'd just abandoned.

Shae's heavy hands press on my shoulders in a silent command to keep going lower. I break the suction and kiss my way between her breasts, over the set of prayer hands tattooed there, grazing my nose across her sternum in my descent.

When I reach the beads, I draw back and marvel at the beauty of the temptress before me. Placing a thumb on each side of the rosary like I'd learned in the one year I attended Catholic services as a child, I freeze. Reflecting on everything that's brought me to this moment.

"Something you need to repent for, Little Fox?"

I smile, licking over the tip of the crucifix inked above her belly button. The irony of the cross's inversion isn't lost on me, but when I look up, her expression is hard to read. Her usual mask is on, but it slips just enough for me to see a hint of worry in her eyes.

She's in control, but still out of her element. *This is for her. I need to keep her out of her head.* "I believe you're supposed to pray before you eat," I tease.

Her flash of worry dissipates into something devilish and hungry. *There she is.*

"Repeat after me." Her voice stirs low within me, my holes feeling empty without her.

I nod, biting my lip.

Fisting her fingers into the loose mess of my bun, she pulls my mouth back to her stomach. "God, grant me the serenity to accept the things I cannot change..."

"God, grant me the serenity to accept the things I cannot change..." The residual heat in my core reignites, the molten intensity pulsing with each word.

"The courage to change the things I can, and the wisdom to know the difference…"

I kiss her navel and breathe the words against her.

Tingles dance across my scalp as she tightens her grip, tugging painfully on the shorter hairs at the base of my neck. "Living one day at a time, enjoying one moment at a time. Accepting hardship as a pathway to peace…"

Her voice is sinfully sexy. Consuming. Gedeon called her the devil, but he forgot one important thing. Lucifer was an angel. *And I'll resign myself to eternal damnation to stay at her side every day.* I swear to myself she'll never be alone again as I whisper the words like they're vows.

"Taking, as Jesus did, this sinful world as it is. Not as I would have it…"

I pepper more kisses between every word, her fingers flexing at each touch of my lips. All of it stoking the fire burning inside us both.

Pain jolts through me as hairs rip from my head when Shaelene pulls my head back, forcing my face up. Her eyes command my attention as if every word she's saying is to *me* instead of God.

"Trusting that You will make all things right if I surrender to Your will."

I swallow, the knot in my throat difficult to get down at this angle. "Trusting that You will make all things right if I surrender to Your will."

"So that I may be reasonably happy in this life and supremely happy with You forever in the next."

My eyes water from the ache in my scalp, but I don't blink them away. I force myself to focus on Shaelene as I recite her words. "So that I may be reasonably happy in this life and supremely happy with You forever in the next."

"Amen."

"Amen."

I'm thrown back against the bed, Shae's solid frame hovering over me as her knees pin themselves to my sides. My thighs rest against her back while she sits lightly on my chest, the rosy shade of her pussy bared in front of my face.

She swipes away the tears that fall down my temples. "Ready to feast, Little Fox?" I nod, but she shakes her head. "Words, Victoria. Use them."

"I want to do this for you, Shae," I confirm, skimming my nails over top her legs. Her hand finds my hair again. Gentler this time, bracing my neck so I can taste her.

My first lick is quick. Timid. But my mouth waters when the taste of her floods it. A confusing blend of sweet and acidic. Sour and citrus-y and salty from her time in the pool. My fingers dig into the flesh of her legs with the same brutal strength she uses to bruise me. *It's better than any of the times I tasted myself on her tongue.*

I suddenly feel starved. Hurried and hungry strokes along her slit aren't enough to satisfy my craving. Sucking her clit out from under its shy little hood, I'm greedy with my need for her. *Now I understand why she turns beastly when I'm in her mouth.*

"Fuck, *ma fraise*. You eat me so well," she moans, her stomach tensing above me.

She tastes and feels heavenly. Slick and velvety soft on my tongue. She churns her hips, grinding without crushing me. Rubbing my nose against her clit with each thrust until we fall into a perfect rhythm.

My tongue explores between every fold, diving deep into her. *Even warmer on the inside, and still so deliciously sweet.*

I gasp for a breath and let her continue fucking my face, my tongue pressed flat against all of her, letting her grind until I see her muscles flex.

I move my arms as much as I can and dig my fingers into the meat of her firm ass. Groping and holding on for dear life as she bucks quicker on me.

"God, Victoria. What're you doing to me?" She grits, stifling a moan as she quivers. I can't stop the prideful moan rippling out of me and rumbling over her swollen, throbbing pussy while it pulses against my tongue.

I want more.

After she stops quaking, she drops my head and lifts off me, tugging me to her and rolling us so I'm on top, kissing me fiercely. Swiping her tongue over mine again and again until we're a mess of lips, spit, and cum.

Giggling against her mouth, I feel her smile while I say, "I love you too, Shae."

69

Shaelene

"You going to share how you're planning to do that?" I ask as Shaun and I follow Shephard down the hall.

He finally came home, interrupting breakfast in the process, and ignoring us all by bulldozing his way straight to his room. Shaun and I were the only ones brave enough to chase him down, leaving Victoria and Luca sitting awkwardly across from each other at the dining table.

"No."

"At least tell us where you're running back to so we can cover for you with Father," Shaun pleads.

The asshole never told us where he went either, though I have my suspicions a certain governor is involved. He's only repeated the same sorry excuse he told Shaun last night. *I'm taking care of the handkerchief situation on my own.'* I'm not inclined to argue with him either. He's doing more in the way of fixing things than the rest of us being held on house arrest are. Father didn't see him come back since he's already left the house to tend to Grigorio, so he won't notice when he leaves again.

"If I do that, you'll be liable when someone starts asking questions," he says, shoving several pairs of shorts and boxers into a duffel bag. "Trust that I'm fine, and everything is getting handled. This is my mess."

"And tomorrow?" I ask, narrowing my eyes on the weeks' worth of clothes he's packing.

"I'll be there don't worry."

Oh, I'm fucking worrying all right. That's not up for negotiation, no matter how good the head Victoria gives me is.

He zips his bag shut and slings it over his shoulder, charging by us toward the door.

"Shephard!" I call when he takes the first step into the hallway. He turns back, his jaw tight with annoyance. My brows draw together, fear raging through me. "Be careful."

He nods and marches down the hall, leaving me and Shaun standing in the mess of his room.

"Think he's gonna listen?" Shaun asks.

"Not a chance in hell."

He chuckles. Our brother is *never* careful. Hence the spit soaked handkerchief in the first place, but when he sets his mind to something, it's easier to step out of the way rather than risk him trampling over you on his way to do it anyway. We can only hope whatever he's up to doesn't land him in any more trouble.

Shaun starts to leave, when I catch his arm. "By the way, if you and Luca are allowed to be horny all over the house, so are we. Quit picking on Victoria."

"I have no idea what you're talking about," he lies, a smile curving his lips as we walk. *Asshole.*

I jab an elbow into his side as I keep pace with him. "I mean it."

He rolls his eyes and shakes his head. "Alright, alright."

He's most definitely going to continue pestering her. As sure as Shephard is stubborn, Shaun is playful. I can't help the smile lifting my cheeks as we make our way back to the dining room.

The rest of the day goes by uneventfully until we get the news about Grigorio's bail being denied.

He's officially booked and awaiting trial in county lockup until the state can prosecute him. Which means this meeting will be just us and his sons. *Nine of us versus who knows how many cronies Gedeon and Maxim will have in tow.* I pick at my nails, thinking of contingency after contingency.

Victoria doesn't know it yet, but I have every intention of keeping her at the manor during the meeting. She doesn't need to be anywhere near the warehouse. I won't risk it.

I wake up and dress before Victoria opens her eyes, strapping on my chest plate before layering a tank and a dress shirt over it. I'm not walking into that warehouse unprotected, especially after Gedeon's antics at The Rosary.

Another reason I don't want Victoria to come. If something were to happen to me—my heart races at the thought—I'd rather her not see it.

Slipping on a shoulder holster and then my jacket, I fasten a second gun to my hip. *There is absolutely no way the Vasilievs will be attending unarmed.* This may be a business meeting, but I'm not taking any chances.

Someone knocks on the door and Victoria stirs under the covers. I crack it open quietly, unable to take my eyes off the bed. Shaun and Shephard are on the other side, dressed and ready to go. The meeting isn't for a few more hours; we're supposed to be at the warehouse at eleven, but the three of us have work to do.

"You ready?" Shaun asks.

I shake my head, still looking at my Little Fox. "She's still sleeping."

"The offer still stands. And everything is already set up—"

I sigh and pinch the bridge of my nose, trying to keep my voice as hushed as possible when I whisper shout, "Shephard, for the last time, I am *not* tying her to your bed."

"I sure hope not," Victoria says behind me, clutching the sheet around herself to cover up. "What's going on?"

"Whoops!" Shephard whistles, and I level a glare at him before slamming the door in their faces and turning to face her.

"You're staying here."

Her head jerks back and she stiffens. "Like hell I am!"

"Ooh, Red's feisty this morning!" Shephard's muffled voice quips through the door.

Shaun chimes in with more unwanted commentary. "You should've heard them the other night."

"Shut. Up," I growl at them, glaring at the ceiling. "And *yes*. You are. This isn't like The Rosary. We don't have a leg up."

"If you recall, Shae, we didn't have a leg up then either and I'm still here."

"She's got a point!" Shephard chirps behind me.

Jesus fuck, *I cannot handle all three of them right now.* I storm to the door, swinging it open and holding up a finger. "One more word and I swear to God, Shep, I don't care how much Father loves the carpets. I *will* shoot you."

He laughs in response and Shaun joins in. The annoying sound tap dancing on my last nerve.

"Good. You're all awake," Uncle says, stopping in the hall behind them. "Your father has called a meeting." He peers in my room. "You too, Ms. Fenwick. Get dressed."

"No."

"Yes, Mr. Laughlin." Victoria and I speak over each other.

I look back at her, but she doesn't budge, keeping her eyes locked on my uncle and raising her chin.

"Did you or did you not say she was a part of this just the other night, Shaelene? She's coming with. Your father ordered so."

He's been the one trying to push her out of every meeting. Why the fuck would he demand she be with us today?

I can hear her shifting through drawers and getting dressed in the closet behind me. I barely contain my growl, watching as Uncle leaves to make his way back to Father's office, his expression closed off and guarded more than normal.

"My door is unlocked. Just saying, all you gotta do—" I shove Shephard's chest, pushing both him and Shaun out of the doorway before he can finish his sentence.

"Get out!" I yell, hearing their footsteps and snickering voices recede down the hall.

When I turn back to my room, Victoria steps out of the closet in an oversized gray, wool sweater, and black trousers with a flimsy waist band, too thin to do more than hold a fashion belt. There's no place for her to holster a weapon, and I don't trust her not to hurt herself with one in the first place.

She starts to slip into a pair of black heels, and I close my eyes in defeat. The weight of the world settling heavily inside my chest. "No. Flats, please. At the very least, *please* wear flats." She arches a curious brow at me as I run my nails along my thumb. "In case you need to run."

70

Shaelene

I DON'T OWN ANY protective gear small enough to fit her, but I manage to convince Victoria to sheath my knife in the front of her waistline, knowing the parachute's worth of extra fabric from her sweater would be able to conceal it. My fingers itch to triple check the harness, but we don't have time. *I just hope she can draw it easily enough if she has to.*

After an hour and a half of my father obsessively going over the layout of the warehouse and his plan of action, still conveniently leaving out any details about the deal itself, we set out to meet the Angelini sons and head for the shipyard.

Our father drives, Simon sitting in the passenger seat next to him. Shaun and Shephard take up the bench ahead of us, leaving Victoria and I crammed into the back. *Same as we were the first time we'd set out to meet Gedeon.*

Her hand is gripped in mine, and I can't say for sure which of us is holding on tighter. *I hate this.* Any other job I'd be able to clear my head and complete it with ease, but with her in the line of fire, I can't sit still. *And I have no fingernails left to bite off.*

The closer we get to the jetty and the imposing Vino Santo warehouse towering near the docks, the tighter the knot in my stomach twists.

We pull through the warehouse gate, driving past a black Rolls-Royce sitting empty with New York rental plates. *Maxim.*

We follow Mass, Gio, Ale, and Luca around the side of the building before Father stops the car and the men file out.

"I love you and I trust you, but I'm begging you... Wait in the car," I plead. My eyes are heavy with fear, tumbling back and forth between hers. *I don't want to fight before going into the unknown.*

I step out Shaun's side with her on my heels, ignoring my request and killing a piece of me in the process.

I grab her elbow before she can step past me, moving her hand to feel the gun at my side, then the one at my hip. When I knock her knuckles against the metal face of my chest plate, I say, "He will do worse than kill you. If you're in there, he will do whatever he can to get to me. I won't let him hurt you. *Please.* Wait. In. The. Car."

I nudge her toward the still open door, but she pulls herself from my grasp. "Be brave *together*. That was the deal, Shae." When I don't move out of her way, she shoves my chest, her fight doing nothing but reminding her of my armor and pissing her off even more. "We had a deal!"

"JUST WAIT IN THE FUCKING CAR, VICTORIA!" I shout, finally losing to the amalgamation of emotions raging inside me.

Silence presses in around us, and for the first time in a long time, she stares at me like I'm a stranger—a heartbreaking mix of fear and hatred in her wounded eyes. Another piece of me dies along with the light in them.

"Shaelene is right. Wait in the car, Miss Fenwick," my father says, coming to stand between us. Her teary eyes slide to him as he reaches us, while mine are too busy memorizing every detail of her face as I watch her realize she was wrong. *She should've left after reading those letters. She should've never accepted the internship at all.*

"We'll lock you in and you'll be perfectly safe so long as you stay inside. Your help and support of Laughlin & Laughlin have been highly appreciated this semester."

My chest locks, my armor suddenly feeling too tight. *Why. The.* Fuck. *Did she need to come if she was going to be left in the car?! Is this some kind of fucking test? Because Daddy's Little Girl stopped obeying his every beck and call?*

My mind feels like a burning cyclone, twisting and spiraling from confusion to fear to anger. *I want to kill him.* My fingers twitch toward my hip, but the unimaginably sincere look he gives as he faces me scatters every thought. An eerie calm settles over me. *I haven't seen that look in years.*

His usually scolding eyes are gentle. The harsh lines always furrowed between his brows softening until they nearly disappear. *It's the same look he gave me after my first piano recital... Before he started demanding perfection from me.* The look that reads 'I'm doing this for you'.

But if he'd really been doing something for me, he'd have made her stay at the manor.

The door closes between us, and I know she's safe, but the cut from my words is festering, growing into a wound I can only hope to mend when this meeting is over. Hope that she can forgive me, even if she's right. My body begs for us to be anywhere but here. *I'm a coward. I can't be brave with her. I want her safe, not brave. Brave means she's at risk. And I'll give up everything for her every time.*

My hand rests against the cool glass of a window, too tinted for me to see inside, but if she's looking, I want her to know—at least one more time—the depths of my feelings for her. I drop my head and whisper, "I love you." To her. To God. To the universe. To anyone that may be listening and will help keep her safe. Hoping for that simple favor feels wrong, my skin crawling as I wait for a response I know will never come. *I don't deserve her.*

I hear and feel the click of the doors as they lock, taking a thankful breath and walking to meet the rest of my family, as ready as I'll ever be to face the danger waiting inside these walls.

Grigorio's warehouse matches Father's description exactly. The same it looked years ago when my brothers, Luca, and I used to sneak in and unseal a barrel, getting stupid drunk on wine that hadn't aged nearly enough.

Thousands of oak casks line the walls on both sides, creating a makeshift double wall down the center of the open storeroom. Eighty-gallon barrels are shelved a dozen high down the length of the space. The only deviation is the small table set up in the center of the closest aisle, three chairs evenly spaced around it, and Maxim sitting facing us, nonchalantly packing tobacco into his pipe.

"*Dobro pozhalovat'*, Brother. I'm glad we could finally meet."

71

MAXIM DOESN'T BOTHER TO stand. He doesn't acknowledge the Angelinis behind us either.

Gedeon stands off to the side, several paces behind his father. This isn't his meeting. Regardless of how much like his father he thinks he is, Maxim is running the show, and Gedeon is back to being nothing more than his messenger boy. Though he keeps that infuriating smirk plastered on his face.

Behind them are several burly men with long hair and scruffy beards, appearing as if they've been fighting each other to pass the time until we arrived. Sweaty, with muscles pumped beneath their shirts. They're of considerable size, and I don't miss the prison markings on the face of the one in the middle, but none of them are bigger than Shephard.

Father and Uncle take their seats, and Father pulls a thick envelope from his suit pocket, no doubt containing the signed agreement from Grigorio to allow Russian access to his shipping routes. But what I'm most curious to hear is who the guns are for, and what the rest of us are getting in return.

"St. Petersburg," my father states. "Vino Santo regularly makes port in Helsinki to deliver to the Italian Embassy. The ship will make one additional stop, in St. Petersburg, to pick up *additional cargo.*"

"If you can get your guns to the border, Grigorio has agreed to get them to Belfast safely on his route back to Italy," Uncle adds.

Belfast. *That's the piece of information everyone has been so conveniently leaving out.* If Maxim is shipping guns to Belfast, that can only mean one thing. *He's aiding the New Irish Republican Army.*

But why? What benefit does he gain? Money? Not a good enough reason to force such a partnership... My guess is to gain connections.

"There is no *if*, Simon," my uncle's name pours off Maxim's tongue like molasses. "The question is how many guns will he take and when?"

Uncle's jaw ticks. "Every four weeks with the next port call being three weeks from now. On the first, the ship will pick up fifty Makarov PMs, forty PP-19s, and ten AK-74Ms."

"That is a fraction of the cache I have ready to send." Maxim's lip curls in disgust behind his pipe. "Tell Grigorio to make more room."

"No more than a hundred on the first trip. The fewer, the better. They'll be easier to hide, and the crew will have a chance to adjust to the customs risk. If anything goes awry, you'll only lose a fraction of your stores," Father presses.

Maxim puffs a thick cloud of smoke from his pipe, giving us all a long once over.

"I expect a bigger transport every time after," he says, sketching his name across the bottom of the paper Father lays out for him. His chest expands under his suit, stretching it tight across his chest as he sucks in another long draw of his tobacco. *He's surprisingly built for a man nearing his sixties.* I glance behind him. His guards are used more as a show of force, an intimidation tactic, rather than true protection. *No doubt he knows his way around a fight.* The slender scar trailing below his ear is an indication of that.

The rings on each of his fingers clink against the tabletop when he slides the paper back to my father. Two minutes in and an agreement has been made. *This was too easy...* Gedeon's grin widens as I stand up straighter. He's been watching, waiting for my reaction. The corner of his mouth cuts in a casually evil smirk; the bastard is more than enjoying my discomfort.

Maxim's dark eyes peer over my father and uncle's heads directly at me before he asks, "And the girl?"

Panic flares beneath my skin, and I dart my gaze back to Gedeon. He makes a show of checking his watch.

I can feel my brothers tense, anxiously waiting for the order from the men at the table. Preparing to fight. The Angelinis shift restlessly beside us, not about to let Gedeon take me like he'd threatened. *Promised.*

"Waiting in my car."

My head snaps back to my father.

All of ours do. Even Uncle sitting beside him.

No...

I take a step and something catches my elbow. *Shaun.* He's holding me back, keeping me from causing a scene. Gedeon shifts in my peripheral, and I'm ready to slice that stupid fucking smile off his stupid fucking face.

Maxim leans back, one brow arched high on his forehead. "And *why*, Silas, have you decided to tell me who she is?"

My body shakes from anger. Or anxiety. *Fear, most likely.* Sweat drips down my back, and Shaun's grip tightens into a painful hold on my arm.

"Mutual benefit for us all. You can use her to keep your new partner in place, Gedeon gets his bride, and Shaelene's contract is nullified."

"Wha—" My voice is so broken I doubt anyone heard me before a loud bang pulls everyone's attention. We all look to the door that swung open and see Kian.

Kian Hughes. The fucking Irish bastard...

Laughlin & Laughlin took his case at the beginning of the year. A case twenty-something years in the making. *Contract killing.* He was guilty; he admitted that much on his first day at the manor, but he said it was our job to prove he wasn't.

He certainly didn't make it easy either. Telling us all the reasons he ordered the kills. He wanted his wife and child dead for betraying him and selling out his militia to the ATF. Even saved the pictures of his wife's corpse when they were released—happy to have proof. My stomach churns. *But they never found the kid...*

Now, here he stands, his face as pale and gaunt as I remember, but his graying ginger beard is scruffier than before. Victoria held tight against his chest, squirming and struggling to pry his arm away from her neck, completely terrified by the pistol pointed at her head.

"'Tis a lovely sentiment of ya there, Silas." His accent tumbles off his tongue, and I might've been able to understand him better if I could hear over my pulse thumping in my ears. "But I think the honor to give away ma daughter's hand belongs to me."

The world goes white. *No. No, no, no, no! This can't be happening. This is a nightmare and I'm going to wake up and Victoria will be asleep in my arms. Come on, Shaelene. Wake up. Wake. The. Fuck. Up!*

But I'm already awake, even if every part of me doesn't want to believe it. Even if fear and gut-wrenching guilt corrode every cell in my body.

Her eyes... They're so scared. Tears cascade from her cheeks and her lips tremble with each press of Kian's gun against the stunning mop of curls tied up on her head. The vibrant, red curls that captured my soul the first time I saw them, still messy from her restless sleep in our bed.

The same coppery strands cover Kian's smug brow, peppering the backs of his hands as he holds her against her will.

I take another step, and this time Shaun lets me. "Victoria..."

Those watery eyes find mine, and I nearly drop to my knees. Every fiber within me hurts. Aches from the pain on her face. Shatters with the regret of bringing her into this. *With loving her too much to let her leave...*

"I wouldn't do that if I were you, lass," Kian threatens, pressing the barrel harder against Victoria's temple. It takes a second to register what he means, but I follow his line of sight, and before I even look down, I can feel the cool metal of my pistol in my palm, still in the holster on my hip, but I'd been about to draw it without a second thought.

Around me, everyone reaches for their weapons except the three men at the table. Maxim's face is bored, unbothered by the sudden hostility. Uncle's is full of shock and worry, his eyes pleading with me to stop. But my father...

His eyes are angry. Not at Kian. Not at all the men ready to kill. At *me*. All traces of the humanity I'd seen in them outside gone.

72

Victoria

"Kian! My sincerest apologies. I hadn't expected you here, or I'd have given you the honors," Silas says, pulling his angry eyes from Shaelene.

The itchy wool of Kian's sweater scratches my neck, the cold steel of his gun pressing harder against my skull every time I try to twist away.

Between crying and his chokehold, I haven't been able to draw a full breath since he grabbed me out of the car. One second, the doors had been locked and I watched everyone file into the warehouse, then they popped open and he dragged me out by my hair.

"It would seem both ya' and yer father thought me stupid. I learned from ma mistakes, Laughlin. If you want something done right, do it y'urself."

Silas stands, shoving unsteady hands into his pockets. "Of course not, Kian! Please, why don't you sit? I'm sure we can find another chair." His voice comes out strained. Unrehearsed.

Kian straightens, tightening his arm and tucking me further into him. My arms shake, my fingers aching as I pull against his sleeve, trying to keep him from completely choking me out.

Silas takes the hint and sits back down. Maxim leisurely raises a hand, and the scary looking men behind him relax a little, but their hands stay on their weapons. Simon turns to his niece and nephews and gives them a cautious look, telling them to do the same. Luca and his brothers follow suit.

The only ones that don't settle are Shaelene and Gedeon. He keeps his hand tucked just inside his jacket. Never taking his eyes off her. She keeps her sights locked on me, her hand never leaving her gun.

"Answer me this, Silas. Why is this one here—" He shakes me violently, and I scream. "—being bargained for instead of cold in the ground wit' her mother?"

Silas lowers his head and looks to the floor; the first sign of weakness I've seen from him. I can't help but feel like I'm seeing the real him for the first time.

His big boss persona is all an act he puts on for the bad guys he lords over here, but to the real villains outside the states, he's a submissive coward. *That's why no one here balks at his presence. Outside of New York, Silas Laughlin is no one.*

Even Simon looks surprised. He has since Kian barreled in here with me as his human shield, his eyes shining with quiet concern, while his brother's only reflect feelings of a conniving man caught in the act. I don't bother to hide my disgust. *This was never for the family or even Grigorio. He's only worried about himself.*

Kian goes on, spitting insults about their father to the point my shoulder is damp with his saliva, vaguely referencing jobs and the woman he claims to be my mother, but I can't understand most of it. His accent is too thick and angry, and the adrenaline pumping through me makes my pulse pound in my ears.

I keep my focus on Shae, at the very least to stop the tears from falling and at most to give me enough courage to keep from pissing myself.

"Breathe," she mouths. And I do. One trembly inhale through my nose, with a long shaky exhale past my quivering lips. She nods slightly, not drawing any attention to herself. Everyone else is still listening to Kian blather, their eyes locked on his gun.

"Brave," her lips silently command this time.

"Enough, Hughes! We did not come here to avenge past qualms," Maxim interrupts the irate monologue, pulling a slip of paper of his own from his jacket pocket and unfolding it on the table. "Our previous contract's divorce addendum, already signed." He flips to the next page. "The new marriage contract, also signed. It just needs the girl's signature."

My knees buckle, Kian's arm around my throat the only thing holding me up. All my focus on breathing goes out the window, leaving only ragged erratic gasps escaping me as Kian starts to force me toward the table.

Silas stands, making room for me sign my life away to Gedeon in exchange for Shaelene's.

My feet scuff against the floor, making it harder for Kian to walk us there, and I'm so thankful Shaelene made me change shoes.

She takes a step toward us, and Kian stops.

"No." Her voice is unnervingly calm.

Silas turns to face her entirely. "Shaelene," he hisses. I'm beginning to realize his aggressive dominance only comes out with his kids. Thinking back to all the times I've seen him around others, he's put on a show of wealth and power, but even around Grigorio he scrambled to maintain control after we'd found Derek's body, rushing to assure him everything would be alright. Talking a big game about plans only for them to go to shit because Gedeon outsmarted him.

Outsmarted all of us.

Shae looks past her father, directly at Maxim, when she says, "I didn't sign anything. That divorce agreement isn't valid. He can't marry her if he's still attached to me."

Maxim barely does her the courtesy of looking up to reply. He rolls his neck as if he were explaining the complexities of the marriage contract to a child. "Your father already signed with his power of attorney." Her lethal eyes dart to her father. "Though, that was unnecessary as well. Gedeon is the sole executor as established within the original contract. He agreed Ms. Hughes was a better match. Congratulations, you are now the former Mrs. Gedeon Vasiliev."

Kian pushes us another step closer, pulling Shaelene's attention back to us.

We take another step.

Then another.

I estimate there's roughly fifteen more between us and the table and my unfortunate destiny. *I'd be saving Shae...* My feet begin moving on their own, obeying Kian's push to move forward. The heat of his breath on my neck no longer noticeable because of the numbing cold trickling from the top of my head. *I'll do what I have to for her sake.*

"Victoria," Shae says, pulling me from my trance. My eyes meet her reassuring ones, memorizing the openness she seems to show only me, when I notice her hand gently tapping against her belt.

The solid weight of her knife bounces with each heavy step Kian urges me to take.

I let go of his arm, abandoning my futile attempt to loosen his hold and fumbling under the fabric of my sweater. The *click* of the clasp as the blade slides out from its sheath is muffled enough beneath the layers and my heavy breathing that I don't think anyone notices.

Shae's hand moves from her buckle to her stomach, pointing a dulled finger to a spot on her middle.

"ENOUGH!" Simon shouts, jumping to his feet and whirling toward Silas, fury sharpening his features. "This was never something we agreed on!"

Ten steps. I twist the knife in my palm, bettering my grip on the handle.

"You weren't a part of the discussion for a reason. She isn't your daughter!"

Simon huffs a laugh. "Doing this doesn't make you a good father."

Nine.

Maxim stands, adjusting his jacket like he hasn't a care in the world. "Gentlemen, let the lady sign, then we can all be on our way."

Eight.

"Now," Shae whispers, and I rip my arm from under my sweater, slicing the hem and driving the knife into Kian's gut. Lower than I'd intended—near his hip and away from anything vital—but it's enough for him to loosen his grip and stumble back with a grunt.

I scramble away from him, rushing for Shaelene, but his hand catches my curls and yanks me back, sending me tripping over my feet back into his chest. "Ya' *feckin smuigín!*"

White hot pain slices across my arm, and we both fall. But I'm on my feet faster. Dizzy from Kian's pull and my ears ringing from Shaelene firing her gun so close. All I can focus on is her.

My shoulder stings, but I make it two more steps before another shot rings out, and Shaelene grunts, crumpling to the floor in front of me.

"Shae!" I scream, collapsing to my knees when I reach her—a red puddle forming on the concrete around us. Blood pools from the hole in her knee.

"I'm fine," she grunts, looking past me. "You need to get out of here." She tries shoving her gun into my hands.

"I can't! I'm not—" I push it away, pressing my hands against both sides of her leg trying to keep pressure on the wound.

Shaelene's eyes widen as she attempts to sit up and reach for me. When I look back, Kian awkwardly lifts his gun with his off hand, his shoulder bloody and limp as he lays on the ground, but the sound of his shot never comes. Instead, it's the crack of his nose beneath Gedeon's boot and the thud of his head hitting the floor unconscious that we hear.

73

Shaelene

GEDEON'S COLD, PSYCHOPATHIC EYES wink down at Victoria.

I scramble for the gun I'd tried to give her, but he kicks it out of my unsteady hands, sending it skidding across the floor and under a shelf of barrels.

The room explodes into chaos. Threats in English, Italian, and Russian spew from each of the men ready to let loose a barrage of shots that could kill all of us in the process. All of Maxim's guards have their weapons aimed, and I know each of the boys have theirs pointed right back.

Maxim slides all the papers but one back into an envelope, tucking it into his breast pocket. "Son, we're done here. Grab the girl. She can sign on the plane."

Gedeon crouches, prying Victoria's hands from the hole he shot through my knee, when Uncle's shot stops him short.

Maxim's body crashes against his chair and falls to the floor at the same time Uncle's elbow slams into the side of my father's head. He catches his brother and flips the table, ducking the both of them behind it.

The volley of bullets starts, the gunfire ringing and echoing off the walls and wooden barrels in a deafening spree of noise.

Gedeon drags me off the floor instead. Victoria clings to my leg, sending white hot pain through me when she refuses to let go.

She only does so when Gedeon hauls me to stand and I wince, the warm barrel of his gun hovering near my neck and his face pressed into my cheek.

My knee explodes with pain, and I can't hold myself up enough to free myself from him. *He fucking shot me, and now I can't get Victoria out of here on my own. I have to kill him. He's not leaving here with her.* I reach for the gun still holstered inside my suit jacket, watching Gedeon through my peripheral.

"Ah, ah! Don't, Shae," he lectures. The arm wrapped around me lowers, and he pins mine firmly against my side as he points his gun at Victoria.

She's still on the ground shaking with her hands covered in my blood. Kian neutralized—*for now*—lying unconscious behind her.

"SHEPHARD!" I shout. Two of the guards Maxim brought are dead beside him and the other three are being chased through the aisles of casks. Sporadic shots echo between their shouts, but I can't recognize who the grunts of pain belong to. He peeks around from where he's crouching with Uncle and Shaun over our father, his eyes widening with rage when he sees me and Gedeon. "Get her out of here!"

"No, Shae! Please!" Victoria cries, tripping over her feet as she gets up, but Gedeon turns the gun back on me and she stops trying to stand.

She grunts as Shephard throws her over his shoulder and bolts for the door. Not stopping to look back. "Thank you..." I heave, hoping he can somehow hear it over Victoria's wails as she hits and claws at his back to get down. I close my eyes and try to block out the sound of her screams before they reach the door and it slams closed behind them.

Shephard will keep her safe.

"Good, *Zaichonok*. It was never her I wanted anyway," he whispers, his tongue licking away the tear running down my cheek.

"Fuck you," I grit.

A chuckle rumbles low in his chest, the sound vibrating against my back and making my skin crawl. "Don't fret, Shae-lene. You'll get the chance soon enough."

Bile rises in my throat. *Better me than Victoria.*

He faces the table Shaun and Simon watch from, both of their weapons drawn and ready. But Gedeon keeps his body shielded behind mine.

"Shae," Shaun calls nervously, his chest heaving as a killing rage builds inside him.

"She'll be fine," Gedeon answers for me, walking us around the table, my bad leg dragging as I hobble along with him. "Grab the papers."

He taps his foot against Maxim's side, humming under his breath, and the body slides the rest of the way down the leg of the chair.

"I can't exactly bend down, dickhead."

He grunts, gripping me harder as he grows annoyed. "Fine. Unc, do us a favor." He jerks his chin at Simon, his jaw smacking the side of my face.

My uncle begrudgingly rounds the table, his eyes restlessly flicking between me and Gedeon. Hate, worry, and guilt seethe off him, tainting the blood-filled air. I try my best to nod, giving him the smallest bit of assurance that I'm fine while pushing through the dizziness of my blood loss.

He grabs the thick envelope—now smeared red and soggy—hesitating before handing it over.

"Here," Gedeon orders, flapping open my jacket with the back of his hand. Simon reaches in, his eyes landing on where Gedeon's hand is clutching mine, resting on my spare pistol.

"I'm going to extend you the courtesy of collecting your wounded. Take that one, too, if you'd like," he says, tipping his head toward Kian. "From what I've seen, they'll have someone new in charge by tomorrow."

"Say the word, Shae, and I'll drop him from here," Shaun growls across the table.

Two more shots fire, echoing down from the far side of the warehouse. Silence falls heavily around us before Massimo's voice shatters the quiet. "LUCA!"

Shaun's head whips around, his entire body frozen in fear.

"Go," I say when he doesn't leave. "Go!" I order, but fear for the both of us makes him hesitate. "Shaun!" I plead, my voice cracking. "*GO!*"

Finally, he listens, sprinting toward the back of the warehouse.

Gedeon pulls us back half a step and Uncle follows.

"Shaelene..." We move another step, his eyes hardening as they shift to Gedeon. "We *will* get her back."

"Just keep her safe," I beg. *I don't care what happens to me as long as she's okay.*

Uncle's eyes don't leave us until Gedeon's back pushes open the door to the front of the warehouse. The metal slams shut, cutting me off from my family—my heart dropping as my entire body goes numb. I'm disarmed and thrown into the trunk of Maxim's rental, Gedeon's eyes rageful at my silence. He delivers a swift punch to my already shattered knee, and I force myself not to scream, sacrificing my bottom lip as I bite through the pain. The taste of iron coats my tongue.

"Get some sleep. It's a long flight."
His fist connects with my face and everything goes black.

445

EPILOGUE

Victoria

"SHEPHARD, PLEASE! PLEASE. PLEASE! PLEASE!" I scream and kick and punch my fists into his back the whole way to the Suburban, but it does nothing to slow his pace or loosen his hold. My voice is hoarse, and scalding tears burn down my cheeks with each step he takes me further from Shae.

The door opens and he shoves me through it, throwing me along the bench seat.

It slams shut before I can sit up, and he climbs into the driver's seat in front of me, the locks clicking as he starts the car and drives around the side of the building toward the continued gunfire.

"Shephard, please. You have to take me back in there. She's hurt!"

"She'll kill the both of us if I let you step foot in that warehouse again!"

The car brakes hard, all the air knocking from my lungs as I collide with his seat back. "I don't like it either, Red," he says panting, utter defeat claiming his voice as he cracks his knuckles and stares unseeingly through the windshield.

Ale and Gio break through the giant double doors and sprint for the car. Throwing open the trunk, they slam the seats down flat behind me. Shaun and Massimo exit, too, much slower because they're carrying—

"Oh my god!"

446

Luca's limp body sags between them, and when they hoist him into the back of the SUV, I can see how pale he truly is. His eyes are shut, and with that much blood on him...

"Shaun," I whisper when he climbs into the back over him.

"He's dead," he deadpans as the rest of the brothers file into the car with us.

I grapple with the blanket as I try to find my bearings, jolting awake in Shae's bed. *Our bed...* I swallow, tears burning my eyes.

My bed.

Ten hours ago, the entire idea of what I thought my life was going to be shattered.

Ten hours ago, Gedeon took Shaelene.

TIME SERVED

Don't panic! This isn't the end of Victoria and Shaelene's story; it's only the beginning. Keep an eye out for book two of the Unholy Triad collection, ***Time Served***, coming soon!

ACKNOWLEDGEMENTS

Wow. This is a place I honestly never thought I'd get to, but here we are! Thank you, reader, for making it this far and joining me on the journey of my first publication. However, I didn't make it to this stage on my own. This achievement was accomplished with the help of many amazing people, so allow me several paragraphs to thank them with words that could never accurately describe my gratitude.

To my editor, Casey, discovering Inked Edits Developmental was the greatest use of a "For You Page" I've ever done. You've helped me bring my book baby and all its characters to life—and death. (Still not sorry for that by the way <3) You let Shaelene and Victoria, and all the others, into your heart and that has made this partnership so much more special to me. You took a chance with me, and I truly do believe we created something incredible. Thank you for the many hours of work, conversation, advice, encouragement, and dinner that one time. (Though we definitely need to make it happen again!) You are more than just an editor to me. You became my friend and one of my favorite human beings. Thank you!

To my mother, where do I start? All the way back to birth? Because there hasn't been a day you haven't fully supported my every dream. Even the craziest of them have been met with an open mind and the encouragement to live my life the way that's best for *me*. And while I probably discovered open door romance a little too early thanks to your Nook (maybe double check the books Ne is reading lol), having books as a bonding place with you means the world to me. You read the first draft of this book—which based on the amount of edits Casey and I went through, was definitely a ROUGH draft—yet you still finished it and raved to your friends about it. No matter how far apart we are, you're always at my side, backing me 100%. I love you so much, Momma. Always.

And now, a few honorable mentions I *have* to add in here because without them, I don't think I would've finished writing this book.

Dakota, my husband, my rock, my best friend. Thank you for lifting me up when I doubt myself and want to give up because life is too stressful. Thank you for giving me the space and time to work while pulling dad duty. Thank you for supporting me as a person, not just as an author. You've accepted parts of me the world we live in loves to hate, and for that I'll be forever grateful. I love you, Koda. To the moon and back infinity X infinity times.

Dr. Thomas, thank you for laughing through my insane creative writing projects at Coastal, and for forcing me out of my comfort zone by publishing my poetry works in the New River Anthology all those years ago. I used your writing aids many a time while drafting this book, and I miss sharing memes and ridiculous short stories with you. It's been so long, but I still hope life is giving you the best of everything. Miss you, Dr. T!

To Katie Hemingway and my ARC readers: Katie, we met via Facebook comments in a mutual book page, and you took the time to read a very unedited, typo-filled, mess of a draft all the way through and gave me amazing feedback that filled my cup until it overflowed. The internet is a wild web, but I'm glad it introduced me to you! As for my other ARC readers, your interest and reviews of *Court Ordered* are invaluable, and I'll cherish you taking the time to support a brand-new author like me every day.

Lastly, credit for the Serenity Prayer is reserved for Reinhold Niebuhr, who penned the original words that became the prayer in 1932.

ABOUT THE AUTHOR

Hailing from wherever the military sends her family, C. Jacoby is a full-time SAHM, part-time author, and hella weird. This not-so-former emo kid has spent a decade writing both academically and recreationally, eventually going pro by publishing *Court Ordered*, book one of the *Unholy Triad* collection. Being a queer woman herself, the characters she writes hold a place in her heart unlike any others. When she isn't conjuring up her next plotline, she's often immersed in the pages of another, anywhere from faerie smut to serial killers, with a little hockey romance thrown in between. She also enjoys crafting and designing bookish things for friends and fans to enjoy.